About the Author

Phil Clinker was born in Alton, Hampshire, and lived in Oxford, Cape Town, South Africa, and Kent before retiring to be beside the sea at Bognor Regis in West Sussex.

This is his third novel, following the success of his Sheriff John Withers series of crime thrillers, *Bakerton* and *Thurlow Junction*, although this book is far removed from that genre.

For more information about the author, go to www.philclinkerwrites.com

Also by Phil Clinker:

The Sheriff John Withers Series

Bakerton

Thurlow Junction

Phil Clinker

A Confusion in Time

Pegasus

PEGASUS PAPERBACK

© Copyright 2024
Phil Clinker

A CIP catalogue record for this title is available from the British Library

ISBN-978-1-83794-069-8

Pegasus is an imprint of
Pegasus Elliot MacKenzie Publishers Ltd.
www.pegasuspublishers.com

First Published in 2024

Pegasus
Sheraton House Castle Park
Cambridge CB3 0AX England

Printed & Bound in Great Britain

*My grateful thanks to fellow members of the
Bognor Regis Writes Club
for their support and unofficial editing
of the manuscript*

*This book is dedicated to my grandchildren
Claire, Harriet, Daniel and Joshua*

my great-grand-daughter Astrid, great-grandson Kai

and to all who may follow

Prologue

A man was walking towards me. He was tall, well over six foot, and ungainly. Thicker than a beanpole, but only just. His pace was slow, almost brooding, as if even the weight of his skeletal body was too much for him. His cheap suit hung off him like he was a badly constructed clothes horse, angular and pointed. I swear, if he had turned round, I would have seen his shoulder blades sticking out of the back of his scuffed jacket. His upper body swayed just slightly as he walked, revealing a puke-inducing puce shirt and, more importantly, the strap to his shoulder holster. He stopped in front of me, feet slightly apart, poised, professional. It was only then that I could take in all the details. For later, if there was one.

His face was thin, of course, but it was smooth, like alabaster. Avon had clearly called. His cheeks were very slightly flushed, giving the impression of two plump peaches stuck onto the sides of a barely-covered skull. There was a livid scar running from the corner of his left eye to the tip of his ridiculously dimpled cheek, a feature which I could not draw my eyes away from. While the scar seemed to pulse with pure evil, the dimple was reminiscent somehow of Shirley Temple.

His right eye, the only one appearing to be in working order, was wide open, focused. It was studying me, almost dissecting me. His lips spread into a wide smile, which seemed to cut his face in half. His teeth shone silver in the late afternoon sun as if a light had been thrown into a cutlery drawer.

"Mr Parks," he drawled lazily, lips barely moving, "they have sent me to kill you."

PART ONE
The Island

Chapter One

The sky seemed to me like a watercolour, its blues and muted yellows appearing diluted, almost washed-out, while a tinge of red sliced across the view, adding a frisson of drama, a lone white cloud supplying an exclamation mark of texture.

The water was cool, clear and refreshing. I bobbed gently on my back, relaxing and soaking up the view. And what a view! Inshore from the ocean, the beach spread out like a pale caramel carpet, dotted with multi-coloured raffia-roofed beach huts and vivid green shrubs which grew at incredible angles out of the sand, courtesy of the vagaries of the tropical winds. In the far distance there were cliffs which threw down incredible shadows or glinting light shows, dependent on the position of the sun.

I had been enjoying this experience every day for just over a week, and I never tired of the calmness and serenity of it all. This surely was paradise…

I floated for a few more seconds, then broke into a leisurely crawl, shovelling the water behind me as I headed out, away from the sandy beach and the people.

It had been like this ever since I first set eyes on this blissful island six years ago, although, on that first occasion, I had the strange sense of coming home, or at least a feeling of familiarity which I couldn't shake off.

The horizon was a haze as I made my way further out to sea, the windmilling of my arms effortless and therapeutic. I gulped in great lungfuls of the clean air, my head spinning with the intoxication of it all. It was such a fabulous place to be, and I almost resented the fact that in a few days I would have to leave.

I suppose, strictly speaking, that wasn't quite true. I could stay on for a further week or even more. Hell, I could stay here indefinitely if I chose. As a man of 'independent' means, I was free to do what I damn well liked. Here I was, nudging thirty-nine, with a few million in the bank and a lifestyle anybody would envy. There was only one drawback. I just didn't have any history.

I turned onto my back and gently flicked my fingers through the water as if stroking an invisible pet, the pleasure forcing a smile onto my face that I could not, *would* not, let go of. Perhaps this really could be my forever home…

The swim back was uneventful but slightly less enjoyable, for it marked the end of my beach-bum existence. The next two days would be spent up in the hills, walking and listening to Denver, my guide, during the day and bivouacking under canvas at night. It sounds sublime until you meet Denver. He's a great guy really, but his mock-Texan accent tends to grind after a while, especially when it's been greased with a bottle of his favourite bourbon, which always seems to be close at hand. I met him on my second day six years ago. He was coaxing a tip out of some poor devil who had somehow been talked into letting Denver relate the tale of a mysterious mermaid that had been found washed ashore twenty years ago. He had offered to take the punter on a tour of the local caves to see if they could spot another one, but the guy had suddenly got wise and was edging away. Seeing the man's wallet recede into the distance, Denver's sharp, deep, hazel eyes focused on me instead, and I was hooked.

So we took a leisurely drive out to the caves in his Moke, which was Denver's pride and joy. It was a four-seater 1980s model, complete with roll-bars and a Stars & Stripes decal across the bonnet and leopard-print seat covers. Not easy to miss. He bought it for fifty dollars, he claimed, from another beach bum down by Santa Monica pier, and had spent that summer cruising for 'company', apparently without success. He blamed the Moke, but I wasn't so sure that was his real problem.

Apparently, it was the following Spring that he'd secured a job as a lobster-catcher on the island, and he mothballed the Moke for a year, fully expecting to return home. But then, like everyone, he fell in love with this place and spent a small fortune shipping the Moke out here, fretting non-stop for the entire time it was in transit as if it was a Ming vase or something. He wasn't lobster-catching when I first met him, but I've never got round to asking about that. Perhaps one day.

I enjoyed exploring the caves, and to be honest, I liked Denver. I made it clear that mermaids were not on the agenda, and nor was a tip, but I did promise to buy him a large shot of bourbon for his troubles. His smile was infectious as he slapped me on the back and nodded his acceptance that I was the boss. The friendship had grown from there, and it is always a pleasure to meet up with him each year, even if I do dread his wild tales of the island's mythology.

Now, he was standing at the water's edge as I came out. He threw me a towel and shrugged. "Man, I didn't think you were ever coming back," he drawled, turning away and walking up the beach to where I had left my clothes, and he had left his bourbon. He flopped down and moaned, "You've been gone for hours. I drained my bottle a while back."

I frowned. "What?"

"Hours, man," he repeated, heavily over-emphasising the first word. "I almost sent out a search party."

"What are you talking about, Denver? I just went for a dip."

He mimicked me badly. "*I just went for a dip.* Hey, man, you've been out there" – he pointedly looked at his diver's watch, the huge face flashing in the sunlight – "nearly three hours. I just don't know where you get your stamina. Are you like that in bed?" he added, a curious look on his face.

"I sleep," I said, not really understanding what he meant.

"Is that so?" he chuckled. "Well, more fool you, man!" he added as he turned and walked away. "I'm gettin' myself another bottle. I have a feelin' I'm gonna need it over the next couple of days." His deep laugh stayed in the air long after he had disappeared from view, and I grinned as I began to dry myself with the towel. I worked briskly, keen to get the salt water off my skin, but I dabbed gently around the two-inch scar on my chest, obtained courtesy of the accident. It didn't hurt any more, but I recalled how much pain it had caused me for months, and I still get the strange tingling every time I rub over it.

I settled down onto the sand, my eyes taking in the rolling waves and cloudless sky, and I thought again of my friend.

I don't suppose I will ever fully understand Denver. But then again, I have never really taken to people in general. Connected with my accident, I guess. The doctor told me I had been very lucky, but I remember nothing of it. I only know that I now have three recurring symptoms: a deep mistrust of people, that weird feeling under my scar, and the dream. Actually, it is more of a nightmare: a tree rushing at me, gaining speed, blurring, and then... waking up in a cold sweat. Fortunately, I have no more details, and I prefer not to dwell on it. Life is for living, the doctor had told me, and he was probably right. On the feelings of mistrust, Denver was certainly making progress in changing my opinion of people, although he might not be the ideal teacher.

Sitting on this beach, looking out across the bay, the sun winking at me over the water, I felt more alive than I have ever done before, even more than last year. Yes, I admit it; I was smitten by the magic of this beautiful island.

I fell back on to the sand, my hands clasped behind my head, my eyes squinting at the shimmering haze, and I contemplated the rogue cloud which perforated the blue like an unwelcome guest. When I eventually felt the sun begin to affect my eyes, I turned to look through my bag for my sunglasses. The towel fell from my shoulders, and my body shivered at the gentle breeze playing over my skin. I gave up on the sunglasses and settled down onto my side, the sun warming my back. I relaxed and watched a couple of girls in brief bikinis trying to play beach volleyball without a net. They were giggling and posing, their gazes drifting towards a group of young men who were watching them with eyes popping. One of the girls made a point of adjusting her bra, repositioning one rather large breast so that she was more comfortable, but which also made the boys more agitated. The games people play, I thought with some amusement. It was then, when my mind was happily unburdened that a shadow fell across me.

"Hello, David."

I turned. "Hello," I said involuntarily.

"Mind if I join you?" He sat before I could answer, an incongruous figure in a three-piece suit nestling into place beside me on a tropical beach. "It's lovely here, isn't it?"

I nodded. "Yes." I couldn't think of anything else to say.

"I have fond memories…"

"Of this place?" I asked, more out of politeness than interest. This man meant nothing to me, but rudeness is not in my nature. Go with the flow, I say.

"Fond memories," he repeated, almost dream-like. "You've been here before, too, David."

I looked at him, stunned. "How do you know that? How do you know me?"

He gave a little chuckle. "History, David."

"What are you talking about?"

"We have history… you and I." His smile was warm but crooked in some inoffensive way. I studied him. He was probably a shade over sixty, medium build, with a kindly face despite his wonky smile. I did notice that he had the same colour eyes as me, but I could see they were wary, and he was on edge.

"I'm sorry, but I haven't a clue…" I began.

He held up his hand. "Of course, you don't, David. How could you?"

There was a pause as we appraised each other. Then I said, "Who are you?"

"To know that, David, you first have to know yourself."

I jumped to my feet. "I don't like riddles, Mister…"

"*Doctor* Allenby," he offered, indicating that I should sit back down. "I need to tell you something, David."

I hesitated, then resumed my place. Despite my misgivings, I was intrigued. "I'm listening."

"I should warn you, this could be painful."

I reddened with anger. "Are you threatening me?"

He raised his hand again. "I would never do that, David. But you must listen."

"Give me one good reason why I should!" I roared.

"Because, David, my name is Rufus. I am your father."

I froze. I didn't have a father, or a mother for that matter. Something to do with me not having a history.

"Is there somewhere we can talk, David?"

I stared at him, my mind scrambled. "Talk?"

He smiled again, and for some reason it felt reassuring and familiar, even while my defences were going up. "I have a lot to tell you. It is most urgent if you'll listen," he said, almost beseechingly.

* * *

The café was small and intimate. That's why I liked it. The door was open, the sound of chatter mingling with the smells of exotic cooking which wafted over my senses. I wasn't sure why I had agreed to continue talking to this man. Perhaps it was the desperate look in his eyes or just the fact that my interest had been piqued. We went in.

It was quite dark, the only natural light coming from a window high up on one wall, a huge mural of traditional dancers beneath it, the colours alive and vibrant. Opposite was the bar, constructed of what was clearly driftwood, the dark knots and the grain embedded in the light, sun-dried timber. Sand, brought in by many bare feet, lay all over the floor. There were seven tables, all covered with linen cloths bearing the orange and yellow national flower, and each table had four wicker chairs. Few of these were occupied, for it was early, but the noise was still intense as the locals discussed life in this particular part of paradise. I sat down and waved at Morice, who gave me a toothy grin and came over with a bottle of my usual, plus two glasses. The owner of this oasis perched on the edge of the stunning beach, Morice, was a stocky little Frenchman who, I assumed, was in his fifties and bore the buzz haircut of an ex-military man, although I had never associated the flamboyant swagger with anything but Parisian élan and a past shrouded in café culture and Camel cigarettes. His voice alone would have given Sasha Distel a run for his money, and I often expected our host to burst forth with a sultry rendition of 'Raindrops Keep Fallin' on my Head'. Sadly, it never happened.

Morice was a particular friend of Denver's – probably his only real one – so it hadn't taken long for me to also fall under his spell. I enjoyed our evenings after hours; the three of us sat around a table, each cradling a shot of bourbon, me listening to their tales of life in wild America and even wilder Montreuil. They never asked for my story, and I never offered.

Rufus had grunted as he entered. He didn't like the gloom, and I could see the look of disdain on his face as he saw the mural. Not to his taste, I assumed wryly. He frowned as he surveyed the place, taking in the rickety old bar and the clashing smells of fish stew and sizzling steaks. He sat opposite me, wiping his troubled brow with a delicately embroidered silk kerchief. He picked at the tablecloth, trying to work out what the flower was. I didn't feel like enlightening him. He tried to say something, but the noise was too much for him, so he sank back in the chair with a resigned shrug.

I smiled with satisfaction. "Are you okay?" I asked, not caring a damn either way.

"Fine," he mimed, but I could see the way he looked at Morice when he came over with the drink. He was obviously out of his comfort zone, and that suited me fine.

"Thanks, Morice," I said. "My friend here won't be staying long."

The room had fallen silent when we entered, as they usually do when something unusual comes in. And Rufus was certainly that. Among a group of semi-naked surfers, swimmers and posers, his suit was enough to attract interest of the highest degree. He wiped his brow again with the kerchief, and somebody offered a wolf-whistle. *Nice touch*, I thought.

After a few seconds, the chatter began again, interest in the new boy waning somewhat, although the noise was more subdued as if they all had one ear tuned our way. I waved the bottle at him, but Rufus placed a hand over his glass, so I just poured a decent shot for myself. I was used to drinking alone anyway, at least before I met up with Denver.

"So," I said between sips, "where have you been all my life, *Father*?"

Our eyes met and locked. I saw pain in his, but that didn't soften me. I waited.

"Do you really want to talk about it here?" he asked, finally.

Now, my glass was empty, and I angrily smashed it onto the table. "Just tell me who you are and why you are here!"

He sat back with a resigned look on his face. "Believe me, David, I didn't want to be here now."

"That makes two of us," I snapped.

"You don't understand." He lifted up his glass. "Perhaps I will join you after all."

I slopped the liquor into his glass, some of it spilling onto his hand. He ignored it, knocking the drink back in one gulp. It was clear that this conversation was going to be difficult and very long if I didn't speed things up. "So," I said, "let's start at the beginning. Are you my father?"

It seemed a ridiculous question. He looked nothing like me. He wouldn't have passed as a very distant cousin, let alone my father…

"In a way," he said quietly, almost in a whisper.

"What?"

"I'm not going to explain. I won't. Not here." He picked up the bottle, poured another tot and sank it like the first. "Let me just say I'm the nearest you've got."

I stared him down. "You know, you really are trying my patience, mister. I could say you're pissing me off, but it's much worse than that." I stood, and the room suddenly became hushed, all eyes focused on our table. I felt like hitting the old man, but something held me back. Instead, I put my hand out just to push him away.

He grabbed my hand with a surprisingly strong grip. "Wait, David," he said, and something in his voice made me stop. "This is important. For you. For the future."

I found myself sitting back down, and I couldn't explain why. It just felt the right thing to do. "Okay, I'm listening," I said through tight lips.

He took an age to speak. "I wouldn't be here if it wasn't critical. I need to take you back with me."

"You what?"

"It's not safe…"

"Says who, the father I never knew existed? Or some madman out to… to do what, exactly?" I poured another glassful and downed it in one, the liquid calming my nerves only slightly. "Who are you – actually?"

He sighed, the sound both weary and resigned. "You need to listen, David. I mean, *really* listen." He reached for the bottle, but instead of filling his glass, he put the bottle on the floor at his feet. He had my full attention now. "I can't tell you everything…"

"What sort of line is that?" I said bitterly. "Sounds like something out of a cheap movie."

He nodded and gave me a watery smile, which was still crooked. "Perhaps, son," he said, then paused as if the last word might have been one step too far. I let it go. "It's complicated, David. But I repeat… it's not safe; *you're* not safe." He reached out to touch my arm, but I pulled back. "Please… you have to trust me on this," he begged.

I stared him down, my nostrils flaring and my hands beginning to form fists. I am not a violent man, but my patience was being sorely tried, and, for once, I wasn't sure what I was capable of. "I've never met you before," I snorted. "Why the hell should I trust you?"

"I was there, David."

I had started to rise, but I stopped. "What? Where?"

"Your accident. I was there."

This was too much. I flung back the chair and reached out for him, my hands grasping at his jacket. He didn't flinch. "I was there," he repeated, this time much softer, almost apologetic. He stood, my grip still tight on his lapels, and gently, he pulled my hands away. I let him. "I'm sorry, David. Truly. But we must go. We don't have much time."

"Tell me about it," I said hoarsely.

"What?"

"The accident. If you were there, tell me. Give me some made-up 'fact' so I can prove you're the lying bastard I think you are."

He began to make for the door, expecting me to follow. His words were like tasty morsels and, like a stupid bird following a line of corn, I obliged, falling in behind him, waiting for him to say something, anything.

"Just as I thought," I hissed. "You know nothing. Get lost!"

We were outside now, the sun waning and clouds beginning to cross the sky. Soon, it would be sunset, and perhaps I would be rid of this man who called himself my father yet filled my head with riddles and probable half-truths.

Denver approached, and I felt relief. I needed support from someone who cared about me. "Denver," I shouted with an enthusiasm I didn't actually feel, "where are you taking me tonight?"

He sidled over and gave Rufus a swift appraisal. "Hi," he said with some warmth.

"Hello," responded Rufus, equally friendly. "Pleased to meet you."

"He's not staying," I said quickly, "or if he is, then we're going."

Denver looked at me quizzically. "Is there a problem here, David?" he asked.

"You're looking at it!" I spat, and I saw Denver and Rufus exchange a look before I turned and walked away.

Denver came after me and grabbed my shoulder, turning me to face him. "Hold it, pal. What the hell's goin' on here?" he asked. "Who is this guy?"

Rufus had caught up, and he thrust a business card into my hand. I raised my fist to him, but Denver took up position between us, stopping me from doing something I might regret – or might even have enjoyed.

"If you won't come with me, then at least go somewhere safe." Rufus's mouth tried to form itself into that crooked smile again, and I realised that it was because he had a very small scar on his top lip, which I had not noticed before. "Please."

I snorted. "In your dreams!"

"You've got my card, David. Take it and go if you must. But remember what I say: you are in danger now, and only I can help you." He paused, and I felt the tension rise between us. There was something there, some connection which made no sense to me. But I still began to walk away.

"You hit a tree, David."

I stopped.

"In a car, a blue Toyota."

I began to turn back.

"I could give you the registration number… but I'm sure you won't remember it."

That was when the gunfire started. It was loud and incessant, like a group of drills going off in my head. For a second, I was disorientated and confused, but then, as I looked back over my shoulder, I saw Rufus go down, one sleeve of his expensive jacket shredded and a spray of blood pumping out of his arm. He was mouthing something, but I heard no sound.

Denver was heading for the café, his legs racing for all they were worth, his mind apparently only on self-preservation. I couldn't blame him. Rufus was my problem, and I realised at that moment it was a problem which might not be around too long, the way things were going.

I ran to his side, ignoring the bullets flying past me, bent down and helped him to his feet. He tried to object, but we both knew he had no strength for any kind of fight. I threw his good arm over my shoulder, and we scurried towards the café, rather like competitors in a life-or-death three-legged race. His face was pale, his mouth stretched in a grimace, eyes reflecting the fear that both of us felt.

"Leave me, David," he pleaded in a voice that I could hardly hear. "Save yourself."

Speaking had taken its toll, and he leant into my shoulder, his legs slowing, so that, by now, I was dragging almost a dead weight. "We're nearly there," I said. "Hang on."

It had all happened so quickly that I never had the chance to see who our assailants might be. The only thing I knew for sure was that we were the targets, and I almost lifted Rufus off the ground in my effort to get him to the café and safety.

"Come on, David!" I heard Denver scream, and I saw him standing in the doorway, waving frantically.

Bloody fool, I thought, but at the same time I was spurred on by his words and show of bravado.

As we got nearer, I was surprised to see Denver being pushed aside, only for Morice to appear holding a twelve-bore shotgun. He raised the weapon and fired over our heads, giving a yelp of delight as he did so. I wasn't sure if he had hit anything, but it certainly helped, especially when he discharged the second barrel and it was followed by silence.

It was then that we crashed through the doorway, and Denver slammed the door shut. We were still alive. I looked round the little café and was greeted with faces gripped by surprise and fear. For the briefest moment, nobody moved, unsure of how to proceed. Then, Morice put down his gun and raced to Rufus's side, gently ripping his sleeve and studying the wound in his arm. "Water! Get me water and some cloths," he demanded, and one of the girls ran behind the bar to oblige.

Denver was looking at me, bewildered. "What?" I said.

"They didn't hit you!" His voice was high, adrenaline-fuelled. "How the hell did they not hit you, David?"

"Don't ask me," I replied, thinking that there were more important questions to be asking, like 'Who are these people trying to kill Rufus Allenby – or me?'

Rufus was hunched on the floor, his back against the wall, as Morice dabbed at his wound and fussed over him. I sat beside Rufus and looked at him properly for the first time. "What have you started?" I whispered bitterly. "Who the hell are you?"

"They're going!" someone shouted, and a muted cheer went up as we heard the sound of a car skidding on the dusty road and driving away, just as a police siren came into earshot. "The cops are coming!" the same person added unnecessarily.

Rufus put his hand on my arm. "Thank you," he said weakly.

"Yeah," I answered without feeling.

"You need to get out of here, David," he whispered, every word a struggle. "Before the law arrives."

"What?"

"There will be too many questions. Go. Now."

Denver was leaning over us. "What the fuck is going on here?"

Rufus pushed Morice away and looked into Denver's eyes. "Get him out of here. Please."

"Sure," Denver said, obviously hoping to calm him down. "Whatever you say, mister."

Rufus grabbed Denver's sleeve. "He must not die."

Both Denver and I knew that whoever was after me would be back. Once the police had left to file their report, we would be sitting ducks. "Get the Moke, Denver. We're out of here," I said.

He didn't need telling twice and was out of the door and running across the sand before anyone else had moved. Morice had tightly wrapped Rufus's arm in a strip from one of the tablecloths, the exotic flower incongruous against the blood that had darkened Rufus's suit.

"You're coming with us," I said to Rufus. "You still have a lot to tell me."

"That can wait, David. I'll be okay here. You go."

"Oh, no," I said, taking firm control of the situation. "You're coming." Suddenly, I felt calmer than ever. "Morice, can I take your shotgun?"

"Certainly not, my friend," he responded with a grin. "She is mine. But I do have something else for you." He raced behind the bar and emerged with a rifle that looked even older than him. "It's a Lee Enfield," he said with pride. "It was my grandfather's." He winked at me. "It works a treat."

I gingerly took it from him. I'd never been anywhere near a firearm, let alone a vintage piece. But it did feel good in my hands. "Thanks, Morice."

"I am sure you will look after it, but just to be sure, I will come with you," Morice announced.

"I can't ask you to do that," I said limply.

"Then I take back my gun!"

"Okay, you win," I conceded with a smile.

Morice ran around the café, cajoling his regular customers to look after the place in his absence, then picked up his trusty shotgun and helped me lift a still-protesting Rufus to his feet. Then, we waited for the tell-tale sound of our getaway vehicle.

Denver parked the Moke outside, and he helped us manhandle Rufus across the back seats, where he slumped forlornly, holding his wounded arm and breathing heavily. To be honest, I was a little worried about him but thought he would survive a short, bumpy ride to the hospital, safe from the men who were following us.

Denver jumped into the driver's seat, and I sat beside him while Morice perched precariously on the back, grinning inanely and whooping with delight. At least he was enjoying himself.

"So, where to, skipper?" Denver asked, looking at me.

I pondered. The black car had headed west, so that was clearly out. North led to the hills, where we could evade them without too much trouble if they pursued us, but it would be a few miles of pretty rough terrain before we could reach any kind of civilisation. I had no doubt the Moke would handle it, but I wasn't so sure about Rufus. "East," I said with an authority I didn't exactly feel.

"Will do!" said Denver, throwing the Moke into gear so that it pulled away with a throaty roar. Or that could have just been Morice giving another whoop.

There was no road, of course, but the Moke hit the sand with panache, kicking it up either side and sliding slightly as we rose over the little dunes and back down again. Under normal circumstances, this area would have been classed as visitor friendly, but not today. The locals and tourists alike had clearly heard the gunfire and had headed for the hills – or at least the safest place available – and our escape wouldn't be witnessed. A good thing because it meant there would be nobody likely to tell tales to the wrong people. I actually started to breathe easier.

"What's the plan?" Denver shouted over the sound of the engine.

"Plan?" I replied. "No plan! Just head for civilisation, I suppose."

"The nearest town this way is Foscana, about eight miles."

"Okay."

"But we'll have to get on to the main road."

"Okay," I said again.

Denver was wrestling with the movement of the Moke across the sand, and I was thinking about Rufus when Morice leant across and screamed, "Car ahead!"

We all looked in the direction he was frantically pointing, and there, sure enough, was what was clearly the same black car, now parked on the side of the highway in front, at the very point we were about to merge onto it. A more urgent aspect, as far as we were concerned, was that the car's occupants had spilled out across the verge, guns raised.

"Shit!" said Denver. "They knew we were coming this way." He began to turn the wheel, causing the Moke to screech its objection, almost throwing Morice off the back. He whooped again, even as his knuckles whitened with the tight grip he had on the roll-bar.

I had been so naïve. Of course, they would be tracking us. These were professionals. They probably had binoculars or had just seen the sand cloud we had kicked up. They didn't need to be rocket scientists to work out where we were headed. I could have kicked myself if my legs hadn't been feeling cramped and twisted inside this uncomfortable vehicle. No wonder Denver had never been able to net the 'company' he so craved.

"Foscana's out, then," said Denver with more than a little sarcasm. "What's Plan B?"

Good question, and one I couldn't answer immediately. I was too busy watching the men scramble back into their car. There were four of them, all big and apparently muscular under their black suits. I almost laughed at the cliché, until it came back to me that their intention was my destruction. Not so funny now.

The sun was even lower in the sky, casting dark shadows over the dunes, like weird alien life-forms that danced across the sand. It got dark quickly in this part of the world, and I knew we had to find somewhere to rest up, away from the elements and the potential of a fatal confrontation with the men in black.

"Where are we heading?" I shouted at Denver.

"You're the navigator, so you tell me!" He grinned, clearly enjoying himself. "But if we keep going this way, we'll be in the sea, so may I respectfully suggest we change direction?"

The car had disappeared, presumably following the winding road that took it, at times, away from the beach and out of our view. I was hoping that if we couldn't see them, then the opposite applied. "Which way to the hills?" I said.

"Right. But they'll be expecting that, surely?" Denver replied.

"Exactly. That's why we're going to the caves."

"Are you serious?" Denver wanted to know, taking his eyes off the driving and throwing me a withering look. "You know they get flooded at high tide, right?"

I slapped him on the shoulder. "You forget, old friend, I did actually listen to you when you took me down there whilst trying to fleece me…"

"Fleece you? What, *moi*?"

"You said that only four of them ever flooded. The two smaller ones are more inland."

Denver choked. "But I never said they didn't get wet, man! We could be up to our knees… or more."

"Better than a bullet, don't you think?" I reasoned, and he had to nod his agreement.

"The caves it is," he whistled through gritted teeth, spinning the wheel sharply to the left, throwing Morice against the roll-bar, stifling the whoop that had started to burst from his mouth. He groaned instead.

Chapter Two

The Korinna Caves are a cluster of six hollows created by Nature in the island's limestone hills, which had been pushed out of the sea by tidal waves and tectonic plate movements many millions of years ago. Each cave boasted its fair share of mesmeric stalagmites, stalactites and flowstone, offering a dazzling lightshow when the sun was in the right position. They were the island's hidden gems.

Right now, though, the sun was barely present as we carried Rufus over the rocks and into the mouth of Cave Five. It didn't really have a name – none of the caves did – but Denver had to differentiate between them for his punters when he was recounting the tale of the mermaid. Imagination was not his strong point.

Rufus was in and out of consciousness, and I was concerned for his well-being. We laid him on a large plateau of rock that we found a little way into the cave, which was both secure from any incursion of the sea and also the most comfortable spot we were likely to find.

"We should have left him back at the café," Denver said.

I couldn't argue with that, so I said nothing.

Morice busied himself, changing the dressing on Rufus's arm. The wound looked bad, and I again felt the guilt. I had only brought Rufus with us because I wanted answers, and I thought I would get them when he was in a hospital bed far away from here; but now it looked distinctly probable that I wouldn't get any closure, and I might very well have a dead man on my conscience. I walked back to the entrance of the cave, deep in thought. Life had been so comfortable, what, less than two hours ago. I had been lying on the beach, not a care in the world when everything was shattered, and here I was now, hiding out in a hole in a Pre-Cambrian hill, putting my two best friends in danger and facing the possibility of annihilation. What the hell was happening…?

I looked out at the sea and then turned to study the lie of the land to the right. More hills, covered in moss and wild lavender, offering just a whiff of scent in the still air. Denver had hidden the Moke well. I couldn't see it, and we would be really unlucky if our pursuers came across it. Of course, they may still be up in those hills, waiting for us to fall into their trap. I hoped so because a quiet night would be very welcome, especially for Rufus.

Him again. It always came down to Rufus. Who was he? What was he to me?

"All quiet, David?" It was Denver, who had come up behind me.

I nodded. "I'm sorry," I said weakly.

"For what?"

I couldn't help a small chuckle. "What, you mean apart from us cowering in a cave, waiting for a bunch of killers to attack, and with a badly injured man in tow."

I sensed Denver's smile. "Yeah, man, apart from that."

I put my arm around his shoulder and squeezed. "You know what I mean."

"Yeah, I do. But remember, pal, it was my choice to be with you."

I nodded again. That really didn't need an answer.

"Besides," he said, "I'm an American. Shit, you know we're all gung-ho guys!"

We surveyed the horizon in silence then, looking for danger, hoping for nothing. The silence was awesome; even the sea kept its peace as the moon began to rise, and the sky turned from a dusty pink to a slate grey in the blink of an eye. It was an amazing sight, and one which would have made my heart race at another time.

I sat on a rock and cradled the Lee Enfield, feeling an inner strength from it. Absent-mindedly, I wondered whether it had ever seen any action with Morice's grandfather. He had presumably been French, born around 1950, I guessed, but I couldn't think of any conflict in which he might have been involved. I knew that France stayed well clear of Vietnam in the late sixties and seventies, even though it had originally been one of their colonies. I, therefore, decided that the rifle, like me, was a campaign virgin. Long may it stay that way.

"I hope that thing works," said Denver.

I looked up at him, brought back to the moment by his voice. "What? Oh, yes, so do I."

He crouched beside me and took out some gum, offering me a strip. I shook my head, but watched intently as he unwrapped his piece and put it in his mouth. Americans and their gum, eh?

"You know," I began, "when I asked you to bring the Moke to the café, I hadn't intended to take you with me."

"What?" he exclaimed with mock indignation. "You were going to take my Muleshoe away from me? I am devastated."

My eyes opened wide. "Muleshoe?"

"Yeah, Muleshoe."

"Really?"

"Yeah, really."

"Why?"

He shrugged. "Man, do I have to explain everything to you? I named her after Muleshoe, a town in Bailey County, Texas…"

"And that's another thing, Denver," I said quickly. "You so don't come from Texas, any more than I do. That accent is about as fake as… as…"

"As Richard Nixon's smile?" he finished for me.

"Well, that's not what I was trying for, but it's near enough. So, where do you really come from?"

He went quiet, and I thought he was sulking, but eventually he said, "I was born in Priest River, Idaho."

"Sounds good," I said, then waited.

"Yeah, I guess. Had a good view of the Selkirk Mountains and spent my childhood along the Priest River."

"Idyllic."

"For some, maybe. Not for me, though. I got out as soon as I could, and ended up bumming it down Santa Monica way. Life was better then."

"The California dream," I said.

"Too true, man."

"So why the Texas drawl?"

He gave me his hippy grin. "Company, man! They loved it. They thought I must have been a cowboy or somethin'!" He nudged me playfully. "Know what I mean?"

"I do," I said with as little irony as I could muster. "But Denver is in Colorado, not Texas."

"Hell, I ain't all fake, David!" he said with feeling. "Denver's my real name. Denver Hardin Miller, at your service."

I swear that if he'd had one, he would have doffed his Stetson and waved it as if he was at a rodeo. Then he went quiet for a second, before saying, "So, David, what about you?"

"Me?"

"Yeah. What's your history? We've never really spoken like this before," he said, and I sensed a slight embarrassment in his voice.

I knew I wasn't about to answer him, even before I saw the glint. It flashed between the trees a couple of hundred metres away, and I brought up my arm to usher Denver back into the darkness.

"What?" he hissed softly.

"They're out there."

Denver peered into the gloom, seeing nothing. "You sure?"

He didn't need a response, as he saw me level the rifle and aim it. "I'll get Morice," he whispered, then scurried away.

I should have known they wouldn't give up. It was clear that they had scanned us with binoculars or something, and they knew we weren't making for the hills. Although the terrain up there was what one might euphemistically call uneven, I felt sure they would have outrun us in their car, considering the disparity in speed of the vehicles. They knew it, too. A four-wheel-drive car beats a Moke any day of the week.

No, they knew exactly where we were, and we were in a noose.

I cursed myself for my stupidity. For one thing, I should have left Rufus back at the café, where he would have been safe. I could have talked to him later, after he had been treated and I had escaped with my life. Now, all I had done was put him in more danger, along with my two friends. I needed to think things through more carefully if we were going to survive.

There it was again, the glint. I might have had the slightest doubt with the first time, but now I was certain. Someone was approaching with the stealth of a predator. I wasn't sure if it was his belt buckle or his gun which had been caught in the moon's rays, but either way, it spelled trouble.

Denver and Morice appeared silently behind me.

"How's Rufus?" I whispered.

42

"Resting," said Morice, which didn't tell me much. I didn't pursue it.

"D'ya see anyone yet?" asked Denver. "Like the whites of their eyes."

I looked at him. "Are you serious?"

We all heard the sound together and crouched further down. It was a twig snapping in the stillness of the night. Professional hunters these guys were not. A plus for us, perhaps.

Before we could stop him, Morice had slipped silently away, his feet leaving the smallest of ripples in the water under our feet. I was about to call him back, but common sense took over, and I stayed silent while bringing the rifle to my shoulder. "I'm sorry, Denver," I whispered, my eyes not leaving the gloom outside. "This is a hell of a place to be without a gun."

Denver sniggered. "Fear not, my friend." As he spoke, he pulled a pistol from inside his shirt and waved it around. "Smith & Wesson Magnum. Came with Muleshoe when I bought her. One previous owner, a Clint Eastwood fan. You know, *Dirty Harry*." I nodded, dumb-struck, as he added, "Got its own shoulder holster, too. I wouldn't go anywhere without it." He then spun it round his finger, Wyatt Earp-style, and knelt beside me, ready for action, his arm brushing mine. I felt the buzz of excitement he was generating, and I let out a breath of anticipation.

"I had no idea," I mumbled.

"I've told you before, I'm an American, pal. It's my inalienable right to bear arms. For defence only, of course."

"Of course," I echoed. I was going to add, "Have you used it before?" But that particular question stayed in my head. I really didn't want to know the answer. So I just gave him a watery smile and gripped my rifle tighter.

In the moment, I had completely forgotten about Morice. I was losing the plot, falling apart. I winced at my own stupidity. Nobody with any sense would have gone into a cave, knowing that they could be trapped at any minute. Morice understood. He had got out. Now, it was our turn.

"Here, take this," I hissed at Denver as I handed him the rifle. "I'm going to get Rufus, and then we are moving out."

Denver said nothing, just looking at me and accepting the weapon. Then he turned to the cave entrance and stood guard.

Rufus was still on his ledge, his breathing heavier than it should have been, his arm hanging down. His eyes were open but sightless. I couldn't make out if he was conscious or in some kind of semi-delirious state between life and death. I exhaled deeply, aware even more of what I had done, what I had put him through. He might be a charlatan, but he didn't deserve this.

I scooped him up with all the gentleness I could muster and carried him to where Denver was still on guard. Denver had obviously reholstered his pistol and was caressing the rifle thoughtfully. I didn't offer a penny for his thoughts, or he might just have told me what a fool I had been.

Instead, I nodded and began to move out of the cave, my steps slow and careful, my eyes trying to penetrate the darkness, looking for whoever might be out there. They knew we were here, so they could simply sit it out and pick us off in the morning. It then occurred to me that Rufus might not actually make it to morning, and my mouth went dry. I had to get him to a hospital.

I sensed Denver beside me and felt a little better. It's strange how another person can give you inner strength, even when the odds are stacked against you. I knew Denver wouldn't let me down, and I hoped he could say the same about me. Right now, I had my doubts.

The ground outside the cave was uneven, small boulders and stones slowing our progress and making us zig-zag, which perhaps wasn't such a bad thing, especially if the bullets started flying.

I stopped and bent on one knee, laying Rufus down. I listened. There was the gentle wash of the water as it lapped the beach, and the almost imperceptible click of the bats echoing out of the cave entrance. Then there was a flash, and the harsh whine of a bullet ricocheting off one of the boulders close by.

Denver sank down beside me.

"Are you...?" I started to ask, before a great boom blocked out all other sounds, and a second later we heard a loud movement ahead. Denver had his rifle raised, but it wasn't necessary. One of the men fell forward, half his face blown away, his gun still in his hand.

"Morice!" we both said together. So he hadn't run out on us. He was out there, protecting us with that wonderful shotgun of his. One down, how many more to go?

I told Denver to retrieve the man's gun, while I lifted Rufus and carried on walking. Speed was of the essence now, even more than before. The darkness was our friend to some extent, but the moon might suddenly appear from behind a cloud, and then we'd be sitting ducks. Denver passed me and took the lead, his footing more sure than mine, considering the many times he had explored these caves and the fact that he seemed more like a mountain goat than a human being. I struggled to keep up with him, although Rufus appeared to be no weight at all to me.

The shotgun blasted again, this time from a different place, but with a predictably similar result. There was a long groan, followed by silence, then the jubilant voice of Morice: "Hey, *poilu Americain, j'ai un autre salaud!*"

Denver chuckled, and I looked to him for a translation. He grinned then. "Morice said, 'hey, hairy American, I got another of the bastards!' And I quote."

"Hairy American?" I queried.

"We all have a nickname, don't we?"

"I don't," I said.

"That figures."

He shrugged and moved on, ending the conversation. I trailed in his wake, wondering what nickname he would give me, and preferring not to know.

Rufus groaned as I lifted him over my shoulder like a fireman carrying a damsel in distress. That thought might have been funny in different circumstances. He began to whisper in my ear, his voice croaking and cracking as he said a name over and over, before he settled back into his stupor, which was hopefully a blessing. This journey couldn't have been doing him any favours, considering the loss of blood. Again, I cursed myself. What had I been thinking of? But, again, that wasn't the leading question, which was: What the hell is going on here?

I had lost Denver for a second. I stopped and looked around. I could see nothing, but thought I could hear someone ahead and assumed it was Denver, so I began to move forward. The bullet came from behind, ripping into Rufus and making me tumble forward, throwing him across a rock, where he lay, lifeless and broken. I let out a cry, but stifled it almost immediately, aware that the next few seconds could be all that was left of my own life. It was then that I realised I had no weapon with which to defend myself. Denver had gone off into the distance with all our firepower, leaving me helpless and hopeless at the hands of trained killers. I lay still, unwilling to move, until some kind of plan came into my head. I guessed that, now I was down, the gunman could no longer see me in the gloom, but I knew he would be approaching with the stealth of a hunter and that my next move would be critical.

I rolled over and crawled forward as quietly as I could, my eyes searching for a place of darkness where I could regroup and perhaps plan my counter-attack. There was a large mound of sand ahead, enough for me to at least get out of the line of fire, so I began to edge towards it, rising up so that eventually I was on all-fours, moving crab-like at what appeared to me to be a snail's pace. Sweat was dripping from me, but I couldn't wipe it away. My hands were engaged in saving my life. I was almost there. I was clutching at the tall blades of grass, intent on pulling myself over the mound, when I sensed rather than felt a boot swing at my body, and I heard the breath wheeze out of me. I fell onto my back and came face to face with a smile so mean that I thought I was already in hell. I hadn't heard him getting close, but now here he was, standing above me, the silhouette of a grinning maniac holding a gun. There wasn't even time to offer up a prayer to the Almighty before he fired again, this time point-blank at my chest. It was all over...

I heard the second shot through a haze, as if a gun had been fired into some kind of spiralling metal chamber, rattled noisily around many corners and emerged the other side, finally bouncing across my brain and leaving a terrible pain in my head. I know I groaned, but heard nothing; felt only a throbbing from deep inside my very soul. Sounds melodramatic, but it's the only way I can find to explain how I felt. But at least I felt something.

I stretched one arm out, then the other. I flexed my chest, then tried to move my left leg. Remarkably, everything seemed to be in working order. Slowly, very slowly, I began to sit up, using my hands as props to hold me in an upright position. My eyes were clearing, although my mind was taking longer to focus.

"David!"

The voice came from perhaps a hundred miles away, and I turned in what I assumed was the right direction.

"I'm here," I gurgled, although I wasn't sure what sound was coming out.

"It's okay, pal. I got ya." That voice again, but closer now. Almost upon me.

I felt hands grabbing me, arms surrounding me in an embrace. "Shit, man, I thought you was a goner!"

Yeah, I thought I was saying, *me, too.*

"Thank God I got him before he could do any damage." Denver, for that was who I suddenly recognised, sounded as relieved as I was as we stayed in the manly clutch for a few seconds. Finally, he let go and stepped back. "We should get out of here."

Yeah, I mouthed, we should. It was only then that I saw the body a few feet away. The corpse of the man who had been intending to kill me.

My hand scrabbled around to get a purchase on the sandy ground so that I could stand. That was when my fingers touched something, and I wrapped my hand round it as I stood. I swayed slightly, my head beginning to clear, and I could see Denver looking at me.

"You sure you're okay, David?"

"Fine." At last, a word had actually escaped. "What happened?"

"I heard a shot and realised you weren't behind me. I came back just after the bastard fired again. Luckily, he missed you, and I was able to neutralise him."

Neutralise? Only an American would say a word like that, I thought, my senses finally getting back to normal. But then my mind went into overdrive. Rufus? He was dead, I felt sure, but why was I alive? The man had been standing above me, for God's sake. He had aimed and fired. He couldn't miss. Even I, a novice at this game, would have finished him off if the roles had been reversed. This was nonsense. I should be dead. I remembered my clenched fist and looked down, opening my hand as I did so. A spent bullet nestled in the palm, and my breath skipped. He *did* fire. I had the proof literally in the palm of my hand. So why wasn't I dead? For some reason I couldn't explain, Denver's words back at the café when all this began came into my mind: "*How the hell did they not hit you, David?*" I hadn't given it a thought then, but now the question seemed more important than ever.

I slid the bullet into my pocket so Denver couldn't see it, and offered my hand to him. "Thanks, pal. I owe you."

He gripped my hand, but shook his head. "No thanks needed, man. We're in this together." A pained expression came over his face. "I think Rufus is…"

I nodded sadly. But then my mind began to race again. Rufus. He had started this by coming to the island. He obviously knew where to find me, which would indicate that he had been keeping a close eye on me. Not because he was my father, but for some other reason I didn't yet understand. But it was worse than that. He had inadvertently brought those thugs after him, intent on killing me. Why? And how did they track him? To get to the island, Rufus would have probably taken at least one car journey before the two flights, as well as a taxi from the airport to get to me. True, they could have just followed him, but that was fraught with possible problems and potential failure. Besides, once we were in the Moke, how would they know where we were heading? There are miles of sand dunes, and we would have been out of sight for long periods – and yet they still showed up at the point where we were going to hit the main road to Foscana. And then there was Cave Five…

"Quick, Denver, get over here!" I whispered urgently as I made my way to the still form of Rufus lying across the boulder.

"What is it?" Denver asked. "We need to get out of here!"

"Yes," I agreed, "but first we have to find something."

"What?" Denver said, as I started stripping the jacket off the body. "David! What the hell are you doing?"

"Think about it, Denver. These guys knew exactly where we were. Back at the dunes… and even in the caves."

"A lucky break," suggested Denver, still staring at me as I pawed at Rufus's clothing.

"I don't think so. Once they knew we weren't going to make it to Foscana, they came straight to the caves. Cave Five, to be exact."

"Straight to us," said Denver, finally understanding.

"Exactly," I said. "Something gave them pinpoint accuracy as to where we would be." As I said this, my hand felt something inside the lining of the jacket. "I don't suppose you have a knife on you?"

"Well," he beamed, "it just so happens…"

It took a matter of seconds to rip open the lining and remove the tracking device. I sighed. "Poor old Rufus.

They must have taken his jacket at some stage and inserted this, before returning it. He wouldn't have known a thing about it."

Denver took the device from me. "It's a gem. Small and beautifully formed. More CIA than Carphone Warehouse."

"I agree, but I doubt even the CIA would send heavies like these men."

Denver shook his head. "You know nothing, oh innocent youth!"

"Yeah, thanks for that," I said. "Now, let's get the hell out of here."

As I said it, we both looked at Rufus. We had to leave him. We had no choice. We knew there was nothing more we could do for him. We would inform the authorities as soon as we could.

As the decision was made, more gunfire reverberated round us, and we automatically ducked, even though it was clear that nothing had been aimed at us. The sound was muffled, coming from somewhere over the dunes.

"Here, you'd better take this," Denver said, offering me the rifle. "Now we need to find Morice."

I nodded, and we began to run, the rifle sloped in my hand, all thought of Rufus banished to a compartment in my brain which was now locked, the key temporarily tossed away. I needed all my energy to tackle the living.

We breasted a dune together, side by side, stopping to gauge our location and listening for any sign of Morice or the remaining thugs. Nothing, save the night whispers of the wind over the sea. Under normal circumstances, it could have been a wonderful experience. Now, it was just a fight for life.

The moon was beginning to disappear completely behind the thick clouds which usually filled the sky at this time of night, so we both strained to make out any recognisable shapes. I had no clue where we were, but I was hoping that Denver would, at the very least, be able to point us in the right direction. Assuming we could find Morice first, of course.

Denver nudged me, and my eyes followed his. In the distance were lights, moving, swaying in mid-air, and getting closer.

"Police!" hissed Denver.

I agreed. There was no way they could not have heard the gunfire. "We must find Morice," I said, urgency in my voice.

"Don't worry about him," said Denver. "He can take care of himself."

"You reckon?" I queried, bearing in mind his age and how out of condition he seemed.

Denver scoffed. "Don't let his appearance deceive you, David. Our friend was in the Legion for twenty years."

I looked at him, my mouth open. "You mean, the Foreign...?"

I didn't have time to finish. Denver was racing ahead, down the other side of the dune, and it took me a few seconds to catch up.

"This way!" he ordered, and we swung sharply left, moving away from the shoreline and onto a flatter, more solid footing. Grass. A welcome feeling, as it meant we could run faster, putting more space between us and the police, not to mention the would-be killers who were still out there.

After a few minutes, Denver put out an arm to stop me. We crouched, breathing deeply, our eyes adjusting to the lack of light. It hadn't occurred to me while we were running, but now I could see how black the sky was, how we couldn't see more than a metre in front of us. Suddenly, I felt safer.

"I need to get the Moke," Denver murmured. "You stay here, David. I won't be long."

"What?" I couldn't believe what I was hearing. "You can't leave me here!" I beseeched him, scared once more.

"You'll be fine. There's a tree trunk over there..."

I couldn't see it.

"Crawl over and duck under it. Nobody will find you, I promise." The last was said with a wide grin; I know, because I caught a flash of his teeth in the gloom. "We're near the track, so I can get the Moke up close. Trust me, David." And he was gone!

I made my cautious way in the direction he had indicated, and eventually my outstretched arm brushed against some branches, and I fell gratefully into a dip in the ground, sensing the trunk above my head as I did so. As I burrowed into my hideaway, my breathing began to settle, although my mind refused to. *Rufus was dead.* Along, almost certainly, with all the answers to my questions. He had been there, he said, at my accident. How could that be possible? It was only an indistinct memory, but surely I would have known if he had been there. I remember the tree, the speed of movement and perhaps someone else… But it wasn't Rufus, I was sure. None of this made any sense.

I don't know how long I remained perfectly still. It seemed like hours, but, of course, it couldn't have been. The sky was no darker – nor, indeed, lighter, which would have signified an approaching dawn – when the unmistakable sound of the Moke brought me back to the present, and probably woke up the whole island as well. I gauged it was perhaps about two in the morning now, and all signs of frantic movement had long gone. The police had almost certainly found the bodies, including Rufus, and were more than likely at a loss as to what had happened on their peaceful island. I imagined them combing the undergrowth close by, searching for clues, before fanning out and widening the search for the killers… and us.

I scrambled out of my hole and sprinted towards the sound of the idling Moke, unsure of its exact location. When all else is silent, one sound can be very difficult to pin down.

"Over here, David!" Denver whispered urgently. "Move your ass!"

I didn't really need that sort of motivational encouragement, as I could finally see the outline of the vehicle, and after negotiating some unseen bushes, I gratefully climbed aboard, Denver giving me a helping hand.

"Glad you could join me!" he said, throwing the Moke into gear and creating sand cascades as he pulled away, the movement jerking me back against the seat before I had time to grip the roll-bar.

When I regained my breath, I looked at him. "What now?"

It was a question he had obviously been chewing over. "We need to get you out of here, David. For all our sakes!" He grinned then, clearly enjoying himself. "Remember my last job?"

It took me a few seconds. "You said something about lobster-catching."

"Right. It was a crap job with crap money. But it did have one thing which could be of use now."

"Yes?" I queried, not exactly on his wavelength.

"A boat, David. Our route out of here!"

"*Our*...?" I started, as if the thought of him staying with me was the most ridiculous thing in the world.

But by then he was steering the Moke away from the beach and heading into unknown territory to me.

We could only be heading for the harbour.

Chapter Three

I sat on an old, gnarled rock which was covered in moss and lichen, my head in my hands. Denver stood some way off, tinkering loudly with the Moke in a vain effort to restore life to its mechanical heart. The sun was beginning to put in an appearance, and I looked down on the bay below, where the boats bobbed gently on the sea, and the locals were just starting to stir. We had been here for nearly two hours now, stranded by a malfunctioning Moke after it had crested one too many rocky outcrops, sending out a jarring screech and causing palpitations in an already wired-up Denver.

I put my hand in my pocket, and my fingers found the business card. I pulled it out, and it suddenly hit me that if Rufus had really been my father, then this flimsy card was all I had left of him. My eyes were watering, possibly from the sun, and I couldn't focus. The writing on the card was blurred. I stroked it, as if some powerful force would take everything away; or, at the very least, explain what the hell was going on.

There were images racing into my brain as if someone was flicking through a photo album in my head. Rufus on the beach... Rufus wounded... Rufus smiling at me through his pain... Rufus dying on my back...

I wiped my eyes with my shirt sleeves and looked at the card, expecting answers. I didn't get them.

Denver finally accepted that the Moke had given up the ghost, and he came over, cursing to himself. He stood above me, wiping grease from his hands with a section of his shirt he had ripped off. "The old beast has had it," he announced. "RIP." He hesitated, studying my face. "What is it?"

I handed him the card. "His name was Rufus Allenby," I said.

"Not your father, then," Denver said unnecessarily.

"It would appear not." I paused, looking into Denver's eyes. "But he's started something that I need to finish."

Denver nodded, and I could see the steel in his eyes, which worried me. He sat down, and we rested in silence for a few moments, watching a circling gull. Finally, Denver turned to me. "We need to talk about this, David."

I shook my head. "No, my friend, we don't. You need to get the hell away from me. It's not safe ... *I'm* not safe."

He smiled then. "It's a bit late for that, don't you think?"

"You've come through it unscathed for now," I reasoned, "but that's no guarantee for the future."

His smile widened. "What's a bullet in the gut between friends?"

"That's not funny."

"No," he agreed, the smile fading, "it's not. But it's how I feel, David. I am closer to you than I have ever been to anybody else in my life. We have a bond of some kind

– I can sense it." He paused, as if building up to a climax. "We go on together."

I opened my mouth, but no words came out. He was right about one thing. I had felt it from the moment I first laid eyes on him. I saw beyond the grifter, working his unsuspecting mark into parting with money for a fable about a creature that had never existed, his silky tongue churning out a web of words to ensnare his victim. I saw beyond the brash American veneer, the loud bravado and the bourbon-swigging. I saw the inner-man. Weird as it may sound, I saw my soul reflected.

"Come on," Denver ordered, his voice crackling with emotion. "We need to move. That boat won't wait, you know."

He was on his feet, pulling me up, grabbing the Lee-Enfield and waving it at me. "Besides, we have to get this back to its rightful owner."

"Morice?" I mumbled, not sure how to react. I had once again forgotten about the Frenchman, and the pangs in my chest reminded me of how selfish I had been. "Where is he, Denver?"

"Oh ye of little faith, bro. Trust me, he is safe. I told you, he was in the Foreign…"

"Legion!" we both chorused together, grinning at each other and falling into a man-hug.

"One for all and all for one," Denver announced haughtily as we began to move out.

I chuckled. "I think you'll find that was some other group of musketeers… but it'll do me!"

The first thing that registered in my mind was the frantic squawking of the gulls as they danced on the salty breeze and dive-bombed the fragile little boats, swooping back up with fish entrails tumbling from their beaks. Then it was the early-morning sun bouncing off the turquoise and white water, creating a kaleidoscope of translucent bubbles which seemed to skim across the gentle waves lapping around the boats.

Then it was Morice, standing nonchalantly beside a pile of old lobster pots, each one leaning like some drunken matelot trying in vain to support himself and his comrades. Morice was smiling.

When we had looked down on the harbour from our hillside vantage point, it had appeared close enough to almost reach out and touch, but it had taken us over an hour to negotiate the narrow pathway leading down to the beach, our footing unsure and our hands scarred by bushes and thorns.

I ran to Morice and we embraced, slapping each other on the backs like two reunited brothers separated at birth.

"David," he said, the word coming out as *Daaaviiid*, due to the Gallic accent.

"Am I glad to see you," I breathed with relief and affection. "How did you get away?"

Denver came between us. "That will have to wait until later." He turned to Morice. "Did you get them?"

60

The Frenchman beamed. "But of course, my friend. It was, as you say, a piece of *pisse!*"

Denver nodded and began to walk away. I shuffled up to him, confused. "What's going on, Denver? What are you two up to?"

He stopped, turned and looked at me. "David, we are saving your ass." Then he was stomping ahead, his trainers sinking into the soft sand at the water's edge.

I fell in beside Morice. "Well?" I asked.

Morice did not break stride. "I have been in contact with Denver since we parted at the cave. Mobile phones are as good as walkie-talkies, are they not? I knew what you were going through, and he knew…"

"What you were going through," I finished for him. "He knew you'd got away."

"But of course."

"So why didn't he tell me?"

Morice chuckled. "Time, David. You did not have the time to think of me. Besides, I can take care of myself."

I understood. "Your training."

"You think a few men with guns are going to frighten me? Bah, I eat them for lunch!" His laughter reverberated across the harbour, causing one or two of the fishermen to look up.

"So," I asked, "what is it that you have?"

"Your means of escape, *mon ami*. Your and Denver's passports."

* * *

We sat on the shore, our legs out straight and our backs against the side of a bright red fishing boat that had clearly not been to sea for many years. By the look of it, the paint had been peeling for most of those years, revealing bare wood which had been weathered and guano-splattered, so much so that it was impossible to identify the actual species of wood used. Along the side, by my left shoulder, I could just make out the name of the vessel, *Calypso*, although, from a distance, the fading script lettering made no sense at all.

Morice took a swig from his bottle of beer, courtesy of a boatman who had kindly donated a few bottles to our safe keeping. We drank his health as we sat there, watching Denver in an animated discussion with one of the fishermen.

I looked at Morice's profile, probably for the first time ever, and marvelled at what he had done for me. "I owe you, Morice."

"Pah!" he replied with a wave of his arm. "We are friends, David, you and I. And besides," he added with a Gallic chuckle, "I am enjoying myself!"

We continued our beers in a comfortable silence, watching Denver's agitated negotiation with the lobster fisherman who had once been his employer, and who now seemed to be casting the American adrift. Denver raised his voice, and I wondered whether I should perhaps go over and offer a calming edge to the proceedings. But suddenly, the fisherman burst into a raucous cackle and slapped Denver on the back with some force. Then they embraced, both laughing and lurching from side to side, as if they were ready to fall over and roll in the sand. This lasted for over a minute, and then they shook hands warmly, almost aggressively, and Denver made his way back to us, a saunter in his step and a wide grin on his face.

Morice was the first to speak. "Ah, I see the *entente cordiale* went well."

"Eventually," I added pointedly.

"Fear not, my friends, Uncle Sam always finds a way," said Denver.

He sat beside us and accepted the beer Morice offered. He snapped the lid and took a long, satisfying swig.

Then, I said, "I assumed it would be easy. After all, you did work for him. At least, that's what you told me."

"They're all the same, these damn lobsterers!" Denver said. "Short memories – and even shorter fuses. Godammit, anybody'd think the two years of my life I gave him meant nothing!" He emptied his bottle, and I thought he was about to throw it at the fisherman. He might have considered it, but, instead, he lobbed it over his shoulder and into the boat we were leaning against, the sound of the bottle causing a discordant note as it nestled among all the other bottles already there. "Just think, guys, the old dog didn't want to know me. After all the early mornings I spent out on that damned boat with him. Not to mention the nights in the bar…"

"I remember them well," Morice said, a dreamy look on his face.

I shrugged. "So, how did you swing it?"

Denver offered a face of such innocence. "I told him the cops were after you."

"What?"

Denver threw his arms in the air. "Well, it's half true. And I have to say, the old seadog was pretty impressed." Then he added, almost as an afterthought, "Oh, and I said you'd pay him a thousand dollars!"

Chapter Four

I felt sick. As a matter of fact, I was pretty sure that I had never felt worse in my entire life. Every time the boat rolled, my stomach went the other way, causing a tsunami of raging feelings deep within me that I knew were going to erupt at some point. I tried to hold my breath; then I took deep gulps of air, but that was even worse, because I inhaled sea spray and the sickly crustacean smell of lobster and other creatures I didn't even want to know about. We had been at sea for twenty minutes, with another two hours of this before we reached the mainland, and I could start to live again.

Denver sat beside me, a comforting arm across my shoulder and a cruel sneer on his face. "You'll get used to it," he said, knowing full well that I wouldn't. "Just think of nice things."

"What, like the *Titanic*, you mean?" I said sarcastically.

He chuckled at that. "Ain't no icebergs round these parts, pal," he said, as if to console me. Then, "Might get humped by a big whale, though!"

"Thanks," I spat, tasting the salt round my lips and retching once more.

I read somewhere that there are around four and a half million fishing boats in the world, and it was just my luck to be aboard possibly the worst of the lot. The decking was speckled with what used to be bright white paint to reflect the sun, but now it was peeling at an alarming rate, shrivelled by the same sunrays. The cabin, tacked about midway along the hull, still had a semblance of the bright orange paint it had once proudly displayed, but that, too, was fading fast, and the glass windows had long been replaced by cheap plastic bearing a layer of tinted vinyl which had bubbled so much that the first mate – or whatever they called him on this kind of vessel – had to peer from side to side to get a clear view of any oncoming traffic.

The captain, barely less dishevelled than his boat, came up to us and said a few words I didn't understand. That might have been because he was using his native tongue, or it could have been that my mind, like my stomach, was addled. He handed a small bottle to Denver, who offered it to me.

"What is it?" I asked through clenched teeth.

"Your salvation, David," Denver said.

"Really?" For some reason, I didn't believe him.

"Take a shot," he urged.

"What is it?" I repeated.

"It's a local concoction," said Denver. "Apparently, a lot of people on the excursions are weedy landlubbers…"

"Gee, thanks for that," I hissed, trying out my own phony Texan accent.

"And this settles their internals like nothing else. The captain here swears by it."

As if he understood every word, the captain lifted his right hand and simulated pouring the liquid down his throat, then belched loudly and smiled, the sun catching the two teeth he had in his mouth.

"Do I have to do that?" I asked Denver.

"The belching, you mean? No, that's a personal choice. I do have it on authority, though, that it does help. What do you say?"

I thought about it for a second, then unscrewed the lid and took a small swig of the liquid, which felt rough on my tongue. "Bloody hell!" I said. "It's revolting."

Denver slapped me on the back. "Just like all good medicines. Try another drop."

I did, and it tasted better, though what my stomach would make of it was anybody's guess. As they say in all the best medical dramas, the next few minutes would be critical.

* * *

I felt much improved. There was no doubt about it. After only ten minutes or so, too. The boat was still rocking, but my stomach was now rolling with the punches. It was a feeling that I could live with. I belched happily and sank back, my arm placed nonchalantly over the side as if I were a life-long matelot. The salty wind was good on my face, and I felt the colour returning. I would survive, after all.

"Better?" said Denver.

"Surprisingly, yes."

"Good," he said. "Because we need to talk."

I looked at him. "Yes," I said. "I owe you."

"You do," he said simply. "You need to tell me everything. Somebody's after your guts, and we need to find out who and why."

"My story won't take long," I said. "Everything before the accident has been lost. My memory has a span of precisely six years."

"Okay," he said, "so let's start with the accident."

I gathered my thoughts. "It's hazy," I started.

"Sure, most serious accidents are. What was involved?"

"Involved?"

"Yeah, was it a car crash?"

I thought about my dream. The fast-approaching tree, waking in a sweat immediately before impact. "Yes, Rufus said as much. I hit a tree…"

"Okay. So where was it?"

"Surrey, I assume," I said hesitantly. "That's where I live." Then, I racked my brain before coming up with something new, which surprised me. "The Hog's Back…"

"The *what*?" he almost choked.

Gathering my thoughts, I said, "It's an area between Farnham and Guildford."

"That means nothing, bud. Geography ain't my thing… especially weird place names in England. Man, you thought I was strange naming my Moke Muleshoe!"

I ignored him. "That's all I can remember."

"How did it happen?" He was back on track now, trying to coax more out of me.

"I don't know." I was desperate to clutch at anything that might help.

"Take your time, David. Relive the moment."

I knew what he meant, so I sank back into the boat, my gaze drifting out to sea and my mind focusing on what I needed to remember. I had never done this before, and I wasn't sure what good it would do, but eventually a picture began to emerge, as if a curtain was slowly being pulled apart, giving just glimpses of what I needed to know.

"I am in a car. I'm sure I'm not driving, so I must be in the passenger seat…" I closed my eyes, squeezing them tight so that no light could penetrate. I was now back in time, reliving it. "I am shouting something. I am hysterical. I'm saying 'Save…', but that's it." I opened my eyes and thumped my fist on the side of the boat in frustration.

"Save," Denver repeated. "Save who, David?"

I sighed heavily. "I don't know," I said, anger in my voice. I had tried so often to evoke the events of that day, but had never recalled so much. This was new and frightening. Who was in the car with me?

Denver was still probing. "You said you were in the passenger seat." I nodded, so he continued, "Then who was driving?"

"I don't remember," I said lamely.

"Male or female? Old or young? There must be something, David. Think!"

I lost my temper then and turned on him. "Don't you think I've tried? God, it's a nightmare!"

69

He eased up a little and let me settle. We sat there for several minutes, riding the gentle waves and listening to the monotonous drone of the engine. The two fishermen were huddled together in the small cockpit, presumably keeping well clear of the madman who was wanted by the police.

Eventually, Denver tried again. "This Rufus…"

"Yes?" I said.

"He told you he was at the accident."

"That's what he said."

"But you don't remember him."

"I've already told you, I just remember the tree and now the car."

"Somebody pulled you out."

"What?"

"Humour me, David. If somebody wrapped a car round a tree, chances are they would need help getting out of the wreckage," he said.

"Okay," I agreed, then took a moment to think about it. "So, what are you saying?"

"Could it have been this Rufus guy? Is that how he knows you?"

Now I understood what he was driving at. Could my mind's eye see Rufus Allenby helping me out of the car?

"It's possible, I suppose."

"So, who was pulling out the driver?"

Again, I thought hard. "I don't remember any movement…"

"Mm," said Denver. Then he went quiet.

"What is it?" I asked. "What are you thinking?"

70

I didn't need him to answer. It was clear. Nobody working on the driver's side, no frantic effort to save a life or remove an injured person from the wreckage. Nothing. Suddenly, I felt a tear in my eye. "She's dead..."

Denver was quick to react. "Who's she?"

"What?" I mumbled.

"You said *she*, David. Who was she?"

My mind was closing down, and I felt nauseous again. "I can't remember," I said, the movement of the boat adding more confusion to my addled mind. "I'm sorry."

The last words came out with such resignation that Denver put his arm around me and said no more. I was grateful the interrogation was over for now.

PART TWO
England

Chapter Five

The boat trip to the mainland and the flights home had passed without incident. I had remained tight-lipped, and Denver had respected that by also staying silent.

Now, we were in the back of a taxi, still silent, but with eyes on the crawling traffic of the M25. Denver was seeing views he had never experienced before; I was seeing danger in every face that turned our way, half expecting a gun to be raised and fired through an open window as a vehicle pulled alongside.

I was still convinced that Denver had actually lost the plot. It was his idea to go to my house – I ask you, how dumb is that? Sure as hell, they'd be watching the place. Staking it out like some cheap TV cop show, but with a much more realistic ending: me covered in blood, stretched out on the drive before I'd even had time to pull out my key, let alone a gun I didn't have.

I'd tried to point out to him that I had narrowly escaped death twice now. "Yeah," he'd drawled, "and you're still with us. It's karma, man."

"So, explain again what your plan is," I'd said, exasperated.

"It's easy! They don't know you're back in the country. How could they? Sure, they may have a guy watching the place, but we can take care of him."

"Okay," I'd said, still not convinced, "but what are we after? You know, in the house."

"Your laptop, for one. There may be something on it you haven't sussed out. After all" – this with a wide grin – "you didn't know you were a wanted man." He had then studied my face. "Relax, David, it's all under control."

We had then continued in silence – mainly because I had nothing else to say.

Now, Denver turned to me and said, "How far is it?"

"What? Oh, another twenty or so miles." I stopped then, wondering. "Do you really think this is a good idea?"

"Yes, David. We need answers. It's the only way we can fight this."

I understood; of course, I did. But that was no consolation. So I used up the next half an hour or so playing through various questions in my head. Like, who was Rufus Allenby, and was he really at the accident which presumably nearly killed me six years ago? Especially if, as Denver intimated, the driver – definitely female, of that I was now sure – had not survived. And who are these men trying their hardest to wipe me out? But, more worryingly, why was I still alive after what happened in the sand dunes?

The taxi came to a halt, the driver swivelling round. "We're here," he said, reaching out a chubby hand, palm up. I dropped a few notes in and climbed out of the car, stretching my legs as I stood up. My muscles ached, and I knew it wasn't just tiredness. My whole body was taut. It was strange: everything in the street was so familiar, so peaceful, and yet my mind was buzzing, and my scar was throbbing. For just a second, I thought of that tree, the car, the dead driver...

"Keep the change, pal," Denver was saying cheerfully, bringing me back to reality. Okay for him, it was *my* money he was splashing.

The taxi took off, and Denver herded me to the edge of the pavement, so close to the hedge that I felt it scratching my cheek. I could also feel his breath as he whispered to me.

"Stay here, David. I'll take a look round and report back."

I didn't argue. Instead, I just stood there as he walked off as nonchalantly as a commuter coming home from a busy day at work. Despite being a brash American, he seemed to fit into the staid Surrey surroundings, and I was impressed. I waited, as instructed.

It gave me time to think, which is never a good thing. My mind was in turmoil, and as I fingered the bullet in my pocket, I couldn't help going back to the sand dune. Surely the man had fired? At point-blank range, there was no way he would miss. And yet here I was, living, breathing, wondering...

Denver was back in a minute or two. "All clear, David. Let's get in and out before somebody notices," he whispered urgently, pulling me along by the sleeve of my coat.

"What would they noti—?" I began, but my voice stopped mid-word. There was somebody lying in the garden, his head at a strange angle. "What the—?"

Denver didn't answer; he just waited anxiously for me to take out the key and open the door, before bundling me through and closing it behind us.

He was puffing heavily, but I was okay. "Who was that?" I said, not sure I really wanted to know.

"They had someone watching the place, that's all," Denver answered, his voice level and matter-of-fact. "Not a problem."

"It is for him," I said wryly.

"Not any more, it ain't."

Denver urged me forward. "Get your laptop and anything else you think we might need," he said. "We have to find out what the hell is going on here."

Of course, the house had been untouched. They had merely placed a guard outside on the off-chance that I made it back this far. The word must have got back pretty quickly after we escaped the gunmen on the island, and they had prepared for this eventuality. Well, almost. The guard may have been there a while and was perhaps a little tired and bored. Either way, Denver clearly had no trouble with him. I was beginning to think differently about my American friend. Especially when I reflected on the state of that guard. To my untrained eye, it looked very much like a professional hit, the way the guy's neck leaned out of kilter.

"Hurry up," Denver shouted. "There may be more of the goons."

Thanks for that thought. I raced up the stairs and into the office, ransacking my filing cabinet, stuffing the paperwork into the old briefcase that lay beside my desk and scooping up my laptop. I figured that nothing else would be of value in the coming days. Pity I didn't have a gun in my desk drawer like they do in some of those thrillers I've read.

I got back to the top of the stairs, my hands full, as Denver appeared in the hall.

"I heard something, David," he whispered as loudly as he dared. "Is there a back way out?"

"Yes," I replied with some sarcasm, "there's a *back* door!"

"Well, I suggest you use it, wise-ass!" he came back with a smile, and I didn't need telling twice.

I jumped the last three steps of the stairs and wheeled towards the back of the house, while I noticed out of the corner of my eye Denver crouching behind the sofa by the front window.

I turned back and stopped. "What are you doing?" I asked, expecting him to be following.

"You go, I'll hold him off."

I was about to argue when a bullet smashed through the lounge window and passed close by me with a whizz. "Bloody hell!" I screamed, and I was in the kitchen and clutching at the back door before the second bullet hit the window. I didn't like it, but now it was every man for himself.

I swung open the door with some trouble, considering the bulk I was carrying, but I knew I couldn't let go. The answer to everything might be in my hands.

I felt the rush of cool air and stepped into the garden, my eyes peeled. It looked like I was clear. I quickly scanned the area, seeing nothing untoward, so I started to make my way to the gate and out to freedom. It was then that I spotted movement by the hedge, and I froze. There was somebody in the shadow, and it was clear, even from this distance, that he was armed and dangerous.

"Stay right there," a voice boomed out, deep and gravelly, as if he'd spent a life-time chewing on lumps of granite.

I had no intention of staying put, but which way to go? Away from him would undoubtedly result in a bullet in the back, while a frontal assault on him would also get me a bullet. I could throw the laptop or the briefcase at him and hope to score a direct hit – but what were the chances? In my admittedly very short memory, I don't recall ever being the sporty type, so that idea was out.

While my mind had been weighing up the possibilities, the man had been standing there, waiting for my response, unmoving but clearly in sight. What was he, about four metres away? How many seconds would it take to cover the ground and tackle him? I didn't have a clue, but realised this was my only option, so I dropped my precious cargo and sprang into action.

He hadn't expected this, and it took a second or two for him to react, just managing to shout, "Hold it!" before I was almost upon him.

The adrenaline was pumping through me at such a rate that I thought I must be moving at an impossible speed, especially as I almost had my hands on him. But then a sound rang out as the gun exploded in front of my chest – but I didn't stop.

I launched myself at him as he pulled the trigger for a second time, and the sound was almost deafening, but I hit him hard, sending him sprawling against the hedge, where he slithered down, coming to rest in a sitting position in amongst the dahlias.

I will never forget the look of horror on his face, and I'm sure it was reflected in mine. I was hyperventilating, my hands on my knees, my body bent forward, my lungs clutching at air which seemed to be evading me. I was gasping loudly, I knew, but all I could do was stare down at the man on the ground, taking in the frozen features and the open but unseeing eyes. I realised he was in a state of medical shock, but I was more concerned with my condition. I stood up straight, rubbing my hand over my chest. Nothing. No bullet hole, no blood. What the hell was going on here? Was he firing blanks? Denver's words on the island came back to me once more: *How the hell did they not hit you, David?*

Finally, wheezing in a huge lungful of air, I reached down and took the gun from his hand. "Who are you?" I demanded, surprised at how loud my voice was in the confines of the hedgerow.

His mouth was open, but there was never ever going to be any sound coming out.

"What do you want?" I persevered, putting the gun to his temple. "Talk, or so help me, I'll finish this!"

I knew it was hopeless. The guy might as well have been brain-dead, and I knew he would never give me any answers. So I had a major problem. What now?

I tried one more time. "Who sent you?"

He almost grunted, but only succeeded in dribbling down his chin. This was hopeless – and there was still Denver to think about.

Like you, I suspect, I had never killed a man, but this one had to be dealt with. In the end, it was easy. I just closed my eyes and pulled the trigger, sensing his body jerking and falling into the hedge. The sound of the gun brought me to my senses, and I opened my eyes. The man had a neat hole in the side of his head, and I again rubbed my chest where I should have been hit and where I, too, should have had a neat hole or two. Nothing. I was sweating, taking in the fact that I was still intact – still alive. I wanted to scream at my frustration and confusion, but I was shaking too much, and my throat was so dry that my tongue felt like a strip of sandpaper in my mouth. I fell to my knees and started to cry – *really* cry, the sobs coming from deep inside and erupting through me so that I began to pummel the body beside me with a fury that I had never experienced before. It felt as if Rufus was lying there, and I was trying to take out my revenge on him for what he had done to me, for I knew it was surely him that had brought me to this point. I just didn't know how or why.

It was then that I remembered where I was and what was happening. Scooping up the laptop and briefcase, gun held tight in my right hand, I raced back into the house, fearful of what I might find.

Denver was still in the lounge, crouching behind the sofa. I wasn't sure what he had hoped to achieve, but I gave him maximum points for both bravery and stupidity, especially as I saw a figure climbing through the shattered window, gun poised.

He was a big brute, filling the window space and cutting out the sun. He wore a rather tight-fitting suit, which was stretched over his ample frame and had the meanest look I had ever seen. That was when I fired.

The bullet hit him high in the chest but was clearly not a fatal shot. He looked up, cocked his gun and aimed before I let off two more shots, which sent him tumbling back out the window and onto the front path. I ran to the window, leaned out and gave him one last bullet to be sure before I stopped and looked down at a bewildered Denver, who plopped onto the sofa, wiping his brow.

"Hell, David! What...?" But he couldn't say any more.

I was still shaking, the sweat pouring off me, and I put the gun on the coffee table, falling onto the sofa beside Denver.

He had got his voice back. "You were bloody marvellous!" he enthused. "But where did you get the gun?"

"You'll soon find out," I said cryptically.

He gave me one of his looks and said, "Okay, pal, let's get the hell out of here. There could be others. This is getting real deep." He stood, albeit a little unsteadily. "Right, where's your car?"

I looked up at him. "I don't have one. I can't drive."

"What?" His eyes were wide with astonishment. "Then how the hell do you think we can make a quick getaway, pal?"

"I have a driver."

He beamed at me. "Now, why doesn't that surprise me? Okay, get onto him and arrange a pick-up point. And make it quick, because the neighbours will have phoned the cops by now."

I took out my phone and dialled the best I could with my shaking fingers. Denver was right: this was going to be a crime scene in a matter of minutes, and guess who was going to be the number one suspect? Shit!

"Hello, Mr Parks."

The voice pulled me back from the brink. "Gregory, I need you here *now*. It's life and death…"

"Did you say…?"

"Yes, Gregory, I did. Meet us at the corner of Foreman and Grange Roads."

"Us?"

"Yes, Gregory. Now hurry!"

"On my way, Mr Parks."

I pocketed the phone, and Denver stretched out a hand to help me up. As we stood together, he wrapped his other hand around mine, and his eyes glistened. "Thanks, David." It was a simple statement but so powerfully said that I choked over any possible response I might have been planning.

Instead, I just picked up the gun and gave it to Denver. "Here," I said, "I have a feeling I won't be needing it."

He looked at me with a query in his eyes, but took the gun anyway and put it in the waistband of his trousers. "Come on," he mumbled as we ran out the back door. I picked up the briefcase and laptop, and we made for the gate.

Denver must have seen the body in the hedge and put two and two together without really finishing the puzzle, but he said nothing. All I heard was a very sharp intake of breath.

We burst through the gate, and I led Denver down the road at a pace which I felt was at least comfortable for him. Although I felt shocked at what had transpired, I was sure he was equally stunned, but we had to keep together, especially now we could hear the faint sound of sirens approaching.

We ducked behind a garden hedge, hoping that the owner wouldn't come to his door and make a fuss, as three police cars raced by. We were lucky and continued on our not-so-merry way to the rendezvous.

* * *

"Hey, Greg," asked Denver, now safely in the back seat of the Lexus beside me, "where are you taking us?"

"My name is Gregory, sir," Gregory responded in a cut-glass accent, putting Denver firmly in his place. My driver was a little younger than me, dapper in appearance in his smart suit, his face animated at all times, as if he was

85

some kind of cartoon character on a permanent loop, his eyes expressing something mysterious as well as inquiring.

"To answer your question, sir," he continued almost without taking a breath, "we are going to Ongar."

"Fair enough." Denver looked over at me and shook his head. I ignored him.

We were travelling along the Hog's Back, heading far away from my home in Ash, which I imagined I was never going to see again.

However, that wasn't uppermost in my thoughts. I was still getting my head around what had happened and puzzling over the fact that I couldn't be shot. Did this mean that I could never be killed? That I would never die? So, who was I? An android of some kind, a freak of nature?

Now, the events on the island were becoming clearer. Running to the café, helping Rufus along, slowing me down – I was almost a sitting target. At least one of those bullets *must* have hit me. And at the dune, lying prone, that killer looming over me. I heard the shot – and yet nothing had happened. Now I knew why. But how?

"Hey, Gregory," said Denver politely, "so who or what is in this Ongar place?"

"My aunt, sir."

Denver and I glanced at each other, and I registered the confused frown on his face, knowing he was lost. "Ongar is in Essex – the other side of London," I explained.

"Right," he said, although, of course, there was no flicker of recognition.

86

"She is expecting us, sir. I took the opportunity to call her before I picked you up." Gregory's eyes flashed in his rear-view mirror as a smile creased his mouth. "I told her you were two celebrities who needed to be incommunicado for a while. All hush-hush, you might say."

"And will *she* be hush-hush?" asked Denver dubiously.

"Oh, yes, sir. My Aunt Grace understands these things."

With that mysterious comment, the car fell silent again, and my thoughts took over. I was trying to piece together a very strange jigsaw, with most of the pieces still in the box. Rufus was the key, of course. But he was nothing but a blind alley now. All I had was…

His business card! I dragged the crumpled card out of the back pocket of my trousers and looked at it. Plain white with simple lettering in black Times Roman:

Dr RUFUS ALLENBY
Physicist
Rufall@denny.com

Hopeless. It told me nothing. I sighed and replaced it in my pocket, deciding that at the first opportunity I would at least try the email address. Perhaps the 'Denny' part might offer up a clue.

It took us just over two and a half hours to get into Ongar, with Gregory slipping off the M25 early and passing by Woodford and Chigwell and on to the village of Stapleford Tawney, maintaining a steady speed through the slower roads. We listened intently to the radio, but little of interest was broadcast. Perhaps the police were still trying to sort out the mayhem that must have greeted them at my house.

"Just three more miles, Mr David," Gregory informed us as we saw the sign to Ongar Bridge.

"So what does your aunt do, Gregory?" Denver asked.

"Do, sir? Why, nothing. She has independent means."

"Okay. That figures."

"My uncle was chairman of a pharmaceutical company, which he sold for a rather large fortune," Gregory explained without a hint of flamboyance. "Then he died."

This sort of took the wind out of our sails. "Sorry to hear that, Gregory," I commiserated.

"Thank you, sir."

We drove on for some minutes until Gregory swung the Lexus through a walled gateway and up a long gravel driveway with manicured lawns and huge oak trees on either side. The gravel crunched as the tyres rolled to a halt in a sweeping arc at the entrance to what Denver would have probably called an ancient castle.

It was, in fact, a splendid eighteenth-century classical Georgian manor house, built of grey stone and brick and set in what appeared to be several acres of beautiful grounds and woodland. It took my breath away.

"Shucks!" breathed Denver. "How the other half live, eh?"

"As you say, sir," agreed Gregory, stepping out and opening my door. "And as I said, you are expected."

As Gregory spoke, the massive oak front door of the house opened, and I envisaged seeing the scarlet livery of a footman or at least a suited butler. Instead, the lady of the house appeared, a tall, elegant woman dressed in a knee-length tartan skirt, a white rouged blouse and with a shawl over the top. By my estimation, she was well into her seventies, but she looked good on it.

"Gentlemen, you are more than welcome. Please, come in… before somebody sees you!" she breathed with an air of conspiracy.

While that possibility was highly unlikely, we did as she had instructed and made our way to her side.

As Gregory got back in the car, Grace said slyly, "I see there is no luggage."

"It all happened so quickly, Aunt. I will arrange supplies in the morning," Gregory tried to explain.

Although giving the appearance of being shocked, Grace ushered us through the door and into a bright drawing room, where she indicated that we should sit on the two armchairs, which were positioned well away from the huge bay window. "One can never be too careful," she said by way of explanation.

"Thank you," I said, "for your kindness."

She stood over us, and I got a sudden feeling of menace. "Now," she said darkly, "perhaps you will return the favour by telling me the truth."

Chapter Six

We sat around the circular oak table in the dining room, the four of us. Gregory had parked the Lexus out of sight in the garage and had joined us, now suddenly confused as to the situation he found himself in.

"Sit down, Gregory," Grace ordered, and her nephew obeyed in silence. "Now, listen to me, all of you, I do not appreciate being lied to, especially by you" – and here she threw a withering look at Gregory – "so I expect you to explain yourselves."

Denver looked at me for guidance, but I knew I had to come clean. It was obvious that we had now put Gregory's aunt in great danger, and the least I could do was tell her my story. I also felt that the unburdening of everything might prove cathartic in some way.

So I explained about the trouble on the island and the problem at my home, making sure I made no mention of dead bodies – and I certainly never revealed the fact of my new-found immortality. That was something I still had to get to grips with myself. And I definitely didn't want Denver to know. That was one complication too far.

When I had finished, Grace looked from me to Denver; then her eyes rested on Gregory. "So, how much of this did you know?" Her voice was sharp, accusatory.

"He knew nothing, I swear," I said. "I just phoned him to get us out of a fix…"

"A fix, you say? So, Mr Parks, can you tell me how this 'fix' came about?"

I hesitated, forming my words. "No, I can't. The first thing I knew about it was when this man came up to me, claiming to be my father…"

"This Rufus, you mean? But you say he is not your father?"

"No. He is… was a physicist. With a different surname," I added limply, falling into silence.

Nobody spoke for a moment, all of us digesting where we had got to in this sorry mess. There were now four of us involved – ignoring, for the moment, Morice back on the island, who had presumably returned to his comfortable and more mundane life behind the counter of his café. I knew I could rely on Denver, of course, and I was fairly confident about Gregory's support, but Grace was the unknown quantity.

However, to my eternal relief, she soon climbed down off the fence. "You say your memory goes back only six years, Mr Parks?"

"Please, call me David. Yes, I remember nothing before the accident."

"And when exactly did you make my nephew's acquaintance?"

"He has been with me for many years now."

"Well, that's not quite true," said Gregory sheepishly, appearing to sink into his chair. "I was asked to be your driver about, er, six years ago…"

"By whom?" I demanded, confused.

Gregory chewed his lip. "Well, I was contacted by telephone at first…"

"Explain," Grace snapped.

Gregory cowered a little. "This man called. He said he wanted to engage me as a personal driver to a gentleman who had just been discharged from the hospital. I was to be available at all times, at Mr David's request."

I was stunned. "I didn't know that. I thought you had always been my driver."

"That's what the man told me. Make it appear that I had always been with you. He said it might help with your recovery."

Denver, too, was shocked. "And you never spoke to each other about any of this?"

"Certainly not!" Gregory said firmly. "I was under strict instructions. The man said that any negative thoughts might endanger Mr David's fragile mental state."

"That was nice of him!" I said with feeling. "So, you never met this man?"

"No, sir. It was all conducted over the telephone."

"Did he say how he had come up with your name?"

Gregory smiled. "I have an impeccable reputation."

"Okay, so how did he pay you?" asked Denver.

"Oh, *he* didn't. After I had agreed to think about it, a lady came to see me with a very handsome cheque as a retainer. She said that they would look after me if I gave up my other work and concentrated solely on Mr David. I agreed at once, of course."

"What about future payments? The retainer couldn't have lasted six years, surely?" I said.

"No, sir, it didn't. I gave the lady my bank details and have received regular payments. As a matter of fact," Gregory added with a wink, "I never did spend that retainer."

Grace was ahead of us. "We can trace the payments!"

I grinned at her, my very own Miss Marple. "Yes, we can! Brilliant."

"Can you remember what account name the money came from?" asked Denver, moving to the edge of his chair with renewed excitement.

"Oh, yes. I remember because it is unusual. Rufall, it's called. I assumed it was a holding company of some kind. I did try to check it out, but without success," said Gregory.

My hands were clammy with nerves as I reached for the business card in my pocket and threw it on the table. "Rufall. Rufus Allenby. So there is a connection!"

Grace was all over the case now. She picked up the card and studied it. "David, I see you have your laptop. I think you should search this 'Denny'."

"Good idea, Grace," I agreed, noting the waspish look she gave me at my presumption at using her given name. Then she softened.

"Excellent," she said, delighted that she was clearly now part of the team.

I brought up the laptop, plugged in the lead to the mains and waited. The battery, of course, was long dead, but a pulse from the wire made the computer surge to life.

I tapped in 'Denny' and got a town in Falkirk and a stream of names spreading over many pages. There were bakeries, snack bars, accountants and plumbers, all vying for a good spot in the list – but there was nothing of value to us.

"Try 'Denny physicist'," urged Denver, but I was ahead of him, already typing in the second word. I found some guy at Yale University, another from Canada who had been nominated for a Nobel prize forty years ago, together with a Chinese scientist, and a physical trainer who had somehow bypassed the system and been hooked up to the wrong heading.

"It must be a company," Gregory said. "What about 'Denny & Co' or 'Denny Limited'?"

Of course! I tried the 'Limited' and hit the jackpot the first time. "Denny Archer Limited," I said, opening up the company's website and beginning to study it.

The others leant in, and I eased them back with an arm which, for some reason, was shaking. "This looks like it might be the one," I said.

"What's it say, David?" asked Denver.

I read some more and then quoted, "Denny Archer, leaders in the worldwide study of particle physics in relation to the structure and behaviour of energy and matter." Then I stopped. Stunned. This was telling me something, and I didn't like the sound of it. *Oh, Rufus, what have you done to me?* I took a deep breath and continued, "They have an R&D department, but mainly manufacture coil ring accelerators and other equipment. Not very exciting."

"Where are they based?" Grace asked.

"Battersea. Judging by the photo, their head office is in what looks like a Victorian house."

"Very nice!" murmured Denver over my shoulder.

"What about the staff, David? Your friend Rufus may be listed," Grace suggested.

I wanted so much to tell her that Rufus had not been a friend, that he was just somebody who had breezed into my life and created a tsunami of destruction that would not be spent for some time yet. I wanted to tell her that I felt guilt and anger over his death, that I was bewildered and broken by the events on the island. I wanted to… break down and cry. But I did none of these things. I just looked at the computer.

There was no mention of Rufus – but then I froze again. *Robyn Newman.* Robyn was the name Rufus had whispered to me at the dune seconds before he died. I had expected it to be Robin, a man, but for some reason, Robyn, a woman, made much more sense.

"What is it, David?" Denver had seen my frown.

"See this? *Robyn.* I think she holds the key."

Denver read off the screen: "Dr Robyn Newman, Head of Experimental Research, Particle Physics." He looked up. "Sounds heavy."

"Yes," I agreed, "but we have to assume that these are the good guys. After all, Robyn Newman's colleague, Rufus Allenby, did come to warn me."

"Agreed," said Grace.

"Yeah," said Denver gravely, "but who are the bad guys?"

We sat back then, exhausted, each with a swirling mist inside our heads. I was suffering the most, I knew, because I had a secret. Something that was so out of this world that I wasn't sure I could handle it. This was the first chance I had been given to digest all that had happened in the hours since Rufus had approached me on the beach, but it was all still a blur. I understood nothing, and felt only the cold shiver of dread and incomprehension. I had a bullet in my pocket which should have been in my chest; I had life when I should be dead; and I had unanswered questions which were not going to be explained away any time soon. I sank back into my chair and breathed heavily.

Grace had taken the opportunity to go out to the kitchen, and now she came back with a tray holding a large teapot, four bone china cups and saucers, a matching milk jug and a sugar bowl filled to overflowing with white and brown sugar cubes.

She poured a cup for each of us – Denver taking it black – and I put in milk and three sugars, stirring furiously, before bringing the cup to my lips and tasting the hot energy going down my throat. *Energy*. There was that word again.

"I think," said Grace, holding her cup daintily, her little finger raised, "that we should plan a strategy."

I couldn't help but notice the delicious smile that played round her lips. She really was enjoying herself.

"I agree," chipped in Denver, picking up on Grace's excitement. "We must go to Battersea!"

I smirked. "That's not a statement I ever expected to hear."

96

"But your friend is right," said Gregory, not quite having the nerve to address Denver by his name. "The answers will be at this Denny Archer…"

"And with the mysterious Robyn," Denver finished.

Grace delicately returned her cup to the matching saucer. "Not exactly mysterious," she said. "Ms Newman does have an online presence."

We looked at her in surprise. "She does?" I asked rather stupidly.

Grace offered me one of her sympathetic smiles, as if she was being asked to explain herself to some kind of inferior being. "One is able to ascertain a great deal in the three minutes it takes for a kettle to boil, young man. It can be time well spent."

I nodded, not daring to show any more of my obvious ignorance.

"You have a laptop in the kitchen!" Denver said rather unnecessarily, the look of admiration deeply etched on his grinning features. It would appear that he had developed a very strong case of auntie love.

"Your Ms Newman is a product of Nottingham-Trent University, where she obtained her BSc about twelve years ago. She then went on to do her Masters in Particle Physics at Edinburgh, before going into research at various non-governmental quangos both here and abroad. She was head-hunted by Denny Archer seven years ago, specifically to launch their research into particle physics."

"Okay," I said, "but who are Denny and Archer?"

We all turned to Grace, expecting the answer.

"Matthew Denny," she explained, "is an award-winning designer and manufacturer of scientific equipment…"

"Everyone's an award winner these days!" Denver said bitingly.

Grace ignored him. "Denny has made a fortune from a number of patents and designs, not least his range of colliders used in the pursuit of the Higgs Boson…"

"Like the one at CERN," said Gregory.

"Indeed," agreed his aunt, almost patting him on the head for being a very clever boy, "but that particular model is not one of Denny's. He specialises in smaller, table-top versions."

"And Archer?" I asked.

Grace smiled. "No such person. Think of 30th November."

"Meaning?" I wasn't sure who had said it, but the word must have been on everyone's lips.

"Matthew Denny's birthday," Grace continued, creating just a little light at the end of the tunnel. "It's on his website for all to see," she added with a gentle turn of her lips, which may have been a smile of superiority, although her breeding surely would not have permitted such a thing.

Remarkably, it was Denver who was the first to respond. "Astrology!" he beamed. "Sagittarius… the Archer."

"Correct. Like we were, I imagine Mr Denny must have been overwhelmed by the number of people and businesses with his surname, so he personalised his company just that little bit more. The Archer, half-man and half-centaur, is considered to be the learned healer whose higher intelligence forms a bridge between heaven and earth, a fact not lost on our multi-millionaire, I am sure."

I was stunned. "And you learnt all this in the three minutes it took to boil a kettle?"

"Very nearly," Grace said with a grin. "Fortunately, I also had the two minutes while the tea was drawing in the pot."

We stopped talking for a minute, each of us drinking our tea and digesting the knowledge we had gained from our hostess. I, for one, was intrigued by the prospect of meeting Ms Robyn Newman, certain that she would be able to enlighten me further as to my extremely strange predicament. I had been dealt a clearly life-defining curved ball, to use Denver's vernacular, and yet I felt so calm and in control. I could sense tingles all over my body, but they were not fighting against me. If anything, they were adding strength to my resolve, and I was ready for the fray. Then Denver brought me back to earth.

"So, who are the bad guys?" He looked around at us all. "Well, for now, we know as much as we're likely to about Denny Archer and this Robyn... but who have we got in the blue corner?"

"A good question," I sighed.

"One thing's for sure," said Gregory, "they're not fighting to the Marquess of Queensberry rules."

"Oh, very good, Gregory!" chuckled Denver.

"Thank you, sir," Gregory said shyly.

I exhaled sharply. "They certainly don't intend taking any prisoners."

"Amen to that," said Denver. "We've been lucky so far."

Without thinking, I rubbed a hand across my chest. "The only thing that is clear is that they are after me."

"But why?" Grace asked.

I now had a damned good idea why, but I kept my mouth shut.

"There is one thing that is puzzling me," said Denver, his brow furrowed. When he realised nobody was going to respond, he continued, "What have you got to do with this Denny Archer? And another thing: if they want something, then why the hell are they trying to kill you? It just doesn't make sense, David."

That thought had crossed my mind on more than one occasion. Clearly, Rufus had wanted me alive, but the gunmen on the island were desperate to see me dead. They had killed Rufus without compunction, and would have got rid of me as well if their bullets had been effective. But Denver was right. It didn't make sense.

"All roads lead to Battersea," I said, trying to sound clever.

"But you must be careful, sir," Gregory said with feeling.

Denver nodded and drew the gun from the waistband of his jeans. "This should do it!"

Grace recoiled in horror, while Gregory just exploded with glee. "My word, a Walther PPK. Weapon of choice of both Ian Fleming and Adolf Hitler…"

100

We all turned to him, bemused. "Hitler?" I queried.

"Oh, yes," said Gregory, warming to his subject. "He committed suicide with one in his bunker."

"Good riddance, too!" said Denver.

"Fleming armed James Bond with a Walther in *Dr No*," continued Gregory, as if he hadn't been interrupted. "Elvis had a silver one inscribed 'TCB'."

I knew I shouldn't ask, but somebody had to. "TCB?"

"Taking Care of Business."

"Which is just what we're going to do," said Denver.

"Yes, but you'll need some reserve magazines," Gregory informed us innocently, almost as if he was talking about the type you take off a shelf at a newsagent. "I can help there. I have contacts." He smiled then, happy with life. "I'll sort it out tomorrow when I get your new clothes."

Not for the first time, I had to wonder about the calibre of the people I had managed to gather round me.

Chapter Seven

I awoke with a start, which came as a complete shock to me as I had not expected to sleep at all. The bedclothes, like my mind, were in a state of turmoil, the sweat still glistening on them as well as on my forehead, the feeling of helplessness still deep within me.

I stretched my legs and arms and swung myself into a sitting position, before rubbing my eyes with my knuckles, trying desperately to focus. I failed miserably and grunted my annoyance.

I had dreamt, of course. Well, more of a nightmare, really, as I reluctantly replayed the last few hours of my life. Had that all it had been? *Hours.*

The night had not begun well. On reaching my room, I had studied the papers in my briefcase: a birth certificate – possibly fake, I now surmised; a few photocopied bank statements in my name; receipts for the television and my laptop; and various invoices from tradesmen who had carried out work on my house – and that was it, basically. I realised how little I had to show for my life on this earth, and none of it shed any light on who or what I really was.

The next hour I spent in front of the full-length mirror, standing naked and vulnerable as I explored every part of my body, concentrating mainly on the scar on my left side.

It was no more than two inches long and started about six inches below my heart. It was red and slightly puffy, which didn't mean anything. I just about recalled the doctor saying it wasn't anything serious, just a result of the accident. *Doctor?* Who the hell was the doctor? He was just another microcosm of my memory that may or may not be real. I no longer knew for sure what was going on.

I had felt my skin, its indentations and contours, searching for some clue as to why I should suddenly be impervious to a piece of metal which travels at around twice the speed of sound and which kills people – *normal* people. But not me.

I had expected round holes in my shirt, but that, too, was pristine, the material unbroken. It was clear that the bullets had been repelled before they got within a few millimetres of me. It made me feel sick, and I raced to the en suite bathroom, where I threw up everything I had inside me and then some more. I was drained.

Eventually, I returned to the bedroom, pulled my boxers back on and lay on the bed, everything still churning inside me, and I gazed up at the ceiling, my eyes not flickering, but my heart racing. I placed my hand on it, hoping that might quell the raging beast, but the rate increased, and I had to sit up again. I had then gone to the window and peeped round the curtain, catching the moon settling serenely beyond the woods in the distance, seemingly without a care in the world.

Shit!

I had thought of Rufus and then of Robyn, this unseen woman who appeared to hold the key to my future; if, indeed, I had one. What is she like? A scientist, of course, so wearing a white lab coat and carrying a clipboard. They all had one of those, didn't they? She would be dressed conservatively: dark skirt, with a pale blouse and sensible black shoes. Glasses? Of course. Almost certainly on a thin chain around her neck. A pencil tucked behind her ear? No, that might be a step too far.

Okay. So how old is she? Grace said she'd got her degree twelve years ago; so she's probably thirty-three, thirty-five, give or take. Slim, I would guess. How many rotund female scientists do you know? Attractive? Yes, I'm sure she is, in a school-mistress kind of way. A fetish for someone.

Then, I had slept fitfully before succumbing fully to my exhaustion.

A knock at the door brought me back from my thoughts.

"Are you awake, David?"

"Yes," I said hoarsely. "Come in, Denver."

He bounced into the room, which threw me. "Top o' the morning!" he sang in a very bad Irish lilt, stopping short of dancing a jig in front of me – but only just. "Time to kick ass, I think!"

"You slept well, I see."

"Like a top!" he grinned. "Spinning and spinning till I tumbled out of bed this morning." His lilt had lost its Irishness by the sixth word, sliding back to his native Idahoan. At this time of the morning, the whole thing was unnerving.

104

"We need to talk with Grace and Gregory," I said in an effort to put the pin back in this crazy American grenade.

"No can do, man. At least, not with Gregory. According to the lady of the house, he had an early start." Denver sat on the edge of my bed. "Tell me, David, what do you know about the guy?"

"Gregory, you mean?" I thought about that one. "Well, like I said, I was under the impression he'd been with me for years."

"Which is what Rufus wanted you to think."

"Yes," I agreed. "But he was obviously a plant."

"Without a doubt. Rufus used him to keep an eye on you. Even if Gregory himself didn't realise."

"Mm," I pondered. "Which would indicate that Rufus was anticipating trouble."

"You can bet on that," said Denver. "But there is one question you need to ask yourself."

"And that is?"

Denver stood up and moved to the door, opening it and half-stepping through before he replied. "Can you trust Gregory, David?"

Then he was gone, and I could hear him taking the stairs two at a time and whistling 'The Star-Spangled Banner' as loudly as his lungs could handle.

* * *

Gregory was back twenty minutes later, rushing up to my room with a couple of bags, which he tossed on the bed as I came out of the bathroom, a towel round my waist.

"I think they will fit, sir, and I hope you will approve," he said, then discreetly retired before I had a chance to say anything.

I dressed quickly, admiring the cut of the Oxford slim-fit white shirt, the Levi jeans, the Derby brogues and the Aran sweater – all of which fitted perfectly – before making my way downstairs.

Grace was gracefully eating a small dish of kedgeree, and I suddenly realised with a start that there must be staff somewhere in this house who looked after her and the property. For some reason, the thought had never registered before, but now I felt just that little bit more nervous, knowing that others might be privy to our decisions and actions.

Grace smiled warmly and beckoned me to a chair beside her. Gregory sat opposite, playing around with his breakfast cereal, his mind clearly elsewhere. Denver was attacking sausage and scrambled egg, chasing a piece of sausage around the plate with his fork without much success. He picked it up with his fingers and slid it into his mouth, sighing with delight. I noticed, too, the bright orange t-shirt that Gregory had felt was fitting for my brash friend.

Grace pointed to the cafetiere, and I nodded, so she poured strong black coffee into my cup, and I added cream from the silver jug on the table. Just two sugars went in this time, before I stirred and took a welcome drink.

"Breakfast, David?" Grace asked.

"Just the coffee, thank you."

"You should eat," she admonished me, rather like a caring grandmother.

I smiled. "You are very kind, Grace, but I'm fine. Honestly." I looked at Gregory. "Thanks for the clothes," I said.

"My pleasure, sir." He was wearing a grey suit, which I assumed he had packed into the Lexus before he rode to our rescue. "I have other items which I will take up to your room later."

"Thank you." I looked at him over my cup as I took another sip. What do I *really* know about him? Can I trust him?

"I also took the liberty…," Gregory said as he produced a bag from beside the table and slid it across to Denver.

"A present?" Denver exclaimed, like a small child. "For me?"

"I like to think it's for all of us," Gregory said with a wink.

Denver opened the bag, took out a cardboard box and read the label. "Thanks, pal, I feel so much better now," he said, before opening the box and taking out a magazine for the Walther. "But how the hell did you…?"

Gregory stopped him with a raised finger. "Like I said, sir, I have contacts. I will say no more." Then, to my astonishment, he deftly withdrew a Walther of his own and pointed it at Denver. "If you don't mind…," he began.

Denver was out of his chair immediately.

"I'll have a couple of those!" Gregory concluded with a wheezy laugh, his empty other hand outstretched. "It made sense to treat myself while I was at it," he explained as the rest of us sucked in all the air around the table, before we all burst out laughing, and Denver threw over a couple of magazines.

"Gregory!" Grace harrumphed. "You could get yourself killed pulling that kind of trick."

"Sorry, aunt," he said, still grinning. "I know I'm among friends."

"Well," she replied, settling back a little, "in future, I trust you will behave yourself in my house."

"Yes, aunt," was his timid response.

Grace suddenly became serious, her face drawn. "David, there has been a development."

"Oh?" I said.

"I am not one for daytime television, but I felt I should see if there was any news of you. After all," she said, poker-faced, "you are a wanted man."

"He is!" grinned Denver mischievously.

Grace ignored him. "The news was brief, presumably because the police are playing their cards close to their chest, but there were pictures of your house in Surrey and a report on three bodies being recovered in the garden."

"I'm sorry, Grace, but we did explain…"

"Yes, yes, you did, David. However, there is one thing that I do not understand." Here she paused, and I could feel her eyes burning deep into me, as if what she was about to say could be life-changing for her as well as the rest of us. "They said that the police were looking for a man named William Daniels."

I raised my eyebrows in genuine surprise. "Who? I've never heard of him."

"Apparently, he owns the house you say you own."

While Grace's tone wasn't exactly accusing, I could feel her doubt almost overpowering me. She had been so welcoming, so understanding, but now I could see she felt only sadness at the prospect of being let down.

"Honestly, Grace, I've never heard of him. I own the house… at least, that's what I've always thought." I stopped then, my mind delving into the six years of my life that I did know about, trying to find an answer which would satisfy Grace – and myself.

I was too afraid to say another word, so I stood up and began to pace the room, each step giving me some time to come up with a plausible answer. I stopped at the window and looked out. Everything was so peaceful and placid out there. If only I felt the same.

Eventually, I started to explain to the best of my ability. "The house is maintained by an agency. I have nothing to do with everyday dealings, like repairs, council tax, and insurance. They do everything."

"Sounds reasonable," said Denver. "For a multi-millionaire."

I shrugged. He was right about the money, but I still felt ridiculously cheap.

"So who is this agency?" asked Grace, still not totally back onside.

"I haven't got a clue," I admitted with embarrassment. "I've never bothered to check. Why would I? As far as I was concerned, I had set it all up long before my accident. I just…" My voice trailed away as I realised how feeble it all sounded.

A few moments of silence followed, before Grace said, "I can see how that would make sense."

I was so relieved. "You can?"

"Yes, David. If Denny Archer – or this Rufus Allenby – wanted to keep you in the dark, then that would be a good way of doing it. Also," she went on, "it would protect you in situations such as the one in which you now find yourself."

Denver nodded enthusiastically. "You're in the clear, David. If the cops are looking for this Daniels guy, then they're not looking for you."

"But surely the neighbours would recognise you?" Gregory said. "Especially when the police draw a blank with this William Daniels."

"Yes, but that might take a little time. Enough for us to formulate a plan, perhaps," I replied, still not sure how this was going to pan out.

Just then, Gregory's phone rang. He answered with his name, then sat silent for a few seconds, listening. Finally, he handed over the phone. "It's for you, sir," he said.

Taking the phone, I held it to my ear.

"David?" It was a clipped female voice.

"Yes."

"I want you to stay exactly where you are. We are fifteen minutes away."

I had a premonition on hearing the voice, but I asked anyway. "Who is this?"

"My name is Robyn Newman."

Chapter Eight

I was in the garden waiting when the three Lexus ESs swept up the drive and glided to a halt by the door. I had decided to stand in full view, much to the dismay of the others, but I did have Grace beside me for comfort. Denver and Gregory, both armed with their Walthers, were hidden in the undergrowth, poised for any confrontation.

However, I expected no trouble, assuming Robyn was indeed a friend of Rufus. Of course, it was entirely possible that she *did* mean me harm, but I still doubted that. Logic would tell you that an assassin doesn't announce her (or his) arrival by telephone. Nevertheless, I could still feel the sweat on my palms, and I rubbed my hands down my new jeans in an effort to control my nerves.

We waited as the rear door to the first car opened, and a suited man stepped out, obviously armed. He didn't even look at me; instead, he reverently held the door as the second passenger emerged. This had to be Robyn, and she was the most beautiful woman I had ever seen. I couldn't take my eyes off her as she walked gracefully towards me, a nervous smile on her lips. No glasses, I noted, but she did have a bob of jet-black hair, which rather suited her. She wore pale blue trousers under a caramel three-quarter-length wool coat, and she looked stunning. I could feel my mouth getting dry as she approached, and I wondered why this vision had not been embedded in my memory.

Nobody emerged from the other cars, but I could sense eyes scrutinising me, and I shivered a little more.

Robyn stopped beside the car and looked me up and down. "Hello again, David," she said, her smile broadening, her voice like a satin sheet, encircling me and creating warmth and desire in equal measure. I had never had such feelings before!

With my mind in conflicting mode, I decided not to respond, so I just stared at her. Not very macho, I admit, but what would you have done, faced with the classic beauty of somebody who looked like an angel?

"I think," she said, her voice silky but authoritative, "we should go inside."

I stepped aside so that she could follow Grace into the house, my eyes trying to watch her and her bodyguard at the same time. He, however, hovered behind, waiting his turn to shadow me.

As we got to the door, he said, "You should call in your friends as well so we can keep an eye on everyone."

* * *

I had somehow known that they would find me. From the moment Rufus turned up unannounced on the island, I had realised there must have been something going on. People just don't get accosted on a beach like that. Rufus had tracked me somehow. And now, so had Robyn.

At first, I had thought that a tracker had been planted in my clothes, rather like the one we found on Rufus, but that was nonsense. I had spent most of my time on the island just wearing shorts or swimming trunks, so there was no way anybody could have infiltrated my sparse wardrobe without my knowledge. No, it had to be something else. It had to be closer to home. I thought again about that scar. Could they have put a tracer *in* me?

Robyn would know, but for the time being, and for the second time in two days, I found myself at the dining room table, facing a feisty woman and feeling tongue-tied. The others had traipsed in after us and taken their places: Gregory sat beside me, nodding as Robyn welcomed him by name, confirming to me that she was indeed the woman who had secured his services with that handsome retainer. Denver hovered behind me, a look of insolence on his face. He refused to sit, and Robyn shrugged to show she didn't give a damn either way. Grace was on the other side of me, looking daggers at the interloper. We had become Grace's brood, and the mother hen wasn't about to put up with any truck from the visiting albatross. She glowered as Robyn looked at me.

The armed guard took station by the door. He had the chiselled jaw and facial features you see on a film extra who is desperately trying to be the star – and failing. I nodded to Denver, and he sauntered over to the door, coming to rest beside the guard and actually rubbing shoulders with him. The guard edged a few inches away, and I knew then that Denver had his measure.

The atmosphere was frosty and toxic, so I broke the ice with a heart-felt, "I'm sorry about Rufus." She didn't answer, but I could see the moisture in her eyes. "More than just a colleague, I presume," I added.

"Yes," she said limply.

"You were close?"

She waved a hand across her slacks, as if swatting away my question. "I am here to talk about you, David." Again, she offered me that smile. "Getting off the island in one piece. I'm impressed..." A very slight nod. "And pleased."

"That makes two of us," I said.

We faced each other across the table like two chess players: her knowing every move there was, and me having just learnt that a pawn could advance two squares on its first move. In short, she knew everything about me, and I knew nothing about her. No wonder my legs were shaking under the table.

I felt as if I had been thrown down a giant plastic chute into one of those children's pools filled with different coloured balls. Each of the balls held a question, and as I juggled them in my mind, I didn't know which one to pick. I plucked the first one that came to me. "Who was Rufus?"

She pondered the question, and she took so long that I thought she wasn't going to respond at all.

"He was a brilliant scientist."

I had gathered that much. "Studying what?"

115

"Pacinian corpuscles." She gave me such a smile then that I couldn't help but return the favour. She knew I was clueless, so she continued, "They are responsible for detecting pressure and vibration stimuli."

"Speak English, lady," said Denver brusquely.

She turned to him. "These corpuscles are found deep in the skin of mammals, and they appear at the end of the sensory neurons."

"So they sense all kinds of pressure?" I asked, more in hope than any kind of knowledge.

"More than that, David. They *react* to pressure. Under certain conditions, they can create local circuits of current which extend through the body."

I was beginning to understand. "And these circuits… they can form a barrier."

She gave me that smile again, but this time I could see that she was impressed. "Absolutely!"

I was on a roll. "So Rufus found a way to harness this reaction."

"Yes."

"And I'm the result."

"You are the most successful result of a very long experiment," Robyn said. "Dr Allenby developed a way to heighten the power of the circuits so that they could repel micro-organisms such as bacteria."

Gregory joined in. "So Mr David is immune to diseases?"

Robyn nodded. "He is."

I couldn't believe it. "Is that all?"

"What?" she replied, surprised. "Is that not enough?"

"No," I said bitterly, "it certainly isn't." I bit my tongue then. It was clear that Robyn knew nothing of my extra immunity.

"What is it, David?" she asked, concern in her voice.

I leant in and looked her in the eyes. "Can we continue this outside?" I whispered.

Her eyes were enquiring, but she shrugged anyway, perhaps sensing I might be more easily persuaded if we carried on the discussion on our own.

She stood up. "Let's take a walk, David," she said for the benefit of the guard.

He was clearly bristling at the suggestion, so I assumed Robyn was stepping out of line here. Denver noticed, too, so he leant in a little more on the guy, who just tapped the gun under his jacket as a silent warning. Denver stayed where he was.

Robyn and I went to the door without looking back, but nobody tried to stop us.

* * *

The sky was remarkably blue and welcoming as we crunched our way across the gravel drive and onto the lawn. The three cars were now empty, their occupants presumably deployed throughout the garden, intent on keeping us in and anyone else out. Nobody broke cover as we walked, but I felt many eyes on us, and it wasn't a pleasant sensation.

When we were clear of the house, I stopped and turned to her. It was time. "Who am I?" I demanded, my voice cracking just a little.

"What?" She seemed genuinely shocked at my question.

"I need to know."

She studied me, worry lines on her brow. "I don't understand, David."

I hesitated, unsure. I was desperate for answers, but as I saw the frown on her face and the slightly quivering lips, I knew she wouldn't be able to tell me everything I needed to know. "I was happy, Robyn. Leading what I thought was a fairly normal life. Then, in stepped Rufus. Now I don't know who I am. I have limited memory; people are trying to kill me for some reason I don't understand; and I find that I don't even own the house I thought was mine. Perhaps you can explain," I finished with a vindictive sneer that made her recoil.

When she didn't answer immediately, I turned away and walked on, feeling the gentle breeze playing against my reddening cheeks. I wasn't sure if I was getting angry or just feeling more frustrated. Then I realised it was both. Robyn fell in beside me, her right hand shielding her eyes from the glare of the still-rising sun, and we said nothing for a couple of minutes.

Eventually, she said, "Your name is David Michael Parks, aged thirty-eight, born and bred in London. You have lived in Ash in Surrey for fifteen years, and you are, as you well know, a man of independent means." She smiled sweetly at that. "There, does that help?"

I wasn't sure it did. "Is that what Rufus told you?"

She looked baffled. "Not exactly, no. It's in your file."

"Ah," I said, "my file." I stopped walking again. "So, what do *you* know about me?" I persevered. "Something that's not in the file."

She took a moment to think, and I could see something register. "Well, not a lot, really. We never had the chance to speak as you were sedated…"

"Sedated?"

"Well, yes. It was imperative that you remained perfectly still while undergoing the procedure, so Dr Allenby gave you regular injections…"

"Bloody hell!" I roared. "What sort of animal was he?"

Robyn broke away, her face as flushed as mine. "How dare you! Dr Allenby was a great man of science."

She began to head back to the house, and I had visions of her getting her gunslinger to give me a good going over to teach me some manners. I reached out for her, grabbing her arm.

"I'm sorry," I said lamely.

She tried to carry on, but my grip tightened. "Please, Robyn…"

She stopped and looked down at her arm, waiting for me to release her. I was reluctant because I wasn't sure which way this was going. Would she carry on to the house or allow the conversation to continue? The third option was that she might slap my face, but somehow I didn't think that was likely, even if I perhaps deserved it. I let go and waited.

"Why are you so angry, David? After all, you did agree to the procedure." Her eyes were hooded, her face solemn.

"Did I? I don't remember," I said, my voice trailing away.

"That is not unusual," she said soothingly. "Your body and mind have undergone a serious transformation."

"No, you don't get it. I really can't recall anything."

The garden seemed serenely silent, as if waiting for something to happen. I saw a squirrel scamper across the lawn and race up a tree, its tail arched for balance. It tasted a freedom I could only dream of.

I took a deep breath. "My first memory is sitting in my house six years ago. I remember nothing of what you and Rufus did to me before that." I wasn't sure whether to add anything else, but before my mind had taken full control, my mouth seemed to act independently. "Well, that's not strictly true. I do remember the accident."

"What accident?"

I sighed, my head bowed. "I don't know" was all I could say.

Her face flickered with what appeared to be sympathy as well as confusion. I was clearly testing her, and I didn't feel good about that, so I tried to ease back. "So," I said with what I thought was a light-heartedness I certainly didn't feel, "what exactly did Rufus do to me?"

She appeared relieved at my more controlled tone. "Nothing terrible, David. He just stimulated your corpuscles."

"Are you kidding me?" My eyes were rolling.

"Not at all."

"How?" I tried to smile. "The shortened, layman's version, please."

She returned the smile. "He designed a machine – rather like an MRI scanner."

"But different?" I ventured.

"Yes. MRI scanners use magnetic fields and radio waves to generate pictures. Dr Allenby's machine uses radio waves only, in a way that *affects* the body rather than merely creating an image."

We had reached a garden seat which looked out over some rolling hills, the view spectacular in the warming light. The house was some distance away, and it was as if we were in a world of our own. We sat.

"Go on," I said, turning to face her.

"I'll start at the beginning. Pacinian corpuscles are the mechanoreceptors..." She caught my frown. "They are sensory receptors found on the hairless skin of mammals."

"Okay."

"These corpuscles are highly sensitive to changes in the external environment and send signals to the central nervous system to take the necessary action to cope with these changes."

"So they defend the body?"

"Under normal conditions, it is not that simple. The corpuscles will react if something touches your skin" –

here she leant over and placed her hand on my wrist – "and the process is heightened the more pressure is applied."

My reaction was difficult to describe. I could sense her hand and her fingers, but there was no pressure, no real *feeling*.

She looked surprised. "Can you not feel that? I'm pressing quite firmly now."

"It feels nice," I lied, although the sentiment was genuine. I could sense that she was reluctant to take her hand away, and I felt the same. "Please carry on."

She pulled her hand back, assuming I meant that I wanted her to continue with her story. I did, of course, but I also wanted her to keep touching me. No sense, no feeling, but there was an urge.

"Anyway," she continued, slightly flustered, "Dr Allenby developed his ground-breaking machine…"

"With Matthew Denny's money."

"Yes. They were a formidable team."

"So, what's your position in the scheme of things?" I asked. "Not just as an assistant, I'm sure."

She chuckled. "I assume you have checked up on me."

"A little," I admitted. "You were Head of Experimental Research at Denny Archer."

"Still am, for my sins. Working with Dr Allenby was a bonus."

I nodded. "So, what was the connection between Rufus and Denny?"

"A shared passion. Plus, Mr Denny had the skill to create a machine capable of fulfilling Dr Allenby's dreams."

"And the finance," I said bluntly.

"Oh, yes," she smiled. "Very much so."

I suspected but didn't know for sure, so I thought it was worth asking. "But Denny doesn't pull the strings these days, I'm guessing."

Her eyelashes flicked in surprise. "What makes you say that?"

"The little army you brought with you, for one. They look too professional to be detailed to a scientific project. If I didn't know better, I'd say this has got political."

She didn't deny it, which was proof enough for me. Instead, she rose quickly, keen to avoid impertinent questions from a mere science lab specimen, I assumed. She stood in front of me, looking down. "This is Dr Allenby's baby, David. It took him ten years, but he got there in the end. His machine is capable of stimulating the corpuscles to such an extent that they become the perfect defence mechanism for the human body. Nothing can get in." There was pride in her voice.

I got to my feet and fell in beside her as she began to head back to the house. "Very impressive, I'm sure, but why was I chosen, Robyn?"

"Believe me, David, you weren't the first – just the most successful."

Perhaps she thought I ought to be pleased with that revelation, but funnily enough, I wasn't. "So how did this machine work?"

"You want me to explain the intricacies of a scientific marvel in a few words?" she asked, her voice suddenly bubbling with humour and amazement. Now we were onto her favourite subject, she was much happier, and I understood; so I gave her what I thought might have been a dazzling smile of apology. I wasn't too sure if it worked, so I tried to put it into words.

"Sorry, dumb question. But you know what I'm trying to say."

She nodded, still smiling. "Yes, David, I do. Actually, the process was simple: you were strapped onto the plate, which was then fed slowly into the machine. You didn't feel a thing. It was all over in twenty minutes each time."

"Each time?" I scoffed. "So, how many times did he put me through this machine?"

"Four."

There was something I didn't understand. As far as Robyn knew, my body had become immune to only bacteria… and nothing else. So, there must be a missing procedure of some kind to explain my current state, one which Robyn apparently didn't know anything about. Or did she?

I stopped walking. "And you were there each of the four times?"

"Yes, David. Why?" Robyn grabbed my arm as if that might help her to understand.

"So what would happen if he had done it a few more times?" I hesitated. "Without you being there, I mean."

She was surprised at this and pulled her arm away. "That's ridiculous. Of course, he wouldn't do that."

"What would happen?" I persevered, holding her attention so that we stared hard at each other, our mouths set.

"That's hypothetical, David."

"Humour me."

We carried on walking as she thought it through. "Well, to be honest, I'm not sure. It might develop your resistance even more, I suppose." She stopped to look at me again, her large hazel eyes full of confusion. "What are you saying, David? Is there something you're not telling me?"

I ignored the question. "Where is the machine now?"

She didn't answer and fell silent, but I could see pain on her face. She wasn't as confident as she had been when she arrived, and I knew there were questions she needed answers to as well.

Eventually, she stopped again and looked at me. "David, you need to come back with me." She was almost pleading.

I reached for her hand as reassurance, perhaps for both of us.

* * *

Back at the house, it was almost as if nobody had moved, except there was an extra guard at the door, barking into his walkie-talkie.

"They're back," he said. "Stand down."

I visualised creepy men creeping out of the undergrowth, holstering their pistols and smoothing down their suit trousers, before gathering at the door to escort me on what could be my last journey. Was I being too dramatic here? Perhaps, but I knew what my decision had to be.

"Time to go, ma'am," the man said to Robyn.

She looked at me. "You will come, David?"

It was almost as if she thought I really had a choice. I gave her a slight nod, before turning to my hostess. "Thank you for everything, Grace, but it's time to go."

She didn't like that idea, and nor did the others.

"What are you doing, David?" Denver spat.

"It's okay. I'll be in safe hands." I smiled at Robyn, who returned it, despite the worry in her eyes.

"We'll come with you," offered Gregory.

"Not possible!" said the guard at the door, a rod of steel and danger in his voice. "We are taking Mr Parks; nobody else. He will not be harmed in any way... as long as you do as you are told."

"Is that a threat?" Denver demanded, his hand hovering near his gun.

I saw the bodyguard beside him react, so I waved an open hand to show my innocent intent. "I'm coming, but on one condition."

Robyn was desperate to get this finished. "What is it, David?"

"I want to keep in touch with my friend."

Robyn wasn't sure what to say or do. I could see the confusion on her face, in her blinking eyes.

"I need telephone contact," I added.

"That's not a good idea, ma'am." The man at the door had spoken in a clipped, official tone, signifying that he

126

was more than just an armed goon.

Robyn ignored him and looked straight at me. "You will come of your own free will?"

I nodded.

"Then I will take your phone – for now. It is safer that way." Her whole body was pleading. "This, David, has to be non-negotiable."

I wasn't sure, but it sounded like Robyn was trying to bend the rules in my favour. I appreciated the gesture and hoped it wouldn't backfire on her, but judging by the company she was keeping, I could see that she was certainly going out on a dangerous limb, so I silently handed over my mobile with a smile of support. I just needed Denver to be accessible, and I hoped this was the best way.

The bodyguard took a step forward. "Ma'am..."

"I will take full responsibility," she snapped at him, then she turned back to me. "Shall we go?"

I gave Grace a hug and shook hands with Gregory, who tried to slip me his gun. I pushed his hand back gently and shook my head. "Thanks, but no," I whispered. "I'll do this my way."

Denver threw his arms around me as if we might never see each other again and breathed into my ear, "We can still get you out of this."

"No," I said softly, "just find out all you can about the accident. Oh, and check out David Michael Parks, aged thirty-eight, born in London. It's something I should have done years ago."

I pulled away and began to follow Robyn to the door,

not really knowing what the future might hold. But then again, I didn't know what my past held either, so in the great scheme of things, what did it matter?

As we emerged from the house, I saw that Robyn's men had indeed broken cover and were at the cars before us. I was impressed with their professionalism.

"Ex-Army?" I asked Robyn.

"Something like that, I think," she replied.

The back doors of the first car were open, and we both climbed in. The two men from the house sat in the front, and I craned my neck to see out of the back window as at least five others took their places in the cars behind. I sighed internally, glad that we hadn't started something, because these guys sure as hell would have finished it. It also emphasised how important I really appeared to be.

Robyn noticed my expression. "You made the right decision, David."

"Time will tell," I mumbled, clipping the seatbelt and looking back at the house as we cruised down the drive. Grace was standing at the door, and I could see the steely look in her eyes. She wasn't going to let anybody get away with this – but I wasn't sure what she could do about it.

I assumed we were heading for Battersea, and I said so.

"No, David, we're going much closer to home." She smiled at me then, and I sensed her relaxing. I took that as a good sign, so I tried to open her up.

"These corpuscles of mine," I began light-heartedly, "I assume they are permanently affected."

"Yes, but you have nothing to worry about."

"I only have your word for that."

She smiled. "You've been okay for six years. There's nothing to say you won't live for another sixty or more. Especially as your body is so well protected."

"Ah, yes, I almost forgot about that." I sensed her smile widening, although I was reluctant to look at her. For some reason, her close proximity was causing palpitations in me, and I knew that had nothing to do with corpuscles. I thought it was time to change the subject. "So, what's with the heavy brigade?"

The men in front bristled, and I took a small degree of pleasure in that.

"They come with the territory, I'm afraid," Robyn said, resting her hand on the seat, very close to mine. I could have reached out... *wanted* to reach out. It wasn't just a physical thing – it was also the thought that Robyn might be a valuable ally in the unknown future ahead of me.

"Another form of protection," I said. "External rather than internal. Seems all my bases are covered."

"We hope so."

We drove on in silence for a long time, the countryside and towns passing by in a flurry as our little convoy made its way. Then, to my amazement, we found ourselves in Surrey.

"Where are you taking me?" I asked.

"To my laboratory!" she grinned.

"Really?"

"Really."

Chapter Nine

To my surprise, our cavalcade had gone down the A31 and across the Hog's Back to within a mile of my home in Ash – sorry, the house that isn't mine. When I saw the 'Welcome to Farnham' road sign, I started to relax. I knew a little about the place, having enjoyed walks down Lion and Lamb Yard, browsing in the book shops, as well as visiting a few of the town's other attractions: the castle, the ruined Waverley Abbey, Mother Ludlam's Cave.

I know a bit about the cave because I've been there and taken a look – not that there's much to see. I suppose that could also apply to the rest of the town, although I have enjoyed my odd trips to the Maltings for the theatre and to check out the artists.

However, our brush with Farnham was all too brief, as we skirted the town centre and found ourselves on a long, winding road that led out of the town. Large, detached houses passed by on either side, then a new-build estate of half a dozen 'executive' homes, then a row of trees and two ploughed fields, indicating a more rural outlook.

"Nice area," I said to no one in particular. "No laboratories, though."

Robyn smiled. "You'd be surprised."

Just as she spoke, our car took a left sweep into a drive where a huge tile-hung detached house sat back in splendid isolation, and two suited men stood at the open gate, waving us in like royalty. I was tempted to give a little 'king wave', but instead, I just shook my head and held back a flippant comment. I was too intrigued by the whole business to complicate things by upsetting the locals, especially as they all seemed to be carrying weapons of some description. It all looked so out of place.

I was invited to step out of the car by the bodyguard with the walkie-talkie, who then led me into the house, where he had a quick word with what I could only assume was the man of the house, before taking up station in the corner, where all lackeys should be.

I paused on the threshold, looking around. The house was old, but real designers had clearly been let loose on the interior, which sparkled and dripped with expensive woodwork and soft furnishings. The hallway staircase would have suited Scarlett O'Hara, as it twirled majestically skyward to an upper floor which appeared to disappear into the heavens. How the other half live, eh?

The new man approached. He was swarthy, perhaps with some Latin blood. He looked around forty, but that could have been due to his hair, which was buzz-cut to an almost US Marine specification, and his face was not so much lived-in, more a rough terrain which could have been the surface of Mars. I would have said pock-marked, but that doesn't really cover it. At close quarters, I could see that the ridges consisted of scars, many years old, and I hazarded a guess that he had been in a fire, or possibly a fire-fight.

He was wearing a combat jacket – which looked totally out of place in the ornate hallway – and a holster, which seemed to fit nicely with his bearing. His voice was strong, commanding, and in a deep Geordie accent. "Miss Newman, I hear you stepped out of line."

"What?" she mumbled.

"You had a private conversation with the…"

If I wasn't mistaken, I could have sworn he was about to say 'prisoner', which wouldn't have surprised me. He looked like a gaoler from a nasty blood-fest movie.

"I needed to persuade him…," Robyn started weakly, but the gaoler cut in.

"You have Mr Parks's phone. Hand it over."

Robyn tried to face up to him. "I made an agreement, Packer."

"That's *Captain* Packer," he said cuttingly. "And I am fully aware of what you agreed." He looked slyly at the bodyguard, letting us all know what a snitch he was. "You no longer have any authority here, Ms Newman. Now, please give it to me."

"I don't understand…"

"There has been a slight change in the hierarchy since you left this morning," Packer said with menace. "Your place in the pecking order has been somewhat reduced, I am afraid."

"What do you mean?"

He was enjoying this. "With the awful demise of the doctor and now the re-arrival of our guinea pig, it was felt that the experiment should be placed on, shall we say, a higher level." He snarled, "The phone!"

Robyn stared Packer down as much as she could, but seemed to wilt in front of him and meekly offered the phone.

"Just drop it," he said with feeling.

She did as she was ordered, and he took a step forward. He was wearing army-issue khaki boots, and I watched with mild amusement as he lifted one foot and brought it down with brute force on the phone. That had no effect, so he tried again, this time clearly irritated by the fact that the phone was resisting his strength and also by the smirk on my face. He was in two minds whether to try again, but decided that bully-boy tactics might be more appropriate, and he moved closer to me, staring me down.

"You may be the poster boy," he snarled, "but I'm in charge here. Understand?"

I waited. Then I waited some more. Just enough to get him rocking on his heels, the anger bubbling across his cracked face and almost pumping steam out of his ears.

"Understood," I said eventually, and I could see the look of anguish on Robyn's face turning to relief.

"Would that be all, Captain Packer?" she asked, attempting to diffuse the volatile situation.

I knew these people couldn't hurt me physically because they had done something to me, which gave me a protection no man had ever experienced before. I was still trying to get my head round it all, but it dawned on me that I held most of the aces, and a jumped-up jerk like Packer wasn't going to cause any real problems. At least, that's what I was telling myself.

I stepped round the bubbling cauldron of anger that was Packer and was about to follow Robyn down the hall and past the sweeping staircase.

"One moment, Ms Newman," Packer said through a sickly smile. "There is someone you need to meet."

Robyn turned back to him with a look of bemusement.

"Please," he said, elongating the word, "come with me. You, too, Parks." He threw me a glower worthy of any pantomime villain, but we meekly followed him through the house, past a multitude of closed doors and a handful of security men, finally coming to rest at another equally benign-looking door.

Packer knocked, and a refined voice responded. "Come."

The door was opened by the resident guard, and we made our way in, Packer, for once, showing due deference.

"Ah," said the man inside, "you must be our national treasure, David Parks."

It was a pleasant enough welcome, but I knew that he was well aware of who I was and almost certainly had a file a mile deep on me. He looked like that sort of man.

He was large, in girth as well as height, his fingers thick and stubby as he held out his hand. I didn't want to, but I shook it and felt the clamminess. I also noted the nicotine stains, which were replicated in his moustache, giving the end of his nose a slight yellow tinge. His eyes were large, orb-like, and his jowls moved of their own free will as he turned to Robyn and offered her a brief wave as if reluctantly accepting that she needed to be in the room despite his fervent desire for her not to be. I wasn't sure whether that was a professional preference or because he clearly preferred men to women.

He was wearing a sharp, black three-piece suit, the waistcoat straining over his corpulence, and the top button of his shirt was clearly undone, despite the huge Windsor knot in his tie trying to hide the fact.

"Please, take a seat. I was just having a spot of lunch. Would you care to join me?" he said jovially, beaming at me. His voice was pure upper crust, straight from the playing fields of Eton, perhaps.

As he sat back down in the heavily upholstered chair behind his huge mahogany desk, he picked up the napkin he had been using and laid it almost tenderly across his lap. "Captain Packer, perhaps you would be kind enough to rustle up something for our guest."

"Yes, sir."

I was hungry, but not yet sure I was ready to sit at this man's table. Not without introductions first. "You have the advantage," I said, standing my ground.

The man looked at me, his cheeks flushing slightly. "Mr Parks, I do apologise. How remiss of me." His eyes sparkled in the light from the anglepoise lamp on his desk. "My name is Wolstenholme – you know, like the television chap: 'They think it's all over... it is now'." He registered my blank stare. "No? Oh, well, never mind." He picked up a cucumber sandwich, beautifully crafted into a perfect triangle and devoid of crust. "Please sit down." It was said in the nicest possible way, but it still sounded like an order. Robyn obliged immediately; I took a few seconds. "There, that's better," he said smoothly, before taking a delicate bite of his sandwich, revealing perfect white teeth and the end of a tongue which wasn't, to my surprise, forked.

We were perched on the edge of a three-seater leather sofa, pushing against what seemed like a hundred cushions which had been scattered across the back. Everything screamed quality, and my eyes fell to the plushest of maroon carpets, and I wondered whether I should have taken off my shoes.

I hadn't noticed, but Packer had slinked out the door, presumably to carry out his master's wish. Perhaps a sandwich might not be so bad after all.

Wolstenholme was talking again. "I can't tell you how pleased we are to have you back, Mr Parks. We did think that, at one point, we might have lost you."

"I didn't think that was possible," I said.

"I'm sorry?" he mumbled, not understanding my comment, as he took another bite of his sandwich.

"You losing me," I explained. "What with the tracker, I mean."

He guffawed then, loudly and unabashed, which was almost endearing. "Of course! I see what you mean. Yes, well, it was Dr Allenby who insisted on that – he wanted to keep an eye on you at all times. After all, you are a medical experiment." His laugh this time wasn't so loud, but it was clear he was enjoying himself immensely. Then he stopped. "I'm sorry, no offence meant." He nibbled another sandwich, and I studied the movement of his thin, feminine lips, before looking into his eyes.

"It's okay," I said. "I've got thick skin."

It took him a few seconds to appreciate my joke, and he seemed amused that I had seen the funny side. I waited while he devoured another triangle of cucumber sandwich.

"I don't wish to appear rude," I said, and he waved an arm airily to show that whatever it was I didn't want to be rude about, it wouldn't bother him. He was the king of this particular castle, so nothing was going to cause him grief. "Well," I continued, "I was just wondering – as you do – who the hell are you exactly?"

He paused, a third sandwich hovering close to his mouth. "I had been told you are rather blunt," he said. "Not a bad thing."

"So?"

"So I am Gavin Wolstenholme, your boss."

"I don't have a boss, Gavin," I replied.

He chuckled then, and his belly moved in sympathy. "Everybody has a boss, David. I am yours. You can trust me on that."

"You think I should trust you?"

"The point is moot, my dear chap. It is what it is." He thought about taking another sandwich from the plate, but decided against it. Perhaps he didn't want to appear a glutton. He delicately dabbed the napkin on both sides of his mouth and then took a long drink of what was probably Earl Grey tea from a Chinese-design teacup, his fingers barely able to hold the delicate handle.

As Packer came back in with a tray, Wolstenholme beamed. "Ah, sustenance for you! Please feel free to tuck in. No charge, I assure you." This was followed by a little chortle of delight.

Packer was not at all happy about being the gopher, and he glowered at me as I looked at the tray he had laid on the coffee table in front of us. Ham sandwiches, again beautifully triangled and crust-less, dainty little cupcakes, and a cafetiere of coffee with two cups. How very civilised. Robyn acted as mother, not out of any sense of gender recognition, more that she was nearer, and in my state of mind, I might just have poured it over the smug man sitting in front of us. I took two sandwiches and bit into one.

"It's not much, I'm afraid, but we will make up for it at dinner," Wolstenholme said.

"I'm staying that long?"

He thought that was mildly humorous. "Oh, yes, David. You are here for the duration."

I wasn't sure exactly what that meant, but I had already decided that I didn't like this place, nice as the décor was. Robyn handed me a cup, and I kept my eyes on her as I took it. She was clearly rattled, and I knew that this development was new to her.

"So, you don't know Mr Wolstenholme, either?" I asked her.

He answered for her. "Like you, David, Miss Newman has no idea who I am. Let me just say that I am her boss, too."

She looked askance. "Since when?"

"Since the passing of poor Dr Allenby, my dear. That sad event has changed things for all of us. I am here to steady the ship, as it were."

"The *Titanic*?" I said. It wasn't very funny, I admit, but nor was my situation.

"I prefer the idea of the *Mary Rose*. I have brought you back from the deep, and now I am going to work on you until you sparkle even more. And you will, David. You will be my crown jewel."

"Would you care to elaborate?"

He thought about that. "Let's just say that you are a work in progress. An unfinished…"

Robyn bristled. "Hold on a minute." I could see the flush of anger spreading across her cheeks and the daggers in her eyes. "Dr Allenby concluded his work six years ago. That is why David was…"

"Released?" I added the missing word, and she looked at me with something like despair in her eyes this time.

"No, that's not what I was going to say. Not exactly." Her voice trailed off.

Wolstenholme offered a sympathetic smile. "It's all right, Ms Newman," he said silkily, "we know what this means to you." He paused. "However, Mr Parks is now our domain, and we wish to pursue and expand Dr Allenby's experimentation. With your permission, of course, David."

I wasn't sure what to make of Gavin Wolstenholme. On the outside, he looked like a cuddlier version of Oliver Hardy, but inside, he could be something much more sinister. I wasn't prepared to make a decision either way.

"I would prefer to go home, Mr Wolstenholme," I said calmly.

His smile was all-encompassing. "I agree that might appear to be a good outcome for you, but there are two factors which make that impractical."

I waited.

"Firstly, of course, you do not have a home to go to." He shrugged as if that had nothing at all to do with him.

"And secondly?" I asked.

"There are people out there who wish you harm. Believe me, David, you are much safer here."

"Fair enough," I conceded. "So, what do you plan to do to me?" I took a quick glance at Robyn and saw her mouth was open, wondering what in the hell was going down here.

Wolstenholme stood and came towards me, his feet shuffling with the weight and his breath a little wheezy. "We believe there is more to be learnt from this experiment, and you are the only candidate." He grinned, his glistening teeth seemingly filling the space between us. "Let's just say that you've got the job – and you start immediately."

I stood up then, my eyes looking down over him. "You are very kind, Gavin, and I do appreciate the offer, but I think I'd like to decline. As you know, a body is a temple, and I would like to treat mine with the respect it deserves."

He appeared not to understand the slur on his appearance, or perhaps he was used to it. Either way, he turned to Packer. "That is enough for now. Please see them out, Captain."

"Yes, sir," Packer said, so obviously piqued. Like me, he clearly had no time for Gavin.

We were chaperoned out of the room, back past all the closed doors, to the entrance vestibule with its sweeping staircase. The front door was tantalisingly close.

"Where are we going?" I asked.

"To your *new* home," Packer said with a smirk. "I trust you'll be very happy."

We set off in another direction and made our way through the house, while I tried to map the layout for possible future use, although what I could do about my predicament I wasn't sure. Just play it by ear, I supposed.

Robyn clearly knew where we were headed, and we soon reached a massive double door which had what I presumed was some kind of speech-sensitive lock on it because when Robyn said, "Open sesame," I heard a loud click, and the doors opened smoothly and silently.

"Neat trick," I said.

"It recognises my voice," she explained needlessly.

"I love the password, too."

She looked embarrassed. "A childhood spent going to Christmas pantomimes, I'm afraid."

"Keeps out the riff-raff as well."

She knew I was referring to Packer and gave a bright little chuckle.

The object of my comment stood stony-faced beside me, hand hovering over his holster, Western-style. I could almost see the tumbleweed rolling down the corridor.

"You will both remain here until sent for," Packer sneered. "My friend here" – indicating one of his robot-like men – "will ensure you comply with all my orders."

"Yes, sir," I responded with a salute to the side of my head, which included two fingers, but not Boy Scout-fashion.

With that, Packer turned on his heel and marched away, no doubt seething at my response.

Robyn tugged at my sleeve, and I followed her through the portal.

After the *faux*-Georgian beauty of the house, I wasn't expecting what I walked into. A state-of-the-art clinical laboratory.

"Wow!"

"Just what I thought when I first saw it," she said, beaming.

I stopped. "That smell reminds me of…"

"Something familiar?" she finished for me.

"Yes," I said, stepping into the laboratory, not understanding what I felt. I looked around, intrigued. It wasn't just the smell; it was the whole place. White walls with no windows, no sign of human habitation except for a long bench filled with scientific paraphernalia, the walls segmented, as if they were created from white plastic sheets, and two upended gurneys at the far side, appearing to stand sentinel over a place which looked like a morgue that had only been opened yesterday. I shivered at the coldness of it all, but there was a slight memory as well.

"This was your home for a few weeks," Robyn said.

"Six years ago."

She nodded. "I'm sorry, David, if it upsets you."

"Not at all," I said, perhaps not convincing myself. This place had clearly been the start of my problem, and God alone knew what went on here. I felt sure Robyn had been kept in the dark regarding some of it, and she definitely knew nothing about Wolstenholme. So who was he? I hazarded a guess that he was some sort of government man, possibly brought in as soon as Rufus died and I went rogue, which would explain why Robyn had never met him. He had obviously arrived after she set out to bring me back so that he was in a position to take over as soon as I arrived. The whole affair was so huge and well organised that it had to be controlled by a central power – and that could mean only one thing.

"Are you government-funded?" I asked innocently.

"A little, I believe," said Robyn. "That's not my field of expertise."

I nodded and continued looking round. It really was a stunning place, and I could see valuable scientific work being carried out here. I just wished it hadn't been on me.

"So, how much were you involved?"

Robyn looked at me. "Sorry?"

"In the experiment on me. I assume, being Head of Experimental Research, you were treated as an equal."

"I was," she said with a smile. "We worked well as a team."

"Team?"

"Well, there were only three of us at the end. We are… *were* merely a monitoring station. What we are now, I'm not so sure." Robyn sighed heavily.

"You say three of you."

"Yes. Dr Allenby, myself and Specs…"

"Specs?"

"Oh, his name's Harry Wilson, but Dr Allenby always called him Specs. For obvious reasons."

I nodded. "So what, exactly, does Specs do?"

"He is the techie. Keeps the computer room going."

"On his own?" I asked.

"Oh, it's pretty basic," she said; then, realising she may have slighted her friend, she added, "And Specs is a real expert."

"What about Packer?"

"He was always here, presumably from the very beginning, but certainly before I arrived. I never liked him."

"I can understand that," I sympathised. "What about his men?"

"He had three when I first arrived. All armed and mean-looking. Frightening, really, but Dr Allenby seemed at ease with them, so I went along with it. A few more men arrived here this morning just before I set out to find you…"

"And there's even more here now," I finished for her, receiving a nod of confirmation. "Wolstenholme's army," I thought aloud.

"Who is he, David? What is this about?"

I didn't have any answers, so I thought I should change the subject. "Tell me, how did it work? The experiment, I mean."

"It was all very simple, really," she said, pulling out one of the stools from under the bench and sitting on it, her back straight, her chest out, but not consciously. I tried not to stare, so I copied her and sat down beside her, closer than perhaps I should have. She didn't seem to object. "Dr Allenby had done all the preliminary work, of course, so I just supervised you in and out of the scanner…"

"It was all done here?"

"Yes."

"So where is this marvellous scanner? I'd love to see what I went through – literally."

Robyn looked a little abashed. "It was dismantled."

"Really?"

She rested her hands on the bench, fingers clasped. "You were the success story, David. There was no need for further experiments. At least, that's what Dr Allenby said."

I sensed her disapproval. "You didn't agree."

"Don't get me wrong, David. I worshipped Dr Allenby and all he had achieved, but I felt there was more to be gained. He, however, was adamant that it was all over…" Her voice trailed off, and she bowed her head, perhaps thinking of the mentor she had lost.

It was at that moment I seriously contemplated telling her the truth: that it was clear to me that, somehow, Rufus had carried out more work on me than she knew, and that I was a living freak, my body internally disfigured to such an extent that there was no knowing what might happen to me in the future, and Rufus knew he had gone too far. I wanted to tell her, but she looked so forlorn and lost that I held my tongue. Instead, I reached out for her hand and stroked it for a few seconds before she looked up at me with a limp smile and mouthed, "Sorry."

I squeezed her hand, and something strange came over me. For the first time, I could actually feel her soft skin, and then a surge of power rippled through me. It was as if I had suddenly come alive, and it almost toppled me from my stool. I regained my composure in a moment, and I was sure Robyn had been too engrossed to notice. I took a breath and then tried to break the spell by looking around. "I can just see you working in here," I said, my voice uncharacteristically high.

"Yes," she mumbled, still upset, "it was fun."

"Dr Frankenstein strikes again!" I realised immediately that it was the wrong thing to say. "My turn to say sorry. That was a cheap shot. I know your work was important to you."

"Yes, it was… *is*."

I tried to regroup. "So, what happened when I left?"

"We monitored you."

"Through the tracker."

"Yes. We have a special room."

"Where Specs hangs out," I said.

"Yes." She felt she needed to defend herself and Rufus. "It was imperative that everything was carried out in a controlled environment. There was a real chance that we were about to change mankind forever."

"I understand that," I said soothingly. "So, tell me how you got involved."

"I had heard of Dr Allenby, of course. I had read several of his articles in the *Journal of Neuroscience* and the *American Journal of Physiology*. He was particularly well-respected in America – certainly more so than at home. I had been working for Denny Archer for a few years when Dr Allenby approached him and asked if he could poach me to work on his latest project. Dr Allenby showed me his notes… and I was hooked. He and Matthew Denny had been friends for many years – I believe they first met at uni – so it was impossible for Matthew to refuse. He had basically been funding Dr Allenby's work anyway."

"He built the scanner," I said.

"From Dr Allenby's designs, yes. It was beautiful, a work of art."

"And it worked," I added without malice. Even considering what the damn thing had done to me, I still had to admit it was a remarkable achievement.

Robyn smiled, a *real* smile. "Oh, yes, David, it worked!"

More than you could possibly imagine, I thought, but I said, "Tell me *how* it worked."

"Well, the bare bones of the matter was that we put you through the machine a total of four times in an effort to stimulate your corpuscles enough to maintain a permanent defence against internal attack. We then monitored and noted any movement in your medical responses."

"What sort of movement?" I asked.

"It was amazing," she said, almost in awe. "Your defence mechanism grew with such speed and strength that it took my breath away. It was clear you were a huge success. Dr Allenby had created inside you a wall of protection which repelled all known bacteria. But only time would tell how the experiment performed in a wider context."

"Out of the lab, you mean?"

"Exactly."

"So you've been keeping an eye on me for the last six years?"

"We have. Although not visually, David!" She seemed embarrassed at the thought, as if she might have caught me with my trousers down.

I saw the slight blush and gave her a smile. "You won't have missed much, I'm afraid." Her blush darkened, so I changed the subject. "You must still have a file on me?"

"Well, yes, of course," she said, jumping up and moving to one wall which appeared to be just that – but then she pressed the surface, and a door eased open silently and smoothly. There had been no indication that the wall held anything within it, and that was the beauty of it. A secret compartment, indeed.

I stepped over and looked in. There were numerous large folders, each one an almost glaring white and bulging with paperwork. On their spines were a series of numbers. I looked at Robyn in amazement. "Paper files?"

"Dr Allenby insisted."

"The old dinosaur!" I said, but fell silent when I saw the look she was giving me.

"He was very particular about his records," she said, annoyance coursing through her voice. "Computers can be hacked."

I nodded. "Fair enough. But surely Specs used…"

"He did," she replied quickly. "Every evening, Dr Allenby would wait for the print-outs, then he would supervise as Specs wiped the computer clean. This cupboard," she added almost lovingly, "holds the only copies of the files."

"And only you and Rufus have access."

"Yes."

"Foolproof," I concluded, although I wasn't really sure about that because erased computer files could always be resurrected.

Robyn took one of the folders out and placed it on the table. I hesitated, still not sure how much I actually wanted to know. On closer inspection, it looked less bulky than the others.

"Is this it?" I said. "If this is my life story, it's not saying much."

"I don't understand," Robyn said, flicking through the pages. "There appears to be so much missing."

"Like who I really am, you mean?" I said bitterly.

She gave me a baleful look, then returned to the folder. "Dr Allenby must have…"

"You mean only Rufus could have done this?"

"Yes," she mumbled, eyes still down. "Like you said, nobody else has access."

"I can understand that! They'd have trouble finding the bloody cupboard!"

She smiled wanly but was still confused. I gently took the folder from her and rubbed my hand over it, as if that might conjure up some answers. It didn't. The number on the spine had been repeated on the front, but then it had been crossed out, and the word 'Goliath' had been written above it in a vivid mauve ink. Intriguing as the name was, the thing that struck me the most was that mauve is my favourite colour. It was as if Rufus was reaching out to me.

"Goliath," I said. "Very biblical."

Robyn hadn't cottoned on. "Sorry?"

I smiled sweetly. "Your Rufus turned David into Goliath. He had a sense of humour, that's for sure."

Almost reluctantly, I opened the folder. Amazingly, the first page had a message, again hand-written in mauve.

Robyn gripped my hand. "What's that?"

I read it out to her. "*Do you get the picture? 37 PWF.*"

"What does that mean?" she asked.

I wasn't sure, but something was playing with my memory. I flicked through the folder. Just page after page of scientific jargon and numbers. "This tells us nothing," I said, exasperated.

Robyn took the folder and studied it. "This is all the data, but where is the rest of it? The personal stuff? I don't understand." She pulled another folder out and opened it, revealing the extensive medical history of number EX43, including a name and an impressive biography.

I grabbed her wrist. "Who was this?"

"A dead end," she replied softly.

150

"A failure, you mean?"

She appeared outraged at that. "He just didn't respond… like you did."

"So where is he now?" I said, thinking the worst.

She turned to the last page in the folder. "Here, see for yourself!" she almost shouted, upset that I was doubting her integrity once more.

I read the last sentence and slowly closed the folder. "Went back to his family in Huddersfield," I said. "Is that a euphemism, Robyn?"

She replaced the folder calmly before turning on me. "This is serious science, David. There are many near-misses before hitting the jackpot. And yes, he is enjoying life back in Huddersfield, like it says."

I wasn't sure if that was an oxymoron, but I kept my mouth shut.

"As with all our subjects, I maintain monthly contact by telephone. They are all alive and well, trust me."

"Are they monitored, like me?"

"No," she said. "None of them reached your standard."

"And they don't know what they were here for?"

"They all signed agreements and received ample remuneration for their time, as I assumed you had been. They were just told it was a medical study on bacteria."

"Okay," I sighed. "I'm sorry. Let's go back to my file. What exactly is missing?"

Robyn replaced the second folder and closed the cupboard. "There is nothing in your folder about you,

David. We have everything about the research, but nothing about who you are."

I sighed. "You mean Rufus has taken out everything which could identify me?"

She nodded. "Yes."

"Don't you know what it said?"

"The file was always full when I used it, but I only ever looked at the back, where I recorded the data. Your personal stuff could only have been taken out recently; otherwise, I would have noticed the folder feeling so light." She pleaded with me with her eyes, and I softened.

"Rufus took the pages out to protect my identity," I said.

She was silent for a long time, then, "I need to get you out of here, don't I?" she said, her eyes watering.

"At least we agree on something," I smiled, and I could see her reciprocating. I liked that.

We knew we couldn't do anything until we were out of the lab and into the wide-open house, so we just talked, firstly about several hare-brain plans to escape, and then about inconsequential things. The lab had its own little kitchen, and Robyn made coffee for us both, so we sat at the bench and got to know each other a bit more. I couldn't bring much to the table on that score, but Robyn more than made up for it, telling me about her childhood in Norfolk and her time at uni, where she met and fell in love with a Polish lad who broke her heart. She laughed about it now, but it had made her wary of men, which was why she had progressed so high, I guessed. Who needs a man holding you back?

In a break in the conversation, I noticed she had been drumming her fingers nervously on the bench.

"What?" I asked.

Without replying, she stood and went to another part of the wall, pressed it, and a cupboard door glided open. A smile creased her face, growing wider and more mischievous as she pulled out a box. Returning to the bench, she said, "There is one door that won't be guarded."

"Really?" I couldn't believe it. "Where?"

"The one place they'd never expect you to be."

I was feeling her positivity, but was still puzzled. "Where?"

"The monitoring room, of course!"

I nodded. "Sounds good. But tell me, why do we need a first aid box?"

Chapter Ten

We had been enjoying each other's company so much that we had no real idea of time. It was only when we heard a loud rap on the door that we broke off our conversation.

Robyn opened the door, and there stood one of Packer's men – tall, gangly, alert, a look of menace on his face and with his right hand inside his jacket, clearly ready to pull out his sidearm if the need arose. This was not the one who had ushered us into the lab earlier. My word, time really must have flown by; they had even changed shifts.

"Dinner is served, ma'am," he said without any of the bonhomie one would associate with a maître d', while his eyes never left mine as I stood behind her. "I am to escort you."

I moved closer to Robyn and quickly squeezed her hand as a signal. This was it – our play for freedom.

We moved into the corridor, and I took up station on the left of the guard, slightly ahead as he had indicated, so he could theoretically keep an eye on me. I held the folder under my left arm, leaving the other arm as a weapon when the time came. Naturally, there wasn't enough room for the three of us, so Robyn tucked in just behind the guard, which is what we wanted anyway.

We walked down the corridor, and then, instead of turning right, which led to Wolstenholme's office, the guard took us left onto a new passageway, which looked just like the other one. Again, we passed closed doors on both sides, leading to what may have originally been dining and reception rooms but were now probably offices for the nameless and faceless. I deliberately slowed the pace, making the guard readjust his step. Any little thing to throw him off his stride.

We turned yet another corner, walking into a vestibule which appeared to match the first one on the other side of the house. It was a stunning room, with a crystal chandelier, Georgian chairs, a long oak table waxed within an inch of its life, and a mix of Old Masters and more modern paintings hanging on the walls. The Old Masters were clearly fakes – even the government couldn't afford ten originals by Vermeer, Rembrandt or Van Eyck. Fascinating as they were, though, my eyes were pulled immediately to a print of a Picasso work from his 'Blue Period'. Ignoring the guard, I went over to the picture and read the brass plaque on the frame: '*The Old Guitarist*, by Pablo Picasso, the original of which is in the Art Institute of Chicago.'

I stopped. *Do you get the picture? 37 PWF*. Rufus's cryptic clue. I looked around and spotted Picasso's *The Weeping Woman*, and a weird feeling came over me. Suddenly, I had an idea of what Rufus was trying to tell me, but I just couldn't quite formulate it.

"What is it?" whispered Robyn, noticing my hesitation.

"An answer," I said, although I couldn't explain how I came up with that thought.

"Let's be moving," the guard said with some force, and I was suddenly being propelled forward, an arm on my shoulder.

"Hold on," I said softly, "please." I went over to one of the Rembrandts, but only to gain more thinking time. "Beautiful, don't you think?"

"If you say so," scoffed the guard.

"Magnificent," I murmured, as if I was studying the work of art with an appreciative eye. Under normal circumstances, I would have, but there was something teasing me. *Do you get the picture? 37 PWF.*

"Come on!" urged the guard, and this time he was not taking no for an answer, pushing me in the back with some force. I fisted my right hand in anger but caught Robyn's glare, so I forced myself to relax just a little, my heart stepping down a few beats.

We took another couple of steps, and then it hit me. Picasso's *Guernica* came into sharp focus. Painted as a result of the savage bombing of the town during the Spanish Civil War, it was my favourite work of art – or was it? Perhaps that was just something else planted in my brain by Rufus. How could I know? Either way, there was a copy of the painting back at my house, and, in my mind's eye, I could see the brass plaque in the frame. *37 PWF*. Of course!

I turned to Robyn and winked. "I love Picasso's work, don't you?"

Her frown let me know that she wasn't exactly with me, but I carried on anyway. "Are there any more examples here?"

The guard seemed not to be interested, but he stopped when I did and we waited for Robyn's reply.

"Well," she said, "there are a couple, I think."

"*Guernica*?"

Her eyes seemed to mist over in confusion. "I haven't a clue, sorry."

I persevered. "Black and white, lots of body parts…"

"Oh, yes," she said, "I've seen that."

"Can you show me?" I pleaded, as much for the guard's benefit as Robyn's. He didn't appear to have an objection.

However, Robyn was not at all impressed. I was going off-script, and she wasn't sure how to play it. The plan had been to proceed as normal until after supper, then make a break for it. Like I said: hare-brained.

She mumbled something I couldn't hear – probably a few swear words – then said, "Are you sure?"

"Oh, yes," I said enthusiastically. "Very."

Shrugging, she turned to her right, and, to my amazement, the guard meekly followed, elbowing me ahead of him so I was within his sight. That suited me.

We walked through another short corridor, Robyn stopping at a closed door on her right. "This is the committee room, David. Just down there" – pointing ahead – "is the room I told you about."

It was all falling so beautifully into place that I could have scooped her up in my arms there and then. *The monitoring room.* Which had a door to the outside world!

I looked at the guard. "Do you mind if I take a quick peek at the painting?" I felt sure my face was a picture of innocence.

He was out of his comfort zone and wasn't sure what the procedure should be. He had been instructed to deliver the prisoners for dinner, and here he was, several corridors and rooms away from his destination, contemplating the prospect of being introduced to a bit of culture. Clearly, his brain couldn't comprehend, but he felt safe in the knowledge that the house was full of his armed friends and any attempt on my part to escape would inevitably end in failure. "Okay," he said. "But be quick about it."

Funny, he still thought he had the situation under control. "Great!" I said, urging Robyn through the door which she had just opened. Before the guard could react, I swept him through the portal, and we stood in a line: Robyn on the left, then the guard, then me. Perfect! That was when I swung my right arm in an arc and caught him across the throat, and he fell to the ground, gurgling. To silence him, I grabbed his head with both hands and banged it hard on the ground – twice. It didn't do much for the parquet flooring, but that was in a better condition than the guard's head, which was spilling blood over it at a rate which alarmed Robyn.

"Have you killed him?" she asked, her breath heavy.

"I doubt it," I said, pulling his gun from its holster. "Keep an eye on the door."

I dragged the body around the room, leaving it behind some chairs, as far from the door as possible. There was little I could do about the trail of blood which followed it.

Robyn had regained her composure and knelt next to the guard, opening the first aid kit.

"What are you doing?" I asked.

"We don't want him to wake up too soon and alert the rest of the house."

She was drawing liquid from a vial into a syringe. "What the hell…?" I stammered.

"It's all right, David. This is just recuronium bromide. It's a paralytic drug. I wasn't expecting to use it so soon, but needs must."

I nodded but wasn't sure why. "I know this may sound stupid," I whispered as she searched for a vein in the guard's arm, "but what exactly does it do?"

"It's a fast-acting drug that paralyses the body for about an hour, with very few side effects – unless he's really unlucky." She offered me a smile. "It's what we used on you before you went into the scanner. It was imperative that you kept absolutely still, and this little beauty did the job perfectly." As she spoke, she fired a spray into the air, then plunged the syringe into the flaccid skin of the guard's arm.

"Is that what caused my memory loss?" I asked.

"What?"

"That stuff. Does it cause mem—?"

"No," she whispered harshly, "of course, not. What are you talking about?"

"I can't remember anything before you and Rufus got your hands on me," I said bitterly, my voice raised. Then I calmed down just enough to say softly, "It must have been something Rufus did to me."

Robyn turned from the guard and grabbed my arm. "Look, David, I know Dr Allenby had you sedated for your own good."

This was no time to hold a conference on what I could or couldn't remember, so I turned away and looked up at *Guernica*.

It was massive, certainly a full-size copy, over three metres long, much larger than my print at home. This one was so much more dramatic that I spent precious seconds just looking in awe.

"It's so majestic, isn't it?" I said. Then I looked at the brass plaque, and my instinct was confirmed. "*37 PWF*," I breathed triumphantly.

"What about it?" she said.

"I knew it meant something to me. Look."

Robyn leant in, so her hair brushed against my forehead, sending impulses through my body. "What am I looking at?" she asked.

"Paris World Fair."

She understood immediately. "PWF."

"Exactly! The 1937 Paris World Fair, to be precise. As it says on the plaque, that was where this picture made its first appearance. Either I had a real love of Picasso in the past, or Rufus drilled it into me so that he could leave me clues if he needed to. Whichever it is, this painting means a lot more to me than it does to anybody else."

I put down the folder and looked behind the picture, running my hand across the wall, my fingers hitting something. I pushed hard, and whatever it was fell away from the wall and became lodged on the back of the frame. I stretched my fingers as much as I could, but it was out of reach.

"Here, let me," said Robyn. "My fingers are thinner."

I stepped aside and let her try. It didn't take long for her to bring out a small package still attached to the tape that had pinned it to the wall.

"What is it?" asked Robyn, handing it to me.

I put it in my pocket. "The answer to everything, perhaps." I took her hand. "We should be going."

"Wait! Take your shirt off!" she demanded.

"What?"

"Just do it!"

"Look, Robyn, much as I like you…"

"Listen," she whispered, "we need to nullify that tracker inside you."

I nodded, although I didn't have a clue what she was going to do. But I took my shirt off anyway.

She opened the first aid box, replaced the syringe and took out a bundle of large plasters and a bandage, all unused and still in their wrappers. "Take your watch off."

I obeyed silently.

"Can you get the strap off?"

"I think so," I said, working frantically to remove the gold-plated bracelet. "Are you going to tell me what you have in mind?"

"It's a little trick Dr Allenby told me about."

Of course, I thought. *Good old Rufus*.

"Explain."

"He said that, in the early days, when he used to lean over to examine you, Specs told him that the tracker seemed to go haywire. It took them some time to realise that it was his watch that was interfering with the monitors, so from then on, he always took it off before going into the lab. It made sense to him anyway because time meant nothing to him when he was working." She took the wrapping off one of the plasters. "Now, hold the watch over your scar, and this will keep it in place."

I winced as she pressed down the plaster. "You think it will work?"

"We'll soon find out," she smiled, opening the bandage. "We'll be okay until we get outside, but by then, Packer and his men will realise something is up."

I sat on the edge of the table while Robyn quickly and expertly wrapped the bandage round me tightly and secured it using several more plasters. I felt the watch dig into me, which, I assumed, was what was needed.

After putting my shirt back on, I patted her hand to try to convey my confidence, although I'm sure she felt as helpless as I did.

We left the room with one last look, hoping that the unconscious guard wouldn't be found for a while, and headed for the monitoring room and freedom.

When we got there, Robyn started typing in the code to open the door. She had pressed only three keys when the discordant sound of a klaxon reverberated through the corridor we were in and, no doubt, around the whole house as well.

"What the hell?" I said.

Robyn looked stunned. "I don't understand. That's the alarm. What is Specs up to?"

She hastily finished the code, and I pushed her aside, at the same time taking the gun from my pocket. I wanted to be prepared for what lay beyond that door because I had the feeling it wasn't going to be good news. I turned the handle and pushed the door open, stepping to the side as I entered, just in case somebody got trigger-happy.

I had no need to worry. There were three men, each in shirt sleeves and wearing ties of the same design. Very professional. And very scared. The one who was closest was short and rotund, with compressed, fluffy white hair and round glasses. I assumed he was the leader. He just gave off that aura. The other two were younger, one of them looking as if he was barely out of his teens, bum fluff on his chin and a pair of hippy glasses perched loosely on the edge of his nose. Like something out of *Scooby Doo*.

The room itself had a bank of computer screens on one wall, each of which was fizzing with static. I assumed this was because they were not picking up signals from my tracker. Robyn had done well.

There were six tables, each holding a console and keyboard, and the two younger men were still seated at their stations, a look of horror on their faces.

That was also reflected on the face of Robyn, who stood in the doorway like a statue. "Who the hell...? Where's Specs?"

We didn't have time for answers, so I waved the gun from one to the other. "Don't worry," I said. "Behave, and you're safe." They all nodded obediently.

Robyn closed the door and raced to one of the monitors, flipping a couple of switches, which made the alarm stop and filling the air with a silence that almost hurt my ears. "Who are you?" she demanded. "What are you doing here?"

I waved the gun to indicate that the young ones should remain seated and headed for the boss. "Answer the question," I said.

The rotund one was sweating as he studied first my face and then my gun. "You are David Parks."

I nodded. "And you are?"

"Steven Green. I run this monitoring station."

"Since when?" demanded Robyn, her face like thunder.

"Since this morning," said Green, trying to sound in control, but his voice was so high it could have been a violin being played pizzicato. "We came in with Mr Wolstenholme…," he stammered.

"Yes," I cut him off, "we know all about Wolstenholme."

"How did you get the code?" Robyn wanted to know.

It was a rhetorical question because we both knew. Somehow, Wolstenholme had wheedled it out of Rufus or Specs, and now he had control of the monitoring. It would be only a matter of minutes before his men realised that this was the only place we were likely to be. We had to move fast.

"Give me your mobile," I said to Green.

"What?"

"Your phone. That's all I need. Then we'll be gone."

He exchanged looks with the two youngsters, as if begging for help and not getting any, before reluctantly reaching behind and carefully drawing out a mobile from the pocket of his jacket, which was draped across the back of his chair.

"Open it up," I ordered. "I want to be able to use it."

He obliged, tapping in the password, and Robyn took the phone from him.

"Time to go," I said, still clutching the folder, which now seemed even more important, and Robyn led me to the emergency exit at the rear of the room. We could hear Packer's men in the house, running blind and angry because they no longer had a track on me, but I wasn't sure what we were going to find beyond this door. I was assuming we would be out in the garden, but who were we going to meet?

I pushed open the door and said to Robyn, "Whatever happens, stay behind me. And don't argue!" With that, I sprinted out, surprised to see a narrow gravel path leading to a low wooden fence and countryside beyond. We had come out at the side of the house, and there was no sign of life whatsoever. Luck appeared to be with us.

I leapt over the fence and waited to help Robyn, although she didn't need me, as she jumped higher than I had done and was soon a pace or two in front of me. That was fine, because if anyone tried to shoot at us from the house now, they'd only hit me, and that wouldn't help them one bit.

Just as that thought crossed my mind, I heard a shout and the sound of bullets. I didn't stop. At first, I had toyed with the idea of facing them down, but the last thing I wanted was to be caught again. The only way to end this nightmare was to find answers, and that meant running as fast as I could.

We were halfway across the field when I decided to look back. There were three of them, spread out and sprinting, guns at their sides. It looked as if they had instructions to take me alive, and that was a point in our favour, although it was also clear that they would have reinforcements arriving by road on the other side of the field now that they had pinpointed us.

"Robyn," I screamed, "get down! Lay down, NOW!"

Without questioning me, she did as I asked, and I knew the men would never be able to hit her the distance they were from us. I swivelled and sank to one knee, aiming for the man on the left. He was the nearest, and I liked the symmetry of working left to right. They had all stopped when I did so, confused by my tactic, and as they reluctantly raised their guns, I pulled the trigger of mine.

The first man fell silently and swiftly, so I swung my aim to the next one, rather like shooting ducks at a fair. They were returning fire now and probably wondering why none of their shots were registering.

The second man went down with a yelp, and I could see the look of horror on the face of the one remaining as he froze. I walked over to him as he came back to life, pumping his bullets at me until his gun was empty, and he could hear the click of nothingness. I didn't want to kill him, but he knew my secret, so I aimed for his heart. Twice.

Robyn finally looked up as I was retrieving the gun from the first man. He hadn't had a chance of firing, so his was the most loaded weapon. And that was something I might desperately need.

"What the hell happened, David?" Robyn asked through her heavy breathing. "They could have killed you."

I ignored the question. "Let's get out of here. The others will have heard the gunfire and will be heading this way."

I began to run to our left, away from the house and also from the road I assumed Packer and his men would be using. It was a calculated gamble, but what choice did we have? I just hoped Robyn was with me.

Reaching the edge of the field, I pushed my way through a gap in the hedge, coming out in the corner of another field, this one filled with what may have been potatoes, the ridges likely to prove a hindrance to our progress.

"We'll go round the outside," I said as Robyn appeared beside me, a couple of small leaves adding a dash of colour to her hair where she had emerged through the undergrowth. I grinned, then gently pulled them away while she did the same for me. It was a bad time, but it was still a moment I will treasure. That was also the second time I had wanted to kiss her, which was strange to me. What on earth was I feeling?

We broke into a trot, Robyn in front so that I could shield her. It was unlikely anybody would appear ahead of us unless we were really unlucky, but there was no doubt Packer would be spreading out his forces behind us, and there was every likelihood that one or more of them would emerge when we least expected it.

But our luck held. We had skirted the entire field without mishap and then found ourselves in another field, this one ploughed but otherwise untouched. I reached out for Robyn and stopped her.

"I'm phoning the police," I said.

"I'm not sure that will be much help," she wheezed.

I smiled. "Just keep breathing like that and tell them you're being attacked."

She understood immediately, and I handed her the phone after I had dialled. "Hello, police, police." Pause. "You've got to help me! I'm being…" She offered up a very theatrical scream, gave them the address and hung up.

"Beautiful," I said. "That should do the trick." I took back the phone and dialled another number. I would have called Denver, of course, but you know what it's like: I only had him on speed dial, so I had never needed to commit the number to memory. And as my phone was no longer in my possession, I called Gregory instead.

"Hello?"

"Gregory, it's me," I said. From all the times I had needed him over the six years of our association, I would never forget his contact details. He was my taxi, after all.

"Sir?" he stammered, surprise in his voice. "This isn't your phone."

Always good at stating the obvious is our Gregory. "I borrowed this one."

"Just a minute, sir."

Before I could respond, the line went quiet, and I shared a look with Robyn as we stood in an open field, expecting a deluge of armed men to descend on us at any moment. Of all the times for Gregory to disappear on me, this was undoubtedly the worst. I held back a cuss, as Denver would have called it.

"Hello, sir."

"What the hell are you up—?"

"Sorry, sir. I just wanted to open the geolocation for your new phone."

"What?"

"I assume you are not in a position for me to offer a lengthy explanation, standing as you are in a field."

I was stunned. "You know where I am?"

Gregory gave a self-satisfied chuckle. "Oh, yes, sir. We've known all along where you are. I have a tracker on your own mobile." He paused. "However, that appears to still be in the house."

Although the word 'tracker' filled me with dread, I was mighty glad that Gregory was on the other end this time. "Long story. Okay, so where are you?" I asked.

"Well, sir," he said extremely slowly, attempting and succeeding in winding me up, "if you go to the end of the field you are currently in, we will meet you in... three minutes."

"Are you serious?"

"Oh, yes, sir. Deadly. Over and out."

Robyn gave me a relieved smile as we made our way through the field. Without thinking, I grasped her hand as we covered the last few yards in the open and headed for the rendezvous. It felt good connecting with her physically. A calming influence in a sea of chaos. I repeatedly looked over my shoulder for trouble, stumbling once or twice, but we maintained a good speed.

Robyn saw the car first. It was a big brute of a vehicle, a two-point-something-litre Daimler or equivalent. Sleek-black and purring like it had lapped up all the cream in the dairy. Although it was beyond the hedge, we could make out Gregory seated at the wheel. I couldn't see Denver, but I knew he would be in the passenger seat, probably nursing his pistol and looking out for us and any opposition. I knew we were in safe hands.

Robyn fell through the gap in the hedge and pulled open the back door, tumbling into the car and offering her grateful thanks. I stopped at the edge of the hedge and looked back across the field.

It was then that I realised Packer had been running after us with some of his men, but now he, too, froze, so that we were like two statuesque adversaries, as if cast in stone, staring each other down. After a couple of seconds, I waved the folder in the air, indicating that I had all the evidence I needed, before stooping into the hedge and disappearing from his view.

Chapter Eleven

The car raced down a narrow road, so narrow, in fact, that there were vehicle passing points at regular intervals, just wide enough to avoid scratching oncoming cars. The state of the road didn't seem to be bothering Gregory much, as he put his foot down regardless of what might have been heading our way.

What I hadn't expected when I had climbed into the car, though, was that I would be sharing the plush back seat not only with Robyn but with Grace, who waved regally as I closed the door and she then stretched over Robyn to put a hand gently on my knee as a sign of welcome and relief. They were feelings I reciprocated.

We had been motoring for perhaps fifteen minutes, my mind bouncing with every jolt and swerve, racing faster even than the car itself. Then I overheated.

"Gregory," I said, "stop the car."

"What, sir?"

"You heard – stop the fucking car!" There, that was much clearer, but I could have done without Grace turning puce and tutting loudly. I had just dropped several notches in her estimation – but I wouldn't worry about that now: I was desperate for answers.

It took several seconds for Gregory to obey my command, eventually turning the car into a gateway, which clearly led to some farmer's prized turnips. He killed the engine, and we sat in silence. I waited for a moment before getting out of the car and standing on the muddy track, clenching my hands into fists, daring myself to punch a hole through the bodywork of what was clearly Grace's pride and joy. I was breathing so deeply that my eyes were clouding, and I could hear the air loudly leaving my lungs. Then I felt Robyn reach out for my hand, and I took hers willingly.

"What is it, David?"

"I don't understand," I said, feeling utterly drained. "What is happening here?"

"I don't know." She paused, perhaps trying to get her head round everything. After all, it was not only my life that had been turned upside down. She, too, was suffering, but I just wasn't in the right place to offer her any comfort. "I'm so sorry, David." I could feel the sorrow and pain in her voice.

I nodded. "I understand some of it, sure. It was an experiment. Yes, I get that. But why am I running for my life, Robyn? What secrets aren't you telling me?"

She tried to pull away, but I maintained my grip on her hand. I might not have known what the hell was going on, but I certainly knew that I needed her close. I was more desperate now than anything else. And afraid.

"Honestly, David, I have told you everything I know. What else do you want me to say?"

That was one question I didn't have the answer to. What more could she tell me? The only person I knew who could have helped me was dead. The man who had started this would not be there to help me finish it. I let out a sharp breath and dropped Robyn's hand. I had never felt so alone.

I got back into the vehicle and sat beside Grace, another woman I knew nothing about. But then again, that seemed to apply to all my companions.

Robyn sat beside me, closed the door and waited. She knew I would be exploding at any moment, and she would be there to pick up the pieces.

I took a deep breath. "Explain yourself, Gregory."

"Explain, sir?" he replied, innocence dripping off him.

"I want to know exactly who you are. Why did Rufus pick you, of all people?"

"Well... sir."

Grace interrupted. "Just drive, Gregory."

I sensed a conspiracy, but I would not be turned. "Just talk, Gregory."

Grace gave a sigh, and Gregory's shoulders hunched. He gave in first. "Yes, sir, perhaps it might be time for a few explanations."

"On your head be it," Grace whispered, but for once, he ignored his aunt.

"I'm listening," I said.

"Well, sir, over the years, I have developed some particular, er, talents," he began diffidently.

"Not driving, obviously," Robyn hissed cuttingly.

"Talents?" I prompted.

I could see Gregory's eyes narrow in the rear-view mirror as he continued. "My talents and my contacts. I have had a… shall we say chequered career."

"Criminal?" I guessed aloud.

Grace sighed heavily again.

"Like I said, sir, chequered. Perhaps we should leave it at that."

"I don't think so, do you?" I leant forward, placing my hand on his shoulder, gently at first but menacingly. "Please continue."

Denver was twisting in his seat, excited at the possibility of getting one over on our driver. Little did he know that he would be next.

"I had fingers in pies, sir, I admit."

"And Rufus knew about your wandering digits."

Gregory thought about that. "In hindsight, I think perhaps that he might have done, yes." He looked distraught. "Honestly, I'm not really a criminal, sir," he added, possibly shame-faced, but I couldn't see as he had turned away from me then.

"Good to hear." My sarcasm was taut.

"I admit I was on the fringes when I was very young. Then a police detective took me under his wing and taught me right from wrong and a few tricks of his trade."

"And a few juicy contacts," I surmised, remembering how he had magically produced the gun and ammunition back at Grace's house.

"He's retired now, but I still have access to him for important things." Gregory tried a smile, and I felt myself soften. Dammit, I couldn't help liking him.

I turned to Grace. "So what about you? What's your story?" I locked eyes with her. "A gangster's moll, perhaps?"

"Don't be facetious, young man. It does not become you. I have merely encouraged my nephew in his endeavours and introduced him to people who matter."

I wasn't sure I needed to know if she was deeply embedded in Gregory's misdemeanours, so I turned on Denver.

"Don't look at me, pal," he barked. "This is all new to me. You know I'd never seen this Rufus guy before he accosted you on the island."

I couldn't argue with that, but there was still something niggling my mind. There must have been some connection, no matter how tenuous. Rufus was obviously a man with a plan, and even my old beach bum Denver came into it somehow. I had already questioned the skills he had, so what if Rufus knew all about them – all about *him*? What if Rufus knew Denver's history long before he came to the island to see me?

It was then that everything began to fall into place, and my stomach heaved afresh now that I knew what must be the truth. Rufus had said we had been to the island before, *together*. He must have pointed Denver out to me before he erased my memory. That way, Denver became a subliminal figure to me, and it was obvious that I would make contact with him. Oh, very clever, Rufus.

"You okay, David?" Denver's concerned voice broke in.

"Never mind," I said hastily, before pausing. "So what did Rufus find out about you, my friend? What murky past did he uncover?"

"Well, it wasn't criminal!" Denver said quickly.

"No," I agreed. Rufus wasn't stupid. He would have searched out somebody who, when it came to the crunch, would defend me with his life. Somebody who would follow me wherever I went, even back to England, to ensure that no harm would befall me. Somebody who would willingly kill to protect me. Someone who *knew* how to kill.

"US Army? Marines?" I guessed.

"Close," was all he was going to say on the matter. "Now let's get moving, David, before the bad guys get wind of where we are."

It sounded so much like an order that I just said, "Where are we headed?"

"We've been doing a little research while you've been enjoying yourself," Denver said mirthlessly as a relieved Gregory pulled the car back onto the road and continued our journey down the dusty lane.

"Okay," I said slowly, wondering what he had uncovered.

"Firstly, as we suspected and you now appear to have confirmed, *you* don't exist. Despite exhaustive investigations, I found nothing online about David Michael Parks – at least not the David Michael Parks sitting in this car. You, my friend, have no social status at all. No Facebook, no Instagram, no…"

"I get the picture," I interrupted.

"Rufus apparently gave you a new persona, probably to protect you," suggested Grace.

"But surely anybody else could have checked me out."

"Why would they bother? As far as anyone knew, you were just a harmless millionaire going about his mundane life. Nothing to see here, folks, move along," said Denver.

"Of course," said Grace, "that no longer applies. You are a wanted man, David."

I involuntarily reached for my stomach, ensuring that the watch was still covering my scar. It wouldn't help if it slipped out of position, but I also knew that this was only a temporary measure. I needed an operation to remove it – and soon. "So, what do we know about Rufus?"

"Ah," said Denver, "quite a lot, as it happens."

Over the next ten minutes, he gave me a detailed portrait of the scientist who, at one stage, had been tipped to pick up a Nobel Prize but who got bogged down with his experiments and began to alienate fellow theorists and would-be patrons with his increasingly bizarre suggestions. While not exactly flavour of the month, he still had a few friends in high places – a fact confirmed by Robyn – and he was able to pursue his work thanks in the main to his association with Matthew Denny.

Robyn then gave us a more personal tour of Rufus, explaining how erudite and charming he was, how meticulous he had been with his experiments, and how welcome he had made Robyn feel. Almost part of the family, she said. I wasn't happy with that reference, but I let it slide. Rufus still meant nothing to me, as I had no memory of him whatsoever. He was a closed book, locked away in a dingy library far to the back of my mind.

"That's all well and good," I said. "But how does any of this help us?"

Denver hesitated, then said, "You talked to me about an accident."

"Yes, I did."

"When did you say your accident occurred?"

"I'm not sure," I said.

Robyn appeared baffled. "I know nothing about any accident."

"Okay, so what day did you start working for the mad scientist?" asked Denver.

Robyn's lips pursed. "Don't call him that!" Her eyes blazed momentarily. "I began on 1st September. Why?"

"As I thought," said Denver. "Then you really don't know anything." He was craning his neck to look at Robyn behind him.

"What are you saying?" demanded Robyn, upset that her mentor was being maligned. Without thinking, she clutched at my hand, so I gently squeezed hers. I had a feeling something unpleasant this way was coming, and my heart skipped for Robyn as much as for myself.

"What have you found, Denver?" I said.

Denver was now in his full Perry Mason mode. "For the record, Robyn, you say you started on the first day of September, six years ago."

Robyn nodded, even though Denver was no longer looking at her. Instead, he had opened the laptop. "Yes," she said softly, hesitantly, willing him to end this charade but fully expecting to be plunged into some kind of dark abyss.

"And you believe that David here came to your laboratory a couple of days before that."

Again, she nodded, squeezing my hand even tighter. When Denver did not respond, she sighed and said, "Yes."

"Doctor Rufus told you so."

"Yes." She was beginning to feel exasperated as well as nervous.

"Well," said Denver eventually, "I beg to differ. David, while you were away, we checked the local papers for accidents that occurred along the Hog's Back that year."

"Okay," I said slowly, wondering what he was getting at.

"There were seventeen," Denver stated almost with pleasure. "Three of them involving fatalities."

Robyn gasped. "What the hell are you saying here?"

"David's accident was all too real. We have it in black and white, as it were."

I was about to say something, but thought better of it. Denver appeared to be on a roll now, so it was best to let him go on. Besides, I could sense at least one answer about to emerge from my dim and so far non-existent past. Denver didn't disappoint.

"According to the *Aldershot News* at the time, on 24th August, a car went off the road along the Hog's Back near a place called Tongham, hitting a tree and coming to rest in the undergrowth next to a field. The occupant was pronounced dead at the scene." He paused then, allowing it all to sink in.

It took me a few seconds, but the cloud lifted. "A woman!" I almost screamed.

"Just so, pal. The woman you have always known about, deep down," Denver said.

Robyn wasn't convinced. "Hold on a second! What makes you think this is the same accident? Come on, talk about clutching at straws!"

Denver sucked air through his teeth. "Tell me the name of the assistant you took over from."

"What?" asked Robyn, taken aback.

"Before he took you on, Rufus had another young assistant. He must have mentioned her in passing, surely. What was her name? No, don't tell me; I'll tell you." Denver turned to face her. "Let's call her Susan, shall we?"

Robyn fell back, a look of shock on her face. "Susan left for another job."

Denver was in his element now, rather like a prosecuting counsel tearing apart a weak witness. "Robyn, Rufus lied to you. Susan Patterson didn't leave her job – she left this mortal coil."

I could feel Robyn's pain, so I stepped in. "You know this because?"

"Because we have the evidence, old friend," said Denver. "Susan Patterson first worked for Denny Archer as a research assistant. More than a coincidence, huh?"

I contemplated for a moment. "But I don't recognise the name."

"No, but you remember her from the accident. She was obviously driving you to or from somewhere when she crashed." Denver paused. "The question is, why did she crash?"

"And why did Rufus cover it up?" I added.

"I've had enough of this!" Robyn broke in. "Rufus was a good man."

"A good man who lied." That was Gregory, who had drily summarised the position on my behalf. Like Robyn, I believed that Rufus was basically a decent man, but there were still questions to be answered. Unfortunately, he wasn't here to answer them.

I felt in my pocket for the small package I had taken from behind the painting, wondering when I would get the chance to examine it. "So, where are we going?" I asked again.

"Frensham Pond," said Gregory.

I didn't ask anything else. It appeared that my friends were taking me on a magical mystery tour, and all I could do was sit back and enjoy the ride as much as possible. Besides, there was so much turmoil going through my head, I didn't particularly care.

* * *

The 'pond' is actually two – the 'Great' and the 'Small'. Very descriptive. Apparently, we were heading for the

'Great', set within a thousand acres of Surrey countryside owned by the National Trust but managed by the borough council. The site is made up of mainly heathland and woodland, while the ponds themselves were created in the Middle Ages to provide fish for the Bishop of Winchester's estate. The area is now an SSSI and an AONB. This was being explained to us by Gregory, slipping effortlessly into tour-guide mode.

"Hold it, bud," said Denver. "What's with the initials?"

Gregory sighed. He didn't like being interrupted when he was in full flow, especially during a geography lesson, and certainly not by someone from a country with no real history.

"For your information, sir" – this last word slurred to show his contempt – "SSSI means a Site of Special Scientific Interest…"

"Meaning it's old," retorted Denver, well aware that he was winding up our driver.

"Precisely."

"Okay," continued Denver, enjoying himself, "carry on."

"Thank you, sir." There it was again, that emphasis. "AONB refers to an Area of Outstanding Natural Beauty, of which there are many in this county and country."

I couldn't see it, but I was sure Denver was grinning. "Sure beats the Grand Canyon and Lake Tahoe," he said, his voice rich with sarcasm.

Gregory fell silent, beaten for once.

I could see the pond out of the window. It looked so remarkably blue and welcoming, but as we continued, the view was quickly screened by trees and then houses, until we were on the road leading away from the water and offering a vista of little charm.

Gregory pulled in outside of a house with a low fence and a small garden. The gate was open, but that was probably because it appeared to be hanging slightly off its hinges, one of the signs that I picked up which gave me the impression that the owner was not particularly DIY-savvy.

"What is this place?" I asked.

Denver climbed out, indicating that I should follow. "The next piece of the puzzle," he said. When I looked blank, he added, "This is the home of Susan Patterson's father."

Chapter Twelve

As we walked up the path, I saw that my initial appraisal had been correct: the garden was a little overgrown, and the paint was peeling off the bright yellow front door, while the wooden window frames were crying out for attention. It all looked very sad and unloved.

The same applied to the man who opened the door. He was probably in his mid-sixties, although you might say that he was trying to look ten years older and succeeding. His hair was tousled – put politely – the grey overpowering what little natural rust colour he had started with. He had shaved, but only just, and his face drooped a little to the left, like someone who had suffered a stroke. His eyes were dark, as if the world was sitting on his shoulders, and he couldn't shift it.

"Mr Patterson?" Denver asked.

"Yes." The voice was as weary as the man.

"I wonder if we might have a word?"

The path was narrow, which meant that I had to stand behind Denver, partially hidden from view. Patterson blinked and studied my friend, then leant round him to take me in. "David!" he screamed, his face surfacing from the gloom.

I was stunned. This was the first time in my life – well, my *current* life – that anybody had ever recognised me, and I couldn't believe it. It was a defining moment, and I could feel my legs shaking and my heart racing. I really thought I was going to fall over.

Patterson was animatedly waving. "Come in! Come in!"

"We have friends…," Denver began.

"Oh, the more the merrier! Come in! All of you!" Patterson was suddenly sprightly, his face beaming as he led us into the house, switching on the light to brighten the place.

The interior reflected the careworn outside, as if a deep melancholy had crept up the garden path and forced its way through the yellow door, damaging everything on its way, including the owner.

We were led into a small lounge, where a two-seat sofa and an armchair took centre stage, the light brown leather cracked and peeling. Cushions were thrown across the sofa, perhaps in an effort to add colour to a dismal landscape.

"Sit! Sit! I'll bring in some chairs from the kitchen." Patterson was sounding like a machine gun, his words rattling round the room, bouncing off the walls. We were picking up on his pleasure.

"I'll give you a hand," said Gregory, and they both disappeared through a door which led to the dimly lit kitchen. Robyn sat with Grace on the sofa; Denver and I stood, leaving the armchair for the man of the house.

Patterson and Gregory came back with two dining chairs and placed them next to the sofa.

"I've put the kettle on," said Patterson, plonking himself ungainly in the armchair. Denver and Gregory took the dining chairs. I perched on the arm of the sofa next to Robyn.

"So, David, what brings you here after all this time?" Patterson asked excitedly. He was on the edge of his seat, quivering with delight.

I looked at Denver, then at Patterson. "I'm not sure you'd believe me, Mr Patterson."

"Oh, please, call me Rex, like you used to."

"Well, Rex, it's a long story…"

"Never mind, my boy, I've got all the time in the world for you."

So I told him about my memory loss, of the last six years not knowing who I really was, of the trauma over the last few days.

In return, Rex took me back in time to a different life when Susan was alive and I was her friend. How we met at the laboratory when I volunteered to be a guinea pig for some mad scientist's supposedly harmless experiment, and she was the assistant desperately hoping to be part of some world-shattering breakthrough in medicine, her youthful enthusiasm so obvious to a doting father. He said I jokingly called her Igor, which she loved, or sometimes Marie, referring to Madame Curie, the greatest of all female scientists, whom she admired. We laughed so much, he said, and her life was enhanced because of our friendship.

"Although," he said with a grin, "I was convinced there was something more."

"Really?" I said, naively innocent.

Rex became misty-eyed. "She was only twenty-four when she died, but despite being a bit younger than you, she loved you, David. I'm sure of that. She changed when she met you, and it was all for the better. I am so glad she had that time before…"

The moment had arrived that none of us wanted. There was a silence as Rex gathered his thoughts and his strength. "Before the accident."

"Please, Rex, I know this is difficult, but I need to know what happened. This is part of my history as well as yours."

"I understand, my boy." He took a gulp of air. "I was upset that you didn't make it to the funeral…" He held up a hand to stop my protest. "It made no sense… until today. I know you would have been there if you were able."

"Thank you," I breathed.

"I first met you just after you began the experiment. Susan brought you over to help celebrate my birthday. She was always thoughtful like that. I remember we sat in the garden – it was a glorious day in July. Sometimes, it can be an unforgiving month, don't you think?"

"Sometimes," I nodded.

Robyn had been restrained the whole time, but now she leant forward. "July, you say?"

"That's right, my dear. The thirtieth. My birthday."

Robyn sank back, defeated, her eyes damp and her lips quivering. Rufus *had* lied to her, and now she had no interest in what Rex was saying.

"Susan made sandwiches and had bought a cake, especially for me. She'd even put a couple of candles on it, which you both insisted I blow out and make a wish." He looked at me wistfully. "I won't tell you what I wished, but it never came true." He gripped the arms of his chair as a convulsion took hold. "You must forgive me. I am afraid I have something called dystonia, which affects my muscles." His face dropped. "I've had it for years, but it became serious when I lost both my wife and Susan. It's stress-related, of course," he finished by way of explanation.

"I'm so sorry, Rex," I said, knowing how inadequate it sounded, while at the same time thinking how that laboratory had affected the two of us in violently different ways.

He rallied a little. "Not to worry, my boy. You have brightened my day. Now, where was I? Oh, yes. Susan talked about what was going on at the laboratory – all way above my head, of course – and you said how you were enjoying yourself, especially the bedside manner of the staff. Susan had a little giggle and a blush at that, I recall."

It was Robyn's turn to wriggle in her seat.

Rex continued, "She brought you over three more times, I think, and then it suddenly stopped…"

"Shortly before Susan's accident," said Denver bluntly.

Rex gave him an old-fashioned look, but nodded. "Yes, it was. The next contact I had with the laboratory was a few days after the crash, when Rufus Allenby made a personal visit to offer his commiserations and to explain what happened."

"He knew all about it?" I said.

"Yes. He said that Susan had left work to go home and had lost control of the car."

"Is that it?" I gasped.

"What do you mean?" said Rex. "What else could have happened?"

I bit my tongue. I had said too much already. The last thing I wanted was to upset this gentle man by implying that I was in the car when his daughter died. That wouldn't help anyone. "I'm sorry, Rex. I just meant that I thought there might have been more details."

"That was enough. It had been just a sad, sad accident. Rufus Allenby was very nice about it all, but really, I just wanted him to leave me in peace."

The conversation had reached its end. None of us wanted to prolong the agony, so each of us sought to find another topic of discussion, something lighter. I went back to the day of Rex's birthday, and he was happy to enlarge on the details, grateful that his mind could turn to happier times. We all joined in, bringing joy and laughter back into a desolate house.

When silence descended, it changed nothing. Silence among friends is a wonderful thing. When talking is no longer needed, you still have the *presence* of friendship. For me, I felt blessed, although my experience of true friendship had been brief. Here was Denver – a crazy American who, I knew, would do anything for me, and I for him. Gregory had been my driver for six years, but it was only in the last two days that I had realised what he meant to me and what he truly felt about me. Grace, too, was a godsend, although I wasn't sure yet what her true role was to be. Then there was Robyn. Where to begin? A beautiful woman, true. But there was more. While she had a place in my immediate past, I was convinced more than ever that she would also hold a place in my future, and I welcomed that thought.

During the lull, Gregory took up all the cups and disappeared into the kitchen, where we could hear the tap water running and the clink of crockery as they were placed in a bowl. Good old domesticated Gregory. One day, he'd make somebody a fine partner.

Rex had brought out a photograph album so that we could all see his daughter's life in pictures. It wasn't enough, of course, but it gave me some semblance of closure as I watched her as a ten-year-old playing at the water's edge – possibly Frensham Pond itself – and, a couple of years later, riding a pony without a safety hat, giving the impression of a true professional. Rex confirmed that riding was her passion, and he regretted the fact that he could never afford to buy her a pony. I was sure she never held it against him. There was love in her eyes: for the pony and for the life she was leading. Rex had no reason to castigate himself, and I told him so.

"You are very kind, David. I hope we can be friends again."

I told him that was what I wanted, too, and it was then that he left the room and came back moments later carrying a photograph frame close to his chest. "Here, David, you should have this," he said in a faltering voice as he handed the picture to me. My breath caught. It was Susan – of course – but there was more. It was a reflection of my past, a view into somewhere I had not been able to visit and had not expected to, for I was standing beside her, smiling, frozen in a moment of time, locked together for eternity. Susan was gone, but I was still here, and as the tears ran down my cheeks, I knew more than ever that I had to fight on.

"Thank you, Rex," I said softly. "I will treasure it."

It was time to break away, to gulp down some air and relieve the tight feeling in my chest. It was also time to see what Rufus had to say for himself. The package in my pocket had to offer up some answers. "Denver, can I have my laptop?" I took it from him, as he nodded. "Rex, would you mind if I went into another room? I need to be alone."

I wasn't sure he understood, but he guided me into the kitchen, where I sat at the table, unzipping the laptop from its carrier and plugging in the lead. Rex took out the kettle plug and inserted the other end of the lead into the socket, before leaving me with a squeeze on the shoulder. I acknowledged him with a "Thanks" before taking the parcel from my pocket and unwrapping it.

As I'd always suspected, it was a USB stick, and my hand shook as I placed it on the table. I booted up the computer and sat spellbound as it came to life. I tapped in the password and then inserted the USB in the port, a drawing of what I could only assume was a corpuscle appearing on the screen as an icon. I clicked on it, and the screen diffused colourfully until Rufus was sitting before me. While that alone was a shock, I was more stunned by the fact that he was at my desk, in my house, under my copy of *Guernica*.

He was still for a moment, his nervous blinking the only sign of life. Then he spoke.

Chapter Thirteen

My name is Rufus Allenby. I am – or was – a particle physicist of some little note. I use the two tenses because either may be equally relevant at this time. If I am still alive, then I am sure I will be going to prison. If not, then…

The fact that you are watching this also means one of two things. Firstly, through the manner of the clues I have left, this memory stick will be in the hands of the intended recipient. Conversely, if the stick was found accidentally at some time in the future, then it may all be over, and one or both of us will be dead.

I fervently hope that the person who is seeing me now is actually the product of my lifetime's work, which gives me a chance to offer my sincere and unreserved apologies for what I have put you through, and I trust that you will watch the rest of this confession with a partly open mind. That is probably too much to ask, I know, but therein lies hope.

Let me introduce myself formally. I am Rufus Immanuel Allenby, of Badger House, Dockenfield, Surrey. I live alone, and nothing of value or interest in this case will be found in the property, I can assure you.

I obtained my BSc and MA at a red-brick university. The name may be ascertained easily enough, but I do not wish to besmirch it here. Suffice to say, I received a thorough grounding in the subject of particle physics, which I have more fully developed since. I studied the physicist Louis de Broglie, who believed in a real physical interpretation of matter-waves. While this may sound like jargon to the uninitiated, I found the subject more fascinating as I developed my own theories. In layman's terms, the idea is that particle velocity is equal to wave velocity, and that if the trajectory of a particle can be determined, then so can the trajectory of a wave. I hope you can bear with me here because this is extremely important.

I then turned my attention to Pacinian corpuscles, which can be found in the skin of mammals and which are responsible for detecting pressure and vibration. I felt that if I could create waves through these corpuscles, then perhaps they could become a defence mechanism to detect and possibly repel bacteria and other harmful cells.

I experimented privately for ten years, before formulating my plan and procuring both the finance and a machine capable of testing my theory. It was time to carry out field trials.

There were, naturally, considerable failures and non-starters, all of which were meticulously filed and subsequently removed from the programme, although my colleague is in touch with all of them on a regular basis to ensure there are no lasting side effects. Thankfully, none have arisen.

However, there was one subject – I shall call him Pablo here, in a nod to the great painting behind me – who responded amazingly to the procedure. And herein lies my dilemma.

Pablo was such an outstanding subject that I... I confess I took it too far. I overstepped the boundaries of science and pursued my own agenda at personal risk to Pablo, and that will always be to my overriding shame. I am here attempting in some small way to make amends.

I have no intention of divulging Pablo's real name. I have removed his personal details from my file and will take them somewhere safe so that if, in the future, Pablo is in a position to retrieve them, he will know of his past.

I have to believe you are out there, Pablo, even if you might be watching this with a mixture of horror and bewilderment.

Because you were so special to me, I had to take measures to erase your memory. This was purely for your own safety because it would do no good to pursue your history as it would lead to a Pandora's box of problems for you, me and science itself. I could not allow that to happen. I am so sorry, Pablo. I hope you will find it possible to forgive me one day.

I sent you out into the world with a new name, enough money so that you would never have to worry... and a secret I was hoping we would both take to the grave.

It all began so wonderfully. I designed a machine which would do untold good, but because I possessed so much vanity I carried the experiment on, thinking that I could enhance the future of mankind even more. The truth is, Pablo, I put you through the experiment more times than I should have so that now I am not sure what I have created.

[It was here that Rufus began to cry, his face contorted in agony, and I felt only pity at that moment. Suddenly, he rallied.]

Pablo, if you are still alive and are watching this, then you will know by now how special you really are. More special than anyone else could know. That, in itself, is an accident of my experimentation, and I have lived with regret ever since. If it is not you watching this, then my heart bleeds, for I will have lost everything.

Believe me, I would have left you in the dark forever if it wasn't for certain people who are set on exposing you and destroying my work for their own aims. I am not sure yet who they are or what exactly are their intentions, but I believe they will show themselves soon, and to that end I have no choice but to break out of the straitjacket they are trying to put me in and I am going to warn you of the dangers. I just hope that you will listen to me.

I winced at the memory. Of course, I had not listened to him. I had thought him an idiot, a man who had taken leave of his senses, and my stomach churned at the thought that I would never be able to say how sorry I am. I froze the picture and waited a moment to pull myself together. Rufus's eyes matched the sadness I could see in mine from the reflection on the motionless screen. In the silence, I heard the others chatting beyond the wall, but I forced myself to listen to the rest of the message, short as it was.

As I said, Pablo, your identity is safe, and I am sure that you will work out where I will hide your file. You are an extremely clever man, and it has been an honour to have known you, even though you may not believe that.

   Please try to stay strong. My thoughts will always be with you.

I sat back and sighed heavily. Rufus had finished speaking, but he had told me very little I didn't already know. He had confirmed that he had been ousted by somebody he knew nothing about. At least I was ahead of him there: I had one name. Wolstenholme. But who exactly was he, and what did he hope to achieve by performing more experiments on me?

Then there were the others, on the island and closer to home, who had done everything in their power to dispose of me. Were they all connected, or was I fighting for my life on two fronts?

I had to find out.

Chapter Fourteen

We had another two hours with Rex Patterson, a time in which I learnt very little about myself but a lot about Susan. She had been with Denny Archer for three years before Rufus came calling, looking for an assistant to help with his new experiment. She had found him fascinating and mysterious; not quite a mad uncle, but very close. Rex, too, had warmed to the scientist, although he had met him only a handful of times, well away from any lab or clinical establishment. On one occasion, they had enjoyed a liquid lunch at The Bull at Bentley, just down the road, but neither had discussed work. Rufus would not be drawn on the subject, which was understandable, considering how things had worked out, while Rex, of course, had no interest in whatever Rufus was engaged in. It would appear they talked of nothing more consequential than football and music from the seventies. Heavy topics, indeed.

Susan had enjoyed her time with Rufus immensely, and had thrown herself into the work with a fervour which had surprised Rex. He had never seen her so happy, and that had apparently been accentuated when I came on the scene. I was embarrassed when he informed me that he thought Susan had fallen in love with me, and I felt helpless that I could not offer him a crumb of comfort by saying that the feeling was reciprocated. The more I thought about it, the more I became convinced that was probably the case, but I was in no position to confirm it to Rex. I also had to take into account Robyn's feelings.

I was starting to think we had overstayed our welcome. I wasn't sure how secure the bandage over the tracker was, and the last thing I wanted was for Packer to pick up on our location and swoop in on Rex and cause him problems.

"Time to go, I think," I said to the room, and Rex looked at me in disappointment. "Sorry, Rex, but we need to keep ahead of some nasty people."

"Yes, yes," he said quickly. "I understand, David."

I stood, and the others followed. "You will be fine, Rex," I told him. "They are only after me... they won't bother you once we've gone."

He smiled at that. "They'd better not!"

We all laughed with him, but I could see the steel in his features as he stood up.

We took our leave with hugs and promises to keep in touch, although none of us had any sound logic for assuming that would happen. I had my doubts, but even over such a short period of time, I had grown fond of Rex, and he was at least one portal to my past, so I promised myself I would definitely return if at all possible.

"Where now?" Denver asked as we piled into the car.

I had my answer ready. "The only other person who knows what the hell is going on."

According to Robyn, Specs lived close by in Aldershot, but to be on the safe side, we drove to a car rental company in Farnborough and took out a nondescript saloon under Grace's name and credit card. Wolstenholme knew I had stayed at Grace's place, but there was no reason to suspect that he had put a trace on her financial movements, so it seemed safe to me.

We drove in convoy to the nearest Holiday Inn to drop off Grace and Robyn to book two rooms. Robyn would pose as Grace's daughter for one room, while Denver, Gregory and myself would bed down as best we could in the other.

I had told them that I thought it was a good idea if Grace and Robyn stayed behind when we went to see Specs.

As we stood in the car park, Robyn let us know that she wasn't at all happy with that arrangement, as she felt – understandably – that it would be better for her to come with us to see Specs, as she was the only one of us who knew him.

We tried to reason with her, saying that we needed them both to carry out more research on Wolstenholme and Packer and anything else they thought might be relevant.

"Grace is fully capable of doing that," Robyn announced haughtily.

"Agreed," I said, sensing danger ahead, "but there is one other thing."

"What?" she demanded, almost like a truculent teenager to her father.

"Your safety."

"Hah!" she said. "I can take care of myself."

I put out my hand to soothe her. "I know that, Robyn, but I won't be able to take care of myself if I'm thinking of you." I stopped then, stunned by my comment.

Robyn, too, looked shocked, but then she nodded and turned on her heel, guiding Grace by the arm towards the reception.

I watched her go, unable to put my thoughts into any more words.

"Wow!" said Denver beside me. "David, you are hooked!"

I ignored him and climbed into the hire car beside Gregory. "Let's go!" I hissed, and he threw the car into gear and pulled away, just allowing enough time for Denver to tumble into the back, the door swinging wildly as we came out of the car park and onto the road.

* * *

The block of flats stood out like the proverbial carbuncle, its bright red brickwork clashing almost noisily with the subdued aura of the Edwardian street it had been dropped into by a thoughtless 1960s council.

It wasn't a large block by any stretch of the imagination, housing perhaps twenty flats on three storeys, but it dominated the area, throwing a shadow over the small park in front and devaluing the houses beside it.

The front door was clearly locked, and a large keypad was fixed to the left wall, its numbers fading after years of use and abuse. Beside it was an array of buttons, each with a computer-generated label bearing the occupant's name. We looked for WILSON, and I pressed the button, wondering what germs I might be introducing to my finger, but knowing that they couldn't harm me anyway. There was no reply, so I tried a longer burst, with the same result.

"Try the one next to it," suggested Denver, although he didn't offer to do the pressing.

"Okay," I said, doing as I was told.

Within seconds, there was a response. "Hello?" a sleepy voice rang out. "Is that you, Wayne?"

"No," I said with a cough. "I want to speak with Harry Wilson."

"Who?"

"Your neighbour… in flat number…"

"Oh!" A spark of recognition. "Do you mean Specs?"

"Yes, that's him." I thought the nickname had perhaps been thought up by Rufus, but it appeared that Harry was known as Specs by a few others as well.

"You're a bit late, mate," the voice said, slowly stirring into consciousness.

"In what way?" I asked.

"He's not in. Haven't seen him for a few days. Probably off on a jolly somewhere. You know Specs!"

Actually, we didn't. I had visualised him as a middle-aged computer geek, glued to his screen and only surfacing for food breaks and the occasional nap, both of which probably occurred in the middle of the night. From what this voice was saying, my vision of the man may have been considerably off-beam.

Gregory pulled my hand away from the button, causing the voice to abruptly disappear as it began a knowing laugh which seemed to confirm my newly-acquired picture of a rampant Specs.

"Leave it, sir," Gregory said. "Give me a couple of minutes."

He had already begun to move away as the last words left his mouth, and Denver and I watched as my driver ran down the road and disappeared inside what looked like a Tesco Express. Denver shrugged as if to say, 'Stupid Limey', but I knew Gregory was far from that. However, I wasn't quite so convinced when he came back with a notepad, a couple of pens and a box of disposable gloves, size large.

"What the hell…?" Denver began, then thought better of it. He waited instead.

"If the man in question is away, sir, then we can at least have a look round his flat," Gregory said with a twinkle. "On the quiet, shall we say?"

"Ah, the gloves," I said, understanding. "But the notepad?"

Gregory gave me a sweet smile. "The walls in flats are notoriously thin, sir. It would be better not to speak once inside."

"So we write notes to each other?" Denver couldn't quite believe it.

"Not *you*, sir; just Mr David and myself. I would like you to stand guard and look after the box of gloves."

"Now, hold on…!" Denver was not a happy man.

Gregory ripped open the box and scooped out a pair of gloves, handing them to me. "There you are, sir. Put them in your pocket until we get inside the building. We don't want to draw attention to ourselves now, do we?" There was that smile again. He pulled out a second pair and placed them carefully in his jacket pocket, before handing the box to Denver. "Look after them. We may need them in the future." There was no smile for Denver, who just stood there, silently fuming.

"So, how do we get in, Gregory?" I asked.

"We will have to bide our time, sir."

So we waited.

It was almost an hour later when the door opened, and a resident appeared. She was a young mother trying to control a pram with one hand and a toddler with the other. I wasn't sure which of them was winning, so I thought I might help out. Gregory held me back by putting an arm in front of me. "No, sir, we don't want witnesses."

I could understand that, so I pulled back. Eventually, the pram was extricated, and the wailing toddler was safely chained to it by a safety harness. The distraught mother uttered a few ripe words, threatened the child with the loss of sweets if he didn't behave, and headed in the direction of the shops.

"Perfect," said Gregory, bolting for the door before it closed. We had been in luck. The woman had to open the door fully to manoeuvre the pram through, so it took some seconds to swing closed, enough time for Gregory to bound up the three steps and place his foot neatly over the threshold. The door glided gently to a halt against his perfectly buffed shoe.

I followed dutifully, slipping in as he pushed it open, and as he came after me, he allowed the door to click back into place, one hand on it to ensure the minimum of noise.

Donning his gloves, he whispered, "I have to be honest, sir…"

"Yes?" I queried rather too loudly, causing a stern look from my accomplice.

"I am not convinced that this Specs has taken a holiday," he finished.

I nodded, also feeling that it may be one coincidence too far.

Gregory arched his eyebrows. "I am not sure what we might find in the room."

I stopped in my tracks, suddenly aware of what he was implying. "You don't mean…?"

He didn't reply, but instead watched as I struggled to pull on my gloves, seeing the distress on my face. He gave me an encouraging smile and then began to leap silently up the stairs, two at a time, rather like a gazelle in full flight. I went after him, more like a bull elephant.

When we got to the right room, Gregory pulled from his pocket a set of key-like implements on a ring, selected one, put it in the lock and crouched down, concentrating.

I watched, fascinated and horrified. It was as if I had been teamed with Raffles, the gentleman thief, and not known a thing about it. I was about to tap him on the shoulder and say something pithy and Victorian, when the door slid open, and I swear a sigh of triumph escaped Gregory's lips.

We waited a few seconds before entering. I shadowed him, not wanting to see what we had both expected – the body of Specs sprawled on the bed, his throat cut from ear to ear; or suspended from the ceiling, swinging lifeless on the end of the cord from his bathrobe; or stretched out on the floor, wallowing in a pool of his own blood, a dagger in his heart...

Gregory grabbed my arm, making me jump almost out of my skin. My eyes followed his to the centre of the room and then all round. Nothing. No body. No table. No chairs. No bed. *Nothing.* The room had been stripped.

I looked at Gregory as if to say, 'What the hell is going on here?'

His blank stare answered my question, and we made a quick exit, Gregory locking the door and following me down the stairs in a role reversal of how we had come up.

Outside, Denver was swift to grill us. "That was quick. What did you find?"

"Nothing," I said, the most truthful answer I could have given.

After we took it in turns explaining what had just occurred, Denver sucked air through his teeth. "This is not good."

We both looked at him. "What?" I asked.

"I think this confirms that Specs is dead." Denver waited while we peeled off our gloves and pocketed them before we moved away to a quiet corner. "I've seen this before," he added mysteriously.

"You have?" I queried, for some reason not really surprised. I had long lost that feeling when it came to Denver and what he knew or did.

"Well, when I say I've seen it before, that's not strictly true," Denver said quietly. "I haven't actually experienced it..."

"Okay," I hissed, "less of the confession and more of the explanation, my friend."

He nodded. "Right, yeah. Well, what I mean is that in a previous life..." He shrugged when I leant into him, silently demanding he got on with it. So he said, "It's something the Russians used to do."

Gregory and I just stared at him.

"I mean when they eliminated somebody."

"Eliminated?" I almost screeched. "What is this, *Tinker, Tailor Soldier, Spy*? We're not still in the Cold War, Denver!"

Gregory held me back. "I think we should listen, sir."

Denver waited a moment, then continued, "They quite often killed someone and then cleared the room of everything. It was the easiest way to clean up a crime scene, David. Or to search for something. What better way than to take out everything so that they could go through it at their leisure somewhere else?"

"You're serious, aren't you?" I said.

"Yes," he replied calmly. "You can bet your boots that Specs didn't pack up and leave on his own. Hell, David, even his next-door neighbour didn't know."

"Right," I said, clutching at any straw I could, "so how did they do it? Clean out the room, I mean."

"Under the cover of normality, of course," Denver replied as if he had the answer to every question the world might ask. "It's a block of flats, for God's sake. People move in and out. All they had to do was wait for the neighbour to go out – to work, or whatever – then the 'removal' people could come in. How long does it take to empty a couple of rooms?"

I exhaled deeply, finally accepting what Denver was telling me, and also realising that Specs probably was dead. I was about to ask myself why, but, of course, it was obvious. Specs knew all about the system that monitored me. In a way, he was probably closer to me than anybody else, and I felt the loss. I pulled my collar up, suddenly feeling a chill. "Wolstenholme," I said with bitterness.

"Probably not," Denver replied, causing me to hold my breath. "Think about it, David. Wolstenholme and his band appear to be the legitimate side in this. They are the ones trying to keep you alive, after all."

I nodded. "Yes, and they already have access to the computers anyway."

"Exactly," Denver said. "We're looking for someone who presumably has milked all of Specs's knowledge and are now trying to keep tabs on you remotely."

I pressed the bandage under my coat, hoping that it was still firmly in place and that the watch was doing its job. My confidence in both was waning quickly.

Gregory had an opinion. "We should think about this, sir. Even if somebody has taken the knowledge and possibly the computer codes from Specs under duress..."

"Torture," Denver snarled.

"Yes, as you say," Gregory agreed. "But even with all that knowledge, they would still need access to the actual computers on-site."

"I'm not so sure about that, Gregory," said Denver. "A damn good hacker could get into the system with no problem. After all, it's not A1 security we're talking here. With all of Specs's passwords, it would be a piece of cake."

I nodded. "So it could be somebody that even Wolstenholme doesn't know about?"

"Certainly somebody not in his orbit," said Denver. "And definitely not in that house. We have to look further afield."

I was about to respond when Gregory's phone rang. I watched as he put it to his ear, and his face dropped almost immediately.

"What is it?" demanded Denver.

Gregory turned to me. "It's Aunt Grace," he said by way of explanation. "She says she's got some bad news."

I took the phone. "Grace?"

There was the slightest pause before she spoke. "David, we've just heard on the news... Matthew Denny has been killed." Her voice caught on the final word, and she fell silent.

"Killed? What happened?"

There was a rustle as Robyn obviously took over the phone. Her voice was strained. "David, it's true. Matthew Denny's yacht was blown up a couple of hours ago. They think it was terrorists."

I couldn't believe it. I didn't want to believe it. "Are they sure?"

"Well," she said, "they haven't recovered the bodies yet – or what's left of them – but there are enough witnesses saying they saw Matthew get on the yacht. I'm afraid it must be true. Sorry."

"No, I never met the man. I'm sorry for you," I said. "You worked with him."

I desperately wanted to be with Robyn, to take her into my arms and console her. She had lost two close colleagues – Rufus and Specs, although I didn't have the stomach to mention the latter, and I hoped she didn't ask – and now this. My mind raced with the possibilities of what I should say, but I was too slow.

"Listen, David, there's nothing either of us can do about it. But we have to stop whoever is after you."

Robyn's words hit deep, and I realised she was right. "Agreed. We need to go back to the source."

"What do you mean?" both Robyn and Denver said together.

"I need to talk to Wolstenholme."

The first part didn't take long at all. We went into a phone shop, where Gregory bought a burner and SIM card, and I phoned Wolstenholme on the number Robyn had supplied. Then, things slowed down somewhat.

I got through to a minion, who mumbled something incoherent when I told him my name. He was probably rubbing his knuckles along the ground. He asked me to wait – at least I understood that bit – until, after some time, a familiar accent came on the line.

"David Parks, it's canny to hear from ye," he said with as much bonhomie as Indiana Jones felt when he ended up in the snake pit.

"Mr Packer," I said. "I've missed you."

He didn't correct me regarding his title, which surprised me. "My men missed *you*," he said, clearly thinking about our escape and the carnage I had left behind.

I smiled. "Better luck next time."

"Oh, be sure of that, laddie."

"Anyway," I said, "enough of this small talk. Please put me through to the organ grinder."

He was silent for a moment. "You can talk to me."

"I could," I agreed, "but let's be honest, where would it get me? You are merely the Pinocchio to Wolstenholme's Geppetto, Orville the Duck to Wolstenholme's Keith Harris."

"You think you're so funny, Parks," he bristled. "I'm going to change that."

He said no more, and I heard a click as he connected me to Wolstenholme. I could tell he was shocked to hear from me, although he remained remarkably civilised.

"David, my boy. How thrilling."

I ignored his syrupy voice. "I take it you've heard about Matthew Denny?"

"Indeed. So sad. But what of it?"

"He was the last connection," I said.

"Connection?"

"To me, Gavin."

He sighed. "Yes, my dear fellow, I understand. May I offer my con—?"

"Platitudes, Gavin, are for novelists."

He chuckled. "You are so erudite, David. You surely learnt that from Rufus."

I sensed my shackles. "Please, Gavin, I would prefer you not to mention his name."

His chuckle subsided. "Ah, so Rufus is your raw nerve, even now."

"At least he knew when to stop." As I said it, I realised how wrong I was, and I bit my tongue.

Wolstenholme took my silence for something else. "Oh, David, so many demons running through your head. I can help. My bedside manner is second to none." He actually giggled then, and I almost dropped the phone.

I felt a sexual intonation to his voice, and I visualised his piggy lips smacking together in anticipation. It made me shiver.

212

"To be perfectly frank, Gavin, I couldn't give a toss about you or your manners – but I do need something from you."

"Really?" he said, clearly bemused. "And what would that be, exactly?"

"Co-operation."

I could sense the permutations that he must have been juggling with. "Go on, dear boy."

I knew it was a long shot, but what choice did I have? "I was hoping you might help me find out who is trying to kill me."

"I would love to, but what, pray, would be in it for me?"

"Your experiment would be alive."

"I appreciate what you are saying, David, but for now, you are Rufus's experiment. You made it quite clear that you object to me getting my hands on you." I could almost see the leer on his face at the double-meaning.

"I might reconsider," I said, dangling the carrot I knew he wouldn't be able to resist.

"If only, David."

"If the alternative is a sticky end, Gavin, then perhaps I might put up with your sticky fingers."

"Tut, tut, my boy," he breathed down the line. "You should tread very carefully if you require my aid."

I dialled it back just a notch. "Fair enough. So, what do you say?"

I expected and got a long silence. Wolstenholme was playing a game of pros and cons with himself while also deliberately keeping me waiting. That wasn't a problem because I knew what his answer would be.

"We should meet," he said eventually.

"I agree."

"Will you come back here?"

I admired his optimism. "Somewhere neutral would be more appropriate, don't you think?"

It was at this point that Wolstenholme was going to suggest a public place, somewhere safe, with people milling about. A street café, perhaps, or outside some well-known high street shop.

Neither would work for me, of course, because I was being stalked by professionals. They had gone all the way to the island to exterminate me, so it wouldn't be beyond the realms of reason to assume that they would be monitoring this conversation and could then install an élite sniper perhaps half a mile away armed with a state-of-the-art rifle and 'scope. No, I didn't fancy that one bit.

I had given this a lot of thought, and before Wolstenholme could offer anything, I said, "Alice Holt."

"Excuse me?" he said, his syrupy voice moving up an octave.

"Alice Holt Forest. It's just down the road from you. Ideal for family walks among the trees."

"David, I do not walk." He sounded offended.

"Gavin, I'm sure you'll do this for me. Meet me there tomorrow at four. I'll be at the Lodge Pond. They tell me it's wonderful at this time of year."

After I had finished on the phone, Denver took great delight in telling me what an extremely stupid boy I was. To be fair, I couldn't disagree.

"What were you thinking, sir?" Gregory said.

"He wasn't," said Denver.

* * *

"You know you can't trust Wolstenholme," said Grace the moment we got back to the Holiday Inn, and Denver spilled the beans. He was sprawled across the bed in Grace and Robyn's room while the rest of us stood awkwardly in the limited space available. I offered the chair by the dressing table to Grace, but she was too animated and hyper to use it. Instead, she paced the room as best she could through the bodies that blocked her way.

"Why did you agree to meet him?" she demanded. "What on earth do you think you are going to get out of it?"

"Answers," I said.

"Hah!" she snorted. "More fool you, David."

Denver nodded sagely as if he was Confucius about to let forth a pithy saying. Then he said, "Bloody idiot."

Robyn looked as if she was going to contribute to the diatribe but held her tongue, and I gave her a brief smile of gratitude. The verbal battering was starting to become overpowering.

Grace wasn't finished yet. "Tell us about Specs."

This was the one conversation I didn't want to have, and it must have shown on my face.

"We need to know, David," said Robyn.

"No matter how grisly," Grace added, clearly fond of her paperback thrillers.

But that was the whole point: it wasn't grisly. It was nothing. Although I could just imagine the horrors Specs may have gone through before they prised his passwords from him. I could feel the bile in my throat.

"He wasn't there," I mumbled. "The room was empty – literally." I paused to let that sink in. "There was no sign of Specs or that anyone had ever been in the flat."

Robyn responded first. "That doesn't make sense, David. Are you saying Specs has run off?"

If only, I thought sadly. I waited for Denver to bail me out here. After all, he seemed to be the one who understood what was going on. However, he remained tight-lipped, leaving me to struggle on alone. "I think whoever wants me has got to Specs. I don't hold out much hope. I'm sorry, Robyn," I said, waiting for her to break down.

Instead, there was silence for a moment, and I will never forget the way she looked at me, her eyes wide, tears forming, her mouth quivering with pain and hopelessness. I would have done anything to have spared her this, but what else could I have said? It was the truth, as I understood it, and she needed to know.

I reached out and wrapped my arms around her. She fell into me, and I could feel her body heaving. I held her tight and waited for her to recover some kind of control. I stroked her back, which made me feel a little better, and I hoped it had the same effect on her.

Grace took Robyn's hand, so I let her go, and the two of them sat on the bed after Denver moved away out of respect and not knowing what else to do. The room hummed with tension, and I knew that, no matter how much Robyn needed me, I had to get away. She was in safe hands, and there was nothing more I could do, so with mumbled apologies, I beat a hasty retreat and went to our room for a shower and some rest. I needed both.

After my shower and the regular check that my bandage was secure, I sprawled on the bed, ready for an hour's peace. It didn't come. There were too many questions and too many distractions. I could hear the buzz of traffic coming in and out of the car park, the murmuring of voices, the distant sound of pounding roadworks, as if a giant was walking across the countryside, each huge step reverberating in my mind.

I turned away from the window, too tired even to close it. I put the pillow over my head, but still my mind would not stop throbbing. I saw Susan Patterson, dead at the wheel; I saw Rufus, dead in the sand; I saw the first man I had ever killed, shot in the head, his final resting place the hedge in my garden. I even visualised Specs, with his sightless eyes penetrating my skull. It was all surreal, impossible. And yet, it had all happened.

I rubbed my temple with the knuckle of my right hand, trying to massage away the pain. I closed my eyes for the fifth attempt, but I knew it was futile, so I sat up and perched on the edge of the bed, my feet stroking the rough carpet.

There was a gentle tap on the door. "David?" The door opened slightly. "Are you okay?"

"Yeah," I said, knowing I didn't mean it.

Robyn appeared, her tears gone, but with a look of concern on her face. "We heard you," she said, her voice distraught.

"What?"

"You screamed," she said, coming in and sitting beside me. She took my hand.

"I didn't realise," I mumbled.

"It's all right."

It was her turn to comfort me, and I willingly let her enfold me, realising without embarrassment that I was crying. It really didn't matter because I knew that whatever I was experiencing, Robyn would be going through it with me, and we held on to each other like survivors of an apocalypse, with no other human in sight.

I slowly lifted my head, and our eyes met. I gave her a watery smile and gently brushed a loose strand of her hair from her face.

"You're amazing," I said.

She smiled, and it was the greatest sight I had ever seen. Then she kissed me. Not hard and sexual, but with such gentleness that it took my breath away, and I wallowed in the pleasure, feeling sensations that I had never experienced before. I pushed forward, the lust rising and overtaking all the other emotions churning within me. I wanted her. We were so close now, and I slipped a hand between our bodies and cupped her breast, kneading it. For a split second, I thought she was responding, but then she pulled away.

"Stop it!" she demanded. "What are you doing?"

I was stunned. "I was expressing my feelings," I said. "Like you were."

She looked horrified for a moment, then broken. "I'm so sorry, David," she said, wiping the back of her hand across her mouth as if to remove the effect of our kiss. "I shouldn't have started this."

"Yes," I said. "Yes, you should have. It was right – for both of us. Surely you know that."

She was on her feet. "No, it's not right. I am mourning friends, and you are fighting something I can't help you with."

She started to turn, but I grabbed her arm. "You're wrong, Robyn. You *are* helping. I don't know what I would do without you."

Fresh tears sprang into her eyes. "Not now, David. I can't handle this." And she was gone: out the door and down the corridor. I could hear her footsteps receding along with my hopes, and I cursed myself.

The door was still wide open, and Denver suddenly filled the space. "What's going on, pal?"

I didn't have an answer, so I turned away, my head in my hands, bad thoughts about Rufus blocking out that stolen kiss with Robyn.

Chapter Fifteen

I awoke with the proverbial lark. Well, that's not strictly true because I was actually awake before the lark. In fact, I had hardly slept at all.

Yesterday, Denver had dissuaded me from chasing after Robyn and, fearing for my sanity, had made me go to bed. Grace had produced a couple of tablets, which she forced me to take with a glass of water. I knew that resistance was futile, so I took the medicine like a man, almost gagging in the process.

"They will help you sleep," she said.

"Yes, matron," I said, offering her my best schoolboy grin.

They didn't work, of course. I tossed and turned all night, sometimes thinking of Rufus, then Wolstenholme, then the car crash – but it always came back to Robyn. What was she doing to me? It was like she was conducting a totally different experiment on me, without the use of a machine or any other scientific paraphernalia – and certainly without anaesthetic.

The morning was bright and warm as I looked around the room. Gregory was next to me in the double bed, snoring like a tank engine, his thumb in his mouth. I won't ever mention that to him. Don't want to embarrass the poor chap.

Denver was hunched uncomfortably on the chair, his legs up somewhere around his neck, his arms flopping over the side like paddles in a small boat. His eyes were only half-open, but I knew he was looking at me.

"Okay this morning, are we?" he asked, his mouth at a peculiar angle due to his position.

"So, so," I replied non-committedly.

He nodded at Gregory. "At least you didn't disturb him."

"So I see," I said, still not wanting to hold a conversation.

"Lucky I don't need a lot of sleep." Denver was trying to make a point about me keeping him awake, but I wasn't particularly interested. "By the way, Robyn's fine."

That made me angry. It sounded like he thought I didn't care – but I did. "Good," I said.

"Yeah, she came back after an hour. Said she walked around for a bit, thinking things through. Not sure what she decided."

I was surprised at that. "What do you mean?"

"She didn't know whether to stay or go," he said.

I was panicking, but he raised an arm. "It's okay, pal. I think she wanted to leave, but Grace calmed her down. You guys sure need to talk."

"Yeah," I sighed.

Gregory stirred at that moment, breaking the spell. He had taken his thumb out of his mouth and yawned expansively as the sheet flew in the air, and he sat bolt upright. "Morning," he said brightly as if he had been awake for hours.

We both looked at him and then began to laugh, and it felt so good that we laughed even more. And when Gregory joined in, not really sure what we were so happy about, the chain reaction led to us rocking back and forth until real tears came down our faces, and the actual reason for our good humour seemed to be lost in the distant past.

Gregory gathered himself first. "I'm hungry. Who's for breakfast?" he said, using the end of the sheet to wipe the sleep from his eyes.

"I'm in," said Denver, and the tension was completely broken as he picked up the pillow I had obviously thrown out of the bed during the night and he hurled it at me. "Last one down pays the bill."

"You're on!" I said, pulling on my trousers. A shower would have to wait until after breakfast.

We had both made it to the door before Gregory said in a sad voice, "That's not fair; everything goes on my credit card anyway."

Denver grinned. "Of course, it does. Well, no need to bust a gut, then," he said, before walking out of the room in exaggerated slow motion, like something out of *Chariots of Fire*.

I hesitated outside Robyn's room. I wanted to knock on the door, tell her how I felt, and explain what I needed. Instead, I gazed at her door for a few seconds, then sighed and followed Denver down the corridor to the restaurant.

He was already seated, studying the menu. There were a few other people – couples, families, single men who were clearly on business trips – but Denver had secured a table well away from anybody else so we could at least talk through what we intended to do next. I knew I was going to get a grilling about Wolstenholme, but I was determined to face it on a full stomach.

Grace and Robyn came in a couple of minutes later, both subdued, unsure of the welcome they would receive. I stood up and pulled out a chair next to me for Robyn, but she made a point of glowering at me before going round the table and sitting opposite, refusing any further eye contact. Grace sat in the chair I had offered and said gruffly, "Thank you, David."

We sat in silence then, until Gregory finally arrived, immaculately dressed in a grey suit and drowning in enough aftershave that even the chef in the kitchen got a whiff. It was amazing how he had been able to groom himself so well in such a short time.

Denver was the first to react. "Smells like a Vegas brothel all of a sudden!"

"Mr Denver!" exclaimed an exasperated Grace.

"Sorry, ma'am, I was forgetting myself," he said, suitably chastised.

Gregory sat between Grace and Denver as if nothing had been said and picked up one of the menus, appearing to look at it, although everyone could see his eyes hovering over the top, taking in everything that was about to happen.

I gave a little cough and looked directly at Robyn. "I'm so sorry," I said with feeling, meaning every word.

"Look here, young man," Grace said, "I don't know what you said or did, but Robyn was extremely upset last night, and I don't think your words are enough to make amends."

"It's okay, Grace," Robyn said, reaching over the table and touching Grace's arm while averting her eyes from me. "I'm only here to find out who killed Dr Allenby."

Even as she said it, I could see into her mind. She was blaming me for Rufus's death, and I knew, no matter how impossible it might be, I had to overcome that. "We will," I promised, wondering whether that was going to be the biggest lie I would ever utter.

Gregory looked up. "I've chosen," he said breezily.

"Not now!" snapped Denver, and Gregory retreated back behind his menu.

"Robyn, look, I will do all I can to make this right," I said, starting to rise.

"Where are you going?" asked Grace in astonishment.

"I will sort this," I said, "then I will come back for you." I looked directly at Robyn, and I could see her start to crumble. Then I turned away.

"Come back here!" demanded Grace, so loud that the other diners looked up from their muesli. I obeyed, but I just stood by my chair, my white-knuckled fists gripping it tightly. Grace took a breath, then said, "Young man, it was you who brought us into this. I appreciate that it was not of your doing, but now that we are here, you will at least allow us the opportunity to help. Now, please sit down."

I had no choice. The whole room was watching, so I

meekly sank onto the seat and averted my eyes from Robyn, although I did get the impression that she was smiling just a little at my humiliation.

"That's better," Grace said gently. "We will partake of breakfast and then discuss – in an orderly fashion – what we intend to do. Are you all in agreement?"

There was a consensus of nods and grunts, the latter coming from me as I petulantly scooped the menu off the table and hid behind it.

Breakfast was taken in almost total silence. It appeared that nobody wanted to raise the ire of the Mother Superior, who seemed to hover above us like a spectre, daring us to break the sacred vow.

It was only when the second round of coffee arrived, and the waiter had beaten a hasty retreat from the frost that Grace spoke again.

"Now, let us recap," she said. "David?"

She said my name as a question, causing me to lift my head. "Grace?" I replied timorously.

"Please begin at the beginning, or at least what you remember or have deduced so far."

"Yes, Grace," I said, then sat in silence as I gathered my thoughts, disparate as they were. I seemed to suddenly gain a little more strength. "Okay. Six years ago, Dr Rufus Allenby carried out an experiment on me. I was not the first, but, according to Robyn" – here I threw her what I hoped was a warm smile – "I was the most successful. Rufus designed his machine and built it with funds from Matthew Denny, an old friend. Rufus's first assistant, Susan Patterson, apparently took a shine to me" – here I averted my eyes from Robyn – "and for some reason took me for a spin in her car…"

"Where she crashed and died," said Denver, ever the tactful American.

"Yes," I agreed solemnly, "but I didn't. I was pulled from the vehicle, presumably by Rufus Allenby."

"Ah," chimed Denver, like the old Liberty Bell herself, "that's one thing I don't understand."

"Only one thing?" enquired Gregory, cup to his lips. "Lucky you."

"Shss, Gregory," Grace scolded, so he did.

I looked at Denver. "What don't you understand?"

"Why?"

"What?"

"Why was he there? I mean," Denver continued, bit between his teeth, "*why* was he there?"

I hadn't thought that deeply, so I couldn't come up with a suitable reply. Denver supplied it for me. "If Rufus was there, then that means he was following you. He had to be."

I chewed that over for a few seconds. "But why?"

Grace was on to it. "Perhaps Susan was trying to get you away – much like Robyn has been doing." She gave Robyn a motherly nod and looked pointedly at me. I blanched once more.

"Away from what, David?" Robyn asked, more perplexed than any of us.

I thought that perhaps I knew the answer, but swerved the question. "I don't know."

"You were in shock, pal," offered Denver. "You were confused."

"Of course, I was bloody confused!" I shouted too

226

loudly, causing the room to look our way again. Grace put her hand on my arm, and I immediately became calmer. She had that effect. "Sorry, but yes, I was probably confused and concussed," I whispered.

"We're just asking you to cast your mind back," Denver said.

I hesitated. "Well…" Suddenly, I have stopped speaking, and my eyes close involuntarily. My mind is tumbling, racing, like that car, head-long into a tree. I am there, next to Susan. My body is swaying; I am sweating. I can see the tree approaching, a massive shape contorting my vision, until it is the only thing I can see: gnarled wood, tendril branches reaching out, like the welcoming arms of the devil himself. Then there is a *crack* as the bonnet strikes, and the sound of twisting metal is like nothing I have ever heard before, a grating and hollow sound which seems to bounce off the tree and screech across the road, coming back like a satanic echo to fill my head with what feels like metal shards. I reach over to Susan, and I hear a soft groan. She is alive. Thank God! "Susan." The word plays round my head but cannot get out. Then her door opens, and I see salvation. Rescue. Someone is there. My prayer is answered. Another groan. She is going to be all right. A voice: "She's dead." No! That's not possible. I heard her… Then I see the glint of metal in a hand…

The hand grabs me…

"David!" It was Denver, gripping me tight, holding me down, pinning me to the chair. "What's going on?"

"They killed her!" I bellowed. "They killed Susan!"

Chapter Sixteen

If my eyes hadn't been so full of tears, I might have seen that the restaurant had been cleared by my outburst; the other diners had scattered in all directions, presumably frightened and intimidated by my screams. In their place stood the manager and two of his more stoic employees, each wondering what nightmare had visited their establishment.

"Is everything all right?" the manager asked nervously, even though he could clearly see that all was not well. "Should I call an ambulance?"

What he really meant was, *Should I call for the police and a straitjacket?* But the locked frown on his face didn't give away what he actually felt.

Denver dismissed him with a wave of an arm. "No, we're fine, pal. Nothing to see here."

"I beg to differ…," began the manager, but he was cut short by Denver's icy stare, so he took the easy way out. "As you wish, sir. Perhaps you would be kind enough to take the gentleman outside for some fresh air."

That sounded good to me, and I was more than happy to feel Denver's strong arms helping me out of the chair and guiding me past the manager and his staff, who seemed to part like the Red Sea as we made our way to the door. My legs felt like jelly, but my mind was clear. I didn't know how, but I had just remembered Susan Patterson's last moment on earth.

They perched me on a low brick wall in the car park, Gregory standing behind me in case I fell back into the nettles. Grace was stroking my hand, and I wished dearly that it had been Robyn. Instead, she was in deep discussion with Denver a few paces away, before they both came over, Denver kneeling in front of me.

"You remember," he stated rather than querying.

"Yes," I said softly. "At least some of it." I gathered my thoughts. "Susan was alive. I know it. I heard her." I shook my head in an effort to clear it. "Somebody opened her door…"

"Packer?" asked Denver.

"I can't be sure, but whoever it was, they had a syringe…"

"A syringe?" This was Robyn, shocked at the latest development.

"I saw it. He said, 'She's dead', and then he injected her."

Denver stood up. "He injected her *after* pronouncing her dead?"

"Yes." What more could I say? I had witnessed cold-blooded murder.

Robyn was stunned. "Dr Allenby would never be a party to *that*."

Even though I had known him for such a short time, I was sure Robyn was right. Rufus was a scientist, not a killer; but God only knew what he had gotten himself into.

I reached out for Robyn's hand, and she didn't pull away. "No," I said, "I don't believe Rufus knew what was going on. While he was helping to pull me out of the car, someone else was making sure Susan never talked."

Denver nodded. "Someone who was conspiring against Rufus."

"Yes," I said. "Probably the same one who is trying to kill me now."

"But who can it be?" Grace asked. "It's not Wolstenholme. He sounds like a real creep to me, but, to be fair, he has been trying to keep you alive."

"Packer?" asked Gregory.

"Quite possibly," I agreed, "but he can't be the mastermind. His IQ's far too low for that."

"But there's nobody else," Gregory sighed. "They're all dead."

We couldn't argue with that logic, although something wasn't right.

Grace broke the spell of despair that was spreading over us. "David, I agree that you need to meet with Gavin Wolstenholme again. This has all got to stop, and I think he might be the key."

Although I wasn't sure Grace was right about Wolstenholme's status in my story, I felt such relief and an overwhelming love for her at that moment. "Thank you, Grace."

She looked genuinely surprised. "For what?"

"For believing in me." I tried not to look at Robyn in case she mistook my words for criticism of her. I was still confused as to how I felt about her, and certainly what she thought of me. But all of that would have to wait. "Okay," I said defiantly, "we go for it – and we do it my way. I think I might have a bit of a plan."

Chapter Seventeen

We spent the late morning walking round Alice Holt, getting a feel of the place and looking for a suitable meeting point with Wolstenholme. I wanted to see the lie of the land and pick a spot which would be advantageous, and I assumed that it would be too early in the day for Wolstenholme – or anyone else for that matter – to be setting spies or traps for us. We found a nice spot in a small clearing and settled down.

After the events at the restaurant and in the car park, I still felt a little unsteady. The fact that I had remembered an important part of my history did not rest well on my conscience. While I felt relief that perhaps things were beginning to become clearer, I still couldn't get out of my mind the fact that I had seen a young woman's life being ended in the cruellest of ways.

After sending Grace, Gregory and Robyn off to prepare for my 'plan', I had gone back to our room with Denver, where he had attempted vainly to bring me out of the mood I had fallen into. We had sat on the bed for probably an hour, with me saying virtually nothing in response to his gentle probing, until I had told him that was enough. I was through with the questioning. Instead, I had spent another half hour in the shower, hoping the water would clear my head. It didn't, but I knew I had to get on with my life. I owed that to Susan, at least.

Now, I was sitting on the grass and looking around. We had picked a pleasant enough spot under the welcome cover of an old tree but with a view that could have graced a Constable or a Thomas Cole. I stretched on the grass and took a peek at Robyn, who was chatting to Gregory as he laid out a tartan blanket. Suddenly, it was more like a Cezanne painting!

I did notice that Robyn took an occasional look in my direction, and I smiled, but she still appeared impervious to my charm, so I retreated back into my thoughts. I wasn't sure what I hoped to achieve by meeting Wolstenholme, but what other options did I have? They were all dead ends – literally.

Incongruously, Grace had insisted on bringing a picnic lunch, which she had bought at the nearby service station before we left for Alice Holt. Looking like a pack mule and grunting like one, too, Gregory had dutifully carried everything in two plastic bags emblazoned with the name of some foreign-sounding supermarket chain.

Grace had justified her decision with, "Well, even in times of distress, one should at least remain civilised," and, "It is what a group of people would be expected to do at a beauty spot."

She had certainly practised what she preached, as she laid out another blanket she had brought from the car and proceeded to disclose the unexpected contents of her bags. We had the finest Stilton, some Brie and, for the less sophisticated among us, a huge wedge of Mild Cheddar, together with a box of savoury wafers infused with sea salt and black pepper. Grace then produced what turned out to be the most delightful fig chutney I had ever tasted, two very large dollops of which stayed on my paper plate for only a minute before I devoured the lot with a grin, amazed at how she had managed to secure such a high-class spread from a low-class outlet. Grace was suitably happy with my response to her food, and fresh strawberries and cream seemed a fitting finale to a very welcome interlude.

Gregory sat beside Robyn on the edge of the tartan blanket and chatted happily, appearing to forget for a moment that I was there. But she was responding to his comments with little giggles that were so obviously for my benefit, and I could see her furtive glances at me each time there was a lull in the conversation. Or was that just wishful thinking on my part?

Denver was away from us in a world of his own. He hadn't said much on the journey, and it was apparent that he didn't like the way this was going. He had his gun in his lap, which would have scared any unwitting passer-by, and I knew he was keeping watch for the slightest danger. That helped to calm me, but at the same time, I didn't want his trigger finger to get itchy, as they used to say in the old penny dreadfuls. 'Carnage in Alice Holt' would not be a sobering headline for tomorrow's papers.

Grace was talking again. "So, David, do you still think this is a good idea?"

I sensed Robyn looking at me. "It's the only way, Grace. You all need to go back to the car. I have to face Wolstenholme on my own. If they see us as a group, who knows what might happen? I won't take the chance of any of you being injured – or worse."

Robyn was about to speak, but Denver beat her to it. "He's right. Wolstenholme is not the enemy here. He might be a slimeball, but I don't think he would harm David. He may even be able to shed some light on what the hell is going on."

I was grateful for Denver's support. "Precisely. I just need to pick his brain."

"I'm not convinced," said Robyn, concern on her face all of a sudden. Perhaps she did care, after all. "And there is always Packer."

"Yes," I agreed, "there is always Packer. I am hoping that Wolstenholme will have left him back at the house. If not, then so be it. I have a feeling I'm going to have to come up against him some time, though."

"I don't think that is going to be easy," said Gregory. "Are you really sure you don't want us with you, sir?"

"I am. You will just have to trust me."

I heard Robyn's intake of breath then, and I took it as a critique of what I had just said. With great restraint, I ignored her and continued, "Please, let me be. I want you to go now."

As they scattered, picking up the detritus of our picnic and moving away, I felt lonelier than I had ever done in my life before.

* * *

I hadn't been in position long before I heard rustling and the sound of breathing. I tensed, expecting Wolstenholme. I was wrong.

A man was walking towards me. He was tall, well over six foot, and ungainly. Thicker than a beanpole, but only just. His pace was slow, almost brooding, as if even the weight of his skeletal body was too much for him. His cheap suit hung off him like he was a badly constructed clothes horse, angular and pointed. I swear, if he had turned round, I would have seen his shoulder blades sticking out of the back of his scuffed jacket. His upper body swayed just slightly as he walked, revealing a puke-inducing puce shirt and, more importantly, the strap to his shoulder holster. He stopped in front of me, feet slightly apart, poised. Professional. It was only then that I could take in all the details. For later, if there was one.

His face was thin, of course, but it was smooth, like alabaster. Avon had clearly called. His cheeks were very slightly flushed, giving the impression of two plump peaches stuck onto the sides of a barely-covered skull. There was a livid scar running from the corner of his left eye to the tip of his ridiculously dimpled cheek, a feature which I could not draw my eyes away from. While the scar seemed to pulse with pure evil, the dimple was reminiscent somehow of Shirley Temple.

His right eye, the only one appearing to be in working order, was wide open, focused. It was studying me, almost dissecting me. His lips spread into a wide smile, which seemed to cut his face in half. His teeth shone silver in the late afternoon sun as if a light had been thrown into a cutlery drawer.

"Mr Parks," he drawled lazily, lips barely moving, "they have sent me to kill you."

I smiled back at him, my fingers playing around the object in my pocket. "It's been tried before, friend," I said, withdrawing my hand and tossing the object towards him.

Instinctively, a bony arm shot out and caught it, his talon-like fingers gripping it as if it was prey. He looked down, puzzled. A used bullet case.

He frowned.

I hadn't noticed it before, but dangling from his left ear was a small silver skull. A self-portrait, perhaps?

"One of your friends," I said, sensing a lack of intelligence, "shot that at me a few days ago. He's dead, of course." I waited for a response, but all he offered me was a look of bewilderment. "I killed him," I added to avoid any confusion he might have been experiencing.

I watched, bemused, as he pulled his pistol from its holster and pointed it at me. It wavered slightly, a sign that he still wasn't sure what I was capable of. So I showed him.

As the bullet left the gun, I waited for the truth to register on that smug face of his, before I walked up to him and punched him hard, my fist connecting with his forehead and sending shockwaves across his eyes. He crumpled, and I helped him on his way by lashing out at his groin with my left foot, scoring a direct hit that must have left his testicles somewhere up near his throat. There was a gargle of escaping air as he tottered for a second before he fell backwards into the dirt with a soft thud.

I retrieved the bullet he had fired and which had bounced harmlessly off me, coming to rest on the grass; then I went back to him. "When will you people learn?" I asked, looking at the skull twinkling in the sunlight and then tugging it from his ear and leaving a trickle of blood. "Never aim for the heart... I haven't got one."

I knelt down and slipped off the man's jacket so I could unfasten his holster before taking off my jumper, checking the bandage under my shirt – again – and putting on the holster, then retrieving his gun and placing it in its rightful place. I took my gun from the waistband of my trousers and stuck it down the sock on my right leg. It stuck out a bit and made it a little awkward to walk, but I thought I might just get away with it when confronted by Wolstenholme if and when he turned up.

I sat beside the unconscious man and waited...

* * *

Five minutes. That's all it took for Wolstenholme to arrive on, of all things, a golf buggy. I couldn't believe it as the cart trundled over the grass and uneven tree roots and came to a halt beside me. Wolstenholme stepped out, while his driver sat rigid, his eyes the only part of him that was moving as they took in the view.

Wolstenholme was smiling. "My boy, I'm so glad you are all right. I heard a shot."

238

"You didn't send it, then?" I said. "This isn't one of your goons?" I didn't really think it was. Wolstenholme might be many things, but even he wouldn't send an assassin into a forest teeming with the general public. It meant only one thing: my real enemy knew the plan and had got here before Wolstenholme.

"I can assure you he is not one of mine. Rogers, kindly take care of this problem if you would."

The driver, Rogers, gave a slight nod and stepped out of the buggy, at the same time withdrawing a small pistol from his pocket. As he bent over, he attached a silencer to his weapon, aimed it at the man's neck and pulled the trigger.

"He'll be dead in three minutes," Wolstenholme said without feeling. "Very little blood externally, which is always a godsend, don't you think?"

I chose not to respond as Rogers dragged the body to the buggy and hauled it onboard. It occurred to me that the man might have been of some benefit, and the idea of torturing him myself to gain information began to form in my brain, but then I realised what Wolstenholme already knew – the would-be assassin would have offered up nothing because he knew nothing. As Wolstenholme might have said, the fellow was an inconsequence.

"Let's take a little walk, David," Wolstenholme said as the buggy drove away. "Rogers will dispose of his load and be back shortly."

"I thought you didn't walk, Gavin," I said.

"Ah, I would do almost anything for you, David. Even put myself out. Shall we?"

As we walked, almost like two old friends enjoying an afternoon stroll, we were silent for a few minutes. I was still taking in the cold-blooded way he had ordered the execution, but why should it surprise me? I was dealing with fanatics of all persuasions, so anything was possible and probable. I sighed internally.

"Perhaps I should try to explain my position," he said suddenly. I nodded, so he continued, "I am a parachutist, David." When I chuckled at the thought, he grabbed my arm. "Metaphorically, I hasten to add."

"Go on." What more could I say?

"All the while Dr Allenby was alive, my employers were happy with the *status quo*. He kept an eye on you, and we kept an eye on him. Then it changed."

I nodded again. "When somebody tried to kill me."

"Precisely, my boy. That put the wind up the sails, I can tell you." He grinned, and for a moment I saw the look of a kindly uncle telling his favourite nephew a risqué joke. His good humour vanished as soon as it had begun. "I'm sorry about Rufus. We never actually met, but I was fond of the old chap." He paused, perhaps as a mark of respect. "Anyway, when my employers knew you were in danger, they tried to protect you. However, we always seemed to be one step behind."

"But you don't know who is responsible?"

"No," he conceded, "unfortunately not."

We walked on in silence for a minute, allowing me to digest what little I had learned. Then I asked, "When did they decide to parachute you in?"

"Oh, that was when you and your American buddy killed those men at your house."

"The house that wasn't mine," I corrected him.

"Just so. My superiors felt that a steady hand was needed. Your Miss Newman was never going to cope with the fallout. Such a shame. She was shaping up nicely if you don't mind me saying."

I did, but said nothing.

He continued, "I had been working behind the scenes, as it were, for some time, but it was decided that I would make my appearance to coincide with your less-than-triumphant return to *our* house." A pause. "I am only sorry your stay was so short-lived, especially as you also removed some of Captain Packer's men."

"Oh," I said, jumping on the point, "they weren't *your* men, then?"

Wolstenholme cackled at that. "Heaven forbid, David. My employers and I are pacifists. Unless, of course, some unforeseen event crops up."

He was clearly referring to the execution of the man a few minutes ago. I just wondered how many other unforeseen events had occurred during Wolstenholme's career.

He was still talking. "No, those guards were Packer's private army, purchased *en masse* by my employers for a ludicrous amount of money to protect the project."

"Didn't do a very good job, did they?"

"No, David, they did not. Now, it is up to me to put things right."

241

We were still walking, and Wolstenholme's breathing seemed to deteriorate with every step.

"Tell me, Gavin, how do you propose returning to your *status quo*?"

He chewed on that for a few seconds. "With your collaboration, dear boy." I could hear a slight wheeze as he spoke. "I appreciate that you do not wish to help us with further experimentation, and I honour your wish. I truly do." The last was added when he saw the look of disbelief on my face. Then he grabbed my arm. "May I be blunt?"

"Be my guest."

"You may have heard that Matthew Denny is no longer with us." When I nodded, he continued, "You may also know that the Cor-AD was dismantled a short while ago."

I had not heard the scanner's name before, but it made sense: 'Cor' for corpuscle and 'AD' for Allenby and Denny, I presumed. Still, it wasn't a moniker that rolled off the tongue.

Wolstenholme continued, "It is my intention to rebuild."

"Really?" I said. "Good for you, Gavin."

"With your help, David."

He had stopped as he said that, possibly because his body was about to give out, or perhaps because of the look on my face.

"*My* help," I spat through clenched teeth. "God, man, you are something else! How on earth will I be able to help you?"

He smiled, a kind of reptilian mock-smile which was not reflected in his eyes as he turned to face me. "Since the last time we met, there has been a development."

I waited.

"Not a problem so much as an inconvenience." He began walking again, looking ahead, his hand on my elbow. "You know how it is, David; these things are sent to try us."

"So," I said, pulling my arm away from him, "what exactly is this 'inconvenience' – or shouldn't I ask?"

He turned to look at me. "I believe you know the whereabouts of some of Allenby's papers… and perhaps something else."

"Me? Why would I know where they are?"

"Because, David." And he stopped there, just like that.

"What are you saying?"

"I just need your co-operation on this," he said with a heaving shrug. "Simple as."

I felt like punching him in his ample paunch to see whether I could deflate him. Instead, I sighed. "In your dreams, Gavin. I'm not going to help…"

Before I could finish, I saw the golf buggy trundle into view with Rogers at the wheel. What I didn't expect was to see Robyn behind him. She looked as if she was dozing, her head lolling from side to side with the gentle movement of the buggy.

She shouldn't be here. I gave explicit instructions…

Wolstenholme offered me a look of pity as he drew a pistol from his pocket. "I'm sorry, David, I did try to play nice. Please, take your place beside Miss Newman if you would be so kind."

He was politeness personified, I thought, *even as he trained a gun on me*. I clambered into the back of the cart and put my arm round Robyn to keep her stable, at the same time trying to look at her to make sure she was all right.

As I did so, I felt something on my arm and turned to see Rogers brandishing a syringe…

Chapter Eighteen

When I finally stirred, my head was ablaze with a fiery pain I had never experienced before. It seemed to dart between my eyes at a terrific rate, from one side to the other, each time rising in intensity as it pierced the back of my retinas. My mouth was dry, and I could feel the sweat dripping off me as I tried to sit up.

After the initial shock, I remained still for several minutes, afraid of incurring more pain. I wiped my brow with the back of my hand and blinked a few times in an effort to get back some of my senses. It took several attempts, but eventually I got to my feet, swaying a little so that I had to put out my hand to the wall to avoid falling back down again.

I felt instinctively that I was back in the house in Farnham, but not exactly as I had planned it. It had been my intention to persuade Wolstenholme to act *with* me so that I could root out whoever was plotting my extermination. I was sure the answer would be found in the house, although it wasn't clear in my mind what I expected. There would be no paper trail, as Wolstenholme had been looking for that himself without success. Rufus had hidden that pretty well. But there must be something.

My prison was a small, obviously sound-proofed room with no windows and what looked like a pretty heavy door. I tried it, of course, as you would, but there was no way it was going to budge from the inside. I was surprised that I had not been tied up, but was allowed to wander round the confines of my prison, even if that wasn't going to take me long.

I had realised immediately that Wolstenholme had frisked me. Perhaps he got a thrill out of it? My guns were gone, as was the bandage round my chest, meaning I was back on everyone's radar. My pockets were empty.

As my head cleared, I started to think of Robyn. Why on earth hadn't she stuck to my plan? I needed everyone to be safe – especially her. Now, she was as deep in the mire as I was, and that didn't give me any leeway when it came to negotiating with Wolstenholme. He would be operating from a position of even more strength now.

I remembered arriving with her and knew that she had also been drugged by Wolstenholme's buggy chauffeur, Rogers; but where was she now? Then, I began to wonder whether she was even still alive. I wouldn't put anything past Gavin Wolstenholme, and right now he was the man I hated most, and I was desperate to get my hands on him.

There was a knock, which seemed incongruous to me, followed by the order, "Stand away from the door."

I obeyed meekly as the door swung open, and three suited and armed men entered. They weren't taking any chances this time. They escorted me out without actually manhandling me, which at least gave them an air of friendliness, even if that wasn't conveyed to the look on their faces.

We marched briskly through the house, one of them in front, the others behind me, guns and eyes acutely trained. I wasn't going anywhere they didn't want me to go, that was for sure. Not this time.

I recognised some of the corridors, mainly by the paintings on the walls, but we never went past a Picasso, so I couldn't be sure exactly where we ended up, although the door we stopped at looked like a hundred others in this house – massive chunks of thick oak with intricate panelling chiselled out by a master craftsman. Like the other doors, this one offered beyond its threshold a mystery which I probably wasn't going to like.

The leader rapped on the door with a gnarled knuckle, and we all waited. One of the men behind me tutted loudly, and I sensed that he didn't like being kept waiting. Too bad.

Eventually, a voice – possibly Wolstenholme's, but it was muffled so that I couldn't be sure – ordered us to enter, but before any of us could move, the door opened, and we were confronted by a very large, very powerful-looking man, built like a tank and probably armour-plated like one, who stepped aside to let us in. I noticed that his suit appeared to be a very tight fit, but the scowl on his pitted face persuaded me not to pass any kind of comment. Fortunately, he took up residence outside the room, closing the door with a hand big enough to shovel coal.

"Ah, David, please join us." The voice had indeed been Wolstenholme's, and now he was sweetness itself as he urged me forward, the men behind me offering physical aid to his request by pushing me in the back. There was nothing dainty about this entrance.

I almost stumbled into the room, just managing to grab the back of a chair to maintain my balance. As I regained my composure, I adjusted the buckle on my belt, before taking a few seconds to look around, seeing one man in the corner, standing behind a chair which was occupied by an awake but very scared Robyn. Although I was still angry with her for being caught, I nodded, hoping to instil some confidence that all would be well, although I don't think it worked. She mouthed, "I'm sorry," which penetrated my anger and made me a little less judgemental, so I nodded again and gave her a reassuring smile.

She wasn't tied to the chair, but it was clear that she was required to remain still, which she did, apart from the trembling hands and the twitch of her lips. I so desperately wanted to take her in my arms.

Wolstenholme sat behind a small white desk. Nothing grand, like the one in his office; this one was what you might call *faux* bijou, out of Warehouse For The Deadbeats via a low-grade version of Walmart. There was nothing on it but his plump hands laid out flat, as if he was about to push himself up from his tight-fitting chair. But he didn't move.

"It is so nice to have you back, David. After your premature ejaculation from our clutches last time." He curled his top lip in delight at this lewd comment, clearly pleased with himself. *Whatever gets you off, Gavin.* He waved an arm in the direction of the chair in front of the desk. "Please take a seat," he invited, and despite my reticence, I was grateful because my legs had suddenly become very weak. I wasn't sure whether it was the drug still working its way through or the fact that I was as scared as Robyn.

"Very good, David. We can at least be civilised." Wolstenholme's bonhomie was jarring, to say the least, but what could I do?

"I'm as civilised as the next man, Gavin."

He chuckled, that strange gravelly sound reminiscent of pebbles being ground together. The last time I heard it, I was mildly amused; this time was different.

While seated, I could look around the entire room, and what I saw was not good news. Packer was packing a sub-machine gun and was poised to pounce as he stood by the door I had come in. Another man, similarly armed, stood beside him, subservient but also ready. As I had never seen such firepower before, I wondered what might possibly go down.

To Wolstenholme's right, a few paces back, was a tall, rakishly thin, rather effeminate man, probably early thirties, dressed impeccably in a three-piece pinstripe suit, just like Gavin himself. Probably a job-lot from Savile Row's poor relation down the Old Kent Road.

Wolstenholme was speaking. "During our little sojourn in the woods, David, you got me thinking."

"Glad I could be of some use."

He came closer, then put out a hand, and I braced myself, expecting what was to come. But instead of giving me a hard slap, his fingers stroked my cheek so gently it was as if a feather had fallen from the sky and was caressing me on its way to the ground.

"You are very special to me, David," he purred. "I hope you realise that."

His voice was soft, almost sensuous, like a lover whispering in my ear. I could feel his breath as he hovered over me, and I half expected him to plant a kiss on my cheek. I turned away.

He gently turned my head back so that I could see his other hand, which was half-open but not quite enough for me to work out what he was holding. He leant in even closer and whispered so that only I could hear. "I want to know about these."

As he parted his fingers, I saw the two bullets and the skull ear-ring he had taken from my pocket, and I nervously tugged at the buckle of my belt.

"Mementoes," I said without conviction.

"Really?" he smirked. "From your holidays, perhaps."

I gave him a cheesy grin. "As a matter of fact, one of them was. The other two are home-grown."

He nodded as if he understood, although he couldn't possibly have known what I was talking about. He wasn't to know that one of the bullets was a souvenir from the island, while the other bullet and the ear-ring had been collected more recently and not too far from home, either.

He drew back and put his hand in his pocket. Without turning from me, he barked to the others, "Get out – all of you. NOW!"

I was as stunned as much as the others by this sudden outburst, and I swivelled in my chair to see the confusion he had caused. Packer, in particular, was clearly agitated, looking hard at Wolstenholme in an effort to understand and perhaps get clarification.

"Get out!" Wolstenholme repeated, and the room cleared in seconds, no matter how reluctant Packer had been. This was one order he was definitely loathe to carry out, and I could hear him mumbling oaths under his breath. Wolstenholme chose not to take any notice.

When the door closed, he looked down at me. He knew he was safe because even if I did go for him, there would be nowhere to run, and I certainly wouldn't get to Robyn before Packer carried out an execution. I was trapped.

"David," Wolstenholme started, his voice smooth, his demeanour even smoother, "we need to talk." He circled round me, brushing an arm across my shoulders, and sat in the chair behind his little desk like some overgrown schoolboy. He rested his elbows on the desk, steepled his fingers and rested his ample lips against them as if deep in thought, and then he looked intently at me. I waited. Seconds ticked by. I wasn't going to break the silence.

"I want to tell you a story," he finally began.

"*Jackanory?*"

"No, David, something a little more serious – more *personal.*"

I didn't like the sound of that, so I refrained from further comment. As someone once said, there's a time for levity – and this wasn't it.

He was silent again for a few seconds. Then, "Once upon a time, there was this brilliant scientist... What do you think we should call him, David?"

I wasn't in the mood, but I knew I had to go along. "Let's call him Rufus."

Wolstenholme chuckled. "Oh, yes, that's a good name. I like that, David. It will really make the story come to life." He rested his arms on the desk, his fingers still clasped. "So, this scientist – Rufus – had been working for many years on an idea involving... Oh, help me here, David. What's the word?"

He knew I knew, but I wasn't going to give him any satisfaction. I really didn't want to be a part of this game, although I suddenly realised that I might actually learn something. "It's your story, Gavin. You tell me."

"You want to know something, David? You're no fun." He paused and took a deep sigh. "Rufus was playing with corpuscles. There! What do you think of that?"

"Are they anything to do with testicles?"

"Oh, David, please don't lower the tone of the story. We both know you are more intelligent than that."

I could have taken umbrage here because it wasn't me who lowered the tone. He did it every time he opened his mouth. No, it was worse than that. Even having to look at him was an affront to decency.

"You've got me, Gavin. I know all about Rufus and corpuscles. Now tell me something I don't know." I glared at him.

"If you insist, my dear boy. Let us start with Susan Patterson, shall we?"

I felt the breath escape my lungs, and I tottered forward, gripping the edge of the desk with hands that had drained of blood. "What about her?" My voice was croaky, almost ethereal, sounding as if it had come from somewhere else in the room and not from me.

"A lovely girl. I hear you were both extremely close. Shame." He stopped and looked across the room as if focusing on a particular spot. "I'm surprised you remember her, David."

It was time for honesty. "I don't, but I've always had this recurring dream about a tree."

"A tree?"

"That's right, a tree. Oh, and an accident," I added bitterly.

"Ah, yes, the accident. Or not."

He left that last comment in the air for me to digest. I waited.

"As I have already told you, I never knew Rufus personally," Wolstenholme said. "However, we did keep an eye on him. I know that he had many failures and even one or two near-misses in his experimentation over the years. Then you came along. We're still not sure where you came from because Rufus was less than forthcoming with his documentation on you, but you were the star pupil, the main event. We all knew that you were the answer to Rufus's prayers, so we let him carry on."

"You were in control?" I asked in surprise.

"We are always in control, David," he grinned malevolently. "Trust me."

That wasn't the first time he had said, "Trust me," and each time I felt even more hatred. It was all I could do to stay in my seat and not get up and throttle the bastard.

"Rufus conducted many preliminary experiments on you, David, and the lovely Susan was in attendance each time. But, as far as we knew, you were never introduced to the Cor-AD. Everything Rufus carried out was, he said, a precursor to you going through the scanner. We believed him…"

I sensed a change in his attitude. "But now you don't, is that it?"

Wolstenholme put his hand in his pocket and pulled out my bullets and the ear-ring, slamming them onto the desk. One of the bullets bounced and rolled off, but I caught it before it hit the floor. I held it tight.

"This is where the story begins, dear boy," he said. "It may not be a hundred per cent accurate, but I am fairly sure it is close to the truth. Tell me, what is the significance of these bullets to you?"

"I told you – mementoes. They have sentimental value."

He leant over the desk. "Bullets that have clearly been fired from a gun but appear to have hit nothing."

"What can I say? Bad marksmanship?"

"I believe," he began, ignoring me, "Rufus put you through the scanner before he said he did."

"That's a wild supposition, even for you. Why would he do that?"

"Perhaps," he said, once more steepling his fingers in that thoughtful pose, "he thought that extra treatments

254

might enhance your body even further. Possibly even protect you in ways that seem impossible to science."

"This is a pretty far-fetched story, Gavin," I said.

"There is a grain of truth in every story, David." He paused, licking his lips in thought. "Just for argument's sake, let us say that Rufus had put you through the full treatment, and his experiment was a roaring success."

"He'd be happy," I said. "Mission accomplished."

"Yes – and no. Of course, he would be ecstatic that his dreams had been fulfilled. All those years of toil, and suddenly he had what he had always craved... But what next, eh, David? What could possibly be his next step?" He slammed his hands flat on the desk, making me jump. "He would put you through the scanner again!"

"You're not serious?" I asked, knowing that he was, and that was almost certainly what did happen.

"Oh, David, *please*. The man was a scientist, desperate to break through boundaries. Of course, he would continue to experiment." He stopped, inhaling sharply as if he had just solved the most complex of conundrums. "Which brings us back to the delightful Susan."

"What?"

"The accident, David. Or not."

I was out of my seat, glowering down at him. "That's the second time you've said that. What do you know?" I spat, reaching out for his throat but stopping myself before I actually touched him.

Wolstenholme had not flinched or moved a muscle, save the minutest upturn of his mouth. "Sit down, David. For all our sakes – especially Miss Newman out there."

I obeyed sheepishly.

"That's better. It's good that you know who is calling the shots, my boy. A terrible expression, I admit, but fitting in this instance. Your American buddy would approve, I'm sure." He attempted a real smile, but it failed on all counts. "Now, where was I? Oh, yes. Susan Patterson. Not a patch on our Robyn, but still a comely wench."

"Get to the point," I demanded, even though I was in no position to do so. I felt helpless and lost. I felt sick at what I knew might be coming, but I had to sit tight and brace myself for the roller-coaster.

"Let us start with some facts, shall we?" He didn't wait for an answer. "Miss Patterson drove her car into a tree. Correct?" He waited for me to nod, then added, "You were a passenger."

"I believe so, yes," I said quietly, nervously.

"I can confirm that, David. She did indeed go head to head with a tree. I can also confirm that the crash was caused by another vehicle ramming her car so that she left the road." He said this with such indifference that I caught my breath.

I was shaking. "Why the hell would you do something like that?"

"Oh, dear boy, you misunderstand me. It was not us who caused the crash. No, we were merely required to tidy up the considerable mess that had been created by the event." He paused for me to assimilate the fact, clearly hoping that this would exonerate him from any blame. Some hope.

He continued, "It is our belief that she was attempting to remove you from the experiment – and the organisation could not allow that to happen."

"I don't understand."

"We do know that she was clearly developing feelings for you, and we are convinced that she was trying to protect you by getting you out." He sighed, as if the whole thing was upsetting his delicate feelings. "So very sad."

"So somebody gave chase... and ran her off the road."

Silence. There was no need for confirmation. I glowered at Wolstenholme, who sat rigid, like an all-powerful demi-god of evil surveying his personal Hades. I waited.

Eventually, he sighed again. "What do you want me to say, David? It is what it is. Rufus pulled you out of the car. Your life was never in danger, but the old fellow clearly felt responsible. And, after all, he was protecting his investment."

Even in the short time I got to know Rufus, it was clear that I was more to him than just a commodity. He sacrificed his life on the island to save me. But that would never have crossed Wolstenholme's mind, so I kept quiet.

Wolstenholme suddenly felt that he needed to offer me a little comfort. "Rufus was not involved in what followed."

"You mean Susan's murder!" I spat with what felt like enough venom to fell a herd of marauding elephants.

He was taken aback by my spite. "What are you talking about? She wasn't murdered, David. I was referring to the story we gave to the media. Poor Rufus was far too upset to be involved in that." He paused, staring at me as if he was the therapist and I was the out-of-his-mind client, which felt about right to me. "What makes you think Susan Patterson was murdered, David?"

My mind was swirling so much that I didn't respond to the question, so when I looked blankly at him, he repeated it slowly, as if he was explaining to a foreigner unused to the language. I took my time answering. "My dream. I remember a syringe…"

His voice suddenly became softer, more sympathetic. "Really? Anything else?"

"No." And that truth really hurt, because I had been so desperate to gather my thoughts into a semblance of order and had failed miserably.

"I am sorry to disappoint you, David, but we are not the ogres you think we are. Miss Patterson died on impact with the tree."

"You were there?"

He began to chuckle, then thought better of it. Perhaps he had suddenly realised that the subject-matter did not warrant such frivolity. "No, I was not there. The troops on the ground reported back to us."

Troops? I couldn't believe what I was hearing. To him, this was like some military manoeuvre. The man was mad. I didn't hear the next few words because a torrent was raging in my head, but I did hear, "There was no mention of a syringe."

"Well," I stormed, "there wouldn't be if one of your troops went rogue."

He thought about that. "That is an interesting theory."

I could almost see inside his head. "A theory that you have considered yourself," I offered.

He didn't need to answer. Now I could see it on his face as well. I felt sure that he had long suspected that he was being betrayed, and the fact that I had voiced the probability of it being true didn't sit well with him at all. His face was so florid that the character Sergeant Beetroot slipped into my mind. He was fit to burst and made a heavy sigh of resignation. Then, remarkably, he was calm once more.

"So, let us get back to my theory."

"Which is?"

He just sat there, and I could almost hear the cogs whirring in his head. He was putting two and two together, and we all know what that adds up to...

"At the time, Susan Patterson's actions were considered those of just a lovelorn woman. We could think of no ulterior motive. However..." He was becoming theatrical, rather like an overweight Gielgud treading the boards at the Yvonne Arnaud. With a flourish, he stretched out his hand, and it took me a while to realise he was demanding the bullet I had been holding. I opened my fist and gave it to him, leaving a deep indentation in my palm where I had gripped it so tightly.

He held the bullet delicately, using the balls of his thumb and first finger to hold it up between us. Then he scrutinised it, rather like an ancient mystic might stare at an artefact given to him by the most sacred of his deities. I was almost mesmerised myself.

"This," he said, his hand wavering slightly with excitement, "could be the key to everything."

I snapped out of my enchanted state. "I'm not with you."

"I think you are, David. In fact, I am sure you are way, way ahead of me. Because you know the truth, don't you?"

"The truth?" I took a deep breath. "You've lost me, Gavin. What truth would that be?"

He held up his other hand and let the bullet drop into it. Then he closed his fingers over it and raised his fist in triumph. "This, David, is proof. Proof that Rufus Allenby exceeded all expectations in his experiment. I know now that he must have put you through the scanner with the help of Susan Patterson…"

"You're clutching at straws that don't exist."

He ignored my feeble comment. "He was going to do it again, but Susan didn't like that idea, so she tried to get you out. She couldn't stand the thought of her favourite guinea pig going through it all again and possibly facing destruction. How romantic."

"It cost her life," I interrupted with bile in my mouth, but he just smirked.

"Her choice, my boy. But I'm right, aren't I?"

I gripped the chair tightly. "I have no idea. I've lost my memory, remember?"

He was fairly bubbling with excitement. "Why else would she risk everything? It's the only thing that makes sense – especially now I know about these." He again stared at the bullet, and I gripped the arms of my chair, knowing he was right and that there was nothing in the world I could do about it. "When Robyn Newman came to the lab, Rufus carried out more experiments, didn't he?"

He scooped up the other bullet and put them both in his pocket. He leant forward and said, "I believe you are a walking miracle."

I tried to chuckle. "I don't think so."

Then, with a speed that amazed me, he pulled out a small gun from his waistcoat pocket. Even in that moment of sheer fright, I could still marvel at the magnificence of the tiny weapon in his pudgy hand. What I could see of the grip was ornately engraved, and the double barrels glinted silver in the light coming through the window. Wolstenholme saw my fascination.

"Beautiful, isn't it?" He waved it nonchalantly in the air, showing it off for my benefit. "It's a replica Philadelphia Deringer, just like the one that killed Abraham Lincoln." He thought about that for a second. "But then that couldn't possibly happen to you, could it, David? You're immune."

"If you say so, Gavin." It was as much as I could do to just sit there, let alone voice an opinion. I just had to think of Robyn, outside with some nasty men, and that kept me in my seat.

"Perhaps we should try it. You know, conduct our own experiment." He waved the gun around some more, this time pretending to aim at specific targets, like the far wall and the door handle, before standing up, leaning forward and directing both barrels at my crotch. "What do you think, David? Shall we experiment?"

This time, I did stand up, and I pushed back the chair in anger. "You're mad!" I screamed, hoping that someone would barge into the room and stop this performance. Of course, nobody did. I had forgotten how thick the oak doors were.

"All that time we assumed you were just extremely lucky, ducking and diving from those bullets," Wolstenholme said, his monotonous voice causing my brain to vibrate. "But, in reality, Rufus had created a... What shall we call you, David? Not Superman – that's been done to death. We need a special name for you. I will have to give that some serious thought."

It was then that he pulled the trigger, and the little gun recoiled slightly in his hand. I recoiled as well, but only from the shock of what he had done. The bullet fell harmlessly to the floor in front of me and rolled away, leaving the most awe-struck look on the government man's face. I really thought he might have a heart attack there and then, but I wasn't that lucky.

"I knew it! I knew it!" he gasped, trying to steady himself. "You *are* immune!"

The door flew open, and a trigger-happy Packer filled the space. "What the hell...?"

Wolstenholme, being the diplomat that he was, quickly regained control. "It's nothing, Captain. I was merely demonstrating my toy." He offered Packer a good view of the gun, before pocketing it once more, then added, "You may leave now."

Packer hesitated, and I could see his shifty eyes looking us both up and down, not a hundred per cent convinced by Wolstenholme's explanation, but then he turned smartly and left the room, closing the door with a sarcastic, "Yes, sir."

Wolstenholme turned his attention back to me. "Don't worry, David. Your secret is safe with me." He paused. "As long as you co-operate."

I was in a corner with no means of escape. But I had to carry the fight to him. "You need to let Robyn go."

He sniggered. "Oh, I don't think so, my boy. At least not just yet. Firstly, let us discuss this…" He picked up the ear-ring from the desk. "Where did you get it?"

I could see that the conversation was moving away from my personal story, so before I answered, I tugged on my belt buckle once more. "The ear-ring? I took it from the man who tried to kill me at Alice Holt. Why?"

By way of answer, he went to the door, opened it, called out a name, and the effeminate man came in. Even in the short distance he had to travel, I could see he walked with a feminine gait, as if he had left his stiletto heels behind but was still trying to compensate. When he reached the main man, he held out a long, beautifully manicured hand, which Wolstenholme took and squeezed lovingly. They continued to hold each other as Wolstenholme spoke. "This is Linton. He is the love of my life. He has been my puppy for several happy years now, so I have allowed him a certain *arrangement*."

I didn't really want to know, so I just stared at them. Wolstenholme slowly lifted their entwined fingers and patted them with his other hand. "I allow him to dally, as it were, in exchange for his unbridled servitude to me. He will do anything for me, won't you, Linton, my love?"

Linton gave the sweetest of smiles and nodded. Wolstenholme squeezed his hand tightly and gave the younger man a long, lingering kiss.

Eventually, Wolstenholme came up for breath and looked hard at me. "So, David, do you see it?"

It took me a few seconds as I studied the young man, but then I saw an ear-ring identical to the one that had been in my pocket and was now resting on the desk. A skull.

Wolstenholme looked crestfallen, even perhaps having a tear in one puffy eye. "I have long suspected there was a rat on the ship," he said to Linton with deep sadness. "I just never thought it might be you."

Linton pulled away. "What is it, Gav?"

"It's the ear-ring! It's the ear-ring!" Wolstenholme was fast losing control.

The younger man, though clearly scared witless, manfully stood his ground. "Gav, what on earth are you saying?"

"See this?" Wolstenholme screamed, grabbing Linton's neck and forcing him forward so that his face banged the edge of the desk, and he came face to face with the ear-ring that matched his own. "What have you got to say for yourself?"

Linton knew it was a lost cause. "I'm sorry, Gav...," he whined.

"Sorry?" roared the big man. "You'll be sorry, all right!" With that, he pulled Linton upright, drew his deringer from his pocket and shot the young man neatly between the eyes.

Linton fell at my feet, and Wolstenholme stumbled back to his chair, trying not to look at the crumpled body beside me. I couldn't have stood up even if I wanted to. My sense of shock was overpowering, and I think Wolstenholme felt the same. He was mumbling to himself something about being betrayed, and I almost began to feel a pang of sympathy for him.

The door flew open, of course, with Packer and the big man both trying to get in together, jamming each other as they did so. It was almost comical. Almost.

Packer pushed his way through and was the first to see Linton's body. "What the hell have you done?" He was looking hard at Wolstenholme, but I could see that he was also keeping tabs on me, his machine gun half raised just in case I tried something stupid.

"He betrayed me," Wolstenholme whimpered, slouched in his chair and rubbing his hands up and down his legs, probably in an effort to ease his pain. By the look on his face, it wasn't helping. "He was the mole."

"You bloody fool!" Packer spat. "How the hell do you think we can cover this one up?"

It was at that precise moment that we heard the sirens. Police cars, at least three by the sound of it, entering the compound and presumably disgorging heavily-armed officers trained in counter-terrorism, as arranged by Gregory according to my finely detailed plan, which I might have scribbled on the back of an envelope. It had been a long shot, but it appeared to have paid off, and I tapped the hidden microphone in my belt buckle to confirm that I was still in the land of the living.

It amazed me how much influence Gregory seemed to carry, but I was grateful for it. At my request, he had talked his police friend into getting permission for full surveillance and a potential raid on this government-sponsored house, no questions asked, and, once more, I was intrigued by the formidable talent that Rufus must have possessed to draw people like Gregory and Denver into my life to offer a level of protection which was nothing short of incredible.

Of course, Robyn had not been part of the equation at Alice Holt. The plan was that she should have gone back to the car with the others – to be safe. That way, they could all keep an eye on me from a distance. Trust her to throw a spanner in the works.

I was being yanked from my chair, a hand roughly but tightly gripping my shirt and propelling me forward. I tried to fight it, but my momentum had been set in motion, and as I came out of my chair I was brought to an abrupt halt by Packer's body as he breathed over my face. "Come with me!" he hissed, close enough that I felt his spittle on my cheek.

"Piss off!" I replied. "It's over."

He laughed then and tightened his grip. "If you want to see your girl again, you'll do as you're told."

I froze for a second and then allowed him to drag me from the room. What choice did I have? I had to protect

Robyn, even though I had no idea where she was and in what state she might be. Packer had full control.

As I was bundled from the room, my last sight of Wolstenholme was of him slumped in his chair, blubbering and broken, his world crushed. Yet even at that moment, I sensed he might possibly escape justice somehow because he had friends in high places, much more elevated than any policeman, be it commissioner or chief constable. Wolstenholme's world was beyond that, and he would walk away like the Teflon-coated rogue that he was. Or perhaps I had got that all wrong.

Packer was pushing me harder, forcing the pace as we raced through the corridors. Everything was just a haze to me as I tried to focus my thoughts on my predicament and not on Robyn. It was difficult, and at one point I stumbled against a wall, but still he forced me on.

I gathered my breath and said, "Where are we going?"

"Safety."

I couldn't believe what I was hearing. Was Packer actually getting me out of this?

We reached a door, and he ordered me to stop. Just another huge oak door opening into another expansive room, but this one was empty and musty, smelling as if it had remained closed for years. He prodded my back as a signal to enter, so I did, although it made no sense to me. The police would be going through this place with a fine-tooth comb, so nowhere was safe.

As I stumbled into the room, I was amazed to see Robyn standing in front of me, guarded by one of Packer's men, his weapon down but clearly poised. Robyn offered a cold stare, which I hoped wasn't for me.

Packer grinned at the bemused look on my face. "In the corner," he ordered.

I spread my arms in exasperation. "Why?"

"Like I said, safety." With that, he put the palm of one hand against the wall, and a gap suddenly appeared, a small section of the wall coming out into the room to reveal an opening. The space was barely large enough for a person to get through, even crouching, but I sensed that it would lead to the outside world, and I still couldn't quite believe that Packer was prepared to let me go. There must be a catch, of course.

Packer was grinning. "I thought you might like a last look at your lady friend before you left us. She will remain behind, naturally."

I edged towards the opening, still not sure how to play this. I was fuming, but saw no way to get Robyn free. She stood motionless as I neared the exit, my movements deliberately slow and almost mechanical, my brain addled.

Then Robyn made her move. I would never have believed it had I not witnessed it with my own eyes. Without warning, she brought up her right hand and delivered the most beautiful uppercut to the man's jaw, the force probably enough to have floored Tyson Fury. I saw her wince with the pain as the reverberations shook through her hand and up her arm, but then she was off, scurrying behind me and ducking into the void so quickly that none of us had time to react. Packer's man was on one knee, grunting and feeling his chin, checking if anything had been broken by the piledriver. I hoped so. Packer had his mouth open, lost in the memorable moment.

I stood at the entrance to the tunnel. "Run, Robyn!" I shouted, admiration and excitement in my voice. "Run!"

Packer's man was up by then, and the two of them trained their guns on me. I stood tall. "You won't get her back, Packer," I sneered. "Not without killing me." I paused then. "But you don't want to kill me, do you? Or rather, you're under instructions not to kill me, isn't that right? Something's changed since this all started. On the island, your people were hell-bent on eliminating me. Now, you want to save my neck. What's going on?" I waited, but Packer wasn't playing the game. He just stared, those cold black eyes trying to penetrate me but failing. He held no thrall over me, so I said, "I'm going to wait right here until she's well away – then I'm going to follow her."

We had reached an impasse, and Packer knew better than to rush past me and try to follow Robyn. His job was to see me clear, and that was what he intended to do. We were frozen in time.

I smiled. It was a pleasure holding the upper hand for once. "So it's you who was the mole," I said. I had suspected this to be the case for some time, but I thought I would just pass a few more idle seconds. "Not Linton."

"It was both of us," he replied. "More intel that way."

"Yes," I agreed, "I can see that. Linton took notes on the inappropriate pillow-talk, and you took care of the rest. All bases covered. Neat." I decided to take a flyer. "Tell me, who is your boss?"

He didn't respond, so we fell silent once more, except for the man in the corner, who was simpering over the loss of his pride and perhaps a tooth or two.

The seconds ticked by as we stood there, facing each other, until Packer finally said, "Time to go. The police will be here soon. I might be under instruction to save your neck, Parks, but I need to save mine as well. You have the girl, so I suggest you get out. We'll give you a head start, and I promise not to interfere."

I harrumphed then. "Promise? You don't even know the meaning of the word!" I turned and bent into the tunnel as Packer's words hit me from behind.

"Just remember, I *will* get you. No matter what you do, we will *always* know where you are."

* * *

The tunnel felt damp and draughty as I made my way through it. After a few metres, the ceiling seemed to rise up, allowing me to stand almost erect, making movement much quicker. There was electric lighting along one wall, which cast strange shadows over the curved roof of the tunnel, and I found that if I used my hands overhead, it compensated a little for the uneven floor, which was basically dirt and stones. Somebody had created a neat little exit strategy but hadn't bothered with the niceties such as tiled flooring.

I could hear movement behind me and knew it was Packer, but as he said, I had won this round, so it was clear he wouldn't pose a threat just yet. I was just happy that I couldn't hear Robyn ahead. I had been a little worried that she might have felt guilty about leaving me behind and would be waiting around a corner, gasping for breath and throwing herself into my arms. In one way, no such luck; in the other, I felt only relief. She was long gone.

The tunnel was getting wider, almost enough for two people to pass, and I wondered what exactly it had been created for. Then I came to a fork. Not what I wanted. I stopped, listening. I took a few steps down the left fork and again stopped to listen. Nothing. So I went right and was rewarded almost immediately with the onrushing sound of wind and, possibly, the distant whoosh of traffic. I ran on, my movement faster as I sensed fresh air, and, eventually, I saw a shaft of light. I was running uphill by this time, and it was getting harder, but I knew I would be leaving the tunnel very shortly, and my priority would be to find Robyn.

I had no need to worry. As I broke into the welcome light, she ran from the cover of some trees and embraced me. "Thank God," she purred, before I forced myself away from her and began to run off in any direction, my hand on her elbow to ensure she stayed with me.

As we fled across a field, much like we had done the last time, I gripped her hand tightly. This time, however, I didn't want to look back, but I was sure that Packer was standing there, watching. Biding his time.

Chapter Nineteen

We were in a safe house. Not the usual run-of-the-mill safe house; you know, the one with plainclothes detectives in shirtsleeves and shoulder holsters, sunglasses and deep frowns, offering endless cups of coffee and caustic comments about the cost of the whole enterprise to the public purse.

No, this was an entirely different safe house, courtesy of Gregory's more lower-class connections. We were, I assumed, somewhere in London. I rather hoped it might be Peckham, home of Del Boy, but it probably wasn't. Our host was Luigi, which should have told me something. He was Italian, of course, not unlike Pavarotti in appearance, being a rather large individual with jowls worthy of perhaps a deep bass rather than a tenor. Every time he passed me, I expected him to be carrying a violin case, which made me smile. He was a jolly fellow, which belied the long scar down his neck and the half-chewed ear which, I had been informed with a great deal of humour by one of his colleagues, had been gouged by a bull somewhere in Spain quite a few years back. How cosmopolitan was that?

He must have been nearing seventy but was remarkably agile, and I could see him running the bulls in

Pamplona or running the police ragged in Sicily. Either way, he looked like a winner to me, and I rather liked him.

We had been in the house for three days now, safe from danger and regrouping. It was a big house, with many bedrooms, and as well as Denver, Gregory, Robyn and myself, there were four further Italians to back Luigi up. I didn't know their names; in fact, I couldn't be sure that Luigi was really his name, but it made no difference to any of us. We were friends. And they were heavily armed.

I wasn't sure how Gregory had made the acquaintance of the Italians. Probably not through his connections with the police, but then Gregory had always been full of surprises. I was just grateful that Packer was off our back, and I could think things through with a relatively clear mind.

Robyn had been slowly warming back up to me, and we would sit in the mornings after breakfast and talk, although I knew not to make things too personal. She had been through a lot and was still reeling over the things that her beloved Dr Allenby had possibly been up to. It was not for me to disillusion her further.

As we were strongly advised not to leave the house, I had taken to my room for hours on end, poring over the folder from the laboratory in the hope that something might jump out at me. There was nothing about me *per se*, of course, but the figures laid out in Susan's tidy handwriting and, later, Robyn's more floral script intrigued me, even if they meant little. Rufus had made what I assumed to be pertinent comments in the margins in his familiar mauve ink, but they were actually indecipherable, and I would need Robyn to translate them. In fact, I knew I would need Robyn to go through the whole folder to find any clue as to what had happened to me. The thought made me shudder because I didn't want Robyn to know the truth – but I *did* need to know myself.

When Luigi, in his wonderful broken English, called us down for lunch, his voice demanding but exquisitely melodic, I took the folder with me, placed it on the table and sat opposite Robyn. Denver sat beside me.

"What, a bit of light reading, David?" he smiled. Since he and Gregory had arrived at the house a couple of hours after Robyn and me, Denver had been more attached than ever, like a barnacle on one of his lobster boats, I thought. Perhaps, like me, it had occurred to him that we might never see each other again.

Escaping from the house in Farnham had been a close-run thing. While Packer himself had given up for the time being, there was the strong possibility that government thugs might still be on our trail, so when we got away, we had laid low for an hour or so, at one time resting in a small, delightful copse, eating a couple of apples we had scrumped from an orchard on our travels. It had all felt so normal. Then we had made our way to the nearest road, where Robyn did the trick as a damsel in distress and secured a hitched ride which took us to the outskirts of Woking. We had no money, of course, but her winning smile paid the debt, and Gregory even managed to call Luigi's boss on the driver's mobile, which meant a car was despatched immediately, once the password had been given. So simple when you have good friends.

Now, in answer to Denver's question, I looked directly at Robyn. "I rather hoped that our resident scientist might take a look," I said with a thin smile, angling for a warm reception. "There's nothing in there about me, but there still might be clues. I know Wolstenholme felt there was something missing. I think that's why he took me… *us*." I could see Robyn blush as I drew her into the equation. It was clear that she was still feeling guilty about getting herself caught, but I had moved on from that after seeing the way she handled Packer's man on the way to the tunnel. She was definitely my kind of woman.

"If you think it would help," she said flatly.

"Please," I said, my smile widening to encourage her. I hoped it might do the trick.

"Of course," she said, adding nothing more.

I slid the folder across the table, and she put a hand on it. I thought for a minute she was about to caress it, but then Luigi and friends rolled into the room with bowls of pasta and sing-song voices extolling the virtues of Italia and the Mafioso.

"*Mancia*! *Mancia*! *Buòn appetito*!" Luigi screamed, crashing the dish onto the table and lifting the lid. "*Mancia*!"

None of us knew what he was saying, but the meaning was clear! So we all tucked in, Italian-style, with much laughter and slapping of backs, until we had sated ourselves, and we eventually withdrew to the lounge for recuperation and a fat glass of brandy. This was how the other half lived, I thought dreamily, as I sank into the plush armchair and gazed longingly at Robyn across the room. She was holding the file tightly, and I was relieved to see that she was looking back at me with something like affection, although it might well have been pity or something much worse. In my state of post-luncheon drowsiness, I couldn't be too sure what she was thinking. But at least she was looking at me.

I awoke about two hours later with a prod from Denver.

"We need to talk, David."

His words found their way in and around my fuddle, forcing out my answer. "What?"

"Wake up, Beauty. There's been a development."

"What?" Again?

I stirred, slowly, very slowly, coming out of the cocoon created by the comfortable armchair and sitting upright, blinking in the late afternoon gloom. "What is it?"

Denver was beckoning me to follow him, so I rose unsteadily and made my way to the small office next door, where Gregory was seated at a laptop, a worried look on his face. Immediately, I was alert.

Gregory started, his voice shrill and excitable. "I just heard from Aunt Grace…"

Grace was in her own safe house, a *real* safe house, somewhere out in the shires, courtesy of the retired police chief who had taken Gregory under his wing and presumably tickled Grace's fancy many years ago, if what my chauffeur had told me was anything to go by. Still, why not? They were both widowed, and at least I had the satisfaction of knowing she was in good hands, even if the mental picture was a bit too much to handle. Grace was also our window onto the world.

Gregory was still talking. "She told me that Gavin Wolstenholme is dead…"

"What?" I said once more, this time with more feeling as I shuddered.

"I've called it up on the laptop. Look." Gregory was pointing at the screen as Denver leant in beside me for a closer look.

The heading was stark – 'MURDERED IN PRISON' – and I greedily read on: 'The Home Office has announced that once-prominent government mandarin Gavin Wolstenholme has been murdered in his cell at HMP Dartmoor by unknown assailants, believed to be fellow inmates. Mr Wolstenholme, said to have allegedly been a member of a shadowy Government faction, died before medical assistance could be administered. He was sixty-two, unmarried, and had been detained in prison for the murder of a much younger man in what had been described as a "lovers' tiff".'

We all let out a collective breath as the news sank in. I was more than happy, realising that he probably took my secret to the grave, but it was still unclear who had taken Gavin out. My bet was the 'shadowy Government faction', and Denver seemed to agree with me.

"They got him before he could spill the beans."

"Yes," I said. "They obviously thought the less the public know about what he was up to, the better."

"Then it's all over." The voice came from the doorway, and we turned to see Robyn. She was frowning, perhaps not really believing what she had just said.

I got to my feet and went to her, gently leading her into the lounge. Nobody followed us. She sat on the sofa at my beckoning, and her big eyes watched intently as I paced in front of her, desperately trying to verbalise my thoughts.

"What is it?" she asked. "If Wolstenholme is dead, then surely it is all over. They wouldn't dare send anyone else... not now."

I was still formulating the words.

"All you have to do," she continued, almost pleading, "is to get that transmitter taken out of your body. Then, no one will be able to find you. We can go away..."

I don't think she realised what she had said. "We?" I queried, a smile forming.

"I mean... you. You can go away somewhere," she blurted, her cheeks reddening.

"It's not that simple," I sighed, flopping down beside her and taking her hand in mine. "There's Packer..."

"He'd never find you..."

"Us," I amended her, and she blushed anew. It was as if, at that moment, two dopey teenagers were occupying the sofa. Then I got a grip. "Packer said something as I made my escape back at the house."

"What?"

"He said they would find me... whatever I did."

"So what does that mean?"

278

"It means," I said slowly, "I think they've planted another tracker in me. Even if we got rid of the one Rufus implanted, they would still know where I was."

There are times in history when 'eureka' can be shouted from the hilltops. I had just experienced one such moment.

"Of course!" I almost shouted, jumping up from the sofa. "Wherever I am."

Robyn looked stunned. "What? What is it, David?"

"Don't you see, Robyn? Packer deliberately kept me alive. He even went so far as to save my neck back at the house. Why? Why would he do that? I'll tell you why," I screeched, not allowing her to answer my questions. "Because they *need* me alive! I am so important to them that they were prepared to let me go – all the time knowing that they would be able to reel me in whenever they wanted."

Robyn took this in, then said, "But they were trying to kill you on the island. What has changed?"

It didn't take me long to work that one out. "You gave me the answer, Robyn. You said there were pages missing from my file. I'm betting that the scientific data of all the other guinea pigs was very light compared to mine. After all, Rufus seems to have invested everything in me as his star pupil." I almost choked on those words, but I was in full flow now. "Wolstenholme grilled me on the missing pages, so you can bet they are important. What are they about, Robyn?"

She looked embarrassed. "To be honest, David, I don't know. They were at the front of the folder, and I only filled in your daily details at the back. Dr Allenby made it very clear that was my only role, apart from keeping an eye on you."

I smiled. "I like that thought," I breathed softly. Then, more forceful, "Whoever is behind Packer was expecting to kill me and then take the file. However, somehow, they got wind of the missing pages; my guess is Wolstenholme opened his mouth once too often in the bedroom with Linton – so it became imperative that they kept me alive in case I knew where these pages were. They are playing a waiting game."

"What are we going to do?"

"I'm not sure, but we need to take the initiative. This won't end until we make it end."

* * *

I spent the next hour in my room, lying on the bed, tossing and turning, trying to clear my mind so that I could think straight. It wasn't easy. I kept getting blurred at the edges, seeing Robyn and almost feeling the touch of her hand. I'd never felt like this before, and in a way it frightened me, especially as I knew that I was placing her in danger every second I was with her.

I sat up. This had to stop, and I knew it was me who was going to finish it, one way or another. I thought of Packer and the late but not lamented Wolstenholme. They both desperately wanted those missing pages. But why? What was so important? Then I knew. I knew what they were planning – and I also knew where to look for the pages.

I slid off the bed and pulled open the door, shouting as I did so, "Robyn, where are you?"

She was in the lounge with the others, playing *Monopoly*, which Gregory was clearly winning. It was such an innocuous sight that I stopped in my tracks. They all looked up at me, Denver holding his piece over the 'Jail' square and looking relieved that he might not have to go there after all.

"What is it, David?" Robyn asked.

"The machine – you said Rufus dismantled it."

"Yes."

"When, exactly?"

Robyn thought for a moment. "I don't know, a week or so before he went to the island, perhaps."

"You were surprised by his actions?"

"Very, yes. It came out of the blue. I didn't understand why he had done it."

I sat at the table, absent-mindedly playing with the *Monopoly* Penguin I had taken from the board in front of me. "You're right; it doesn't seem to make sense. After all, anybody could have got access to the blueprint and rebuilt the machine – just like Matthew Denny did in the first place."

"This is leading somewhere," Denver said. "I know how your brain works, pal." He smiled.

"Rufus was a very clever man. Too clever to let somebody else into his secret." I stopped fiddling and looked at my friends. "He knew that somebody was after me – and, more importantly, his machine. He managed to save me, although it cost him his life." I paused, realising exactly how much I owed to that mad, mad scientist with a conscience. "So, how could he save his machine?"

Blank faces stared back at me, until Robyn suddenly found my wavelength. "Microchip!"

"Exactly! Rufus kept the one piece that he had designed and produced himself, the beating heart of the machine. Packer and Wolstenholme weren't just looking for missing pages – they were after the microchip or whatever it is that ensures the machine can be used."

"That makes sense, sir, but where is this chip now?" asked Gregory.

"Ah, I think I know, but we'll need confirmation. Let's get Luigi in here – I need to use his phone."

Gregory left to find his Sicilian cohort, while the rest of us waited in silence, save for the ticking of a clock on the wall. I thought about time: with my friends on the island, with Robyn, with Wolstenholme... ah, the one man who had learnt my secret – but it had done him no good whatsoever. I thought of the short time between his arrest and death, relieved that he had obviously not told anybody else, because they would surely have been banging on the door long before now. I thought of Rufus again, but what came to mind was the confusion he had sown, was still sowing even in death...

Luigi came through the door at a rate of knots. "*Il telefono*," he said, tossing it to me. "Gregoree says it is urgent."

I managed to catch the missile before it hit Denver on the chin and waved my thanks with my other hand. "Very," I said, getting my bearings with the phone and then dialling.

It took several minutes to make the connection, but eventually I heard the Gallic tone of Morice.

"Bonjour, my friend," I said, and I heard the sharp intake of breath.

"David," he moaned, "will you ever learn to say the word correctly? *Bonjour*," he corrected me, and I grinned despite myself. "So," he continued, "you are well? And what about our American hombre? Is he still with you – or perhaps he is riding the range down in Dodge City or somewhere?"

I had set Luigi's phone on speaker, so Denver was able to put the Frenchman right. "I'm here, bud. And I'll be riding over your range when I get back, so watch yourself!"

Both men chuckled, and the sound of their very different voices was a heady mixture indeed. The rest of us joined in, all except Luigi, who stood beside me with a face like granite and bewilderment in his eyes.

"*Pazzo Americano!*" he whispered.

I could only agree, but then Denver had always seemed a little mad to me, in the nicest possible way.

Morice was speaking. "What is it you want of me, David?"

"Rufus Allenby must have booked a room on the island. There was no way he could get a flight back home the same day."

"That is right, David. We are not as sophisticated here as you are – only two flights a day, and one of them is an island-hop, which is not international. Your Rufus would have needed to find a room or pitch a tent on the beach, as some of your compatriots tend to do."

I smiled. "I don't think that was Rufus's style, Morice."

"I am sure you are correct, my friend. So, there are two hotels…"

"Hah!" blurted Denver. "Call the 'Harrison' a hotel? More like an east-end dive!"

My own appraisal of the place might not have been so brutal, but it was a point well made. "I agree. Rufus would have stayed at the Viscount, I'm sure."

"So, what is it you want me to do?" asked Morice.

I had given it some thought. When Rufus came to the island, it made sense to me that he would try to keep his two valuable possessions as close as possible: his paperwork, and me. That could only mean one thing…

"Can you see if Dr Allenby left anything in the hotel safe?" I said.

"I can, but they will need some proof, my friend. They will not accept the word of a louche Frenchman, as Denver often calls me."

"What is it you Brits say, 'If the lid fits, put it on the kettle'?" smirked the American.

We ignored him.

"Morice is right. They will need a password at the very least," Robyn offered helpfully.

I immediately thought of my folder and the mauve ink on the front. "Try 'Goliath'," I said.

"Goliath?" Morice echoed.

"It's just a hunch," I said.

Chapter Twenty

We had our answer two hours later, when a breathless Morice phoned to say that he had just taken possession of a parcel. At first, the hotel had been reluctant to open the safe, but Morice, using the wiles every Frenchman learns from birth, tickled the female manager enough to make her relent, and she threw open the safe as if she was throwing open her arms for an embrace. At least, that was how Morice described it. The truth may have been a little less colourful.

"David, the password was, as you say, 'Goliath'. You are indeed very clever, my friend."

"Thank you," I said in all modesty, "but I couldn't have done it without Rufus."

"So, what shall I do with this now?" he asked.

"Can you keep it safe somewhere?"

"I can do that, yes."

"There is one more thing you can do for me," I said.

"Name it."

I told him, then added, "*Merci*," before clicking off the phone. We could have talked longer, but I had plans to make, and, with luck, we would be seeing Morice again very soon anyway.

I handed the phone back to Luigi and gathered everyone round the dining room table. It was reminiscent of our discussion at Grace's house, which seemed a very long time ago now. But this time, it was a little more urgent.

"I want you to listen to me," I began, trying to lend authority to my voice. "I am going back to the island."

There were the expected rumblings of discontent and disapproval, but my mind was made up. I really needed the nightmare to end, and this was the only way. I raised my hand to allay any comments.

"Denver, I want you to come with me – if you would."

"Of course," he responded immediately.

"Hold on!" Robyn spluttered, clearly shocked at what I had said. "Have you lost your mind, David? If they know where you are, you'll be…"

"A sitting duck?" I finished for her. "That's exactly what I want them to think. They're very clever, but there is one thing that they can't control – and that is their greed. They will come after me because they are desperate to rebuild Rufus's machine. Now that I have what they need, they will follow me to the ends of the earth if they have to. I aim to make sure the island is their last port of call."

"Oh, very macho," Robyn scoffed. "You think you can stand up to all of them? You're mad, David!"

I could see the hurt in her eyes as well as the panic. I reached out for her, but she flinched and brushed my arm away.

"I'm sorry, Robyn, but it's the only way. You must see that. We can't stay in this place forever. Something has to be done."

She didn't soften, but she finally said, "If that is the way it has to be, then I am coming, too."

"I won't allow that!" I said tartly.

"You will have no say in it," she replied, her tone as caustic as mine had been. "Gregory, please arrange flights for the three of us."

"Yes, miss," Gregory replied sheepishly, seeing that the balance of power had shifted. "Whatever you say."

I sighed deeply. I had lost the battle.

"Now," said this new Robyn, "what's the plan?"

To be perfectly honest, I didn't have much of a plan, as usual. Just jumping on the aircraft and leading my enemies a merry dance on the island. That was it in its full glory.

Robyn and Denver were not at all impressed.

"Well," I said tetchily, "what's *your* plan?"

"For a start," Denver said, "all you'll do is attract Packer and his goons. You won't get to the brains of the operation."

"Mr Big, you mean?" I said.

"Yeah, pal, Mr Big. The man who's controlling things."

Denver was right. In order to come out of this, I needed to reach into the very depths of this poison ivy and pluck out its heart, the man at the top who kept the whole thing beating. *Now*, I had a plan.

Admittedly, it wasn't cute, and it certainly wasn't foolproof, but it was the best I was going to come up with, so I was prepared to go with it.

I went to the window, pulled back a small corner of the net curtain that Luigi had thoughtfully installed to ensure our privacy, and looked out on the road. The black SUV was still there, as I knew it would be; it had been staking out the house barely minutes after we first arrived, the trackers in me doing their job to perfection. I knew that the men in the car weren't there for me – they were waiting to see if one of my friends would be foolish enough to take a walk so that they could grab them and use them as leverage. I also knew nobody would be that stupid, and I was also confident that Packer's men wouldn't raid the house and upset what was almost certainly a fairly prominent Italian gang. Let's face it: Gregory would never mix with low-level riff-raff mafioso. That would have been beneath him.

"Luigi," I called, and the man himself was framed in the doorway almost immediately. "I would like you to convey a message to our friends outside."

* * *

The knock on the door, when it came, was more sedate than expected. Not the heavy thump of an ex-army knuckle, more like the almost gentle tap of a persistent woodpecker. But when one of Luigi's men finally opened the door, Packer strode in as if he owned the place.

He was shown into the dining room, where I sat in anticipation and trepidation, not knowing exactly how this would pan out.

Packer stood before me. He wasn't packing a firearm, of course, but in all other respects he was the consummate commando: camouflage fatigues (naturally), military poise, eyes taking in everything through narrowed lids, a scowl on his face and a growl in his voice. "I don't take kindly to being summoned."

"It's simple, captain. I have something your boss wants, so you do what I say."

He didn't like that. Orders from his superiors were accepted without comment, but it went against the grain to be manipulated by a pest that he would like to squash under his boot. He said nothing.

"I'll keep this short," I said. "I will give you what you want if you stay away from my friends."

"We have no interest in them."

"Nevertheless, I have enough evidence to get you put away for a very long time. It is in a safe place – as I trust my friends will be."

"Fair enough," he said, although we both knew that his word meant nothing. "What have you got?"

I beckoned for him to sit, but he refused. Perhaps he thought he was holding the high ground.

"Firstly, I want you to tell me exactly where your tracker is in my body so that when this is all over, I can get it removed. I know where Rufus Allenby put his, but yours is not so obvious."

He laughed at that. "Because we are professionals." He waited for a few moments, pretending to contemplate my request, before saying, "I will tell you – although you know it will be a waste of time because you will be dead before you get the chance."

I had expected some kind of comment like that. "One of us will be dead, I agree."

This he found really funny. "You think you are a match for me? If I could take you outside…"

"Ah, but you can't do that, can you, Packer?" I cut in. "Your job is to follow orders, and that means keeping me alive." I paused, revelling in my power. "Now sit down!"

We locked eyes like two stags, far from rutting, before he scraped the chair from under the table and reluctantly sat, the testosterone escaping from every pore.

"That's better," I said smoothly. "Now we can talk man to man."

He squirmed. "Get on with it, Parks."

At that moment, I had no intention of doing any such thing. I liked the fact that he was squirming like the worm he was, so I leant back on my chair and looked out of the window. "Such a lovely day."

"So?" he squeaked.

"It would be nice to get out and enjoy it, that's all. Nothing complicated. Just feel the breeze on my cheeks and the rays of the sun on my brow. Don't you think that sounds rather poetic?"

He didn't reply.

"You know, it's every man's right to feel free. Don't you agree?"

Again, he said nothing.

"I don't feel free, Packer. My friends don't feel free, either. Want to know why?" This time, I didn't wait for an answer. "Because of arseholes like you and your boss, that's why. Sad, isn't it?"

"Get to the point."

"What was it that Moshe Dayan said? 'Freedom is the oxygen of the soul.' So true."

I stood and started to pace the room, knowing that I was adding to his frustration. As an ex-army man, he needed to be in control, to know what the next move was going to be. I was about to throw him completely.

"Freedom and oxygen. Oxygen is life. They go together, don't you think?"

"Yeah." It was a half-hearted attempt to stay with me. Now, he needed a jolt.

"So, captain, my second request – no, my second *demand* – is that you tell me what happened to Susan Patterson."

He was almost off his chair. "Get lost!"

I pushed him back, and the glint in his eyes became red-hot with anger. He was desperate to get at me, but the soldier in him was winning, so he shrugged and stayed put. "I don't know what you mean," he said unconvincingly.

"You were there, weren't you?" I sighed. "You know Rufus took away my memory. Oh, yes, I remember things from history, from life in general, but nothing about my own life before Rufus got hold of me." Again, I leant in. "Except, I keep having this nagging dream, Packer. More of a nightmare, really, because it keeps me awake sometimes and gnaws at me, testing me to see if I can get the whole story. But all I get is a car heading towards a tree – until the other day, when something else came into my head. A hand with a syringe. Was it your hand, Packer?"

I knew straight away that I had scored. His face told me everything I needed to know.

"So, while Rufus was getting me out of the car, you were murdering Susan." I paused. "Wolstenholme told me that his 'troops on the ground' had been responsible, and I had always believed it was you. Now I know."

"Yes, now you know," he said without feeling.

"But why?"

It was obvious that he had no qualms. "She was jeopardising the experiment. Simple as that."

"Simple?"

"We needed Allenby to continue his work. There was no way we would allow a girl to stop us. We didn't know what was in her mind, but when she drove off in a hurry, we had to follow her."

"And stop her."

He grinned. "Permanently."

I held my tongue – and my fists.

"We had to get you back so that the doc could work his magic," he said, as if it was the most natural thing in the world to extinguish a life. I suppose, to him, it was easy, having been in the army. It was then that I remembered exactly how easy it is to kill, as I had done just that myself. I shuddered.

"Did Rufus know what you had done?" I demanded.

He chortled over his answer. "He didn't have a clue. We told him she had died in the crash, and the old fool accepted it. He even went along with us when we suggested he keep it from his next assistant, the lovely Miss Newman."

"So," I said, "how did you get it all past the authorities? What about Wolstenholme? There would have been questions…"

He didn't let me finish. He was in full flow now. "You think we don't have contacts? Man, you are dumb. We had a doctor in our pocket. He signed the death certificate, and everything went away – in a puff!" He emphasised the last word with a wide sweep of his arms and a smile that almost matched the gesture. "Wolstenholme didn't have a clue what we had done."

"The experiment was that important?" I scoffed.

"It worked, didn't it?" Packer said.

I wasn't sure how much he knew, so it was time to move on. "Your boss?" I said.

"What about him?"

"This is my third demand. I will hand over what I have from Rufus, but only to him."

"He won't agree."

"He won't get the parcel." I stood up and opened the door, letting Packer know that it was the end of the discussion. "So you might as well go now."

He pondered for several seconds, not moving. Then he said, "Sit down." His voice was soft, almost friendly, but it definitely held the tone of a defeated man. I sat, and he studied me. "What have you got?" he repeated.

"I'll tell your boss."

"He'll think you're bluffing. I need something."

That made sense, but I didn't want to give him too much. "Paperwork," I said.

"And?"

He obviously had a good idea what Rufus had taken away. "I haven't seen it, but I believe it's a microchip," I said.

He was amazed. "You haven't got it?"

"Ah," I said with a thin smile, "that's demand number four. I want safe passage back to the island. I need you to call off your dogs of war so that I can pick up the parcel."

He was slow to comprehend. "It's on the island? You have to pick it up?"

"Yes," I said. "I know where it is; I just have to pick it up." I felt as if I was talking to a class of five-year-olds, but that would probably be insulting the youngsters. Packer was even lower on the evolutionary table. "Can you remember all this? To relay to your boss, I mean."

Once more, he was lost for words, but from his expression I could see the fury bubbling beneath the surface. The twitch gave it away. Slowly, he began to get a grip. "Why should we believe what you're saying?" he asked, just for something to say while his mind found the right gear.

"Because we don't want to be holed up in this place for the rest of our lives. We all need closure, and this is the only way. You'll just have to trust me."

"Trust you?"

"I'm afraid so. I'm just lucky it's not the other way round, Packer. Trust would be in very short supply if it depended on you." I stood once more, and this time I wanted to make sure the discussion was over. "Tell your boss, once I'm on the island, he can show his face. He'll know where I am," I sneered, "because, like you told me, you always know. Good day, captain. My friend will see you out."

I opened the door to see Luigi hovering – my guardian angel. He smiled at me, scowled at Packer, and said roughly, "This way!"

Packer followed without comment, but his face gave away the churning inside, no doubt contemplating how he might rip me limb from limb when his boss gave the okay. He could cherish that thought, but it would never happen.

When Luigi slammed the door on him, I finally let out a sigh of relief. Even within the safety of this house, I still felt something strange when I stood next to Packer. It made no sense, but then again, that was what I was feeling about this whole sorry saga. I leant against the doorframe, gathering my thoughts as well as my wits, and Luigi offered me a comforting smile.

"He is gone. You may breathe again, *amico*."

I nodded, but before I could say anything, Robyn was at my side, pushing past Luigi and taking my hand. "Well?" she said.

"Looks good," I replied, not fully convinced. "We just wait for the okay from his boss. If not," I added wistfully, "we could be spending the rest of our lives here."

Luigi laughed nervously. "I hope not! I have no wish to be a full-time wet-nurse!" With that, he spun around and disappeared like an Italian Houdini.

Robyn chuckled; it was such a warm, intoxicating sound that I just had to reach out and pull her towards me. To my astonishment, she didn't resist, and I found myself wonderfully entwined with her, our faces so close that the tips of our noses almost carried out an Inuit welcome. We stood like that for several seconds, with me wondering how far I should push it, while my arms were pulling her ever closer. It was the right time. I tilted my head slightly and leant forward so that our lips met so lightly that the tingle I felt was exquisite, and I didn't want it to end. I pushed a little harder, and Robyn responded, her mouth opening slightly as a satisfied breath escaped. Then she was as desperate as me, as we kissed with such passion that nothing else mattered. It was as if all the problems that had built up over the last few days had been miraculously erased, and we were now in a place of serenity and love. I held her tight as long as I could while our tongues carried out their own explorations.

I just couldn't believe how good it felt. I stroked her back, her hair, then her face as we parted, breathless, excited.

Then Denver joined us, and the bubble burst.

"Sorry," he said lamely. "I hope I'm not interrupting," he added, knowing full well that he was.

Robyn was the first to react. "No problem," she said, shaking her hair back into place and bringing calm to the passionate seas that we had been sailing. "I need to be doing something anyway."

As an embarrassed Robyn pushed past him, Denver gave me a sly smile. "At last, pal," he said. "You sure took your time!"

I gave him a less-than-playful punch on the arm in reply and sat at the table. I had a lot to think about.

Chapter Twenty-One

Packer's response came via a note presented at the door by a scruffy minion with a scowl on his face and halitosis on his breath. Dressed in the almost regulatory dark-coloured suit and open-neck shirt of the gangster, he gave the impression of being a down-market mafioso postman – no offence meant, Luigi. He said nothing, just outstretched a hand bearing a tattoo naming a girlfriend, or perhaps his mother.

I got this report from Luigi's man, who had taken the proffered note and slammed the door as a way of shutting out the vermin. I had also been bending the curtain for a glimpse through the window, so I saw the skeleton ear-ring which the Italian had missed. He passed the note to me, and I read it to myself before proclaiming to my expectant audience, "We're on!"

"What does it say?" Robyn asked.

We were all sitting round the table – me, Robyn, Denver, Gregory and Luigi. Coffee had been consumed with Garibaldi biscuits (appropriately), but now I had something else to digest. The discussion had centred on Packer and how we were going to play out our strategy. I say *strategy*, using the word loosely, as I did with most decisions I had to make. I suppose that comes with being a multi-millionaire who has spent the last six years doing absolutely nothing of worth – and who knows how many years before that.

"It says," I summarised, "that they will allow me safe passage."

"Only you?" Denver said.

I nodded.

"Are they crazy?" he asked rhetorically. "You can't go alone, David."

"They have booked me a flight with BA at eleven tomorrow morning. One way."

Everyone began to talk at once, the voices mingling and rising in a crescendo of disbelief. Robyn's was the loudest. "This is madness!"

I reached across the table for her hand, which she gave me without hesitation, squeezing mine in solidarity.

I was thinking quickly. "You booked our flights, Gregory?"

"Yes, sir. We were due to fly out the day after tomorrow." He frowned. "I didn't realise it was going to be this critical."

"None of us did," I soothed him. "I will just have to stall them until you get there."

"What?" Robyn's voice sounded even sharper.

I made an effort to ignore her, as difficult as that was. "Gregory, see if you can get an earlier flight. Luigi, we need to come up with a plan to get Denver and Robyn out of this house before I leave tomorrow morning. When I get to the island, I don't want to be alone for too long."

"No problem," he said, although I had my doubts.

As it turned out, he was right.

* * *

Denver left the house three hours later, after an Italian make-over which included eye-shadow, colouring and a beautiful fake moustache which he said tickled. It tickled me, too, when I saw it. He looked more Sicilian than the man standing next to him, which was just as well, because he *was* that man when he walked through the front door with another of Luigi's men, both belly-laughing at a supposed joke and Denver's colleague uttering the immortal words from *The Godfather*, "Te voy a hacer una oferta." *A nice touch*, I thought, especially as Packer had made me an offer I couldn't refuse. Denver's laughing response to the line was perfection as the two of them sauntered down the road without attracting the slightest interest from the guys in the black sedan parked nearby.

It was clear, however, that Robyn was going to need a little more finesse with her escape. Because Packer's guards were well aware that she was the only female in the house, her departure would attract a lot more interest. Luigi solved this with his usual aplomb. He held a party!

As dusk began to settle, there was a knock on the door, and when it was opened, a stream of Italians made their noisy way in, laughing and waving bottles of champagne and Prosecco as they greeted Luigi with hugs from the women and high-fives and fist-bumps from the swarthy men who looked as if they had just come off the set of a Versace advert. The women were absolutely stunning, and both Gregory and Robyn gave them the once-over for two very different reasons. Gregory was almost salivating at the beauty, while Robyn was appraising the cut of the dresses on display. I have to confess, I, too, was taking more than a passing interest.

From their arrival, the ambience of the place, along with the volume, went up a few notches. Music from the eighties blasted the ears, and swirling dancers dazzled the eyes as everyone was intent on having a great time. I couldn't believe what I was seeing, so I took Luigi to one side.

"What the hell…?"

"Relax, my friend," he said in a melodic tone, as if he was speaking in sync with the music. "You not like?"

"Yes," I found myself saying, "I do like. But what is your plan?"

"To have fun, *mio amico*! What is that famous line? 'Enjoy life today, for tomorrow we die'."

"Mm, something like that," I smiled. "Although I'm not too happy about that prognosis. Tomorrow I get on a plane…'

"*Sì*, and tonight your lady gets out. Trust me."

I did, implicitly, but, somehow, that didn't stop me worrying.

With a wide grin, Luigi sashayed elegantly across the room and hooked up with one of the women, placing one arm around her waist while also gripping her right hand, before swinging her round and beginning what I could only guess was some kind of Italian folk dance. Whatever it was, the couple remained very close, and I couldn't help wondering what it would be like with Robyn.

With my mind transfixed on that thought, I wandered over to the window and pulled at the corner of the curtain for probably the thousandth time that day. The view hadn't changed too much. The two goons were in their car, as usual, but at least our loud music was causing them some concern, for they had the window down, and one of them was leaning out, looking our way, phone at his ear, presumably giving Packer a running commentary on the shenanigans taking place in this den of iniquity. I couldn't see the other man clearly, just a shadow in the other front seat, but it seemed to me that he was rocking to the beat.

I felt a tap on my shoulder. "David, I would like you to meet my niece, Constantia."

I dropped the curtain and swung round to come face to face with one of the most beautiful women I have ever seen – and a grinning Luigi. I took her proffered hand, so soft and slender, and shook it gingerly, careful not to break the delicate bones within.

"Hello, David," she said in such a seductive Italian lilt that I inwardly gasped, if not outwardly.

"Hello... Constantia," I babbled.

She was probably only a couple of years younger than me, so I doubted if she really was Luigi's niece, but perhaps the Italians use the word differently to us. She wore a simple smock dress of green chiffon, short but not excessively so, marking her out as sophisticated but tantalising at the same time. Her face bore little make-up, and her hair was jet black, mid-length, and cut into a layered bob, which framed her face perfectly. I was amazed that I hadn't noticed her when she came in.

As if reading my mind, Luigi said, "Constantia has just arrived. She walked here."

"I'm very glad you did," I said to her, still holding her hand.

She smiled sweetly and pulled her hand away. "Uncle Luigi wanted me to help you, David," she said softly, mischief in her eyes.

I didn't have a clue what she meant, but then again, it didn't seem to matter. Belatedly and somewhat guiltily, I looked round for Robyn, but she was nowhere to be seen, so, almost reluctantly, I said, "I should go and find..."

"Oh, never mind that!" Luigi broke in. "The night is young, my friend. Let us party!"

He whisked Constantia away in a blur, and I was lost in myself again. So much had happened, and yet here we were, enjoying ourselves as if nothing else mattered. No wonder I was confused.

I was also missing Denver. How sad was that?

The music, if anything, seemed to be getting louder, the voices more raucous, as if everyone else was contemplating the end of the world and were desperate to wring the very last ounce out of life before the Apocalypse. Gregory was throwing himself into it all with gusto, his twinkling toes waltzing round the room, his partner holding on for dear life, a look of panic on her face.

Me? I just stood there for some time, drink in hand, until finally turning my back on the crowd, my mind so far away that nothing registered until I felt a tap on my shoulder.

"David, I would like you to meet my niece, Constantia."

I swivelled, about to tell Luigi that I had already met her, when I came face to face with one of the most beautiful women I had ever seen. The green chiffon dress, the layered bob hairstyle – it was Constantia, and yet it wasn't.

"Robyn?" I gulped.

Luigi slapped my back heartily and gave a loud laugh. "You took your time recognising your own girlfriend!" he chuckled. "My plan is obviously working, David."

"Your plan, Luigi?" I spluttered. "I'm not sure I'm with you."

"Duplicitousness, David."

"That's easy for you to say!"

"Not for an Italian, it isn't, my friend. But I understand the word and its meaning. You remember I told you that Constantia – the real one," he said with a wide grin, "walked here?"

I nodded.

"All part of the master plan. I wanted the *hombres* outside to notice her so that when she leaves this place, they will perhaps ogle from a distance, but they will not realise that Constantia is not what she seems. Simple, no?"

"Simple, yes," I said. "But will it work?"

"You have trusted me so far, *amico*."

"Yes," I said hollowly, not feeling the confidence that Luigi was emitting. Without thinking any further, I took

Robyn's hand and led her out of the noisy room to a sanctuary where we could talk. She sat on my bed and looked up at me. I could see the warmth in her eyes, but also the trepidation. I assumed that she, too, had doubts about Luigi's plan.

"It will work," I found myself saying as I sat beside her, taking her hand and stroking it. "We must have faith."

Robyn gave a watery smile. "It's not that, David." Her voice trailed away in despondency, but I could still see a spark in her eyes. Then I realised. She wasn't worried about the plan or scared for herself; she was fearful of what might happen to me. She was looking into the unknown and seeing nothing but shadows and darkness. I had to do something to allay her fears.

So I told her. Yes, I told her everything. From the moment Rufus accosted me on the beach, to the gunmen who chased us across the sand dunes and into the caves, to the moment when Rufus breathed his last. I explained how we had got away on a lobster catcher's boat, how I took a man's life for the first time, and how I had no qualms, no conscience about doing so. I told her how meeting her was the most precious moment of my life. Then, with my heart in my mouth, I confided in her my greatest secret, and I waited.

She took a long time to digest it all and to respond. She eventually asked, "Your body can repel bullets?" Her face was a picture of amazement and awe.

I nodded, not sure my voice would work again. Then I pulled her close, so close that her next question was

306

muffled by my embrace. "Final proof that Dr Allenby did lie to me."

"Yes," I mumbled, fully aware that I was breaking part of her heart. "He must have put me through that machine enough times to make my bloody corpuscles immune to everything." I was surprised by the sound of my voice; it was full of hatred, and I hated myself for that. Yet I still couldn't stop myself from feeling some respect and admiration for the man.

Robyn pulled herself away from my grasp. "It's time," she said with a resolution that astounded me. "I will be with you on the island, David."

"Yes," was all I could say as she stood and stroked my cheek before making her way to the door.

"I love you," she said softly, then disappeared from view without a backward glance.

My mouth formed the same words, but nothing came out.

I had never felt so alone.

Chapter Twenty-Two

The next morning, I awoke remarkably fresh. Last night, I had half-thought about accompanying Robyn to the front door and giving her a kiss goodbye, but Luigi and common sense would have squashed that idea. Instead, I sulked in my room with a bottle of scotch until I fell asleep just after midnight.

Now, getting out of bed, I felt the effects of the scotch, but a long and soothing shower rekindled my energy and set my mind to the task ahead. I dressed quickly, aware that I had a flight to catch, and made my way downstairs.

The kitchen was quiet, apart from the scraping of a butter knife across toast as Gregory tucked in as only he could. He nodded briefly at me before returning to his job at hand.

I poured myself a coffee and sat beside him, nursing my cup thoughtfully.

"Good news about Robyn," Gregory said without looking away from his breakfast.

"Yes," I said. In her guise as Constantia, Robyn had made good her escape last night, as Luigi had loudly and triumphantly confirmed when he relayed the coded text message she had sent him late in the evening. I found out later that she had made her way from the house to a waiting car with nothing more than a wolf-whistle molesting her, and I could imagine that must have been bad enough.

Luigi came in at that moment, a smile and what looked like relief on his face. "David, welcome to your last day with us. Did you sleep well?"

He gave the impression of someone who had spent many hours toiling in the fields. His sleeves were rolled up, revealing a fair amount of muscle for a man of his advanced years, and he had sweat on his brow. The scarlet bandana round his neck added to the picture of a rustic idyll.

"Yes, thank you, Luigi," I said between sips of the life-enhancing coffee. "Been busy?"

He grinned. "Oh, yes, my friend. Always busy. Like a bee, as you say. Removing all traces of your stay."

"That's nice," said Gregory out of the corner of his mouth.

Luigi threw him a disarming smile. "So we can get back to normal, *mio figlio*."

I look at Gregory. "*Mio figlio*?"

"A term of endearment, sir. 'My son'. Not literally, naturally."

I shrugged. Anything might have been possible in this crazy world.

I finished my coffee and went back to my room. It was time to pack the few possessions I would be taking with me: clothes, wash things, a book for the journey. How *normal*. The folder from the laboratory I was entrusting to Gregory. It would mean nothing much to Packer and his boss, but I valued it for sentimental reasons because it was the only potted history of my life I would ever have. Perhaps, one day in the future, I could sit on the seashore while Robyn explained all the figures to me as I wallowed in the sweetness of her voice and the breezy balm of that tropical island.

I was brought back to the present by a tap on the door, and one of Luigi's men informed me that the car had arrived. I stood up, almost reluctantly, and looked around. This room, this house, had been a safe haven for us all, and it seemed mad to be leaving. The Italians had built a protective wall around us, and, one by one, we had breached it ourselves, leaving safety for an unknown destiny. And yet, it had to be this way. I saw no other alternative. It was time to face up to my past... and my future.

Downstairs, Luigi, Gregory and a couple of others appeared to be forming a guard of honour for me as I made my way to the door. I shook the hands of Luigi's men and nodded my gratitude. They appeared embarrassed at the show of feeling and took a step back. Luigi was not so reticent, wrapping me up in a huge bear hug, which almost took the wind out of my sails. Then he slapped me hard on the back.

"Good luck, my friend. We have enjoyed your company," he said, and I swear I could see a tear in his eye, although he would have denied it vehemently had I commented.

I broke away and took his right hand in both of mine. "I don't know why you have helped us, Luigi, but I'm mighty glad you did," I said with feeling.

A look passed between him and Gregory, and I knew not to ask. There was something that they shared, and, once more, I sensed the overpowering skill that Rufus

Allenby must have had to bring us all together.

I looked through the open doorway. The two goons were still there, sitting in their car, watching the proceedings with slightly less enthusiasm than previously. They knew that this particular job was coming to an end, and they looked relieved at the prospect. Now, perhaps, they could go back to cracking skulls and breaking fingers for their leader's pleasure.

The car waiting for me was a white saloon, quite innocuous, the driver standing by the open rear door, his hand gripping the handle. He was a big man, his face like concrete, pitted and world-weary, and I knew that he wouldn't take any nonsense, a fact emphasised by the holster I could see beyond his open suit jacket.

I pulled Gregory aside. "You know what you have to do?" I whispered.

He grinned. "Don't worry, sir. Aunt Grace and I will tidy up this end."

I had no doubts of that. The closure of Gavin Wolstenholme's nest of vipers was in safe hands. Grace and Gregory, with help from their police buddy, would be more than enough to see off any government interference, especially now that the facts were becoming public knowledge. I could rest easy on that score.

I shook Gregory's hand and walked hastily to the car, my bag in my hand and a worried look on my face. I couldn't be sure if I would ever see any of my friends again... and that point hit home with brute force when I slipped into the car seat and found myself next to Captain Packer himself.

PART THREE

The Island

Chapter Twenty-Three

It wasn't an enjoyable trip. Six hours on a regular BA flight, then ninety minutes on an island-hopper, all in the company of the one man I hated most in the world, who stuck closer to me than a limpet mine to the hull of an enemy ship.

There was no conversation, of course. Packer just sat there, rigid, a permanent scowl on his face. It was enough to frighten the children.

I tried to read my book, but my eyes wouldn't focus, so I gazed out of the window and across the aisle at some of my fellow passengers, most of whom were clearly on their way to a holiday in paradise. I was going their way, but I didn't have a clue where it would lead me.

I thought of Robyn and Denver. Their flight wasn't until tomorrow, and I wondered what they were up to now. The taste of freedom must be wonderful for them, and I briefly held the thought that they might not come to the island at all, opting instead to stay well away from me. I felt guilty for harbouring such an idea.

I was sure that Packer hadn't been alone on the planes. On the BA flight, I saw one or two devious-looking characters who might have been his accomplices, although only one of them joined us on the shorter flight. Perhaps I was doing the others a disservice, and they could have been innocent after all.

The change of plane went smoothly enough, Packer matching my steps as I made my way to the smaller craft, this time with far fewer people to contend with, but I could see the other man loitering at the end of the queue, trying to look nonchalant, and failing dismally. I could even see the worry lines on his face and hoped they were because he hated flying. Serves him right.

Packer crunched his tall body into the bucket seat behind me, and I heard an audible groan. At least I didn't have to look at him on this flight, although I could feel his eyes drilling into the back of my head.

I had spent most of the journey wondering how I was going to play this. I wasn't going to throw off Packer and his goon, that was for sure, but I needed to come up with a plan. However, after seven and a half hours, nothing had come to me.

When the island-hopper touched down, I was still in a quandary. I deliberately took my time undoing my seatbelt, retrieving my hand luggage and shuffling down the length of the plane. I could hear Packer tutting behind me, and I also noticed that his associate had carried out a quick exit, presumably just in case I made a dash for it.

It was around mid-day local time, and as I emerged from the plane, I blinked away the sun's glare, but I could not avoid the humidity, which always caught me unawares whenever I came here. Already, my shirt was beginning to stick to me. I stopped in the doorway and put on my sunglasses – designer Italian ones loaned to me by Luigi.

Very swish and macho, but they still only did the same job as the cheap ones from down the high street.

I felt a nudge in my back and immediately stiffened, waiting a few more seconds before moving. I took a small delight in annoying him, but, in the end, I knew I had to get off the plane, so I edged forward, inches from the woman in front, who was manhandling two young children as well as several bags. It couldn't have been much fun for any of them being cooped up in such a small plane, and I sympathised. I hoped they were going to have a good holiday.

The airport was extremely small, so it didn't take long to disembark and walk across the tarmac to the arrivals hall. It was a new building designed by some American architect with a double-barrelled name and an expensive outlook on life. There was tinted glass everywhere, as well as what looked like native teak forming the frame and the internal furniture. Heavy and beautiful. It was like walking into a new temple dedicated to some ancient god of flight.

There was a surprising amount of activity, so I assumed there was an imminent outbound flight, but even so, there was still no room for escape. Packer had teamed up with his friend, and they stood behind me as close as they could get. I could feel Packer's hand on the small of my back. I knew he didn't have a gun, but I still felt intimidated enough to remain where I was in the queue, waiting patiently for the official to stamp passports and scrutinise faces. *Perhaps Packer had a record and would be detained?* I held that thought.

I felt rather than saw the three men as they approached, and, as I turned, I could see that two of them were wearing the uniform of the island's police force. The third man, a tall, wiry individual, was in a short-sleeved shirt and grey slacks, the stand-out item being the huge buckle on his belt, which could almost have been his badge of authority. He radiated officialdom, and I noticed how the locals moved apart for him as he strode purposefully through the concourse, the click of his expensive shoes playing music on the marble tiles.

I didn't take a lot of notice, but I could see that Packer was agitated by the sight, and he shuffled closer to me, his grip on the back of my shirt getting tighter.

As we stood there, I suddenly began to feel a sense of doom, and it didn't surprise me at all when the small deputation came to a halt in front of us.

The wiry one spoke. "Mr Parks? David Michael Parks?" His voice was remarkably cut-glass, like that of an Oxford don.

I turned to face him and saw the steel in his eyes. "Yes." My voice faltered.

"Mr Parks, I would like you to accompany us, please." The last word seemed superfluous, as there was no chance of me saying no to him.

"May I ask what this is about?" I said.

"You need to come with me, Mr Parks. Please, let me have your passport."

I had been holding it tightly, ready to show to Customs, but the wiry man whipped it away and put it in the breast pocket of his shirt. "Thank you," he said with a shrug, as if I had happily offered him my passport, and this was an everyday occurrence.

"I would like to know who you are," I said, "before you drag me away."

His grin widened. "Oh, Mr Parks, we can most certainly drag you away if that is what you wish." He paused, the smile disappearing. "I am Inspector Munroe," he said, flashing his warrant card, "and I have been asked to detain you on behalf of the British Government in respect to certain crimes committed there."

I could feel Packer's grip releasing my shirt just as my heart sank. "Crimes?" I said, my throat dry.

"I will not go into detail here, Mr Parks. Please do not make this awkward... for you or me."

Packer was moving away even as the policeman was speaking, distancing himself from what was going down. I could just visualise his scowl getting larger with every second. I took a brief glance in his direction, and I could see him making for the door, his accomplice fast on his heels. This should be something to report to his boss.

There was a small crowd gathering, not too close, but within earshot, and it was clear that Inspector Munroe was hoping I wouldn't make a scene. His officers had their hands on their holsters to enforce the intimidation in the inspector's eyes.

"Mr Parks?" he said, and I turned back to him.

"Yes, of course, Inspector. Whatever you say."

The crowd looked a little disappointed as I went willingly, matching Munroe's stride and followed by his officers as we made our way out of the building and into the waiting police car. I was bundled into the back, sandwiched between the officers, while Munroe got in beside the driver and ordered him to move into the traffic, lights blazing and horn blaring. I couldn't see Packer.

"So, Inspector, perhaps you can tell me what this is about now," I said, not really expecting an answer. I didn't get one.

It took about fifteen minutes to get downtown and into the yard of the small police station. The island had a reputation for being fairly crime-free, no doubt because of the armed policemen and the demands of the tourist industry. What little unlawful activity there was usually involved drugs on the beach or in the darkened car parks of the numerous night clubs after they closed at the legal time of two a.m. I had experienced no problems at all... until now.

The police station was old, perhaps from the 1950s, and sad. The paintwork was patchy, a soft peach colour turning green in places, and the window frames were paintless, the bare wood cracking from the incessant sunshine. It was as if somebody had sand-papered everything in readiness for a new coat of paint and had then stopped, deciding they weren't going to bother. The place looked unloved.

I was allowed to get out of the car under my own volition, but then the officers grabbed my arms and led me through the almost-black door and into an air-conditioned lobby where a rather large sergeant resided on a podium behind a huge counter. He stood to attention the moment he spotted Munroe, at the same time giving the evil eye to the miscreant who had just been brought before him.

"Name?" he rasped.

"David Michael Parks," I murmured in response.

"What?"

"David Michael Parks," I said a little louder.

The sergeant looked at Munroe. "Charge, sir?"

"No charge... just yet. We are holding him," Munroe said.

"Yes, sir," said the sergeant, and he wrote something in his ledger. He looked down at me. "Right, empty your pockets and remove your watch and belt, as well as your shoes."

I complied with his order stone-faced, not wanting to antagonise them and make matters worse. It meant that my trousers were hanging a bit loose, but that was the least of my worries.

"Take him to the holding cell," the sergeant ordered the two officers, his voice of authority booming round the room, and they responded immediately by marching me down a dim corridor to a cell that looked like it had been taken from an old James Cagney movie. There was a metal bed with the thinnest mattress I had ever seen, together with a multi-coloured blanket that could be conservatively classed as moth-eaten. Beside it was a small, rickety table, while in one corner was a chemical toilet which was giving off obnoxious gases, and in the other corner was a stained sink with one tap and a constant drip.

I offered the officers a beseeching look, which they ignored, and I found myself being pushed into the cell, before hearing the dull thud of the door closing and the clunk of a bolt being thrown. This was desolation.

I sat on the bed and surveyed my surroundings. It didn't take long. I couldn't fail to notice the lack of windows and the bare brickwork with mortar missing in several places, as well as a number of artworks left by resident artists from years gone by. One or two had been etched using a primitive tool of some kind – perhaps the sharpened handle of a spoon – but most of them had been created using paints probably stolen from a distant art room, or blood, or... I didn't want to dwell too long on that. All I knew was that no matter how bright and sunny this island was, I now found myself well and truly on the dark side.

* * *

I had lost track of the time. I had tried to rest on the bed, but that didn't work, so I sat on the edge, feeling the cold floor on my feet and the churning of my stomach. I was certainly out of the frying pan, and I didn't understand how it had happened. One minute, I was being chaperoned rather heavily by Packer, and the next, here I was incarcerated in a cell, with no rhyme or reason as to why. Munroe had talked about 'crimes' back home. I presumed he meant in the house with Wolstenholme, but I had thought I was in the clear on that one, so I was baffled. I would just have to wait and see what developed.

An hour or so later, a guard brought me a meal of

some kind of plastic-flavoured curry with rice, laid out on

Chapter Twenty-Four

Munroe was toying with me. As I sat back on my bed, I wondered how much he knew, how much he suspected, and how little I had going in my favour. Now, I was in a place of desperation, facing Packer on one flank, the British government on the other, and Inspector Munroe pushing hard at my rear. Even the Duke of Wellington might have crumbled at such an onslaught. I longed for the peace and tranquillity of Luigi and the Italian Mafia.

The bed was still uncomfortable, but I tried to make the most of it. I roughly estimated that it had probably been close to midnight when Munroe spoke to me – those diplomatic soirées do tend to go on a bit, and the inspector definitely looked tired – and here I was, tossing and turning, almost certainly several hours later, my mind more active than my tired limbs as sleep eluded me.

The next thing I registered was a shout of some kind and the door opening. I assume the guard had told me to keep back like before, but everything was a bit foggy, as I had obviously nodded off. I blinked several times and then sat up. "What time is it?" I asked, my mouth dry.

"Breakfast time," a new guard said without feeling, and, as he stepped aside, a second new guy came in with my plastic breakfast and placed it unceremoniously on my little table. They looked smarter than the evening crew: neatly pressed shirt, top button done up, tie straight, as if they had just passed muster at Police Academy. No humour, though.

"Thanks," I mumbled, grateful to see that a steaming mug of coffee was on the tray. "I need that." I scooped it up and drank thirstily, oblivious to the heat and the eyes watching me, until I emptied the mug. It was certainly a step up from the tap water I had been sipping during the night.

I put the mug back down on the tray and looked at the breakfast. Not very appetising, and I wasn't hungry anyway, so I said, "You can take that away, thanks." I could have added 'and feed it to the dogs', but that would only antagonise them. Instead, I said, "Time for the next grilling, is it?"

The guard who had picked up the tray gave a hollow laugh at that. "No, not yet. The inspector is elsewhere this morning. You're safe – for now."

With a straight face, the other one said, "This is your time for rest and recreation." Then they left, chuckling among themselves, and slammed the door shut. Silence.

Dreadful silence. Enough to drive a man mad. In anguish, I made a fist of my right hand and thudded it several times into the mattress, coughing on the dust particles that had been disturbed. I had had enough of the bed, so I crouched against the door, surveying my domain and swearing under my breath. Robyn suddenly came into my mind, and my breathing began to settle. It occurred to me that it might not be so bad after all. Then, without warning, I began to well up, feeling a cramp in my stomach and a sense of utter defeat in my head, until I started to cry uncontrollably, rocking from side to side with my knees up, my hands cradling them, and my head bowed. Perhaps I was going mad.

It was the second time I had broken down, and I felt a maddening sense of frustration for letting myself get into that state. It sure as hell wasn't going to get me through this, and I fought against it so much that by the time the guards came again, I was as near as possible back to sanity.

I was expecting lunch, but instead got another surprise.

They cuffed me and led me back to the Interview Room. There was no communication, of course, but I somehow sensed a variation in atmosphere, a lightening of the hardness, as if they were aware of a change in the circumstances. I didn't know if this was a good thing.

When they knocked and then opened the door, the first person I saw was the sergeant, sitting behind the desk formerly occupied by his inspector. He looked uncomfortable, as if he was usurping his superior, and I took a little delight in his fidgeting.

I hadn't noticed the other man in the room, who stood to the left, almost as if he was trying to be unobtrusive. He was a dapper-looking man, quite old, I thought, dressed in a designer woollen coat which was open, revealing a charcoal-coloured three-piece suit, a fob watch chain hanging from the waistcoat. He wore a navy tie with a crest, and as he stepped out of the shadow, I saw a pair of sparkling eyes, an aquiline nose, and a top lip almost hidden by a chevron moustache which had been neatly trimmed but which still dominated his face. When he spoke, his British voice carried authority.

"David Michael Parks?"

When I nodded, he said, "You do not have to say anything, but it may harm your defence if you do not mention when questioned something which you later rely on in court. Do you understand?"

"What the…?"

"Do you understand, Mr Parks?" the man pushed, his eyes never leaving mine.

"You're cautioning me."

"Yes," he said. "I am Superintendent Neil Starkey, and I have just cautioned you prior to escorting you back to England."

The sergeant looked as shocked as me. His mouth was open wider than mine, and I could only imagine the conversation he was going to have with his inspector.

He gathered his wits a little quicker than me. "You cannot do that, sir."

Starkey turned on him. "You think, sergeant?"

The local man cowered, so Starkey pressed home. "This man is wanted in connection with serious crimes, sergeant, and I intend taking him back to face justice – now!" His voice was authoritative, booming, and even the little room seemed to wither at the sound of it. I gave the sergeant an A+ for attempting to withstand the onslaught.

"I will need to speak with my superior… sir."

Starkey was having none of it. He was clearly on a mission. "No, sergeant, I cannot wait. We have a flight to catch. We go now. Draw up the paperwork." He looked from the sergeant to me and back again. "And remove the 'cuffs."

"But, sir…"

"That is an order, sergeant. This man is now under my jurisdiction."

"Yes, sir," the sergeant bleated like a lost lamb. He went to the door, opening it to reveal the two guards, now standing crisply to attention as if in the presence of an icon. Well, it was a Metropolitan Police Officer. The sergeant whispered something to one of the guards, who performed a perfect about-turn and raced away. After another word from the sergeant, the second guard dutifully came in, took off my handcuffs and resumed his station outside the door, not a flicker on his face. The sergeant, on the other hand, was fuming.

"My inspector…"

"Is out of the office," Starkey finished for him, although I was pretty sure that wasn't what the sergeant had intended to say. "You are in charge here now, and you are handing over a suspect to me. You are fulfilling your obligations, sergeant, for which I am grateful."

It was only a matter of minutes before the guard tapped politely on the door and came in with a sheet of paper. It was clearly a standard-issue form. He also handed over my belt and shoes, which I quickly put on. The sergeant indicated with a nod of his head that the form should be given to the British policeman, and Starkey took out an expensive-looking fountain pen and signed it. Another nod from the sergeant dismissed the guard, and an uneasy silence filled the room. It looked to me as if Starkey was enjoying himself.

"Thank you, sergeant. I will inform your inspector how well you have undertaken your duties," he said, guiding me to the door.

"Yes, sir," the sergeant said, although there was no enthusiasm in his voice.

We made our way to the front door with no further conversation, and it gave me time to understand fully the predicament I was in. Here I was, heading back to England, while Robyn and Denver might very well have already arrived on the island. My future was uncertain, to say the least, and I still wasn't sure what the police had on me. I thought they didn't have any records, especially as I didn't even own the house I lived in. Perhaps that was it. The police had connected the place to me somehow, and I was being held to account for the men we had killed there. If that was the case, I would, of course, plead self-defence, but I wasn't convinced that would stand up in a court of law.

The sunshine hit me hard when I stepped outside. After hours in a windowless room, it was a shock to my system, and I blinked hard and held my hand over my eyes. For some reason, I had expected a police car to take me to the airport, but a local taxi had pulled up, and I vaguely recognised the driver. How ironic that somebody I knew was taking me away from paradise.

"Get in, Mr Parks," Starkey ordered, and I slid into the rear seat with a heavy sigh. It was all falling apart. "Thank you again, sergeant," Starkey was saying as he took his place beside me and then closed the door before the local policeman could respond, adding to the driver, "Let's go."

As the car pulled away, Starkey gave me a satisfied smile, and I felt like punching him there and then to add to my charge sheet. Then he said warmly, "That went smoothly. Oh, by the way, David, Grace sends her best wishes."

It didn't register at first, but then I said, "Grace?" My voice was several octaves higher than normal.

"It was all her idea. She realised that you would be alone on the island for a while, so she concocted a plan to keep you safe."

"Involving you," I said. "You're Grace's retired policeman." I thought he looked old!

"I am," he confirmed with another smile. "Grace asked me to phone the local police, tell them who I am – or *was*, I should say – and that you were a wanted man, and then I hopped on the first available flight. I do hope your overnight stay wasn't too uncomfortable."

Uncomfortable wasn't exactly the word I would have used, but with the threat of Packer having been taken from my mind for a few hours, I found it easy to laugh with him, and at the same time, I gave a silent thanks to my saving Grace.

One thing niggled, though. "So, how did you know Munroe would be out this morning?"

"Oh, we knew," he grinned. "The good inspector received a phone call."

"From you?"

"No."

"One of your colleagues, then?"

"Well, not exactly," Starkey said. "It was young Gregory, offering the inspector information on the whereabouts of your gang."

"*My* gang?"

We were both laughing. "Well," he said between bouts of euphoria, "he had to go check it out, didn't he?"

Indeed he did.

As my eyes began to water from the laughter, I looked out the back window and could just about make out the sergeant standing at the door of the little police station, phone to his ear. He was probably trying to explain to his inspector why, rather than going towards the airport, we were actually heading for the coast road.

Chapter Twenty-Five

We had picked up a tail. It was inevitable, but still annoying. I wasn't sure yet whether it was Packer with his tracker or the local inspector hot on our heels. Our driver, Logan, offered to try to lose them, but I knew that wouldn't work with Packer, so I asked him to maintain a steady course while I spoke to Starkey.

"So, what's the plan, Neil?" I said. "I assume Grace has thought of everything." It came out wrong, implying a slight on Grace I clearly didn't mean, and I bit my tongue for a second before trying to offer an apology. "Sorry, that wasn't very gallant of me."

Starkey didn't take umbrage on her behalf. "Actually, her only plan was for you to be safe until your friends arrived."

"They're here?" I said excitedly, rather like asking about the arrival of the guests at my fifth birthday party. Not that I remembered that, of course, but you know what I mean.

Starkey merely said, "That's where we're headed. They are waiting for you."

Logan lifted both arms from the steering wheel and waved them around triumphantly. "Morice has prepared everything, sir. It will be a humdinger!"

331

It was then that I remembered our driver. I had seen him a few times around the café, running errands for Morice and sometimes wielding a broom, usually in the same excitable manner I was witnessing now, although in the café he never put my life in danger. I was relieved when he put his hands back on the wheel.

"Hold tight, sirs!" Logan suddenly shouted, at the same time throwing the car sharply to the left and onto the sand, causing Starkey and me to collide and perform an almost balletic roll with the vehicle.

Before we could say a word, there was the sound of gunfire, and Logan pressed on the gas, kicking up sand, pebbles and dry seaweed in our wake. I tried to sit up, but Starkey was pressing on me, so I had to wait for him to right himself before I could look out of the rear window.

The car behind had stopped in the sand, at least one of its tyres deflated, and several men were running for their lives, heading for a tiny outcrop of rocks. We were increasingly moving away from them, so I couldn't make out who they were, but my strong feeling was that they were probably Bandits hired by Packer. They had separated, zig-zagging across the sand, dodging the bullets that were zinging past their feet and over their heads.

Logan was whooping as he drove the car with one hand, the other arm now waving furiously out of the window. "Go get 'em, ombres!" he screeched, and I felt the influence of both Denver and Morice in his sentiments.

"A planned ambush," I surmised.

"Apparently so," Starkey said drily. "Something I was not aware of when I signed up for this."

I grinned at him. "Grace will be very proud of you." And he actually blushed. Perhaps old love was in the air.

Two minutes later, Logan brought the car to a halt behind a dune, and we all took the opportunity to breathe again. Then we heard a honk, a sound I knew so well, and Denver's Moke swung into view, the driver performing a perfect wheelie in the sand.

I couldn't help myself. I jumped out of the car and was on the running board of the Moke before it had settled. "Muleshoe!" I exclaimed. "You're alive!" I ran my hands lovingly over the bodywork, cooing and purring like a love-struck swain.

"Very funny," Denver dead-panned. "You English are so fickle, throwing your love away to any beat-up jalopy you meet."

I pretended to frown. "Oh, don't listen to him, Muleshoe. He's just a tough-nut Yank." I stroked her again and said to Denver, "I thought she was a goner."

"Me, too, pal. But Morice knows a man who knows a man who used to maintain Kumass jets for the Israeli Air Force."

When I looked blank, he added, "That's Phantom jets to the uninformed."

"Okay…"

"He fixed her up good and proper. Shame he couldn't add the Phantom's firepower," he lamented, half-seriously.

I climbed in next to Denver and, despite the cramped conditions, gave him the biggest man-hug I could, and we held the pose for some time, both gripped by emotion and relief.

Finally, Denver pushed me away. "Shucks, man, what would the neighbours think?" His grin was as wide as mine as he said it.

I put on a cowboy accent for his benefit. "Sure was a warm welcome you gave us, pardner."

"Best we could do under the circumstances," he said. Then, "And stop with the voice. You sound like Cheryl Ladd doing an impression of Alan Ladd!" He went suddenly serious. "We need to get out of here. Those clowns will soon get their car back up and running. It was only ever a diversionary tactic to buy us a bit of time. I would have preferred gunning the lot of them down, but my country adheres to the Geneva Convention."

We got out of the Moke and said a fond goodbye to Neil Starkey. He had done us proud, at the risk of being struck off the Metropolitan Police Good Conduct List, but his time was over. He could return to England and the love of a wonderful woman – as long as Inspector Munroe didn't put the boot in. I just hoped that Starkey would get to the airport unmolested.

Logan took little time in driving his charge away, the sand scudding skyward as he accelerated, while we jumped into the Moke and headed in the opposite direction. The sun was low in the sky by now, and hunger was gripping my belly as I realised I had not eaten for many hours. It was a painful feeling, but I kept it to myself. There was something more pressing ahead of me.

Chapter Twenty-Six

I've never grown tired of the view. The golden beach, the gently lapping water of the ocean, the sky so blue it takes your breath away. Then there are the caves and the distant mountains, standing proud and majestic, as if surveying their own front garden with a fondness born of millions of years of nurturing and careful planning. There is nothing to spoil it. No human expansion or destruction, no pollution or corruption. *Pure*.

Denver stopped the Moke about half a mile from the caves. We had gone through a dense clump of palm trees into a clearing he obviously knew well but of which I had no knowledge as he had never brought me out here before. I could only imagine that the clearing was man-made, created by careful deforestation, which ensured seclusion while maintaining the natural beauty of the area.

At the centre was a small hooch which was leaning at a pronounced angle. The roof was corrugated, the walls' wooden trunks split lengthways, still with the bark, and all rusticly nailed together and covered with what appeared to be pitch, giving the place a dark and uninviting exterior. The creaking door opened, and there was Robyn, her face alight with relief, and we fell into each other's arms.

"I was so worried…," she began, but I silenced her with a kiss so powerful that it took us both by surprise.

"It's okay, it's okay," I said, as our lips reluctantly parted, but I made sure that I was gripping her hand tightly as we made our way into the hooch.

Inside, it was white and clean, the distempered walls smooth where the bare wood had been covered by some kind of render, which gave off a vague smell of cedar, which wasn't unpleasant. In one corner was a crumpled sleeping bag and a thick blanket, which I assumed Denver used when he crashed out here, and in the other corner, there was an old Welsh dresser, empty save for a frame which held a large picture of a stunning landscape I assumed was Denver's homeland, and beside it stood a couple of glass tumblers and the largest bottle of bourbon I had ever seen, half-empty. In the centre of the room, there was a chunky table with six mismatched chairs around it, some with quilted cushions, others just plain wood with years of use chiselled out of them. Morice was sitting on one of them, with two of his friends I recognised from the café standing behind him. Gregory sat a couple of spaces away, grinning as I entered. Like Robyn, he was very pleased to see me.

I couldn't hide my surprise. "What are you doing here? You should be with Grace…"

"Fear not, sir. She has all bases covered."

"Nice baseball reference, Gregory," Denver offered.

"Thank you, sir," said Gregory, pleased. Then he turned back to me. "I wanted to be here, Mr David," he said with feeling.

I gulped. "I'm grateful. Thank you."

Denver corralled me into one of the seats, and Robyn sat beside me, still holding my hand. Denver remained standing while he spoke.

"We need to be quick, David. Packer will be close behind, as you know."

"Yes," I said, "and a certain local police inspector might not be far behind him, either."

"Munroe?" Denver scoffed. "We don't have to worry about him." There spoke a man who sounded like he had experienced a few run-ins with the local constabulary and had come out on top. Why didn't that surprise me?

"This place," Denver continued, arms spread as if to embrace the entire building, "is an internet black hole. Nothing gets through – that's why I like it so much. I am also hoping that this will blind-side Packer's tracker, meaning he will have to hunt us down using more traditional methods."

"Sounds good," I said, not exactly convinced. "I will wait here for him and his boss. As per the plan, I need you all to be outside, nullifying his men. Inspector Munroe told me that they are using the local thugs…"

"The Bandits," Morice spat. "*Vermine!*"

"Agreed, pal," said Denver, "but I would have put it stronger than that."

Morice and his men picked up the rifles that had been leaning against the wall, shook my hand, and left in silence, knowing what was expected. Somehow, that made me feel a little less stressed. The Foreign Legion had my back. Gregory, keen as mustard to get in the action, picked up the last rifle and followed them out, offering a wave as he stepped through the door.

Denver went to the Welsh dresser and opened the cupboard doors at its base, and I was stunned when he pulled out a weapon I'd never seen before. He caressed it rather like a glass of fine wine or a fine woman, and his smile was almost flirtatious. "Beautiful, isn't she? This is my AR Five Seven; I picked it up in Venezuela a few years back."

There were so many questions in my mind, not least how it came into his possession, but I just asked, "How did you get it here?"

"What you Brits might call subterfuge, but what we call bribery. A friend of mine taped it to the engine of my Moke when they shipped it over. I get the cartridges online, like all criminals." His teeth shone through his wide grin. "Never been fired in anger... but that could be about to change!" He became serious. "We'll be out there, David. You just take care of yourself in here."

We shared a silent hug before he went through the door, leaving it open for Robyn to follow. She came close, and I took her in my arms.

"We shouldn't be doing this," she breathed in my ear. "There must be another answer."

I pushed her away, but only to arm's length. I needed to hold on to her as long as I was able. "I have to find out who is after me, Robyn. Only then can I start to see a way out of this."

She gave the slightest nod, accepting the fact that I was right. "Be careful, David," she breathed, planting a kiss on my cheek. I wanted to share more with her, but now was not the time, so I just squeezed her hand and let her go.

I was on my own.

* * *

It seemed that over the last few days I had spent so much time waiting, and now here I was, sitting in a strange building, on a seat with a plump red cushion, at a table… *waiting*. My life had almost become *Groundhog Day*. But at least it allowed time for thought. I could think of Robyn and the life ahead. I could think of endless days on the beach with my friends. I could think of Packer… and then the depression set in. What the hell was I playing at, waiting for a bunch of killers to walk through that door, rough me up more than a little, force me to talk about Rufus's microchip, then kill me any way they could, even if they couldn't shoot me?

I was sweating. My friends were outside, but they might as well have been a million miles away. And who knew how safe *they* were? Packer's Bandits could have wiped them out. Denver, Gregory, Morice… Robyn.

No, not Robyn! I wouldn't let that happen. Suddenly, I was back, my mind active once more with what I had to do. I slammed my hands on the table, feeling the blood rush and the adrenaline pump. I was ready. I had never been so ready.

It was at that moment I saw the door handle turn, and I was focused. The hinges squealed as the door swung away, and I could see the distant trees with just a glimpse of the sea through them, all dancing in the shimmering heat of the afternoon. I waited.

"We're coming in, Parks," Packer said from somewhere outside.

"Be my guest," I said. "It's an open house."

He stepped in, all camouflage gear and machismo, as if he owned this clearing and the whole of the island. Ever the soldier of fortune, as well as the military fatigues, this time he also wore a kepi to match and had a sub-machine gun slung over his back. He stopped in front of me, his legs slightly apart, hands behind his back, inspecting me. I stood and was pleased to see that I was at least two inches taller. I hadn't had time to notice before, but it gave me the confidence to smile at him.

"Welcome, *Mr* Packer," I said, knowing it would annoy him. A small but satisfying victory.

He ignored me, as I had expected, then came closer, taking a moment to survey the room to ensure I was alone. Then he barked, "Arms out, Parks."

I stood firm while he expertly frisked me. He wasn't gentle with it, either, and I could see the pleasure he was drawing from it. I stood my ground, if only to deny the man just a little of the satisfaction that was showing on his face.

He finished with me, rather like a child tossing away an old toy, before crisply shouting, "Okay to enter, sir!"

I waited. This was the moment when everything was going to fall into place.

A figure appeared in the doorway, his features obscured by the lack of light in the windowless room and the bulk of Packer standing in front of him. But I knew.

"Matthew Denny," I sneered.

He stepped round Packer, a smile on his face. "Very good, David. I am impressed. Rufus always spoke very highly of your intelligence." He moved into the room and paused to look me up and down, before pulling out a chair and sitting. "How did you work it out?"

I shrugged, as if my deduction had been child's play. "Your death in the boat was too convenient, too sudden. Too obvious."

Denny looked different. Over the last few days I had imprinted him on my brain after studying articles about him. I was convinced he was behind everything, and I wanted to be able to pick him out of a crowd if I needed to. Now he was here, next to me, and he was a changed man. Gone was the grey quiff, slicked down at the edges, the pencil moustache and the smile of bonhomie that had emanated from the photos that accompanied articles about this man-about-town entrepreneur, the multi-million-pound superman who controlled great swathes of industry both at home and abroad. He must have been in his sixties, but now he appeared even older, with a shaven head that sparkled from the sweat created by the humidity of the island, something he was not accustomed to. Without the hair, his ears looked larger, his eyes smaller, and the word rodent seemed to fit in so many ways.

I sat across the table. "It had to be someone who knew what Rufus was up to. Someone who had a finger both in the pie and on the pulse. It had to be you, Denny."

He gave a mock round of applause. "Bravo, David." His fixed smile stayed on me, encouraging me to continue.

"I assume Specs is outside," I said, causing his face to drop just slightly. "He's not dead, either, is he? You needed him as much as you needed the heavy brigade." I stared at Packer. "Probably more so. Specs was your inside man. Tell me, Denny, when did you turn him?"

The smile was still there, but was a little askew now. He chewed over my words and almost spat out his answer. "No, Specs is not dead. He is outside, monitoring your heartbeat. I am sure that it is racing, because you look frightened, David, and you do not know how this is going to end."

"And you do?"

"Oh, yes, David. I have total control."

"Or you think you do."

He leant back on the chair, the front legs lifting off the floor. "Specs was not a problem. I knew that money would talk, and if I dangled enough in front of his snout, he would be mine. Like everybody," he added with a look of distaste, and I sensed Packer stiffen.

"Is that what this is all about – money?" I said, watching him rock gently on the two legs of his chair.

"For some, of course," he replied with a sneer.

"But not for you," I stated. It wasn't a question. "So, tell me, why now? Why, after six years?"

342

He crashed the chair down and stood, the movement fluid and fast, surprising both Packer and me. He walked to the dresser and nodded at the bourbon. "May I?" he asked politely.

"Knock yourself out," I said.

He smiled at the thought, then dispensed a large tot of Denver's liquor before offering it to me. I declined, so he caressed the glass for a few seconds before returning to the table. This time, he didn't sit, but he hovered over me, his face close. "Why now, David?" he repeated my question. He took a swig of the bourbon and swirled it round his mouth, savouring the taste before swallowing. "Because the time is right."

"Meaning?"

He put the glass down and sat, but this time he was beside me, not across the table. I didn't feel comfortable with his close proximity, but I said nothing.

"The world is ready for change." He smiled. "The world is ready for me."

I waited.

"I want to tell you about my friend Rufus, David. I do hope you will bear with me."

I tilted my head. Not a nod, more a sign of resignation.

"I was very close to him in the early days. He was a savant, of course, but at the beginning he was a joy to be with. We would talk about his work. We discussed politics, we debated deeply on everything, even though we would probably have been seen as polar opposites."

I was mildly intrigued. "So what happened?"

343

He sipped his drink, presumably reminiscing the good old days with his friend. "Rufus came up with his formula, his solution to the ills of the world."

"That was for the greater good, surely?"

"Perhaps." He paused, looking me in the eye. "Perhaps not."

I waited.

"Tell me, David, are you happy with the world we live in?"

I didn't know how to answer. "On the whole," I said, non-committedly.

"But is that enough? Should we not all strive for a *better* world?"

I wasn't sure where this was going. "I don't follow."

"A *better* world," he repeated, as if it was some kind of mantra. "Surely we should all want that."

"Of course," I said.

"I believe that Mankind can create a new world, David. A new order."

At last, I saw where Denny was heading with this. "Communism," I whispered, as if the word itself was a poison stuck in my craw.

His eyes seemed to be beaming, his whole body alive. "It is the answer. I have long felt this to be the case, but recent events have led me to be much more optimistic."

"Events?"

"Putin in Ukraine, China controlling the world's computers and about to take over Taiwan. These are landmarks in history, David. We are on the march at last."

I stifled a laugh. "You're serious, aren't you? My god, Denny, you really are deranged."

He didn't rise to my comment. In fact, he chuckled, as if I had passed on the best one-liner he had ever heard. "Hitler was deranged. Stalin was deranged. Me, I am just – how can I put this? – a man with a mission. With Rufus's magic formula, I can protect whole armies, conquer nations and destroy unstable governments…"

He was going off into dreamland, and I couldn't help but wonder if he knew the full extent of what Rufus had done to me. If so, then he would certainly know how devastating his army could be. I brought him back to earth.

"But you don't have Rufus's formula," I said. "At least, not all of it."

"True, David," he said sweetly, as if he was talking to a favourite child. "But I soon will. Thanks to you."

"I don't think so," I said, trying to sound hard and decisive.

"You came here for a reason, David. To meet me, yes, but also to defeat me." He grimaced. "Oh, you poor fool. I know you have your ragtag army outside. My men are scouring the hills, looking for them as we speak. They will be of no help to you. Once we have rounded them up, you will be alone. At my mercy," he added with venom.

Bearing in mind what I knew about Denver and Morice, I very much doubted that Denny's Bandits would have the intelligence to overcome them, but I didn't say that. "The microchip is well hidden. You'll never get your hands on it."

Denny moved over to the dresser and poured himself another generous tot. "Let me tell you a story, David," he said from behind me. "Once upon a time, many, many years ago, there was an old ruler who wanted to reward one of his vassals for his bravery. 'What do you require as a prize?' he asked the man. 'You may have anything you wish.' The man looked at the ruler's chessboard. 'Sire, give me one grain of rice for the first square of that board, then double it for each subsequent square.' The ruler considered the man extremely foolish and agreed to the terms immediately." Denny was breathing over my shoulder, the smell of liquor mixing with the sweat to create a fug. "Do you know what happened, David?"

I knew, because I had heard the tale before. Should I burst his bubble by finishing the story? Hell, yes! "At square sixty-four, the servant had so much rice that he became richer than the ruler."

"Very good!" He didn't sound disappointed that I had stolen his thunder because he was about to come up with his own ending. "Now, we are going to play our own version of that game, David. On square one of the board, I shall execute one of your friends. Let me think… ah, yes, Miss Newman would do nicely. What do you say, David?"

I couldn't say anything.

"If the microchip is still not forthcoming, then for square two we will exterminate two more of your friends. Square three will be interesting because, by then, you will be running out of friends. This means we will have to take random shots at the public. Woe betide you if we get to any other squares, David. On your head be it."

346

Packer was enjoying this as well, and there was nothing I could do. I had to make a decision. "Okay, I'll take you to it. But I want assurances."

"Of course, you do," Denny leered. "Name your price."

I didn't hold out any hope that my wishes would be honoured, but I needed to sound like I was desperate. "You'll leave my friends alone?"

"In exchange, yes. A fair price."

"How do I know you will keep your word?"

"Ah," he sighed melodramatically. "That is something you are going to have to trust me on, I'm afraid, David."

There was that word again: *trust*. It was something I had in short supply. "And what of me?" I asked.

"Non-negotiable, I'm afraid." He left it at that, and I certainly didn't want him to elaborate. "Shall we go?"

I nodded and stood up. I had always wanted to tackle Denny in the open, where I had at least a fighting chance, but now the time had come my feet felt like lead, and my heart was pounding. I could imagine poor old Specs out there somewhere, rocking to the beat.

Packer opened the door and waited for me to step through. I hesitated, still unsure of the outcome, then carried on, knowing that Packer and Denny would be close behind, watching my every move.

I could have tried running... but then something unexpected happened.

Chapter Twenty-Seven

"Hands in the air!"

The cry came from beyond the trees, a disembodied but curt voice with a native twang and an official air. I recognised immediately the strident tone of Inspector Munroe. Where on earth had he sprung from?

"Stand where you are and drop your weapons!" An altogether different timbre, the vowels spread over a slightly higher-octave pitch. The sergeant.

It was only then that I realised Packer had swung his machine gun to the front and was brandishing it in a way that was not conducive to a happy outcome. Denny, too, had produced a firearm and was pointing it vaguely in the direction of the voices.

For a second, we were all immobile, confused. Then Packer opened fire, raking across the trees as he darted in the opposite direction. Denny didn't look too pleased with that, but he joined in, obviously hoping that the policemen would keep their heads down, before he raced after Packer and around the side of the hooch.

I was in two minds: give myself up to the police or go after Denny. The first option didn't rest well with me, as I knew it would not bring an end to my woes. No, I had to bring down Matthew Denny once and for all.

I looked around for the Moke, but Denver had obviously moved her to a safe place, so I ran for my life.

I was on Denny's tail, running haphazardly as if to avoid any bullets that might be coming our way. It was purely for show, of course, but it came naturally, along with the fear.

As I ducked past the hooch, I could see Packer ahead, firing into a clump of trees, from which fire was being returned tenfold, and I realised that Munroe must have brought his entire force with him. But where were Denver and the others – and where were the Bandits?

Using all his wiles, Packer offered one more burst of gunfire, then dived down and rolled expertly into the shelter of a bush, from which he maintained covering fire for the now-desperate Denny, who was slowing visibly, his age catching up with him at a rate of knots. He wasn't built for this sort of life, and I wasn't sure how long he would survive. He wasn't ready to quit, though, and finally, with a loud wheeze, he slid down next to Packer.

That just left me, out in the open, on my own and unarmed. I should have surrendered, but I needed to stay close to Denny. It was highly likely that anybody looking on from the hills would not have recognised him, and if he got away now, then that would be it. He would return to obscurity, from where he could wreak as much havoc as he wanted. I had no doubts that even without Rufus's microchip, Denny would find a way to obtain what he needed by securing the services of some foreign scientists to work it out for him. I couldn't allow that.

The firing had stopped momentarily, as if all parties were taking stock of the situation. It was then that I saw Packer turn to me and raise his gun. Perhaps Denny had come to the same conclusion – he didn't need me. Then I saw the look on Packer's face, and I knew that the parameters of the situation had definitely changed. It was clear that he wasn't going to let me get away this time.

I couldn't be sure if Packer was now calling the shots, but I knew that to have any chance of survival, I had to get to Specs and nullify his tracker. I couldn't beat Packer while he held all the aces.

I turned, feinted to go left, and then made a dash to the right, just as the guns began again. I wasn't sure who was responsible, but it was as though I could feel the bullets fired by Packer as each one whistled harmlessly past or off me.

Luckily, I found a narrow passage between some palms, and I scurried on, my footing firm in the sandy soil. I stopped for a moment, listening. The gunfire was still loud and close, but it was off at an angle, so I took the time to think the situation through. I had to assume that Specs was somewhere out front of the hooch, in a place where he had a wide view of proceedings. He would always know where I was, but I felt that he would prefer to keep Denny in sight at all times as well, so that narrowed his choices. He was presumably in touch with Denny – and probably Packer – through earpieces, so I anticipated that they were even now telling him to circle round the hooch in order to track me, knowing how bad the reception was here. That could work in my favour. Specs would need to be wary of

Munroe and his men, but I assumed they did not know of his existence, so he did have an advantage. After all, Munroe had come looking for me, not some mad megalomaniac and his gang.

I guessed that Specs would be heading to my right – the shortest path from his point of view – so I crouched low, regaining my breath, then worked my way through the trees, as silently as I could, in the general direction of where I thought my quarry was going to end up. I encountered no policemen or Bandits, but, more importantly, Packer didn't cross my path, either.

I made slow progress through the denseness of the forest, pausing against some of the trunks now and then as I listened for the sound of movement. There was silence all around me, as even the birds had flown from the outburst of gunfire. I controlled my breathing and steeled myself to remain calm, and I waited. In the distance, I could hear muffled voices, but they were a long way off and posed no threat. I couldn't be sure who they were, but I hoped it might be Denver and the others mopping up the last of the Bandits, or perhaps Munroe doing exactly that.

I heard the slightest sound. A twig cracking? A mole rat scampering? No, it was a continuous noise, a soft purring, not of an animal but of a machine. Then, I could see legs a few metres in front of me, and I raised my head to peer through the foliage. It was Specs. He had stopped, and I could see he was agitated. He was gazing at the machine in his hand while, at the same time, he was drawing a pistol from his belt. His breath was ragged, and I suspected he had been running so intently that he had

351

failed to look at his machine and had suddenly realised how close I actually was.

I took a moment to survey the area to make sure Packer wasn't looming, before I launched myself at Specs. Caught totally unawares, he stumbled backwards, dropping the tracker but holding tightly to his gun. He managed to get off a shot into the air before I tumbled into him, both of us hitting the ground with such force that we gave a chorus of grunts, before we rolled over, arms entwined, the pistol flying harmlessly away.

He was younger than me but smaller and less agile. Not quite a wimpy kid, but not far from it. His brain might have been bigger than mine, but in the world of Darwin, it is always the stronger who prevail.

We finally stopped rolling, and I ended up on top, astride him, pinning him to the ground. He had lost his glasses in the struggle, which allowed me the opportunity to swing my right fist into his face, causing untold damage to the bridge of his nose as I heard a bone crack and saw blood start to run down to his mouth. He stopped struggling, but I hit him one more time, just for the hell of it, before jumping off him and retrieving his tracking machine.

It was a dinky little thing, small enough to be held in one hand, and I could see orange and red lights flashing, as well as numbers. Co-ordinates, perhaps? It didn't really matter what the machine displayed; I knew I had to disable it immediately, before Packer and Denny arrived. I pulled the earpiece from Specs and put it in my ear, and I could hear heavy breathing and the dulcet tones of Packer swearing like the trooper he was.

Then Denny said through his deep breathing, "Specs, where are you?"

I ignored him and inspected the machine. I looked for a battery compartment, but there wasn't one. I turned it over, examining all sides.

"Specs, come in."

I shook it, held it to my clear ear and listened for tell-tale rattling where I might have dislodged some important component. Nothing.

"Specs? Specs?"

The lights were still flashing, so I hurled it against a tree, watching it bounce off undamaged. I put it on the ground and jumped on it. The lights still winked at me, untroubled by my heavy hands or feet. I shrugged with defeat, put the machine in my pocket, took one last look at the comatose Specs, retrieved his pistol, and moved on. At least with the tracker in my pocket, they wouldn't have access to my whereabouts. We were at last on a level playing field – but I still had the advantage of immunity.

I knew I had to aim for higher ground. To gauge where I was and to locate any other human being, I needed to be above everything, where the panorama would spread out below me, almost like a living map, so I headed for the hills.

My progress was slow, the terrain rough and mainly untouched, except by a few animals that roamed free. I stopped several times to rest and listen, but the silence was eerie, as if I alone walked the earth. Where was everybody?

As I stumbled on through the gorse-like features of the hill slope, I sensed that I was not alone any more, but still there was no sound or movement. Again I stopped, this time crouching, fully aware that something was out there. Then I saw him. He was prone, his rifle pointing not quite at me but at an angle, as if he was studying someone else. I got down on my belly and crawled slowly into some undergrowth, spending at least five minutes watching him. He didn't move, which I felt was strange. Only a trained sniper could remain motionless for that length of time, and I was sure that the local Bandits had not received élite military training. I also knew it wasn't any of my friends.

Cautiously, I crept forward, keeping my head low but my eyes sharp. If he moved now, I wasn't sure if I could get to him before he fired, and I could do without the whole area being alerted to my location.

Still, I had luck on my side, and I managed to get within a metre of him, closing in from the side. But, as I got nearer, I saw that there was something wrong. No matter how stealthy I thought I was, there was no way he would have missed my clumsy approach, and yet he still didn't turn or make any noticeable movement.

I was close enough now to rush him, fairly safe in the knowledge that I would reach him before he could raise his rifle and get a shot off – so that's what I did. I took a deep breath, then jumped up, ran as fast as I could and hurled myself at him, falling across his back as I raised a fist to punch him into submission. But I was too late.

Before I could land a blow, I saw that this Bandit was beyond pain as his body rolled slightly to one side, and I could see the deep gash across his throat and the massive pool of blood beneath him. Now I understood why there had been little gunfire in the hills – my friends were waging a guerrilla war against Denny's men, eliminating them with the knife rather than the bullet. I could almost see the killer pouncing, sitting astride this man's back, grabbing his hair and tugging at his head, before wielding the knife almost in the same movement. Swift... and deadly. I winced.

I tried to visualise Denver carrying out the attack, but my mind kept coming back to Morice. He had spent many more years on the island and probably knew all about the Bandits, as well as receiving thorough training in the Foreign Legion. Yes, this had Morice's DNA all over it.

I thought I was going to be sick but only retched once before I sat next to the corpse and rifled through his pockets. Nothing much: just a few cents and a mobile phone, presumably a burner given to him by Denny. Then I saw the skull ear-ring, and, for some reason, I just lost control. I ripped the ring from his lobe and threw it away, cursing under my breath. Suddenly, I was so angry, and I could feel tears in my eyes. I balled my hands into fists and was poised to use the body as a punch-bag, but I managed to regulate my breathing and began to calm down. Desecrating a body was not something I could do, but I did give it a gentle kick as I stood up, although that didn't make me feel any better. The only saving grace was that my friends truly had me covered, which meant I could concentrate on Denny and Packer.

I surveyed the valley below. The trees blocked the view somewhat, but I thought that perhaps I might pick up some movement. I didn't exactly expect to see metal glinting in the sunlight or hear the rustle of leaves, but I hoped there might be something. I spent possibly fifteen minutes just looking, my gaze going from left to right, then back again. Nothing. I couldn't wait any longer, so I rolled the body over a little more so I could get at his rifle, then I fired it twice in the air before resuming my station. Surely, that would bring results?

I didn't have to wait long, as a figure broke cover a few hundred metres below and to my left, looked my way, and proceeded to climb the hill. He was too far away to recognise, but was obviously an enemy of some kind, be it police or one of Denny's mob. Not Denny himself, nor Packer, and he didn't appear to be wearing a uniform, so I scrambled further right and prepared myself for his approach. I needed to be absolutely sure before I launched an attack.

I held my breath as I heard sounds below me, getting closer. I was well hidden, the rifle pointed in the direction it needed to be. Whoever he was, he was being very cautious, and that made me even more nervous as I flexed my shoulder muscles and tried to remain relaxed. I attempted to see if he had picked up a colleague on the way, but my vision was sorely limited, and I was resigned to the fact that I was on my own and I had to take things as they came. My finger actually itched as it was poised over the trigger, but I maintained my stance, as well as my concentration.

Eventually, after what seemed like a lifetime, he broke cover and came towards me, still hunched down as he moved and gripping a rifle much like the one I had in my hands. He was clearly a native, but not in uniform, so I still didn't know for sure what I was facing.

"Police. Stop!" I screamed, almost frightening myself as much as him.

He stopped in his tracks, and I knew this was the moment of truth. If he was a lawman, he would say something to that effect. If not...

He dived for cover, opening fire haphazardly in my direction, although it was unlikely any of his shots would have found their target. In response, I aimed carefully at his moving figure and squeezed the trigger, my heart in my mouth and sweat pouring onto the stock of the rifle. I was surprised at the recoil, as pain whipped through my shoulder, but the other guy was in a worse state, as he appeared to swivel in mid-air before landing spread-eagled in a bush, his gun falling harmlessly beside him.

I felt deep satisfaction, which quickly turned to repugnance as I realised that I had destroyed another life. I dropped the rifle and turned away from the sight, prepared to walk away. The crack of another gun brought me back to reality, and I realised that someone else was shooting at me. How stupid! Why did I not expect there to be more of them? Okay, I had tracked the one man I had seen, but I never gave a thought to who might be outflanking me, closing the pincer movement without my knowledge. I was untouched by the shot, of course, but I fell to the floor as if the gunman had scored a direct hit, and I lay as still as I could, waiting for him to come closer. Surely, he would check that he had completed his task?

Moments ticked by, and I sensed that he was waiting to see if I responded before approaching. It was a wise move, but it meant I had to play dead for longer than I had hoped. I wanted him completely in the open before I retaliated, so I remained motionless, even holding my breath so that there was no visible sign of life.

It was then that I heard two voices.

"Is he dead?" said one, clearly a native, but with a very deep tone.

"I think so?" came the reply, this one higher-pitched and sounding nervous, as if killing wasn't part of his everyday life. "Go check on him," he added, trying to show that he was in charge.

The deep voice chuckled at that. "Come on, Vince, we'll both go – and then you can put another bullet in him to be sure."

I couldn't see them, but I heard the bushes rustle, and I sensed movement. They weren't the lightest on their feet. Then they were standing above me, and from the corner of my eye I saw a puny little guy and one built like a brick outhouse, almost as wide as he was tall. I couldn't get all of him in my range of sight.

The puny one held the pistol, and he raised it, his arm shaking, trying to point the barrel at my head. In the end, he couldn't go through with that particular shot, so he lowered his aim to my chest and fired twice, visibly relaxing now the deed was done.

The bad news hit him between the eyes as I rolled over, at the same time pulling my pistol from the waistband of my trousers and pumping on the trigger. He actually sank to his knees, like they do in the movies, and I watched as he tried to say something, before falling forward and kicking up a little dust as his face hit the ground.

There was no time to admire my handiwork because the big one was on the move, his huge body crashing into me, sending me flying, before he pinned me to the ground, his breath hot on my cheek. He was remarkably agile for such a big man, and I had been caught unawares. My gun had been knocked from my hand by the impact, so I found myself at his mercy.

I struggled to free my arms as I looked up and saw his massive fist heading towards me. I turned my head to one side, hoping to deflect the blow, but he caught me on the temple, and I winced as I waited for it to register. It seemed like a punch that would have floored most heavyweight champions, but instead of an excruciating pain, I felt the softness of a feather brush across my head. My corpuscles were holding up just fine.

He was leaning back, shaking his right hand as if it had just smashed into an invisible wall, and the look on his face was a picture. There was surprise, anger, frustration and fear, the mixture creating a deep scowl. It also meant that, for a moment, he had lost control, and I scurried out from beneath him, scooping up a handful of dirt and hurling it in his face. It wasn't particularly successful, but it added to his overall discomfort, and I compounded that with a hard kick aimed at his nether regions, which narrowly missed the target but caught him on a beefy thigh, bringing a rumble of profanity from his lips, some of the words being new to me, so I assumed they were a local delicacy.

I stood in front of him, urging him to try again. He did. He had got rid of the feeling of shock, so the anger was taking over. As any fighter will tell you, that is not the way to win. Aggression must be controlled; movement must be fluid. This guy was like a bull, rampaging forward and offering haymakers as he got close. I side-stepped and put out a leg, and I hardly felt a touch as he was bowled over and tumbled to the ground, his momentum causing him to roll over twice before he came to a halt, face-down.

I picked up my pistol and went over to him. He was struggling to get up, bewildered as he was, and by the time I reached him he was on his knees, shaking his head and still cursing. I put my pistol to his temple.

"You should be dead," he wheezed.

"Bullet-proof vest," I told him, hoping that would satisfy his curiosity, at the same time offering a grateful prayer that the other guy hadn't aimed for my head. I wouldn't have been able to explain that one away.

"You have a choice," I said, my voice ragged. "Die here with a bullet to the brain, or you get to live."

"Hey, man, what sort of choice is that?" He sounded scared.

It was clear what I had to do. "I have one question. The right answer will save you."

He thought about that for a microsecond. "What question?"

I bent down closer, the pistol pressing into his scalp. "Where can I find, Matthew Denny?"

"He's gone."

"He can't have gone far," I said. "I was with him a short while ago."

"He's with Captain Packer," he offered.

I was losing patience. "Where?" I demanded, tapping him not so gently on the head.

He growled and swore again, before offering up a deep sigh. "You'll kill me anyway," he said.

"Try me," I countered.

"He was meeting up with his tech guy," he said quickly. "They are tracking you."

"Not any more," I said, tapping the monitor in my pocket. "So, where are they due to meet?"

"He has a speedboat…"

"Of course, he does," I murmured to myself. "Where?" I demanded loudly.

"A cove…"

I knew there were at least eleven small coves on this side of the island alone, so I needed him to be more specific. "Which one?"

He hesitated, no doubt weighing up the consequences. Then he came to a decision. "Jessiman's."

I knew where he meant. Denver had always called it 'Jesse James Cove', but, in fact, it was named for Samuel

Jessiman, one-time governor during the island's long-remembered colonial days. As with many places they occupied, the old British rulers had brought some bad things with them when they arrived, but also much good for the island, such as education and agriculture, and, on the whole, the locals were pro-British, happy to retain place names which reflected their past.

Jessiman's Cove was one of the larger inlets, although still small by international standards. It was shallow, with a slight current, which ensured only flat-bottomed craft were able to get anywhere near the shore. This meant two things: that Denny must have a larger boat anchored further out, and also that the smaller vessel in the cove would not be able to carry many passengers – a pilot, of course, plus probably one other man as well as Denny and Packer. I didn't think the odds against me were too great.

The big man was talking. "We were supposed to take you there." With the slightest of pauses, he finished with, "Dead or alive."

So, Denny *had* changed his tune. Presumably, he had tired of trying to keep me alive. My bet was that he thought he would be better off with me out of the way, even if it meant he didn't get his hands on the microchip. He was going to be unlucky.

I allowed the big man to get up, which he did reluctantly, no doubt expecting a bullet for his troubles.

"There is a policeman somewhere down there," I said, waving my free hand to indicate the valley below. "I suggest you go find him." I pulled the trigger, and a hole appeared in his shirt sleeve, followed by a steady flow of blood. "With luck, he'll have a first aid kit with him."

He looked at me, then down at his bloodied arm, shocked at what I had done and, more importantly, what I had *not* done. "You're letting me go?" he asked, incredulous.

"You've served your purpose," I said, before I heard something behind me. It sounded like a slow handclap...

"I'm touched," said Denver, emerging from the bush and still putting his hands together in a show of admiration. "Me, I would a shot the guy in the nuts and be done with it. You, man, you give him a kiss on the arm and let him walk away. How very British." He said the last three words in such a ridiculous attempt at poshness that I burst into laughter. Denver looked at the big man, who was still frozen to the spot. "Hey, arsehole, begone!"

He didn't need any more prompting, and he scampered away, stumbling and lurching, clutching his bleeding arm while trying to avoid the overhanging branches and tree roots littering his way.

I dropped the gun and swept Denver up in a hug. "I'm so glad to see you," I blurted.

"Yeah, me, too," he replied, clearly embarrassed. He broke away, but kept a warm smile.

"How did you know where I was?" I asked. Stupid question.

"Just followed the sound of gunfire. It's a real giveaway, David. I'm surprised you hadn't thought of that!" His grin was infectious, but I needed to remain serious.

"It's Matthew Denny," I said sharply.

"What?"

"Denny, he's behind this."

"But I thought...?"

"He was dead?" I finished for him. "Unfortunately, no. He's very much alive."

"Well, I'll be..." He stopped there, holding back the cusses he was obviously thinking.

I slumped to the ground, one thought on my mind. "Where is Robyn?"

Denver sat beside me, crossing his legs. "Sweet talkin' the local inspector, last time I looked. She and Greg are working miracles."

"I can imagine. How was the inspector taking it?"

"Remarkably calmly, I'd say, considering we've managed to stitch him up over you. The prisoners of war we handed over will have helped."

"Prisoners?" I said, shocked.

"What, you think we smoked them all?"

"Well..."

"What do you think we are... animals?" he said with mock gravitas. "Nah, we just wanted to make a gesture, is all. Morice needed to keep his hand in. You know, it's like riding a bike..."

I knew Denver wasn't being serious, but there was something I needed to know. "How many...?"

He looked at me, his head at a strange angle, as if studying me for the first time. "David, you know a soldier never tells." He punched my shoulder playfully. "Anyway, the inspector has enough of them left to put on trial, so we're all happy."

I supposed he was right. They were out to kill me, so, in all honesty, they got what they deserved. Still, there was a pang in my gut, especially as it had all been so clinical, without a shot being fired. The Bandits had been no match for my Commandos.

"What are we going to do now?" Denver asked.

"I'm going after Denny," I said. It hadn't gelled in my mind until that moment. Now, it was my be-all and end-all, my reason for living. I had to stop him, because it wasn't just for me or my friends. I realised with mounting fear that the future of the whole world could be in my hands. If Denny got the machine working and sold it to the highest bidder, then Armageddon could be at hand. I shivered.

Denver grinned. "*We're* going after Denny!"

"No," I said gently, ignoring the thunder building within me. "You have to trust me on this one, my friend. I go alone."

He was about to say something, but I stopped him with a hand on his arm. "Please, Denver."

There was silence, save for the twitter of a pair of birds in a nearby tree. I waited for his response.

He took a deep breath. "You're serious."

"Extremely."

He took another breath. "Okay, pal. Whatever you say."

I could see he didn't mean it, and he was struggling to come to terms with what I had asked, so I removed the tracker from my pocket and handed it to him. "I took this from Specs. I want you to give it to Robyn; she might be able to work it, which would mean you will at least know where I am." I smiled.

"Hey, man, it looks pretty beat up," he said, looking down at the mangled mess in his hand.

"Yeah, sorry about that. It got caught in the crossfire." I didn't have the nerve to tell him that I had tried to destroy the thing while I was going through a fit of anger. "It might still work," I added lamely.

"It might at that. I'll pass it on."

"I'm sure Gregory's devious mind will bring it back to life."

He gave me a watery smile. "Yeah, that's a fact!"

We stood and shared another less embarrassing embrace before I said, "You'd better go. The sooner you get back to Robyn, the sooner you can get your beady eyes on my movements."

"There's one more thing," he said, his voice breaking just a little. He went back to the place from which he had emerged only minutes earlier, stooped down and came up with Morice's Lee Enfield. Handing it to me, he said huskily, "The mad Frenchman wanted you to have it."

I nodded my thanks as Denver dug into his pocket and pulled out more cartridges, which he stuffed into my pocket. "Just in case you don't get the bastard with the first one," he said softly but with a mischievous smile.

"I'll get him," I said, "and Packer."

Denver touched my hand in respect and affection, before turning and moving away. I watched him go, my heart pounding; but just before he ducked into the undergrowth, he swung round to face me. "There's only one reason I'm letting you do this alone, David," he said with feeling.

I looked at him, unable to speak, so I waited.

"Robyn told me how special you really are." His voice and his face were full of disappointment mixed with awe. "I only wish you had told me, old friend."

I gulped. "I wanted to, Denver. Really."

"Yeah," he sighed, then rallied. "Go get 'em, pal." With that, he raised his arm in salutation and disappeared through the bush.

"I'll get them," I whispered to myself, the words not quite drowning out the sounds of the birds above me.

Chapter Twenty-Eight

The way down from the hill was not as quick as I had hoped. In fact, it proved more challenging, as the slope and uneven ground acted against me when I attempted to increase my speed. My real problems were tree roots and the clumps of sagebrush with their needle-sharp branches reaching out to ensnare me. Some I could jump over, but others were so huge that the many detours round them took away my time and my speed. I was desperate to get to the cove to confront Denny and Packer.

At last, I could see the shoreline, and as I got closer, there was the speedboat, bobbing gently at anchor as if merely caressing the water. Before breaking cover, I stopped to get my bearings and took the opportunity to check that my rifle was loaded. It was the second time I had done so, and I realised that nerves were kicking in, causing me to doubt things. I told myself sternly to get a grip, stepped out of the undergrowth and began jogging again, hitting the beach at a reasonable speed, so I still had the advantage of surprise.

The speedboat was barely thirty metres ahead and maybe fifteen metres offshore. I could clearly see the pilot, his arms resting on the wheel as he relaxed. Another man, who was turned away from me, was obviously talking to Matthew Denny, who sat motionless in the back seat, presumably listening to the latest report. I knew he had already realised that Specs was out of the picture, so I was wondering what his next plan might be. I knew what mine was.

I crouched on the sand and levelled the Lee Enfield, stroking the stock for luck. Then I shouted. "Denny, it's all over."

He swivelled to face me and stood up, a smile playing round his lips. "David, we knew you'd show up. Welcome to the finale."

The man beside him had levelled a sub-machine gun and was already firing before Denny had finished speaking. The sand around me erupted, and I felt sure several of the rounds would have cut through a lesser man than me. I smiled and held my ground, then pressed the trigger of the Lee Enfield. Under normal circumstances, the old weapon would not have been a match for the machine gun – but these were far from normal circumstances. Again, I recoiled from the shot and saw that the bullet had annoyingly failed to hit its target, probably due to my inexperience as well as the gentle swaying of the boat on the water.

I tried again, with more concentration, and this time felt a little more satisfied as I watched the windshield shatter and the pilot fall back, either from the bullet or the shards of glass that were flying everywhere. The boat rocked even more, and Denny struggled to remain standing. It appeared that he had been struck by some of the glass, as he was dabbing at his cheek and looking at the back of his hand, which I assumed and hoped was covered in blood. With his other hand, he gripped the side rail and swayed with the boat. The man beside him was busy changing the magazine on his weapon. The pilot was motionless.

I took careful aim, satisfied this time that the gunman was in my sights, but, before I could fire, there was a devastating explosion, and, in front of my eyes, the speedboat was lifted out of the water and blown apart, the flotsam and body parts falling back down to make a series of hideous splashes in the blood-tinged sea.

I was stunned. No, it was more than that. I was mortified. My ears were popping with the sound of it, while my eyes watered uncontrollably as I thought of the loss of life, no matter what scum it might have been. I lowered the rifle and bowed my head in silent prayer.

"Ironic, isn't it?" a voice boomed behind me.

I turned to see Packer, legs apart, machine gun at the ready, and what looked like a detonator in his other hand.

"Matthew Denny, the only man to die in two boat explosions!" His laugh was mocking, hollow.

"You?" I asked, my voice sounding far away, as if on another island.

"Of course!" he growled, offended that I had not automatically attributed the atrocity to him. "I didn't need him any more, so *boom*!" His maniacal laugh echoed across the cove, bouncing off the cliff and coming back to slap me in the face. "I waited for you to arrive first because every spectacular event needs an audience, don't you think?" Then he added, "Besides, I hate Commies."

There was a pause as we calculated the next moves as if we were indulging in a macabre chess game.

"I have access to the machine," he continued as if I was actually listening to his confession, "and I have the men lined up to work out the missing part your friend Allenby has hidden; so everything else is superfluous."

From deep inside, I summoned up the energy to speak to the monster. "Denny did it for a warped cause. My guess is you're doing it for money."

He shrugged. "Nothing else matters. Money solves all ills," he said with a grin. "Talking of ills, now it's your turn." He became suddenly quiet and menacing, the gun rocking comfortably in his grip. He stepped forward, now only a few paces from me. I hadn't even had time to stand.

I watched as he aimed, my eyes trained on the trigger, which he pressed with fervour, expecting me to dance like a marionette as the bullets riddled my dying body. Poor, misguided fool.

I rose, scooping up my rifle, and stood before him. His face was a picture, all wide-eyed and full of amazement at what he saw. That was when I fired. Three times. Expecting, like him, to see a body crumple at my feet. It was my turn to be the poor, misguided fool.

Packer was still standing, and his face changed to one of triumph. "So, Allenby *did* work on you more than he said. I should have known."

"And Denny did the same with you," I countered.

"No, not Denny," he said. "He was only ever the money man. No, I had inside help."

"Specs," I guessed.

"Someone else, too," he smirked, knowing he was about to upset me.

"Oh?"

"Susan Patterson."

I was stunned. "Susan?"

"Oh, it's okay, she was just a patsy. Specs asked her to help when Allenby wasn't around. She thought she was aiding and abetting a couple of friends. And she knew how to operate the machine."

"So why did you kill her?" I demanded.

"Because she tried to get you out. I couldn't allow that. Our little secret had to be protected. Little did I know that Allenby had already put you through the machine several times before then. Naughty doctor." He laughed again, but there was no humour in it. "So, it just remains for me to dispose of you."

As he was speaking, I had tried to shuffle my way towards the water, knowing it was probably my only chance. Packer was heavier than me, obviously stronger, and had received military training, so my options were severely limited. I just had to hope he wasn't a strong swimmer as well.

"This is going to be interesting. I can't kill you with this," he said, tossing away the gun, "so I will have to find a way round that."

"Truly a conundrum, Packer. For both of us."

This time, his laugh carried a tinkle of jocularity. "What? You think you are a match for me?" He stepped forward. "No chance!"

He tried to bundle into me, but he just bounced away, our bodies not touching at all. He tried again, with the same result, and we stood there, eyeball to eyeball, neither of us knowing what to do next. He threw a punch, but it fell harmlessly away, so I had a go. The same result.

My mind was in overdrive. I recalled the tender touch and kiss I had enjoyed with Robyn, feeling again the intensity of it all – and yet I could not hit the man I hated most. It was those bloody corpuscles! They must have been controlled by my emotions: the touch of love I could feel, while the touch of hatred was rejected unilaterally. None of which was helping.

I attempted to punch him again, just for the hell of it, and as his reflexes caused him to sway to one side, I took the opportunity to duck away from his flailing arms and race into the surf to begin my swim for life. I didn't dare look back, so I quickly got into my rhythm and immediately felt better. I had always been comfortable in the water.

My strokes were strong, and I made good progress despite the fact that the tide was coming in. I tried to avoid the detritus from the speedboat, but it was spread over such a wide area that there was no way I could miss it all. Thankfully, I only brushed against splintered wood and what looked like part of the back of one of the seats, the fabric drenched in blood and flapping helplessly as I pushed it away.

Beyond the wreckage, I decided to stop and check out Packer. If he was close, then I had no chance, but I would try my hardest to take him down with me. I need not have worried because he was still on the shore, watching me watching him. He was running one hand through his hair, perhaps contemplating whether to follow me, but he didn't move, so I swam on.

I breasted the headland and entered more familiar territory. I was now in the cove where I had spent many happy hours with Denver, swimming and chatting, enjoying a barbecue, or just lying back with a couple of beers to the accompaniment of the toucans on the cliff face and the tropical kingbirds hidden amongst the nearby trees.

I slowed my pace so that I could see the lie of the land. The beach was empty, almost serene, but I still waited. I was in no hurry to meet up with Packer again until I had a clear plan in mind. It's funny, throughout all of this, I never once had a plan that seemed remotely workable – and that applied now, as I trod water and looked around.

On one side was the cliff skirting the bay I had just left, while on the other was Denver's infamous caves, cut into an equally expansive cliff. Whichever route I took, I would have to come ashore, so I decided to swim a little further on so at least I would have the partial cover of the rocks as I negotiated the last few metres of water. It seemed like the only plan I was going to come up with.

Once I had reached the point where I felt reasonably safe – using the term very loosely – I stopped and just floated, flexing my shoulders and legs for the final stretch over the rocks. I was fairly confident now that Packer hadn't followed me into the water, but I couldn't be sure whether he could get here overland quickly enough to intercept me. However, I couldn't stay in the water forever, so I had to take the chance.

I swam to the shallows and crawled the rest of the way, keeping as low as I could while maintaining a reasonable speed. I would be a sitting duck if I was caught on the beach.

My mind was racing. Packer did have one weakness, and I suddenly realised there was a way to exploit it. I scrambled to my feet, ran the last few metres across the sand and dived behind some boulders. I waited, watching, then I set off.

The rocks, formed over millennia into quartz-bearing limestone, were remarkably smooth, and I had difficulty clambering over them, my grip slipping on occasion as I tried to maintain my speed.

The fact that I had been here before gave me a slight edge, but I was convinced that Packer wasn't far behind, and he was a resourceful and dangerous opponent.

As I dropped into a dip between the rocks, I stopped for a few seconds. To my surprise, I felt a little out of breath. I climbed up to peer over the next rock and realised how far I had come. The sand wasn't any drier here, and the rocks were thinning out a little, leading to the entrance of what Denver called Cave One, the largest of the six Korinna caves. The one he told me to keep clear of.

I reached up, my hand searching for any small crevice which might give me a purchase to get my body over this rock and on to the next one. There was nothing, and I realised that I would have to go round it, forcing me into the open for several seconds. Once more, I looked for Packer, but I was alone with just the wind whistling through the opening to the cave ahead, so I made a dash for it, falling in behind another of the boulders nearer to the cave's entrance. I could see inside it now and marvelled at the walls, which had been etched away almost artistically by eons of winter rain trickling down from the clifftops above and the salt from the sea water below.

I had to wade through the sea to get into the cave, but it felt like the safest place to be, the darkness inside likely to be an ally. I tried to make as little noise as I could, but the echo of the sploshing water came off the walls with each step I took, making me wonder if I was supplying a rallying call for the man following me. I stopped. Was he following me? Or had he given up and gone away, around to a different cove, where, no doubt, he had another boat to whisk him away to Beijing, or Moscow, or Pyongyang, or some other god-forsaken place? To create havoc in the world. I shivered, praying that I was wrong, but I huddled behind a few rocks as I waited to see if I was right.

The sound of the lapping water was somehow calming, and my body began to relax, which seemed strange to me, considering the predicament I was in. Hell, I couldn't think of tranquillity, not now.

I wasn't sure how long I had been there, but I could feel the cramp developing in my legs, so I tried to adjust my position. That was when I heard it. It was almost inaudible, but there was movement in the water at the entrance to the cave. If it was Packer, he was using all his skills to camouflage the fact; but, as I stared intently, I still couldn't see a thing out of place. I saw water and a darkening sky, but no sign of life. In frustration, I edged my body to a more acute angle, my eyes never leaving the shimmering archway of light which signified the opening to the sea and the evening beyond. Then, I saw a shadow. Just for a moment, as if a phantom had crossed my mind and left merely a whiff of memory on it. I cursed myself, wondering what I had seen, if anything. A bat, perhaps, or just a figment.

I silently rolled back to my original position, feeling the sweat and the anxiety welling up through me.

"I know you're in here, Parks."

His voice sounded *so* close that I actually stopped breathing for a moment.

"Thanks for the directions. Led me straight to you." His laugh reverberated, a ghastly sound ricocheting off every rock, almost defecating the history of the place.

My footsteps in the wet sand had guided him straight to me. He must have thought it was as if I had put out a sign, 'Hey, Packer, I'm here – come and kill me!'

The intention had been that he would follow me, but now I wasn't so sure. I had never been confident that I could handle Packer, and that was especially so now, in the confines of this cavern with the light fading fast. However, the proximity of death was something I had to live with, so, in for a penny…

"Come on in, Packer, the water's lovely," I purred sarcastically, moving away from my rock and scrambling deeper into the darkness of the cave, knowing he had no choice but to follow. Suddenly, I felt more optimistic.

I could see him now, a few metres back, awkwardly negotiating the natural obstacles in his way. His army training obviously hadn't covered potholing. I pressed on, trying to gain some high ground and managing to clamber up on a small ledge so that I at least had a slight advantage. I scrabbled round for any loose stones, scooping up a couple I thought might make good missiles, although I knew they wouldn't be much good.

Packer came into view. Like me, he wasn't at all out of breath, and once again I wondered what I was doing here. Rufus had dubbed me 'David', but I didn't like the look of the 'Goliath' chasing me, and felt that the contest would probably go the other way this time. I girded my loins.

Below me, Packer had stopped, looking a little bewildered. He was clearly out of his comfort zone, but more than that, he didn't know where I was, and for a soldier, that is not good news. He was looking around when the first stone bounced off him, so I tried another with the same result. Nothing was going to get through. But worse, I had given away my position.

The ledge led nowhere, so I jumped to the ground and began running again, knowing that he would be able to outrun me if the surface ever became more amenable. Fortunately, that was not the case, and I maintained my lead as we went deeper into the cave's interior, the light receding and the water rising so that I could no longer see where I was treading.

Then, I stumbled. It was stupid, but I had lost concentration for a second and went tumbling over some loose rocks, landing on my right shoulder and rolling, before coming to rest in the water against a giant stalagmite covered in lichen and seaweed, like some huge verdant statue. I was unhurt, of course, but my co-ordination had been thrown out, and I was still shaking my head in annoyance when Packer came to a halt in front of me, a smile squirming around his lips.

He was clenching his fists, but apart from that, he didn't know what to do. We were impervious to each other.

I got to my feet and aimed a throw at him, even though I knew it was pointless. I could feel my soaking clothes gripping me tight as I swung my arm, only to see my fist stop a few millimetres from his face.

He tried to grab me in a bear hug, but I kicked out, a spray of water the only thing that touched him.

That seemed to stir him somehow, and as he looked down, I saw the panic mount as he realised how much water had poured into the cave since we had entered it. The tide coming in was almost a torrent, and he screamed at me, "I can't swim!"

I took this as my cue, and I was off again, racing through the cave, wondering if I would ever escape this madman who was in hot pursuit, the sound of the sloshing water ringing in my ears as he got closer. I could clearly hear his breathing, which came in bursts, like someone turning a steam pump on and off, on and off...

There was a channel to the right, so I had to make a decision without breaking my stride. I turned down it, hoping this was the correct decision. The walls were closing in, making the track narrower, which worked for me, as it would also slow Packer down. Every little helps. The roof of the cave was becoming much lower, forcing me to crouch and revise my speed. It was an awkward way to run, especially now the water was fast approaching my shins, but I seemed to be making good progress. There was no way I could sense how close Packer was because of the noise I was making in the water, but I could see something sparkling in the distance as if welcoming me, so I carried on in hope.

I emerged into a chamber but kept running until the ground suddenly gave way, and I found myself plunging into deep water, the coldness of it waking senses within me which had begun to dull from the relentless challenge I was facing. I quickly recovered, treading water and checking my surroundings.

The chamber itself wasn't massive, but, in the dim light, the walls looked immense, and my first thought was that the only way out would be back the way I had come. I soon realised that I was in an underground lake, the water rising with the incoming sea, but the lake still being there when the tide receded. There was a thin shaft of light beyond my left shoulder, so I turned and saw what appeared to be a hazy film of moonlight breaking through a gap in the rockface. I had forgotten how night falls so swiftly in these parts.

I was brought back to the present by the sound of a curse and a splash as Packer joined me, his screams of shock and fear rippling across the lake as he gulped in mouthfuls of the salty water and his writhing body caused minor tidal waves. Now I knew for sure that he couldn't swim.

But that, of course, left me with a dilemma. I could swim away and watch him sink without a trace, or I could try to rescue him, probably giving him the opportunity to finish me off later.

The decision was abruptly taken out of my hands as I felt Packer's arms around my legs, pulling me down. I heard him gurgling as he tried to maintain a firm grip, holding on for dear life. He was fully under the water, but he began scrabbling up my legs and then over my body until his head plopped out, and I saw the terror in his eyes. His hands went round my neck, but there was no malice this time; he was using me for buoyancy, grasping me with a fervour that turned his knuckles white and set his teeth chattering.

There was no way I could get him off, so I began swimming back towards the path we had stepped from, but the current against me was far too strong, and I found myself twisting in the swirling water and going with the flow, hoping that it would lead us to salvation. I was carrying a deadweight, but I couldn't feel him, and that was strange. Again, I thought of Robyn, of how we had kissed, and the sweet taste her lips left on mine, and I wondered how that could be possible.

I was dreaming. There was the tree, racing to meet me at breakneck speed. I was in the car, watching the story unfold through the windshield. Susan was beside me, desperately struggling with the steering wheel, trying to bring the vehicle back under control. There was the thunder of the crash, Rufus pulling me out, Susan slumped over the wheel, the syringe…

I opened my eyes and realised I was sinking. I had stopped swimming, lost once more in the nightmare of the past. As I forced my way back to the surface, I gulped in fresh air and knew that Packer was still there. He wasn't moving, but I could see his arms around me, clinging tightly. I had Susan's killer on my back, threatening my very existence. I contemplated the idea of rolling over so he was submerged beneath me, but that would only make me as bad as him, and my conscience would not allow it. So I reached out my arms and swam on, my progress slow but steady, even though I had no idea where I was going.

After perhaps ten minutes, my luck changed. As my left arm reached its forward arc in the water, I felt something. A small ledge. And then another with my right arm, a little higher, as if I had stumbled on a secret stairway. I clawed desperately at these lifelines, to be rewarded with yet another flat rock, and another, until, by some miracle, I found footholds to enable me to inch my way out of the water and onto a rugged plateau, where I fell down, the relief overpowering me.

Packer had let go and was rolling around, coughing and gasping, before eventually leaning over and vomiting sea water and everything else from his body. It took us some time to come to terms with what we had experienced and survived, lying there together, our hands almost touching, but our philosophies worlds apart.

Packer spoke first, his voice croaky. "This doesn't change anything."

"What," I said softly, "me saving your life?"

He nodded. "I'm still going to kill you."

"I could have left you in the water."

He sat up, clearly recovering. "Yeah, but you didn't. Bad move."

I looked around. The opening to the outside world above us was much closer, but I knew we still had some climbing ahead, and I wasn't even sure if there was a safe route out. "You know this chamber will flood eventually? When the tide is fully in," I said.

He harrumphed dismissively and replied, "I'll be long gone by then."

"You think?"

He stood, looking menacing and back to his military stance. "I *know*. Only one of us is getting out of here, Parks."

I jumped up. The water was beginning to trickle over the top of the lake, onto our ledge and around our feet. From what Denver had told me many times, high tide would fill the cave remarkably swiftly, so I calculated we had perhaps twenty minutes to half an hour before it was too late. Time to climb.

"We need to help each other," I told him. "It's the only way to escape from here."

His response was to kick out wildly, causing me to lose my balance and tumble back into the water. He hadn't actually touched me, of course, but the motion of his body was enough to send shock waves through me, and I plunged backwards, the cold water jarring me into life. I began swimming back to the rocky steps, angry that I had fallen for such a move but also desperate to get after Packer.

I scrambled back up onto the ledge and saw him at the far end of the narrow tunnel, starting to climb out of the chamber. He had negotiated the first part of the ascent, reaching a small promontory perhaps three and a half metres above the floor of the cave. He didn't look back.

The water still hadn't got a hold yet, so I could make good progress in my pursuit. When I reached the point where he had started to climb, I stopped to quickly study the terrain. The wall was very uneven, allowing me many

384

opportunities to gain hand- and footholds, so I reached the promontory in good time and without trouble. Packer was not so far in front now, so I began to plot my strategy for when I finally caught up with him. That was going to be a problem. Any wrong move, and one or other of us, or both, would be hurtling down the cave wall to fall into the water that was relentlessly gaining a hold. I could swim, but I wasn't sure I would actually be conscious after that. Still I climbed.

He was slowing, the ascent getting more difficult as he neared the top, but it looked as if he would get out onto the clifftop, which was bad news for me. I would be a sitting duck.

I renewed my efforts, at last getting close enough to reach out for his ankle. He kicked out wildly, so I swerved away from him as much as I could while maintaining my grip, and his leg flew harmlessly past my face. I heard him growl as he brought his leg back, still passing me but almost missing the ledge it had been on. He wobbled but remained in control, and his arm reached out for a higher ledge so he could continue the climb.

I looked up, then foolishly down, the sight causing me to almost swoon. Something about a rock and a hard place raced through my mind, but I shook it off and carried on with my pursuit. He was barely a hand's length away, but also within touching distance of his goal. I reached out once more, this time wrapping my hand round his boot and sensing the laces against my fingers. I tugged, hoping they might loosen and cause him at least a small problem.

We were so high now that I could scarcely see the torrent of water gathering below us, but I could hear it, as well as the warm night breeze tinkling through the opening above, while the moon's rays were throwing strange beams of light across the cavern walls, like a weird *son et lumière* of nature.

He was struggling to push me off, but we had reached an impasse. I could not stop him from getting to the top, but neither could he remove the appendage that I had become. We paused, both knowing that the slightest aggressive move could mean disaster. I could hear his breathing, which was somehow strained, and I assumed mine was the same. We had both been carved out of the same experiment and had more in common than either of us would admit, but it was still going to be a fight to the death.

I was about to renew my assault by grabbing Packer's other leg when I heard it.

"David!"

It was above us, a voice so welcome that I gasped. American. Then there were flashlights, criss-crossing, and more voices, one of whom I recognised with a rush of blood to the head.

"David!" It was Robyn.

I couldn't trust myself to speak and still maintain my grip, so I just held on to the rock, letting go of Packer's leg. *To hell with it; he can go where he likes. I just want to be out of here.* I waited for him to continue the climb, but he had other ideas. He was turning so that his back was against the cliff, and then he started to push his foot down in an effort to dislodge my hand. I could see his boot approach each time, but it never connected, as he must have known it wouldn't. We were two of a kind, Packer and me. Indestructible. Almost.

He swung his leg one more time, but he had overplayed it, and I could see him losing his balance. His fingers clawed at the rock to hold on, but his body had already begun to twist, the momentum pulling him away from the cliff so that, for a split second, he was suspended in space, his face contorted in hatred and horror before he started to fall past me, his hands reaching out for salvation but finding none. I waited for the inevitable sound as he hit the water, but first I heard the sickening thud as he must have collided with the cliff wall on the way down. I held on to both my breath and my grip.

A head appeared above me. Denver. "Hey, buddy, stop hangin' around, will ya!" His grin almost blotted out the moon.

Yeah, I thought, *sounds like a plan*.

* * *

It took them fifteen minutes to pull me through the opening. Perhaps not the longest fifteen minutes of my life, but pretty close.

I rolled on the shrub, grinning like the Cheshire Cat and thumping the ground with a drumroll of victory. To be fair, they left me to it, revelling in the pleasure they got from my pleasure. Then I hugged Denver, Gregory, Morice and anybody else who was on that clifftop, before pulling Robyn to me and almost throttling her with my embrace. We kissed, oblivious to those around us, and it was the most sensational feeling I had ever experienced. I wanted it to go on forever.

We finally separated, but only because we were both starting to feel the excitement rise, if you know what I mean. Denver spoke first.

"You'll have to tell us all about it, pal."

I acknowledged what he had said with a shrug. "I know, but let's leave it for now, eh?"

Robyn gripped my hand and wrapped her other hand round my arm. She wasn't going to let go in a hurry.

"I have one question, David," she said, loud enough for all to hear.

"Yes?"

"Gregory was tracking you all the way. But how did you know how to get out of there?" she asked. "Denver told me that cave is massive."

I had wondered the same thing. Of all the routes I could have taken, I had chosen the correct one. Luck? Or something else?

My thoughts were with Rufus as I said, "Perhaps my corpuscles are more special than we thought."

Epilogue

Now, I'm sitting in the same place, on top of the cliff. Rufus's folder is beside me, complete with the missing pages. That's all there is left from the parcel Rufus had deposited at the hotel. Under my instructions, Morice destroyed the microchip as soon as he'd found it, so Denny was never going to get his hands on it, whatever the outcome.

Over a drink in the café two days after Packer's fall from grace, as it were, Morice gave the missing sheets to Denver, who put them back in their rightful place in the folder. I am grateful to them both, but I still haven't looked at it. I'm not sure if they ever read the pages, but I have made it clear that it will never ever be a topic of discussion.

I am relaxing in the afternoon sun, watching a gull circle above me and the sea like a painting below me. I am content. In fact, I have been content for very nearly four months now.

I have had two operations to remove unwanted items from my body. The first was easy, as the scar left by the insertion of Rufus's tracker acted rather like an 'X marks the spot'; the second was way more complicated, the surgeon eventually finding the other monitor behind my left ear. I will never know whose handiwork that one was down to: Denny or Wolstenholme, or some other faceless monster pulling the strings of a rogue doctor. It doesn't matter now.

I have spent wonderful moments with Robyn: walking and talking, making love, but most of all, being together. Yes, I am content.

I think of Rufus quite often, wondering how it might have been if he had lived, if we had been able to talk properly about our shared past. Whether my life before him made me what I am today, or if I was just the shell of a human being, taken and moulded exquisitely into a man by someone whom people still refer to as a 'mad scientist'…

I suppose I should tell you the rest of the story. You have been good enough to stick with me this far, so it is only fair. I'll start with the bad guys; get them out of the way.

They didn't find much of Matthew Denny – just about enough to identify him. The two men with him weren't so fortunate, as they had no records, being local Bandits. No tears were shed, anyway. Denny's super-yacht, which had been anchored further out to sea, awaiting his return, was impounded and is likely to be sold to a Middle Eastern billionaire.

They didn't find Packer at all. I am sure that he survived the fall, knowing how his body worked, but I can't bring myself to believe that he managed to win his battle with the water. General consensus is that he was washed out to sea with the tide, but I have a feeling he's at the bottom of that underground lake. We may all be wrong, of course, and he could be somewhere now, plotting my downfall – but I'm not losing sleep over it.

Specs is, as they say, awaiting His Majesty's Pleasure. He'll be doing that for many more years to come, considering he aided and abetted a killer. I believe he is also due a touch of rhinoplasty, but the way I left his nose, I'm not sure he'll be able to wear glasses from now on.

After Gavin Wolstenholme's 'unfortunate' death in prison, the UK government allegedly cracked down on rogue departments. Yeah, I don't believe it, either. Anyway, the house in Farnham closed immediately, and the last I heard, the government were looking to demolish it and sell the plot to developers. Nice place, Farnham.

The good news is that Neil Starkey, ex-Metropolitan police chief, has moved to Ongar. To be more specific, he now shares space with a remarkable woman named Grace. Apparently, I hear on good authority, they make a formidable bridge team, while in their spare time they like to look at criminal cold cases. A perfect pair in every way.

Gregory, you might say, has turned a corner. He is no longer my driver – I don't think I'll need one of those again – instead, he is a freelance hearse driver, ferrying celebrities and the well-heeled to their final resting place using all forms of transport. Fancy saying goodbye in the back of the Batmobile? Gregory's your man. He's probably your man for more nefarious deeds as well, but I don't ask.

Morice is down on the beach, organising the largest barbecue the island has seen in years. It's a celebration, he says, to show his respect for some great people. His fortunes have changed immeasurably since he brought down the Bandits single-handed. It's okay, we've let him get away with that one. After handing over six local thugs and pinpointing the whereabouts of the bodies of three others, he was fêted by everybody, especially Inspector Munroe – now chief inspector, promoted for his work in crushing such a dangerous cabal. Morice has now gone into partnership with the policeman in a new venture, *The Hideaway*, which will be a high-class restaurant with a museum attached, detailing the two men's daring deeds. The tourists are going to lap it up.

Denver is still bumming. What else can he do? It's in his blood. The lobster fisherman wanted him back, but didn't dangle enough bait. So Denver passes the time offering beach jaunts in his Moke with a running commentary on how he almost brought down the British government after killing a hundred men in leafy Surrey. The Americans love him, especially the girls.

I sigh with the memories as Robyn approaches. She is a picture, and my heart races once more. I have been so lucky.

She sits beside me and looks into my eyes. "They're ready for you."

"They'll wait."

"Not too long, Pablo."

There, so now you know. I have a new identity and a new passport, courtesy of Chief Inspector Claude Munroe. He managed to wangle island residency for me; he felt it was the least he could do after what I had been through. Nice man, the Chief Inspector.

Robyn is gripping my arm tightly. She does that often, perhaps worrying that I could leave her at any moment. That's not going to happen.

We are gazing out to sea, watching the tide and the changing sky. It is getting warmer and more intoxicating, and then I hear the raucous sounds from down below. All my friends, from both the island and England, calling me to their celebratory barbecue: Morice, Gregory, Grace and Neil, Denver, and Rex Patterson, resplendent in Hawaiian shirt and chino shorts. A roll call of honour.

"We should go, Pablo," says Robyn gently. She loves saying my new name.

"Yes," I agree, rising.

She stops me. "Your folder."

I look down and pick it up, rubbing my finger over the mauve writing. *Goliath*. Inside is my history, but I still don't open it.

I smile at Robyn, and she understands, squeezing my hand tighter. She gives me an almost imperceptible nod, then moves away, offering me the space I need.

I look down. Then, with one sweep, I toss the folder into the air, and we both watch as it catches the wind and flies out, fluttering for a second like a dying bird before dropping over the cliff and out of sight into the ocean below.

Hand in hand, we begin to walk back down the cliff to our friends, to a way of life I am fast getting used to.

Who needs a past?

I have a future.